Courting Fae Thieves and Crowns

JOANNA REEDER

REED IT & WEEP

Reed it and Weep

Courting Fae Thieves and Crowns
Copyright © 2021 Joanna Reeder
joannareeder.com

Cover Art by Angel Leya
angeleya.com

Edited by Kristen J. Dawson, Nicholas Reeder, and Madeline Mortensen

Dedication

To Kristin.
For believing in this story and believing in me.

Author Foreword

Courting Fae Thieves and Crowns was originally published as a serial story on Amazon's Kindle Vella. Due to the nature of serial fiction structure differing from novel structure, portions of the story have been edited.

I hope you fall in love with Amberle's story as much as I have in writing it.

—Joanna

(And don't tell my other stories... but this one just might be my favorite.)

THE REALM OF FAERIE
Summer Court
Spring Court
Winter Court
Underwater Court
Autumn Court
SIGMUS RIVER
INFERNUS FOREST
ISI AURA
AURA POND
SIGMIS LAKE
OHM MOUNTAINS
EMERALD RUN
HERDAN
ORIS LAKE
VERDANTHEARTH
CARBONNE CHANNEL
ROSEWIND
MOIRA RIVER
CLIO
ERATO
The Sea of Neptulus
CALLIOPE
EUTERPE
TERPSICHORE
MELPOMENE
THALIA
THE GRAY VAULT
THE HARSH LAND
NEPTULUS
LUMINARIA
FROZE MOUNTAINS
ADIUM LAKE
CERAUNA LAKE
AVALA
AUTUMN WOODLAND
GRAYCREST
TUMAL DESERT
FORESTS OF NIGHT
ATMOS MOUNTAINS
SANDTIDE
W
S
N
E

Prologue

The high king's voice booms through the town center, seemingly out of nowhere. Spring fae everywhere stop what they're doing to step out of shops and cottages, or turn from their work to listen as their sovereign materializes with what some call witch magic, but no one dares speak it aloud.

"Greetings," he says, lifting his youthful and smooth elven chin.

Their ruler, High King Estelar of the Summer Court, isn't actually in the center of Rosewind, far away in his western palace with a glittering sea behind him. The Summer King claims he has come to an agreement with the Winter Court, thus the use of their illusion magic, but some still think something nefarious is going on. Fae cannot lie, and 'illusion' also means deception. Misdirection.

"The wait is over." King Estelar raises both hands in his grand gesture and flashes a dazzling smile at no one in particular because, although they can see him, he can't see them. "Even as I speak, hundreds of invitations are being sent to eligible young fae who will report to their court capitals in a fortnight. At that time, I hope all of Faerie turns to watch as we choose fifteen lucky females as contestants in the upcoming Consort Tourney. The winner will become the bride and mate of my son, the crown prince, and will someday be the High Queen Consort."

A murmur of gossip spreads like summer fire as the spring fae speculate what this means. One of their own could be chosen. One of their own could find herself on the High Court throne. Everyone knew this was a possibility, but it's been seventy years since the Tourney was first announced. And now it's upon them.

"I look forward to this Tourney and may the best fae win!" says the king before evaporating into the spring air.

One

I crouch on the balls of my feet with my toes gripping the edge of the ledge and peer into the room through the window. Balancing is easy with the dragonfly wings I was born with. They're the perfect color of iridescent blue and are nearly invisible after sunset. Still, I quiet them so the hum doesn't give me away. No one likes a spy.

The sky is dark, but a shadow catches my attention.

I flick my right wing once with a quick signal. Wait. He hasn't left yet.

The shadow retreats.

I adjust my feet and watch the fae called Nightfall inside. My stamina is good, but after six hours and nine nights of waiting for Nightfall to leave, with his twitching lion's tail and permanent frown, my joints are stiff from disuse.

I have memorized his routine. He never leaves his cottage. He rarely leaves this room or takes his eyes off the locked trunk. He opens it often, so I know where he hides the key. Nightfall is like a dragon the way he hoards his treasure.

A loud, ear-splitting commotion sends a shock through me, and for the first time, I lose my balance. Jerking backward, I push both wings outward with force to right myself before settling back on the ledge.

Breathing heavily as blood rushes through my veins, I listen for any sign he heard me. I wait for the fae to peer out the window and catch me. A door slams deeper in the house and I dare look back into the room. Nightfall is gone. Likely rushing off to see whatever caused the racket.

Now is my chance.

I dart forward, propelling myself through the open window and into the room, landing quietly on my feet. I rush to the bookshelf and reach up for the red-spine, hollowed-out book on the top shelf and retrieve the key.

A door below slams. I freeze.

Did Nightfall leave? Has he come back?

Heavy boots sound on the stairs. The footsteps are ascending.

"Amberle!" Clay hisses from outside the window. "He's coming back!"

I don't look at my partner and fall hard on my knees before my wings can soften my fall. They crack painfully on the wood floor. My fingers are quick and still as a seamstress as I shove the key into the lock and twist it with a satisfying click. Jerking the lock away, I lift open the trunk expecting to see a glittering diadem encrusted with diamonds, a ruby-hilted sword, or even a sack full of gold coins, but I see none of those. Just the leather-bound bundle of papers I'm here for.

The footsteps reach the top landing. I only have seconds.

I grab the papers and tuck them under my arm while fumbling to replace the lock. Then I stand and press myself against the side of the bookshelf as Nightfall enters the room. The key is still clutched in my hand.

To better conceal myself, I suck in a breath and press harder against the wall, crushing my wing and a radiating pain shoots up my left side. I bite my lip to stop myself from crying out.

As expected, Nightfall glances at his trunk as soon as he enters the room but seems satisfied that nothing is amiss and goes back to his seat, hovered over his desk, pouring over a book.

My heart hammers in my chest. If the fae glances over, he'll see me. I hold my breath. Even a small twitch might capture his notice. A pit forms in my stomach.

No one likes a spy, but everyone hates a thief.

Movement at the window catches my attention. I scowl at Clay, the pain still thumping in my back. He's up to something.

What are you doing? I want to scream at him, but know that even if I could, he's stubborn enough to do whatever perrifool thing he's got his mind set on.

I hear the same commotion just outside, causing Nightfall to fly from his seat and rush to the window. I don't hesitate and fly out the door and down the stairs, keeping my feet just off the floor so my steps don't make a sound. My adrenaline is pumping so hard I barely notice the throbbing of my wing. When I reach the bottom landing, I slow and plant my feet back on the ground, fold my wings protectively against me and crane my head to listen for signs I'm being followed. Whatever Clay did to distract him has stopped, and the cottage is quiet. Slowly, I turn the knob to the front door and pull it open, cringing as the hinges whine from desuetude.

But I've disappeared back into the night without bothering to find out if I was heard. If Clay has been found out or captured, it won't do either of us any good if I am too.

Clay and I lounge in the shadows of a high rooftop, eating rainbow fruit-tarts and dividing the payout between us. Thankfully, whatever distraction my partner created, he wasn't caught or even seen. He tosses the key I never returned upward, then catches it.

"Why didn't you put this back?" he asks, tossing it again. The action is becoming irritating. Although Clay is an expert at thieving, it's times like this that I'm reminded of our age gap. He's like the irritating younger brother I never had but felt responsible to take in. Although I'm nearly grown now, I wasn't much older than him when they took my father and forced me into this life—alone—on the streets to thieve for survival.

"I ran out of time," I say, taking a bite of blackberries and puff pastry. At least my wing is feeling better. My injury was like stubbing a toe. Painful in the moment, but it didn't last long.

"But the next time that fae looks for his key, he'll know he was robbed."

"The next time he looks for his key, he probably plans to open his trunk again," I say. "He'll figure out someone robbed him, anyway. I might have bought more time by keeping the key because he won't know the deeds are missing until he breaks the lock to look."

Clay ignores my triumphant look. "Did the client say what the deeds were?"

"Just that they were for some undiscovered land in the human world. Nightfall planned to wait until the humans found it and settled, before announcing himself as their king."

"Classy. Ruling a bunch of humans." Clay scoffs and shakes his head.

"You're part human," I snap. "Why did you say that like humans are worthless?"

"I never said they were worthless," he says, tossing his blue-black hair out of his eyes. "And you're half-human too. It's just like a lowly fae like Nightfall to exploit the humans in their own world to make himself feel powerful."

"It's better than exploiting star fae like us."

"Is it? At least we have a chance of fighting back. Humans have no chance."

He has a point.

"It's a good thing they stay in their realm. For their own safety."

"Maybe now," I point out. "We'd both be full-blooded fae if they never stumbled into Faerie."

"True." Clay throws the key again. I snatch it mid-air and pocket it. He scowls at me, but says nothing and reaches for another rainbow tart and changes the subject. "Well, if keeping the key was the only mistake then I'd say—"

"What do you mean?" I interrupt. "The only mistake?"

"I'm just saying, if not for me, you would have failed tonight."

"Yes Clay, we make an excellent team," I drone, but he's wrong. I could have done it alone. Clay's distractions just helped speed up the process. "But I wouldn't call it a mistake."

Clay makes a noncommittal grunt.

"It wasn't a mistake," I protest, sitting up and shooting him a challenging look.

"That's not what I meant," he says sincerely. He sits straighter to drive the point home. "Still, after the king's announcement today, I thought best-case, you'd postpone the job for another night."

"And worst-case?" I aim an eyebrow at him and twitch my wings in annoyance.

"You'd get us both caught and sent to a cell."

"I assure you I don't care about some silly Consort Tourney."

"I think you do. Whenever it's mentioned, you excuse yourself or disappear," he says. "Do you want to be chosen or something? Do you think you can woo and win the heart of Prince Orion?"

"What? No!" I nearly shout but keep my voice down. We're not likely to be heard so high on the roof of this inn, but I'm not taking chances. But if Clay wasn't such an asset, I'd strangle him for even mentioning it. "You know they won't let star fae into the competition, anyway."

"You're right," he says. "I heard invitations were already being delivered. Raine Hazelfalls received one."

"Well, she's practically spring royalty. It's not unexpected," I say, then lean back. "Why do you care?"

He shrugs. "I like to know what's going on. This fancy magic they intend to use so we can all watch the competition has me on edge."

I pull my knees up to my chest and wrap my arms around them and press my wings against my back. Now that the thrill of the job has worn off, the night chill is getting to me. "It bothers you?"

"Yes. It feels... deceptive."

"Ha! Everything the full-blooded fae does is a deception! I don't even want to imagine what Faerie would be like if one of them could actually lie!"

Clay picks invisible dirt from his shirt, then brushes his hand along his sleeve. "You know how I created a ruckus to distract Nightfall? This entire competition feels like the High Court is doing the same thing just to keep our attention away from something else."

"What do you think they're hiding?"

"I don't know," he says, then glances at me. "What are you hiding? Why do you always clam up when someone mentions the Tourney? I mean, besides now?"

"I don't want to talk about it," I say and flit my wings outward to aid my balance as I stand to leave.

"Is it because of your father's disappearance?"

"I don't want to talk about it," I repeat and turn away, touching the skin next to my right eye to feel the edge of my promise mark. It's an unconscious habit whenever my father is mentioned to trace the curves and lines of the inked mark.

"Amberle, I'm your closest friend," Clay says, pulling at my arm. "I'm pretty sure I'm your only friend, but all I know is that your father went missing seventy years ago—" He jerks his hand away as something occurs to him.

I whip on him and see the look of epiphany on his face.

His eyes rise to meet mine as my vision blurs. "He disappeared the same year they announced the Tourney, didn't he?"

"He didn't disappear," I say. "He was taken. He was imprisoned."

Clay's eyes widen. "Do you think it's connected? His imprisonment and the Tourney?"

I pump my wings, taking off from the roof.

"Amberle!" Clay calls, threatening to wake up all of Rosewind. But he doesn't have wings, so he can't come after me.

My eyes burn as I push myself higher into the sky. Clay can't be asking me questions like that. Not if he doesn't want to share a cell with my father. Because if he knew they took my father the same day they announced the Tourney, not just the same year, he'd know the two were connected. It's the reason I'm a thief. It's the reason no one, not even Clay, knows where I live. Because if the high king found out that I suspected anything, I'd disappear too.

I take the long way home, stopping on rooftops far from my neighborhood to watch the streets and ensure I'm not being followed. Even by Clay. So, when I finally arrive at the small, unused storage room above the bakery shop I call home, the sky is the color of pale lavender, announcing the rising sun. I already smell the bread and pastries in the oven down below and envision what delicacies I'll buy after I get a few hours of sleep. Maybe I'll send that youngling who lives down the street to buy them for me.

My fluttering wings send a piece of refuse sliding across the floor, just another piece of parchment blown in by the wind from the bustling city below. I go about my routine, picking up the jug of water from the corner and pouring the rest of it into my makeshift washbasin. I take my time scrubbing my face and hands before glancing at the broken mirror-glass leaning against the wall. My silvery hair could use a wash too, but my water is gone. I'll have to get more soon.

I sit on the edge of my mattress and eat one more tart before lying down for some much-needed sleep. My eyes trail to the rectangular paper still lying on the floor and my mouth goes dry when I read my name in curling calligraphy across it: Amberle Kindra.

My heart jumps into my throat.

I swallow and my tongue sticks to the roof of my mouth. I inch forward to pick it up.

It's a letter. Addressed to me.

In the seventy years since my father was taken, I haven't received a single package or letter from anyone. When I became a ghost—aka the infamous Silver Shadow—to keep my freedom, I trusted no one. I disappeared from the village where anyone knew what happened to me and my father.

With fumbling fingers, I turn it over and break the seal I'd recognize anywhere. It's the royal seal of a sun wearing a crown.

Amberle Kindra,

You are hereby requested to report at Herdan in a fortnight as one of the potential candidates in the upcoming Consort Tourney. At The Choosing, fifteen young fae will be selected from the candidates to compete in front of all of Faerie for a chance to win the heart of Prince Orion Illuminae.

—Signed, King Estelar Illuminae

Two

All thoughts of sleep flee as I stare at the invitation. My hands shake and the letters blur. Thousands of questions fill my mind as I contemplate what this means until I nearly go mad. Shoving the letter into my boot, I grab my pack and hooded cloak to conceal my head and wings, then emerge into the already crowded streets of Rosewind.

It's market day. Everyone wakes early on market day. I buy some pastries from the bakery shop owner, but I doubt I'll be able to eat them anytime soon. My appetite is gone. Still, I need a distraction so I make my way to the erluitle booths for chamois goat cheese.

Why was the letter sent to me? I wonder as I lose myself in the crowd. The erluitle's stall is at the far edge of town and I'm not in a hurry. Was it a mistake? Was it meant for someone else, but made its way to my hideout?

No. I think, feeling the edge of the letter dig into my ankle. The jabbing reminds me the invitation is real, and I didn't imagine it. It's addressed to me by name. Amberle Kindra. It wasn't a mistake.

So why me?

I come up with nothing that makes sense in the time it takes me to arrive at the erluitle booth. I purchase my cheese, but the red-faced, stocky creature's constant twitching and shuffling of their feet makes me nervous, so I quickly shove the cheese into my pack and turn back into the crowd.

If I dared fly away, I would, but the few faces who might recognize me don't know I have wings—and that the Silver Shadow does. I need to remain unforgettable. Wings on a star fae are rare. I force myself to calm and walk back to my hideout the same way I came. When I'm lost in the crowd again, I ease and slow my steps, but my thoughts are still a mess.

How do they know where I live? It's the most terrifying question of all. Even Clay doesn't know where I sleep at night, so how did the king's messengers find me?

And again, why me? I'm a nobody. I'm a star fae. I'm a thief.

A flash of light catches my eye and I notice the fine jewels—likely emeralds and sapphires—carved into beads wrapped around an elf's wrist with sea-foam colored hair piled in a high coif.

I'm not out to lift anything today since I have enough coins from last night's job to support my needs for weeks, but she oozes an air of entitlement. When she lifts her chin and looks down her nose at a shop owner, her disdain could cut glass. She's pure elf, by the looks of it. The shop owner meekly lifts a carved wooden hair comb in a humble presentation. It's intricately designed with a deft hand, one of the many fine adornments on the table. The extravagantly dressed elf's nostrils flare just a bit, the only indication of her ire before she tosses the spring fae's table, spilling the owner's wares all over the pathway. The more delicate pieces shatter, while the busy foot traffic crushes others. The elf shouts, each word punctuated with venom.

The devastation on the spring fae's face breaks my heart. With a loud wail, she rushes to salvage any of her beloved pieces, scooping them up while risking being trampled. The fae who caused the damage, the elf with the arrogant hair and expensive beads, presses the ball of her slipper onto a delicate pendant and grinds it into the cobblestones. The sound of a hundred tiny scratches signals the death of its value. Then she scoffs and walks away.

She should pay for that. For many spring fae, selling wares at the market is their only way to support themselves. It's their way to survive. And now that poor fae might go hungry; her entire family might go hungry because of a rich and spoiled elf's tantrum.

I set my sights on the elf with the too-fancy beads. Snatching that bracelet will be the perfect distraction, but I lose her in the push of the crowd. Still, I keep moving in the direction the elf went, watching for her ridiculous hair.

Lifting jewels and picking pockets is child's play, so my thoughts wander back to my dilemma as I track her.

I could probably just ignore the invitation. I try not to act like I'm in a hurry as I meander through the crowd. In the king's announcement, he said that hundreds of invitations were delivered. If I don't show up at The Choosing, no one will notice—

There.

The elf has stopped at a booth to examine another artisan's craft. I pivot my direction to bring myself closer to her without being too obvious.

That's it. I won't go to Herdan. The prince, let alone the king, doesn't want me in the Tourney, anyway.

My fingers are quick and make light work of removing the bracelet as I pass behind the elf. In a half-breath I've pocketed the precious jewels and make a wide berth to turn back the opposite direction. Slipping these jewels into the spring artisan's pocket will only heighten my good mood now that I've decided to ignore the invitation.

"Thief!"

My heart stalls.

I recognize the shout. Moments ago it rang out when the rich elf shouted at that poor shopkeeper before tossing her table. I make the mistake of turning my head and meet the elf's eyes. She points a long finger directly at me.

"Thief! She stole my property!"

I run.

"She stole my jewels! She just admitted it! Stop her!"

Footsteps and more shouting pursue.

How did I slip up? I chide myself as I weave and push through the crowd. That was supposed to be a simple job! A quick lift! I was supposed to be long gone before the elf even realized she was missing her bracelet. What did I do wrong?

I scan the area for a booth or alley I can duck into and slip away, but I feel them practically breathing down my neck. They can see me. If I duck anywhere, they'll see where I go.

I make a sharp turn down another street lined with more stalls and lose them. I only have a moment before I'll be in eyesight again. A strong hand grabs my wrist and jerks me downward. My already bruised knees crack on the stone street.

I cry out and try to pull away, but my captor's grip tightens.

"I'm trying to help you. Just trust me," he says. He's hooded too, so I can't see his face, but his voice is too low to be Clay.

This fae sounds older. Closer to my age.

He watches for something, then says, "Come on," and pulls me back to my feet and into a very narrow space between two booths and farther back between the stalls. Keeping us more concealed.

If I break free and run back into the street, my pursuers will see me for sure. I have no choice but to follow this fae, whoever he is. I must trust him.

Without releasing my wrist, he slips through a curtain into the back area of one stall, then finds a hidden door that leads to a secluded alleyway that opens up to the next street over. When the hooded fae releases my arm to sprint, I follow. It goes against my better nature not to slip away now that I've lost those who were after me, but I'm curious about this fae who saved me. Why did he help me?

He turns left on the street, then takes another hard right, then left again before slowing his steps. The noise of my pursuers and the market quiets and we soon slip out onto one of the less crowded streets lined with small houses and hovels.

The fae slows—as if we haven't just been running for our lives—to walk beside me and removes his hood to reveal a mess of walnut-brown hair and familiar golden cat-like slit eyes. I can't place him though. I don't know how I recognize those distinct eyes because I don't think he's from Rosewind. He's not a spring fae. Summer, maybe?

"Now, we act casual," he says.

I nod and remove my hood, letting my own silvery hair spill around my shoulders, but keep my wings tucked underneath the cloak. My heart still pounds, especially having my face in full view, out in the open and in broad daylight, no less. But I understand what he's trying to do. He doesn't want us to seem suspicious.

"Why are you helping me?" I ask, trying not to look like a paranoid fae by darting my head and eyes at everything that moves.

When he looks at me, directing his gold eyes paired with a full smile, I have to tell myself that the flip of my stomach and the pounding of my heart have more to do with what I just escaped.

He shrugs and pushes dark hair from his eyes.

I look away.

"I stole the gems from that elf. I'm a thief." When he doesn't comment, I ask again, "Why did you help me?"

"It seemed like she deserved it."

Don't let the high court hear you say that, I think, but don't voice. "Who are you? What are you doing in Rosewind?"

He remains silent for a long moment before answering, "My father has business here, I came with him."

We walk up to the entrance of one of the famous spring orchards with trees forever covered in pink and white blossoms, and meander in to catch our breaths. The stranger stops at a tree and leans against the trunk. I should keep moving, but my feet won't obey. A blossom flutters down and lands in his windswept hair. My fingers itch to remove it, but I refrain.

"So why did you steal the bracelet?" he asks. "Is it for your drinking habits and shady activities?" He winks and I'm nearly undone, but I keep a stoic expression. "Weren't you ever taught by your father or mother that society breaks down when the fae steal?"

I only have few memories of my mother, but the mention of my father smarts, and I wince and close my eyes against the prick of pain in my chest. "No, I steal to survive."

We hear the ringing shout of the Rosewind authorities just outside the orchard.

"Come!" my self-designated protector says, pulling up his hood and gripping my arm again to run.

"I can run very well on my own, thank you," I say as I pull my arm away to put my own hood up.

He scoffs but makes sure I'm trailing him as he weaves through the trees, and we put more distance between our pursuers again. His movements aren't predictable, and he moves in a roundabout way that leads us back into the heart of Rosewind.

This guy is good, I realize and wonder if Clay would be opposed to adding a member to our unofficial team. Although, this stranger mentioned he isn't from Rosewind.

"But I didn't steal to survive today," I say when we press against a building as two enforcers pass by. Sucking in a breath, I pray to Vejo I'm not seen and recognized. I sigh when they pass without incident. "You were right. That elf deserved it because she destroyed one of the artisan's booths."

His cat-eyes widen, revealing the points at either end of his slitted pupils.

"The elf was angry and tossed the table. The spring fae's work and livelihood were destroyed, so I took the bracelet with the intention of slipping it into the pocket of the artisan. To pay for what she had destroyed."

I don't know why I'm telling him any of this, but it just spills out.

"That's very noble of you," he says, holding my gaze.

"The street is clear," I say to break his spell.

He nods and we move further down the road in the direction of the market, but after a few steps, I slow in hesitation. How can I get the jewels to the fae without being seen? Without being recognized and caught? I won't help anyone if I'm carted away to a dungeon.

"I can take it to her for you," he offers, as if reading my thoughts.

I clutch my pack tightly. "Or maybe you'll take them and keep them for yourself."

He smiles. "One can never be too careful."

I raise an eyebrow. "You still haven't told me who you are. Why are you helping me?"

"I'm just someone who wants to help." His hand hovers in the air between us, but I don't move to hand him the jewels. "They're not looking for me, they're looking for you. If you try to go back to the market, you'll get caught. I promise I'll get them to her. You have my word." He winks again. "And I think I've proved that I'm capable."

I consider his offer, but we've only just met. It doesn't require much to gain someone's trust in a few moments, only to betray them at the first opportunity. I know nothing of him that tells me he wasn't helping me escape, only to keep the jewelry for himself. For all I know, he's new to town, ready to take over my territory here in Rosewind. I'd be a fool if I trust him this quickly because he has a nice smile.

"No, thanks," I say, and walk swiftly away. Clay can slip the string of emeralds and sapphires into the artisan's pocket tomorrow. With that thought, I reach in my pack to feel for the jewels, but only feel the now-smooshed pastries and erluitle cheese. Frantically, I lift my pack to search more thoroughly, but they're gone.

Looking up, I see the mysterious fae slip them into his pocket as he hurries back to the bustling market.

Thief!

But I can't follow him into the crowd. I can't demand that he give back what isn't even rightfully mine. I can't do anything! Scaling the cottage next to me, I crouch on the rooftop so I can peer over it and get a bird's-eye-view of the market. I can watch, but I'm powerless to do anything to get the bracelet back.

My eyes search the crowd for the dark-haired fae. I spot him strolling through the press of bodies with his hood back up. When he reaches the stall of the artisan, he stops. She's hunched over, still in distress over her broken wares. Has he figured out who I wanted to give them to? Does he plan to do what I can't?

The artisan jerks in surprise when he addresses her and looks up. He doesn't hand over the bracelet. Instead, she riffles through her broken pieces and hands him a couple of her creations, which he pays for with a few coins. When the spring fae turns her back and before he walks away, I watch the mysterious fae slip the gems into the pocket of her dress. She didn't even notice. I can't help but smile.

Three

Maybe some fae can be trusted.

A familiar shadow appears in my peripheral, but I don't turn or greet him.

"What was that, Amberle?" Clay's voice comes from behind. "Did you want to get caught?"

"It was nothing," I say, climbing down the back part of the cottage, dropping the last few feet.

Clay lands next to me, placing a hand on the ground to brace his fall.

"They almost caught you," he says.

"I made a mistake."

"The Amberle Kindra I know doesn't make mistakes."

I whip on him. "What about last night? You were pretty sure I made a mistake last night!"

He backs up a step, but stands his ground. "I know what I said last night, but that was in jest. I thought the king's announcement would put you out of sorts, but you were focused, as always."

I turn on my heel and keep walking, tucking my hair back into my hood to better conceal myself.

"You should've been caught last night," Clay adds. He catches back up to me and gestures with his hands. "You were right there in the room with that fae and he never saw you!" Clay whistles low. "But today? From what I heard, it was a simple lift. What happened?"

The sounds of running boots pricks my ears, making my heart rate spike, so I duck behind some barrels and hiss at Clay. "From what you heard? Who is talking?"

He crouches beside me. "Everyone in Rosewind. Those jewels you stole belonged to some relative of an autumn princess."

I grip his shirt front, bringing his boyish face smattered with freckles closer to mine, but I don't know what I want to ask. If whatever he knows is hearsay from a bunch of witnesses, a likeness of my face could be plastered on bulletins all over Faerie.

Clay laughs. "I don't think they got a good look at you."

I loosen my grip. "Why do you say that?"

"Because everyone is looking for a silver-haired troll with pockmarks and warts."

I release him and sit back against the barrel. "I could've sworn the elf got a good look at me."

Clay shrugs. "Someone important swore he saw a troll with the jewels. Between his report and what the elf saw of you, the description quickly distorted."

"Well, that's a relief."

"So, are you going to tell me what's really going on?"

I adjust my foot and feel the sharp edge of the invitation for the Tourney in my boot.

"Why were you so distracted?"

"It doesn't matter."

"Was last night not enough?"

I know what he's thinking. That I've become greedy. That I have enough to last me a while, but I want more. "No, it was a thing of principle. I don't even have the jewels anymore." And thank Vejo that stranger stayed true to his word. "I made sure they went to someone who needed them."

"And it couldn't wait?" Clay is becoming frustrated with me. "You're not telling me everything. Amberle, what's going on?"

"It doesn't matter." It's not like I'm going to Herdan, anyway. I've already made that decision.

"You don't want to tell me, but if you're in trouble, I'm the only one you've got." He stands up to walk away.

He's right. He's my only friend, and it doesn't matter if I tell him about the invitation since I'm not even going. "Clay, wait."

He turns.

I look at him, then at the ground and bite my lip as I reach down to pull the note from my boot and hold it out.

Clay doesn't take his eyes off my face in silent question as he walks back toward me and takes the paper, unfolds it, then drops his eyes to the words.

His eyes widen.

I snatch it from him and shove it back into my boot.

"Where did you get that?"

"It was in my hideout after I returned last night," I say. "But I'm not going. I'm a star fae, I'm sure it was a mistake. The prince and the king don't want me—*er*, someone like me there."

"Is it wise to ignore it?"

"Yes. Clay, it's a mistake. It must be."

"But it was sent to your hideout. Even I don't know where you live!" He pauses and leans forward, placing a hand on mine and showing maturity and soberness beyond his years. "I doubt it was a mistake."

I don't have to force the yawn that comes. "I'm tired and I need to lie low for a while," I say and scan the area before standing. "I'm going to get some sleep."

When I walk away, Clay puts a hand on my shoulder. "Amberle." He pauses as if carefully choosing his words. "I don't need to remind you how dangerous it can be to ignore the high court."

I nod at his unsaid words. If the king found me once, he can find me again.

To be safe, I take the long way home and Clay doesn't follow.

I keep to the shadows and make sure not a single soul sees me. Whether they're looking for a troll or not, I'm not risking getting caught. It takes hours to get back to my hideout, and I'm absolutely dead on my feet when I reach the bakery.

I walk around the back so I'm not seen when I fly up to my window, daydreaming about my lumpy bed and the even more lumpy pillow waiting for me. At least I won't be caught off guard by a ridiculous invitation to the Consort Tourney this time, and now that the shock of that and the excitement of the day has worn off, I'm sure I will fall asleep the second my head hits the pillow.

That is, if I can get those *slaugh* golden eyes out of my head. The memory of that mysterious fae who saved me from a thief's punishment when he had absolutely no reason to is sure to keep me up for a little while. I just hope the mere fact that he's not in Rosewind long and that I'll likely never see him again is enough to help my brain shut down and finally get some rest.

I lift my cloak to free my wings and flutter up with all the energy I have left, landing hard on the floor of my sanctuary.

But for the thousandth time today, my heart attempts to flee my ribcage.

Someone is in my room.

And not just any someone. This someone I saw only yesterday in the middle of town with fancy winter fae magic as he announced the Consort Tourney.

Only yesterday he wasn't *actually there*. His image and likeness and message were projected with some illusion magic while the king spoke to his kingdom from the comfort of his palace in Isi Aura. In the Summer Court.

He wasn't in the center of Rosewind yesterday, but there's no doubt the high king of Faerie, King Estelar Illuminae, is real and very present now.

And he is standing in the middle of my bedroom.

Four

I don't think, I just step back to escape out the window, but one of the king's guards steps in my way, blocking my path. The king has brought six with him. All who are crammed in my small little hideout/bedroom.

I kneel. Six guards is a lot. Only two guards came when they took my father away.

"Don't worry," King Estelar says. "I just want to talk."

I don't respond and keep my eyes glued to the floor. My mind spins as I contemplate the best way to escape. I know my home, my hideout, better than anyone and while the guards are blocking the obvious exits—the two windows, and the door that leads to the balcony and down the stairs out the back—they don't know about the trapdoor beneath the threadbare rug that leads directly down to the bakery.

I've never used it because I didn't want to be caught using it by the baker, but after today, this is no longer my sanctuary.

One guard stands on top of it, but as soon as she moves, I'll slip down and out before any of them knows what happened.

"You may stand, Amberle."

I obey and dare raise my eyes to meet his.

"You've grown up," the king says. "I almost didn't recognize you. And this is new." He points at the side of his right eye, indicating my ink marking. My promise to get my father freed.

"Are you here to take me too?" I don't mean for it to come out hoarse, in a whisper like a coward, but I can't help it.

The king turns on his heel and clasps both hands behind his back while looking at the floor. "Did you receive your invitation to the Consort Tourney?"

Of course, that's why he's here. "I'm baffled I was considered."

And for the first time I ponder what it would mean to be a part of the Tourney. My memories are flooded with visions of a dark-haired boy. Intelligent, practical, mostly arrogant.

"You won't be, but I want you there." He straightens and looks at me.

"Why? It's been a long time since I've seen the prince." And I didn't particularly like him back then, but I keep that little tidbit to myself. "Plus, I'm a star fae, I assumed you wanted someone full-blooded on the throne."

"You are correct," says the king. "But I want you there because I don't trust the fae."

I eye his guards briefly, but none of them slip out of their stone-like expression. And the one still blocks the trapdoor.

When I turn back to the king, he continues. "I expect the contestants will act one way when all of Faerie is watching. I expect they'll act a certain way with my son. But I also expect they might have ulterior motives that only the other contestants might see."

"Ulterior motives?" I bite back the urge to scoff. "Like not caring about the prince and only wanting to become the high queen?"

"Like winning the crown, then planning assassinations."

"I see how that could pose a problem."

"My son is a romantic and he wants to marry for love, but it's imperative that he chooses the right fae."

"Why do you need me?"

King Estelar smiles. The smile lights his entire face, pulling me into his glamour. Making himself look more benevolent, more trustworthy as he manipulates the light around his face to create what I know is a farce.

Slaugh summer fae magic, the specialty of his kind.

"Rumors of the great Silver Shadow have made it all the way to the High Court, Amberle."

I can't help but squirm at the mention. I thought Clay was the only person who knows I'm the Silver Shadow. No one else. And especially not the High King.

"I'm impressed with you and I trust you," he adds.

"Why?" I ask. It just flies out.

"Because if you do as I ask, exactly as I ask, I'll release your father."

The room seems to spin as his words sink in. This could be my chance to free my father. This could be my chance to live up to my promise. Absently, I touch my fingers to my inked mark.

But what will it cost? "What if I say no?"

"Then you'll never see him again. Simple as that." The king snaps his fingers, bringing all his guards to attention.

"Why did you take him?" I plead. The one guard lifts the rug and pulls up the hatch. It feels as if rocks have been dropped into my stomach. Apparently, they knew about the trap door all along.

The king's head snaps to me, and the light shifts around, sharpening his features and making him look fierce. "That is not your concern."

But it only lasts a second before the easy smile returns.

"I don't need an answer now," he says as two of his guards descend. "I'll know your answer when you arrive in Herdan for your name to be drawn." He pauses before also descending and approaches me. "But I know you'll come."

That comment alone makes me want to refuse him immediately. But if this is my chance to free my father? To see him again? I'm not sure I have a choice.

"But you cannot go into this thinking you'll easily stay," King

Estelar warns. "You must do well in the trials and act the part. Questions will be raised if I'm giving special treatment to a star fae."

Trials. Tasks. All part of the competition. I swallow over the acrid lump that forms at his insult, pushing it down in self-preservation, and nod. "I'm not a youngling anymore. I am grown and adept at fulfilling the jobs I'm hired for."

I have no concerns for whatever the high court throws at the contestants. I may have to play down my skills to keep my true identity a secret.

King Estelar seems satisfied, but moves closer, stopping only inches away from my face. I smell sharp citrus on his breath. "Yes, but Prince Orion also must like you enough to keep you, so don't do anything foolish to get yourself sent home before you've completed your task."

I hadn't thought about the reality of that. My pride falls a few rungs because this isn't like other jobs. I'll have to play a part and pretend to be interested in a gangly, spoiled little princeling. Last I remember, he hated me. That part could be tricky. "Yes, Your Majesty."

"But don't make him like you too much, because you won't be the one he chooses."

Obviously not in the realm of possibility, I think, but merely nod.

He moves away, turning to leave, but flashes one last self-satisfied smile. "And I would advise you not to fall in love with him either. I'd hate for you to run out empty-handed because your broken heart couldn't stay long enough to free your father."

It's all I can do to keep the incredulous laugh from escaping. "I assure you that won't be a problem."

I pack my few possessions and leave my hideout for the last time. It's not my safe haven anymore. It's not my home. Too many dangerous fae know where it is, so it will never be my home again. I'm not too heartbroken about it. After what happened at the market, I was going to find a new place, anyway.

It's unwise to go there, but I climb up Wild Rose Hill, my favorite overlook of Oris Lake after the sun sets and the sky goes dark. Looking out at the lake and glancing up at the stars fills my thoughts with memories of when my father and I visited once soon after we left the palace in Isi Aura.

Pondering on the king's proposal sets my teeth on edge and twists my insides. He wants me to be on display among all those other fae in the Tourney. All my years of hiding, and I'll be unmasked, in a way. Yet as a spy, I'll have to keep my true intentions secret, not just from the contestants, but from all of Faerie.

"I thought I'd find you here," Clay says. He keeps his distance between us, but sits next to me, glances at my bag, then at the dark lake. "You're leaving."

"I have to."

"But why?" he asks. "Just lie low. No one even saw your face, remember? They're looking for an ugly troll. There's no mention that the Silver Shadow had any part in it." He grins at me, waiting for me to look over. When I do, he continues, "and how could they? The Silver Shadow doesn't make silly mistakes like almost getting caught with a simple lift."

I reach over to shove him and laugh.

"But that's why, isn't it?" he asks, sobering and gesturing at the invitation to the Tourney I forgot I had clenched in my hand. "That's why you were distracted in the market today."

I nod and swallow hard, blinking away the burning tears, and look out at the lake.

"Are you going to Herdan?"

I sigh. "Someone paid me a visit."

"Who?"

I glance at him. "It's safer if you don't know."

"Alright, what did *this someone* want?"

"I'll just say that *this someone* is a person with high ranking in the high court and they asked for my help."

"Ha! They asked for your help? Is the high court in need of a good thief?" he jokes.

"They know I'm the Silver Shadow, which worries me. But I uh…" I sigh and pull my legs close to my chest, hugging my arms around them.

"Amberle, what is it?" Clay asks. I feel his eyes on me, but I can't look at him. I'm afraid if I look at him, I'll give in and tell him everything. And not only that High King Estelar himself paid me a visit, but that he's known me since I was a youngling. I might tell him I grew up in the palace. I might tell him that the prince—the one the king is posturing this Consort Tourney for— was someone I grew up with. "Will you be one of the competitors in the Tourney?"

"Officially, yes."

"But actually?"

"No." I explain the concern about potential political killings. I have to admit the king's worries are valid. The courts are brutal.

Clay's brow furrows. "Wouldn't any of the fae turn in a traitor for treason?" But as he speaks, I see that he knows the answer to that question. "Why you?"

"I think I'm also there to make sure whoever the prince prefers, whoever he falls in love with, loves him too," I say. King Estelar didn't explicitly say that, but when he said his son was a romantic and wanted to marry for love, it seemed the king has his son's best interests at heart.

"Huh. I didn't think the king cared."

"Apparently he does."

"Are you going to do it? Or do you have a choice?"

"I have a choice," I say.

"But?"

I glance at my friend and can't help but allow the tears to build. I hastily brush away the one that escapes. "But if I do this… he'll release my father."

Clay inhales sharply, then leans back on his hands. "So what are you going to do? Woo the prince?"

I laugh once, grateful my friend knows how to lighten a heavy mood. "No. I'll get to go eat fine food and wear fine dresses and do what I do best, with the permission of the high king of Faerie."

"What? Steal the crown jewels?"

"Steal information. And my reward will be getting my family back." I grin wide.

"You're doing it, then. You're going to Herdan." I can see Clay is excited for me.

"Yes, I'm going."

Five

I sit crouched on a rooftop, watching the city and clutching the key tied to a string around my neck. Clay suggested I take it. There's nothing particularly unique about the key. There are thousands just like it in Faerie, so he didn't seem worried about it tying me to theft of the deeds. No, it felt like a sort of don't-forget-about-me type gesture. Not that I could ever forget my long-time partner, especially since it's only been a week since we parted.

From high on my perch, I've observed the spring fae of Herdan bustle to and fro. Even from up here a collective electric mood is amplified as it bounces along every wall and every fae—pure-blooded or otherwise—down below. The bubbling bundle of nerves and excitement make the air thick and nearly suffocating as all anyone can talk about is the upcoming Tourney choosing.

The choosing that will happen in the center of Herdan in only a few hours.

But I don't need their buzzing energy to feel the nauseating thrumming within my core, because I know the king plans to use his mysterious magic to project this historic event to every city and every town within the realm. So, in only a few hours, all of

Faerie will see my face. Me. Amberle Kindra: star fae, half-blood, urchin, thief, and soon-to-be spy for the High King.

My palms are clammy. My heart races. After traveling from Rosewind to the Spring Court capital while hugging the shore of Oris Lake, I took the time to prepare myself for this. I thought the time alone on my trek would be enough. I thought I would be ready. I should be ready. But as soon as the towering buildings of the city came into view, my instincts kicked in. I couldn't even enter Herdan through the front gates, and instead skirted the edge and snuck in the back way to observe without being noticed.

Just like always. Well... always since my father was taken.

But I can't sit up here on this roof forever. I must go down. I must make my way to the center. I must present myself for my name to be called. I must do everything the king has asked if I'm ever to see my father again.

Touching a finger to my inked promise, I steel myself.

First, I need more suitable clothing. I know the precise shade of gray my skirt is without even looking. I don't remember the original color, but it wasn't gray. Whether it was black and faded with washings and the sun, or if it was white and has merely absorbed the dirt and grime over the decades, I can't remember.

I'm afraid I might stand out as a star fae. Some won't recognize my heritage at a glance because wings on star fae are so rare, but it's bound to come out eventually and I don't need to stand out more by looking drab and pathetic. But I can't steal a better dress. It won't do me any favors to look presentable only to have the shopkeeper recognize their stolen property and call me out for what I really am. Besides, the king would probably have me murdered with a snap of his fingers if I disgraced the Tourney before it even began. So I force myself to move out of the shadows and deftly scale the rooftops until I find a shop.

I locate one off the main roadway—which means fewer prying eyes—but I can see the finery of silks and satins through the window. The shop might be off the beaten path, but it's nothing to stick my nose up at. Even from my distance, I see fabric in colors that would give the Silver Shadow's position away in a heist, but will blend right in amongst courtiers and royals. It's perfect.

A few buildings away, I climb down a vine, making sure I'm not being watched. Then I take a deep breath, straighten my shoulders, and pull my hood away from my head, revealing my silver hair. I must appear to have some pride and confidence when I walk in.

The door chimes when I push it open. I pause as my eyes adjust to the lower light and watch dust motes fly around in rays of sunshine coming through the windows.

"Can I help you?" a small wood elf asks, stepping from around a curtain.

"Yes, I-I need to purchase a dress." I expect the shopkeeper to rove her eyes over me with scrutiny since I look either poor, like a criminal, or like some other low-life creature. But I see no judgment on her face. And although her hair is a striking ivy green and her skin is the texture and color of aspen bark—two very obvious signs she's full-fae—it's the color of her eyes that gives me pause. Rimmed in brown, her irises are a striking pale blue full of obvious... kindness. It's a rare trait in any fae. Especially the pure-blooded.

"Yes, it looks like you need something new," she says with a smile that squints her eyes so dramatically they almost disappear. Immediately she goes to work, flipping through dresses on a rack, looking at me as she appraises each one. "No, that won't do," she says, then replaces the midnight blue gown. She frowns when she holds up one that is jade green. "Not that one either." She doesn't even speak when she considers an ivory dress and merely shakes her head.

But then her eyes light and she lifts a finger.

"I have just the thing. Wait here a moment." The pale-eyed elf scuttles to the back through the curtain to the concealed room.

Wringing my hands together while I wait, I shuffle my feet back and forth, darting my eyes around, looking for all the exits.

Two windows, one door. Unless there's another door past that curtain. I wipe my hands along my skirts to calm myself, but it isn't working, and I nearly dart behind a shelf when the shop-keeper reemerges.

"This one will look enchanting on you!" She holds up the dress, a deep mulberry with lace in the bodice flaring out with a full-length silk skirt.

My eyes widen. "It's exquisite. But no, I think that's too much. I don't think—"

"Nonsense," she interrupts. "It's exactly what you need as one of the possible contestants of the Consort Tourney. You should stand out."

"How did you...?" I ask, but can't finish the question.

She smiles. "One can just tell." She wags a bone-white finger. "I had a feeling about you the moment you walked through the door."

My adrenaline spikes, and I step backward.

"No need to be so frightened, dear. Besides, I've had several young fae in my shop since they sent the invitations out. It's a little unwise, searching for a dress this late." When I don't respond, she continues, "But, it'll all work out. And if it's a matter of cost, I'm sure we can work something out."

"Cost is not an issue." I still have funds from my most recent job. But I don't want to stand out. Still, I'll stand out more if I arrive in my current drab. *You must act the part*, Amberle, I remind myself. Forcing myself to calm, I say, "The dress is perfect," and hand over the coins for the purchase.

"Do you have a place to ready yourself?" she asks before I turn to leave.

Am I that obvious? My plan was to find some back corner alley where I can quickly change, and hopefully find a trough some-where to wipe the grime from my face and hands. Not ideal, but I don't have many options.

"I know you aren't from Herdan," she explains. "You are more than welcome to ready yourself here." She walks toward me, placing one hand on my shoulder and gesturing to the back room with the other.

"No, I shouldn't." I start, my heart rate spiking.

"I insist. You're safe here."

"I uh..." But I can't afford to say no. If I can't find a suitable place to get ready, I might be late, and then it won't matter how fancy my dress is. Fae can't lie, so I know her promise about my safety is sincere. I should also get used to allowing others to help me, since there might be servants to aid the contestants once we enter the palace. Might as well practice now. "Yes."

She leads me toward the back and through the curtain, revealing a small storage room that also serves as a bedroom with a simple mattress, a vanity with a mirror and a porcelain wash basin decorated with painted blue flowers. Without a word, she picks up the matching porcelain jug off the floor and fills the basin, then leaves me, closing the curtain between us to give me privacy.

All I can do is stare at the washbasin as if I've never seen one before. It's nothing compared to the one I kept in my hideout back home in Rosewind, but that's not what has me staring. I recognize the jars sitting next to it and know they're filled with different smelling soaps and oils. The sight of them—the familiar, yet foreign sight—causes a deep ache that fills my breast. The last time I saw jars of smelling soaps and oils, they were common, everyday items. Such things aren't exceptionally lavish, but as a thief, a ghost, I could never afford such luxuries. But they were in every washroom where I grew up. In the palace.

Since my youth in the palace, they have become but a memory.

I take my time washing my face and hair with the rosemary-scented oils—my favorite. I scrub under my fingernails, my legs, my feet. And when I'm done, I stare at the glass in front of me. My promise mark shines, my silver hair glows, and when I remove my tattered clothing to stretch my dragonfly wings and clean them too, their coloring becomes immediately vibrant.

Slipping into the mulberry dress, I'm enamored by the way it covers my shoulders and dips into a delicate scoop neckline below my throat. The key is perfectly concealed below the fabric. The back is low enough for my wings to be free, but I fold and tuck them in. Crushing them. Gritting my teeth against the pain, I finger-comb my damp tresses. The pain builds until I can't take the binding anymore and pull my wings out, fluttering them several times to shake out the hurt. I'll just have to wear my cloak to keep them concealed. It's in better shape than my former dress.

The wood elf's white tree-bark face lights up when I emerge from behind the curtain, carefully tucking the visible parts of my wings beneath my cloak.

"Oh dear, you shouldn't hide those. They're beautiful."

I stare at my feet as my cheeks flush. "I just I..."

"Why do you hide them?" she asks when I don't finish.

Instinct. In Rosewind, my dragonfly wings could easily give away my identity as the Silver Shadow. But perhaps that's foolishness to worry about that here. "I am a star fae. Star fae rarely have wings and... I didn't want to stand out."

She studies me for several moments. Long enough that I fear she can read every emotion, every thought, every secret. "You are frightened to be seen, but the star fae need someone like you to represent them. Someone who isn't afraid of who they are." She pauses, still reading me. "You are not frightened of who you are, but you distrust too deeply."

"I—"

"You should stand out," she interrupts. "And learn to trust."

I'm baffled. With her ivy green hair and wide smile, she is so clearly a full-blooded fae—or *pure*, as they call themselves. So why is she being so kind to me, a halfling? A star fae.

She seems to read my thoughts. "Like I said, I have a feeling about you. Don't conceal your wings."

"Why?"

"I hear the prince has a thing for wings." Her smile crinkles her face. "Now, please allow me to brush your hair."

I open my mouth to speak, but nothing comes out.

The prince has a thing for wings? That might have flattered me if I didn't know Prince Rion personally, and I'm not going to the palace to win his heart, anyway. But to hear he has a thing for wings? Surely, it's a rumor, a gossip. In all the years I knew him, he never once admitted to favoring them.

I turn so the wood elf can attend to my hair. She takes her time with slow, methodical strokes until my hair is as smooth as a waterfall cascading around my shoulders. I can't remember the last time my hair was brushed so thoroughly.

No one other than myself has combed it since my mother died. And I barely remember her.

"You should go," she says. "The king will announce the contestants soon. You don't want to be late."

"No, I don't." I follow her to the door and take several deep breaths, bracing myself. I glance at her once more, but I can't leave without asking, "What is your name?"

"Maeve. Now go! Keep your head high and your chin up."

When I spy my cloak draped over Maeve's arm, she quickly folds it and shoves it in my pack so I can't even think about hiding my wings again. Then she opens the door.

I walk out into the bright sunshine. I turn back to offer a token of my appreciation, or even a thanks, but her shop doors are already closed. She's already gone. When I turn forward again, I run smack into something hard and firm.

"Oh!" I say, jerking back. My face flushes when I see who I've run into.

It's the stranger from Rosewind. The one with the golden cat eyes and walnut hair.

Six

I fold my arms and narrow my eyes at him. "Are you spying on me?" I ask, realizing too late that it's a poor choice of words since I'm about to become a spy for the king. Thinking quickly, I say, "Or does your father have business in Herdan too?"

He laughs and pushes back a lock of his dark hair. "Yes, my father has business in Herdan. But I'm here to watch the Tourney choosing. Why are you here? You look... different."

The way he says *different* doesn't sound bad, but when he looks behind me, I want to hide. My wings are not small and when I don't keep them concealed, they fan out on both sides. I want to run. I want to cover them up and not let them ever come out again for fear of whatever he's about to say about them.

"I didn't know you had wings," he says, glancing back at me with a confused expression mixed with another emotion I can't name.

Oh no.

He's smart and everyone knows the infamous Silver Shadow has wings and has been thieving in the outer parts of the Spring Court this past decade. He also knows I'm a thief. What if he puts the two together and turns me in?

"Yes, well, we knew each other for less than an hour," I say, pushing past him. "You probably didn't notice them." *Because they were hidden beneath my cloak*, I don't add.

"Do you plan to watch The Choosing too?" he asks, catching up.

"I am." I can't look at him, but he matches my stride and clasps both hands behind his back.

"Why did you travel all the way to Herdan when you could have stayed in Rosewind to watch?"

"If you remember, I was nearly caught stealing in Rosewind. I can't show my face there for a while."

"Is that why you've changed your appearance?" he asks. "Is that why you wear finery now?"

"I did not steal this dress, if that's what you are implying."

"That was not my presumption," he says with a smirk. I may not be able to lie, but he doesn't think I voiced the entire truth. He still sees me as what I am, a thief, which shouldn't bother me, but I worry it could create problems later. Especially since I'll be on display at the summer palace soon.

He hasn't been forthcoming about his identity either. I know neither his name, nor where he's from. By his clothing, I can't guess because his shirt and trousers are well kept, but not exorbitant. For all I know he could be a rich merchant... or a thief too. But since he's about to watch The Choosing, if I don't tell some truth, he will only become more suspicious.

"Somehow my name got thrown into the mix of eligible young fae for the Tourney," I say as an explanation for wearing the pretty mulberry dress. "And before you say anything about the likeliness that it was a mistake to invite a street urchin and a thief as one of the prince's choices, just know that I was confounded at the invitation too."

He ducks his head. "I admit that notion was far from my thoughts." Carefully arranging his features to hide his emotion, he continues, "What's your name? I'll listen for you and hope you're one of the chosen."

Now I'm nonplussed. *He hopes I'm one of the chosen?* I shove my mixed feelings away. "You'll know my name after I'm called and step forward."

I turn away. Even without my name, I've given away too much.

"Such confidence!" he shouts at my back, and I hear the pleasure in his voice. "I wish you luck, noble thief from Rosewind."

Part of me wishes I could bury him—the one person who knows what I am and where I've most recently been thieving. He's dangerous. Instead, I hurry away, before he can yell any louder about my sticky fingers.

I walk toward the center of Herdan, following the slow-moving crowd. The words *noble thief from Rosewind* echo in my head, but I push them away along with the image of the stranger's impish smile and walnut-colored hair.

Focus, Amberle.

Someone turns and stares at my exquisite dress. I cringe, hating that I stand out after years of blending in. I remind myself that anyone who stares at my dress will assume I'm one of the possible Tourney contestants.

Which is the truth.

When I arrive at the center, a large platform has been constructed, likely with spring magic. Most of the crowd wears typical whimsical spring attire, but a grouping of dozens of females toward the front draws my attention. They're clearly the ones who have received invitations. My elegant dress will blend in with the finery of theirs.

I take a breath.

Pushing my way through the crowd, fae let me pass as they recognize me as another of the possible chosen. But I stop on the outskirts of the gathered hopefuls. I'm not ready to begin pretending and spying and appraising the girls just yet. Besides, it won't do any good to pay much attention until I know who's going to the palace and who's staying behind.

A spring girl with long, neatly arranged red plaits spots me and pushes her way through the press of bodies until she stands next to me. She's short and stocky and her smile is electric.

"Isn't this exciting?" she asks, letting out a quiet squeal.

I press my lips together in a smile and nod.

"My name is Didi Beechriver," she says. "What's yours?"

Here we go. It's time to act the part, Amberle. Instinct tells me to avoid the question, to avoid answering. But if this girl is also one of the chosen, she can't know the real reason I'm here. I must give her my name willingly.

"Amberle," I say. "Amberle Kindra."

"I'm glad to meet you, Amberle. Aren't you excited to see who is chosen?" She grips the crook of my arm tightly. "Isn't this romantic? The chance to win the heart of Prince Orion?" She sighs.

My attempt to hide my astonishment at her calling the prince by his formal name is weak, I'm sure, but I don't think she notices. Everyone who knows him well calls him Rion. Except maybe the king. But romantic isn't a word I'd use. The king mentioned the prince was looking for love despite this unusual way of finding a bride, so maybe it is romantic, but all I can manage is, "It is exciting."

"You know for forever I thought he would marry Princess Arielle Lieawarin, you know, from the Summer Court?"

I nod. Some fae live under literal rocks and don't know the names of all the different court royals, but the majority know the big players, and Arielle is one of them. Of course, I know her more than some because the princess and I were once caught sneaking pastries together. Actually, I was never caught—I was good at thieving even back then—but when they discovered Arielle, she turned me in as her accomplice. Still, we remained friends until my father and I left Isi Aura.

"Yes, they do seem an obvious match," I say. Arielle told me once the idea of her and Rion forming a union was a possibility, but this Consort Tourney makes me believe either the king doesn't approve of her or something else is going on. Still, I imagine Arielle will be in the running at least for show.

"But you don't think they are?" Didi catches my careful choice of words. "Do you think he prefers the other summer princess? Mora Rolen?"

"I have no idea who the prince will wed." Although it wouldn't surprise me if Mora's fanatic crush on Rion turned into an obsession. Still, with her status, she is likely to be chosen too.

"Do you want to know what I *really* think?" Didi asks, lowering her voice.

"I'm sure you'll tell me."

"I think Princess Arielle is the only actual choice. I think the king just wants the other girls to think they have a chance."

"Why?" I ask, turning toward her. "Why would the king go to so much trouble with the Tourney?"

She shrugs, but I can see the excitement in her face at my increased interest. "If the courts think one of their own might end up on the throne, they'll be more agreeable. Don't you think?"

"Do you believe the Consort Tourney is a political move? Something to appease the courts?"

"Possibly. That or a distraction."

I turn toward the empty platform, lost in thought. Didi is an observant fae. Smart too. "You might have a point."

Perhaps the king intends Rion to make a match with Arielle all along. Perhaps this is just a show to do exactly what Didi suspects: appease the courts. But if that's the case, why bring me in? Why ask me to spy and find out who is worthy of the crown? He doesn't think Arielle is capable of an assassination plot. Does he?

"But I hope that's not the case." She snaps out of her hushed tone and turns into a giddy, lovesick girl. "If I'm chosen, I hope to have a real chance. Can you imagine? Having the crown prince of Faerie fall in love with you? Humble beginnings leading to true love that just so happens to come with a crown and a throne? Love conquering all and everything?"

Thinking of the prince I knew, all scrawny and entitled, falling in love? I have a hard time imagining it. "I admit, it feels unlikely."

"Well, the first step is being chosen today, but after that, with your pretty face and wings..." She trails off as if the mention bothers her.

Another comment about my wings? Maybe there is something to it. I could safely assure her I won't be the one to catch his eye, but keep my mouth shut instead. If I'm not careful, I'll end up telling this stranger everything.

"Do you have any guesses who will be chosen?" Didi asks.

I look at the crowd of girls, but don't comment. There's no point telling her I'm going. She'll find out soon enough, even though I won't be her competition if she's chosen too.

"I know some girls here," she says. "Raine Hazelfalls is a definite shoo-in."

I nod, remembering Clay mentioning her.

"I also think Clove Farabella and Pansy Rimwarren have a good chance. But since only three will go and I'd like to be one of those three..." She nudges me. "Then obviously one of them won't be chosen."

"Three?"

"Yes, with the five courts, Summer, Winter, Spring, Autumn, and the Underwater Courts, three girls from each will be chosen to make up the fifteen who get to compete."

I'm glad she doesn't ask why I don't know any of this. It seems like she enjoys talking about the Consort Tourney and I get the feeling it's been a common topic of hers for a long time. It might have been a topic I also enjoyed if they hadn't taken my father the day the Tourney was announced.

Although I know Prince Rion more than most. Maybe I would have been indifferent either way.

"Do you think the other princesses will be in the running?" I ask. Didi might be an asset if she's chosen because she knows so much. Still, I should get as much information from her as I can in case she isn't. The odds aren't favorable. Hundreds of fae received invitations but only fifteen will be picked.

"Princess Shay of Winter will, but not Princess Tanya of Autumn because she found a mate last year."

"I'm impressed," I say. "You know everything."

"Not everything." She eyes me suspiciously. "I didn't know about you."

I swallow hard.

Seven

"You must've recognized my name. *Beechriver*," Didi says, flicking one of her red braids over one shoulder and folding her arms. "My father and mother are ambassadors to the king. But I don't know your name." She directs her full attention to me. "I haven't heard the name Kindra in any of the circles of Herdan."

My mouth is dry.

Think quickly! Am I to be found out so soon? It's not uncommon for star fae to leave the court of their heritage, not like it is for the full fae, but mentioning that will give more away than I'd like. Is this girl, the first girl I've even spoken with, going to find out the real reason I've come? Sweat breaks out along my brow. I can't help that, though I force myself to look casual.

"I'm uh... not from Herdan—"

A hush falls over the crowd, interrupting me. I turn toward the platform and close my eyes momentarily in relief and gratitude. It's imperative that the contestants don't ask me too many questions. I'm not a human, so I can't just come up with a cover story and lie through my teeth. There's a reason fae pay well when hiring thieves and spies like me. The moment a fae is caught, even star fae, we immediately confess our sins.

It was a close call, but I shift my thoughts to the moment, expecting to see a similar event like when the king announced the Tourney two weeks ago. I expect to see our sovereign materialize out of thin air whilst he addresses the realm from the comfort of his palace in the Summer Court. But I realize the hush that fell over the crowd has nothing to do with winter magic projecting the image of our leader.

Because the king is here. In Herdan.

Why is he here? Why is he announcing the contestants in the Spring Court? Sure, he visited me in Rosewind two weeks ago, but he's had plenty of time to go back to his glittering palace since then.

What is he doing here?

I realize with a jolt that the prince might be here too. I scan the area where the king stands, looking for the gawky, haughty boy prince I knew as a youngling in adult form. But I don't spot him among the hulking guards that are an intimidating presence around the king. I recognize them as the ones who filled my tiny room above the bakery.

"All of those who received an invitation, please join me on this platform," says the king, gesturing toward the press of elegantly dressed females.

I hesitate long enough that Didi grabs my hand to pull me forward.

"Come on!" she whispers. By her tone, I can tell all suspicions of who I am and why I'm here have fled her thoughts, or no longer matter. Maybe she assumes I'm enough of a nobody and won't be one of the chosen.

As we walk up to the platform, our group multiplies until four other groups of fae materialize and stand with us. By the amazing and mysterious winter projection magic, they're not actually here, but standing on similar platforms in their court capitals.

The sheer number of possible contestants—in the hundreds —is daunting, and the expression on every single fae has varying degrees of hope and arrogance, and a few of terror that they'll be one of the selected fifteen.

I wonder if they know the king is in Herdan and not Isi Aura? Not that it matters. It's just... unexpected.

When the king spots me, a small smile graces his face. Coming to Herdan for the choosing was my answer to his proposal. It's my agreement to his terms. Spy for the king. Ensure the prince ends up with the female that King Estelar approves of, and he will release my father. It's official.

I now work for the king.

The pressure of the king's eyes on me and my acceptance to do what he's asked forces me to look away and into the crowd where I spot the mysterious dark-haired stranger. We lock eyes. He smiles at me, and I have to look away for a different reason. I can't stare off into the crowd—at another male, no less—when the High King calls my name.

"Where's the prince?" someone shouts.

The king frowns, but says, "You must excuse my son today. He will not meet the chosen until a specified date and time at the palace in Isi Aura."

"That's disappointing," Didi whispers to me. She's still clutching my hand. "I was hoping he'd be here. Maybe they worried how the ones not chosen would react?"

I shrug when she glances at me. "I don't know."

"But I assure you the prince is watching this event now," the king continues. "It will give Prince Orion the opportunity to form opinions before he greets you." His answer seems to appease the crowd. "I will now read the names of the chosen fifteen, beginning with the Autumn Court. Will the following please step forward?"

Even in the projection, I see the entirety of Autumn hold a collective breath, waiting for the king to speak their name. But even the spring fae around me have fallen silent. Didi squeezes my fingers as the king unfurls a scroll to read the names.

"Juniper Faeven, Cerule Rostina, and Tierney Doryra."

"No surprise there, especially Juniper, since she's a powerful Faeven," Didi whispers as three jubilant smiles push their way toward the front of the autumn fae and the ones behind—the ones not chosen—blur in the background. It must be another effect of the winter magic.

"From Winter Court," the king continues after only a slight pause. It feels like he wishes to get through these names quickly. "Princess Shay Malov."

I nod. Didi was right about the Winter Princess.

"Luna Diables, and Frost Neige."

"Underwater will be next," Didi whispers. "Although none of them have a chance. There's no way the Summer King will allow a fish on the throne."

I snap my head to her. Does she know the high king is pulling the strings? Does she know that of the fifteen there's likely only one or two the prince will be allowed to 'choose'?

"From the Underwater Court," the king booms. "River Lyn, Aqualis Duxor, and Lily Strom." The king barely takes a breath before continuing. "From the Spring Court…"

"How much do you bet he will call Raine first?" Didi asks, squeezing my hand tighter. I hear the nerves in her voice and in the pulsing of my trapped fingers.

"Raine Hazelfalls."

"See?" she hisses.

"Clove Farbella, and Didi Beechriver."

Didi squeals next to me, looking wide-eyed. But then realizes something. She offers a sad look and mouths, 'I'm sorry', before releasing my hand and taking her place at the front of the Spring Court grouping.

Since I'm in the Spring Court, she assumes I'm spring fae. Whether Didi has realized I'm star fae or not, she doesn't know my fae heritage isn't spring. It's summer.

I straighten my shoulders. I imagine I'll soon stand next to the two princesses.

"And lastly, from the Summer Court, the following ladies will be the final three contestants in the Consort Tourney," the king says. He no longer seems in a hurry and takes his time speaking. "Lady Pepper Islandwort."

I try to hide my gasp, especially since I'm the only one dumbfounded. I imagine the rest of Faerie assumes the two princesses, Arielle and Mora, will be the final two called, but I know I will take one of their places. The question is, which one?

"Princess Arielle Lieawarin."

I don't even have time to think about how I'll get to see my former friend. We haven't seen each other in decades, but she's a contestant now and I'm about to be one too.

"And finally... Amberle Kindra."

When I step forward, my eyes immediately flit to the cat-eyed stranger in the crowd. I didn't think I cared about his reaction, but I also didn't expect the disturbed, shocked look I see. His smile has vanished.

And just as I gasped silently when Lady Pepper's name was called, an audible gasp reverberates throughout the crowd, with an obvious outcry and anger the moment they realize I was chosen over Princess Mora.

"Congratulations to the chosen!" the king says, lifting both hands. "I'm sure you'll agree with me that these are the best candidates for the crown prince, my son."

At that, all disgruntled noises cease.

"And now," the king continues. "I would like to hear a few words from several of the chosen."

What? I didn't prepare a speech! I glance around at the other chosen. Did they know, or at least have an idea they'd have to address the crowd? Princess Shay looks calm, which isn't a surprise. Two of the Underwater Court girls duck their heads together, looking alarmed, and I spot my new friend, Didi, biting her bottom lip.

The king said several, not all of the chosen, I tell myself. The princesses are used to giving speeches; Arielle and Shay were probably warned in advance and spent the past fortnight perfecting theirs. He won't ask me—

"Amberle Kindra?"

My stomach flops.

"Would you like to go first?"

"Yes, I will," I say. It's not like I have a choice. Walking toward the front of the crowd, my thoughts are a jumbled mess. What is the king doing? If he wants me to keep my cover, to stop the others from knowing the true reason he chose me and doesn't want anyone seeing any special treatment, why is he doing this? And why call on me first?

This is a test. The king is testing me.

"I am glad for this opportunity, Your Majesty," I say. "I look forward to meeting the prince and I hope that Rion—that Prince Orion finds what he's looking for." I look at the king, but I can see I've already failed. He doesn't like what I've said.

Suddenly I understand why the king is here in Herdan to announce the chosen. First, he came to ensure I agreed to his terms and second, he's already watching me. He wants to see for himself if I'm up to the task of being his little spy while convincing everyone—the other contestants, all of Faerie, and even the prince himself—that I'm here for the same reasons as the other fourteen: to win the heart of the prince.

If for one second I'm doubted, if anyone ever suspects that I'm a part of the Tourney for any other reason than for the prince, it will ruin everything. The contestants will clam up and I won't find out who is truly worthy of the prince.

By forcing me to give a little speech, the king is saying, 'convince me.'

"I'm sure many fae find this Consort Tourney very romantic," I say, borrowing Didi's words. When I glance at her, she winks back. "The idea of catching the eye of the crown prince and having him fall in love with one of us is... thrilling." The words surprise even me. But they must be true. Still, I can't look at the dark-haired stranger. I can't worry that he's listening because I must be convincing. Besides, I'll likely never see him again. "Humble beginnings leading to true love... with the prince."

The king's face thaws. It's working. I'm playing the part he wants me to play.

"Whatever happens, I hope love conquers all," I finish. Because I do want my childhood friend to find his happy ending, but this is already harder than I expected. I wish the human part of me allowed me to lie. It would make this so much easier.

Before I back away, I search for the mysterious stranger again. I'm a glutton for punishment to see what he thought of that little speech. But he's gone.

Eight

PRINCE ORION

Sleep evades me.

Typically, I enjoy the solitude and the time to myself when I don't have to act the part of crown prince, but tonight is different. Tonight I yearn for an escape from my thoughts that bounce and echo and fill every corner of my mind.

It's not new; I've walked the silent halls of the palace since I was small, while the rest of fae escaped to dreamland or blissful nothingness. But it's different being in a different court as a guest at a noblefae's estate. I can't simply wander the corridors of a house that's not mine in the dead of night, but I needed to move. And I needed an escape.

"I would have trouble sleeping too at the thought of courting fifteen fae women all at once," Wyn Firetail—one of my longest and closest friends—says as we traverse the streets of the city.

I feel guilty for waking him to accompany me, but going out at this hour without some type of protection would be worse for him than losing a few hours of sleep. At least he's in a good mood.

I give him a side-eye. "I thought you'd jump at the chance."

"Oh, I would! I never said I'd hate it. I said, I'd have trouble sleeping."

"Yes, and talking about it isn't helping."

"Noted," he says, then takes a breath before adding, "I should tell you that I'm off to Avala in the morning."

My head snaps to him. "The Winter Court? You won't come to Isi Aura for the Tourney?"

"I thought you didn't want to talk about the Tourney?" He smirks, but it quickly falls. "The ladies won't be there in competition for *my heart,* after all. You'll have your hands full anyway. You won't need me to rescue you from your boredom."

"Right. Of course," I say, and we fall into silence. I'm grateful Wyn doesn't say more about the Tourney, but whether we verbally discuss it or not, it's all that fills my head. Tomorrow I will travel back to the Summer Court, where I will be expected to formally meet all the contestants and it will finally begin in earnest.

I prepared myself for the commencement of the Consort Tourney. I sat dutifully in discussions and planning sessions for the beginning trials and outings that await me and my would-be-brides.

I even prepared myself for the possible names my father would announce. Most of my assumptions proved to be correct, but I am in turmoil at the one name I never expected to hear. At least not in connection with any type of future with me.

Amberle Kindra.

The silver-haired, iridescent-winged fae with the bluebell-colored eyes who always knew how to set my nerves on edge and create chaos that seeped straight to my bones.

And she accepted the invitation to be courted by me. To participate in the trials and revels and outings of the Consort Tourney with the aim to have a future... *with me.*

If I had not seen and heard it with my own eyes and ears, I would have never believed that she was in a carriage, on her way to Isi Aura right now.

"Let's go back," I say. Clearly this walk is not having the mind-numbing effect I had hoped for. "Perhaps someone in the kitchen is awake and has some sleeping aid I haven't tried."

Wyn nods and we turn to head back to the Hazelfalls estate.

But when we make our way to the kitchens, it isn't only servants who occupy the room.

"Prince Orion!" Lord Oak Hazelfalls says, standing to greet me. "Are you always up at this early hour?" He snaps his finger at a small brownie and orders some tea before I can protest. "Come. I didn't want to disturb the house, so I came here, but since the two of you are awake, we can move up to the dining room."

Wyn glances at me, but I see no point in refusing the master of the house now, so I raise a hand. "Lead the way."

"We have been beside ourselves since the invitations were finally sent out, Your Highness," Lord Hazelfalls says when we're in the dining room and seated near the head of the table. "Of course, we knew Raine would get an invitation since she is of age and our family is of great importance within the court, but it was pleasing to hear her name called by the king."

"Yes, I am sure you are one of many families pleased with the chosen tonight."

"Many of them came as no surprise, but I was concerned at first when I heard the *other kind* were thrown into the mix."

Wyn shifts in his seat next to me.

"The other kind? You mean the star fae?" I ask.

"Yes, but then Raine's mother explained that it was an easy way for the king to garner favor with them. By allowing them to believe that one of them has a chance at being on the throne." He glances at Wyn before turning back to me. "It's brilliant."

In other words, he doesn't think a star fae has a chance at being the one I choose. I wonder what my father would think if he learned some of the fae think the Consort Tourney is at least partially rigged.

At least Lord Hazelfalls thinks his daughter is a legitimate contestant because he drones on about how Raine would be the best fit as my future bride and queen. Surprisingly, listening to him is just the thing I needed to shut off the incessant thoughts in my head, so when a lull in the conversation arises, I excuse myself to finally get some sleep.

Wyn follows silently, but I know my friend enough to know something weighs on his mind. I beckon him in my quarters and shut the door. Sleep can wait a little longer.

"What bothers you, Wyn?" I ask. "Was it what he said about the star fae?"

"It's not that." He folds his arms. "You know us star fae are born with thick skin. Being insulted by the full fae is just a part of our existence."

"Then what is it?"

"I guess I'm still getting used to the reality of the Consort Tourney." He drops his hands and fingers the vines attached to the wall that run floor to ceiling.

"The king's announcement seventy years ago wasn't enough?"

He shrugs. "It just seemed that nothing would change an arranged union between you and Princess Arielle." He waves a hand and speaks quickly. "And of course she's also in the mix, but it was Amberle's name that shocked me the most."

My mouth has gone dry, and the grogginess I felt while listening to Oak has suddenly fled again.

"Hearing her name shocked me too."

Nine

Living in the palace most of my life, my father had very little time to prepare me for feelings of disappointment, fear, and discomfort. Life at the high court wasn't all forever blooms and pixie dust, of course, but it was simple. It was happy.

When we left and my father was taken, I had to learn how to cope on my own with the cruelties and sadness and hardships of living outside the sparkling walls.

Despite decades of practice, none of my usual tricks cast out thoughts of the walnut color-haired, mysterious stranger and his reaction to my participation in the Consort Tourney. Especially the memory of my speech and my use of the words *romantic* and *thrilling* to describe the Tourney. Or that he disappeared in the middle of it.

But I cannot think about it. Instead, I allow dread to fester in my gut, contemplating that I'll soon see two fae from my childhood—Prince Rion and Princess Arielle.

Aside from my misery, the journey from Herdan to Isi Aura is uneventful. Shortly after the king's announcement, the three chosen spring fae and I were ushered into a carriage immediately to take us to Isi Aura. I suppose after waiting seventy long years to begin the Consort Tourney, the king doesn't want to waste another second in finding a bride for the crown prince.

Being immortal, the full fae are funny about time.

"I admit, it was unexpected to hear your name called, Clove," Didi says, halfway through the trip.

I try not to look like my attention has been piqued.

Clove flashes a small grin at Didi, showing off her pointed teeth. "You mean you're surprised I was chosen and not my sister?"

Didi nods.

Clove continues, "Cicily is currently in love with some apprentice architect," she says, waving a hand. "She rejected her invitation."

"Rejected?" I ask.

"*Perrifool*, right?" Clove's eyes are wide with incredulity when she looks at me. "But it worked out for me."

"I hope the architect is worth it," Didi says.

Clove shrugs. "She'll fall out of love with him within five years, then she'll regret turning down the invitation for the Tourney. Her loss."

I nod. It makes sense that the king would allow for invites to be discretely turned away. He wants the most eager, well-connected fae.

The temperature rises as we head further north, and the pink and white blossomed trees turn into leafy green and fruit-bearing ones.

I haven't been to the court of my heritage in decades, but the heat and humidity doesn't bother me the way it bothers my travel companions.

Raine fans herself in the corner while Clove dabs her face with a handkerchief. Didi hasn't complained, but the flush on her cheeks tells me she's uncomfortable too. All three of them chattered incessantly about the Tourney as we traveled, but gradually became quieter and more withdrawn with the rising heat. I imagine the autumn and winter fae are cursing the weather.

The familiar scent of the plumeria flowers growing all around the Summer Court gates tells me we're nearing the glittering city of my youth.

But the carriage stops before we enter.

Raine stops fanning, Clove stops dabbing, and Didi sits forward, craning her neck to look out the window.

"Why aren't they taking us into the city?" Didi turns back to whisper.

"I'm not sure," I say, but it's making me uneasy. It's unexpected.

What's the delay?

When several moments pass without movement or direction, I become antsy and decide to investigate. I don't enjoy being trapped in a box. I move to open the carriage door right as a faun approaches. "Yes, yes, please exit," the faun says in a rush, waving her hands. Her dark hair curls around her horns with such precision and her sharp navy-colored dress is neatly pressed. The golden royal crest on the corner of one collar tells me she's part of the king's staff.

I don't recognize her. I suspect the king has assigned only the staff members who are unacquainted with me to deal with the Tourney contestants. That thought makes me sad that I won't see anyone from my past unless I seek them out, but imagine it's the best way to keep the king's secret a secret.

The king's secret being me.

I look back at my fellow passengers, who exchange quizzical glances, then open the carriage door and step down. Didi, Raine, and Clove descend after me.

"The king wants a grand spectacle of all the chosen to walk through the Summer Capital and into the palace," the faun says, impatiently. "But it's not only for the sake of the spectators who line the streets. The king has directed that all of Faerie may watch."

I suck in a breath. I thought the king would wait to use the winter magic until the Tourney officially began, but of course he's arranged a parade. Another spectacle.

"From now on, you will be watched often," the faun continues, standing tall with her hooves close together and her hands clasped in front of her. "Fae in all cities, in all courts, and even in some select private spaces will see every important moment, big or small. So, I would advise that you mind what you say and mind the movements you make at all times."

I glance at Didi. She glances back. With the king's frequent usage of the winter magic, I had assumed it would play a role in broadcasting the Tourney to the entire realm during significant moments. Like, as Rion dismisses individuals, or during grand events like revels and balls. But I didn't know we would be watched to this extent. How am I supposed to do my job while being watched so closely? What is the king thinking?

As the other contestants pepper the faun with questions, I mull over how I can possibly do what the king wants while fae from every court watch my every move.

Will we have private rooms?

"Yes."

Will we have a seamstress on hand?

"There will be several."

When will we meet the prince?

"That question will be addressed after we arrive at the palace."

"Will they assign us lady's maids?" Raine asks with an air of entitlement. "Or are you it?"

The faun smiles widely, but it looks forced. She's clearly a master of her emotions and has shown extreme patience with the questions, but this one irritates her. "I am not a lady's maid. I'm Gnacia Evernet, the king's private secretary."

It's difficult to hold back the smile that threatens to erupt when Raine's mouth clamps shut. Even in my secluded life as a thief, I know who Gnacia Evernet is. I've never seen her face, which is why I didn't recognize her, but she's famous for being ruthless and smart. She's an autumn fae but is the king's most trusted assistant. Rumor is she literally clawed her way to the top, beating out every eligible summer fae who thought they had a chance. None of the girls—including me—expected Gnacia to be the one to greet us.

We all know she does the king's dirty work.

I suppose they consider greeting us as the king's dirty work.

"And yes, you will each have two or three maids to assist you," Gnacia says.

Two or three? I assumed there would be some servants, but multiple helpers watching every contestant closely is yet another complication. I clamp down on a groan and wonder if it would draw suspicion if I asked that my maids be dismissed.

"If you will excuse me, the carriages from Autumn and Winter are arriving, and I must greet them too," Gnacia says. "They will join your court, and you'll enter the palace together."

"What about the Underwater Court?" Didi asks.

"The other two chosen from Summer have already met them at the edge of the Sea of Neptulus and have made their entrance from the north." Gnacia walks toward the glittering gates before they can bombard her with more questions. I think she's trying to get away from us, but then a black-as-night carriage pulls up.

Gnacia doesn't hesitate before approaching it and instructing the winter fae to exit.

Luna Diables is first. Her dark complexion, which matches the Winter Court carriage, is sprinkled with pale freckles over her nose and cheeks like powdered sugar, giving away her dark elf heritage.

Frost Niege is next, and is Luna's opposite, with her winter dryad white face, hair, and wings.

If the prince likes wings, she could be a serious contender. I make a mental note to pay attention to Frost.

But when Princess Shay Malov, crown princess to the Winter Court throne, emerges, everything quiets. Even the songs of the sparrows and chirping of the cicadas stop. Power and prestige and a blast of ice-cold air radiates from the princess. The air turns so frigid, I'm concerned about the fate of the plumerias several paces away. They can't survive that much cold.

Gnacia gives the same speech to the winter fae, but when she explains the part about the winter magic and having all of Faerie watching, none of the winter contestants seem concerned. Probably because they're winter fae and know how it works. I wonder if they have a way to control it. Or a way to disrupt it. Maybe even a way to hide from it. Perhaps I should befriend one of the winter fae to find out. Frost seems an obvious choice, since the prince might favor her. My job will be easier if I can move about without worrying that every step I take is being scrutinized by fae throughout the realm.

When the Autumn carriage arrives, prompting Gnacia to instruct the last group of contestants, Didi walks toward Luna to strike up a friendly conversation. I hang back and fall into my role as observer. I trust my observation skills better than my conversation ones to get a feel for the personalities and intentions. It's the truth I tell myself, anyway. To really find out the intentions of the fae, I'll have to converse with them all, eventually.

But Princess Shay breaks from the group to fall back. As she approaches, I note she towers at least a head taller than me. Her green skin is also more vibrant than I remember from the winter magic projection at the announcement of the contestants.

"Does anyone else know you're a halfling mutt?" she asks.

It's not the greeting I expected, but I don't flinch at the insult.

"Apparently you do," I say, keeping my voice low. I don't want Raine or Clove, standing just behind us, to overhear.

"Why were you chosen over a summer princess?" She directs her penetrating dark eyes downward at me. "Mora must be livid."

"I assure you; I had no power or sway in the choosing." I must carefully arrange my words. One slip could ruin everything.

"I just can't help but think there's some sort of conspiracy."

"Don't let the king hear you say that," I warn, but my chest tightens. She's uncomfortably close to the truth.

The princess scoffs. "A halfling nothing chosen over an eligible summer princess? It's not hard to wonder."

I grit my teeth. "Like I said, I didn't force the king to say my name."

Without another word, the winter princess lifts her head and walks away.

Even I know the best way to do my job is to be neutral and not make enemies on my first day. I should be a piece of the background. I should be seen as someone in the room, but not as a threat; not as someone they should watch closely.

But I know that's exactly what the Winter princess intends to do. To watch me closely. I need to gain the trust of every contestant so they might spill their true reasons for being here. But Princess Shay already has it in for me.

I'll just have to keep a close eye on her, too.

Ten

Gnacia Evernet claps twice, capturing our attention. "Ladies, it's time to make your grand entrance," she says. "You must act like you haven't been sitting in carriages for days. One of you might someday become the queen consort and she would not let her subjects see her weariness."

Princess Shay takes the lead while I position myself at the end. I don't want to get glares from her while we walk through the city. I'd hate for anyone to see her suspicion of me and the tension between us.

The air still seems thicker, hotter, as we walk through the gates. I feel summer fae eyes trained on us as we walk. But there are so many more watching—every fae from every corner of the realm witnesses this event.

Autumns in Graycrest, Winters in Avala. Is Clay watching from Rosewind? Is the stranger with the cat-slit eyes and walnut hair still in Herdan? Or has his father's business moved on?

Sweat forms along my brow. I straighten my back, but inside, my pulse quickens. Touching a finger to my promise mark, I remind myself that I'm here for my father and not for any of them. It's why I'm uncovering my silver hair, my wings, and my face. It's why I'm no longer in shadow.

I try not to squint at the bright lights from Isi Aura's buildings. The spires on the palace are nearly blinding as they reflect the hot sunlight in every direction. It's magnificent, as always, and seeing its glory and knowing the power that comes from the magic of that light; it's no wonder the summer king rules us all.

"Princess Shay!" someone calls from the crowd. "I hope you win!"

The winter princess turns, and I glimpse a practiced smile as she waves at her admirer.

Another repeats her name, and she turns the other direction.

This prompts other fae to call out their favorites until there's a cacophony of names shouted all around.

Arielle-Clove-Raine-Shay-Pepper-Arielle-Frost-Cerule-Arielle-Raine-Shay-Didi-Juniper-Arielle-Pepper-Clove-Luna-Shay-Arielle-Tierney-Arielle-Shay-Arielle-Tierney-Shay-Clove-Shay-Arielle!

The girls turn to wave when they hear their name. It seems not only summer fae are present in the crowd because I hear names from all three courts shouted as we walk through the city.

I don't hear my name on any of their lips, but it's no surprise. Being a thief, a nobody, a shadow for so many decades, didn't leave room for many friends, let alone admirers. I keep my face forward and my expression neutral.

Arielle-Cerule-Frost-Arielle-Shay-Didi-Pepper-Mora!

Didi's grin is wide and her hand is raised as she waves. She's beaming, and though I have only known her a short time, I'm glad to see her glowing and happy.

Tierney-Shay-Arielle-Raine-Mora!

I keep my chin up and my eyes forward, though my ears prick on the name of the summer princess who was not chosen.

Shay-Raine-Arielle-MORA.

Mora.

Mora.

Mora!

Princess Mora's name becomes a chant that ripples through the crowd. My stomach lurches, but I keep all emotion off my face. It feels like they're chanting at me. As if it's my fault their beloved princess isn't in the running for the prince's heart. I don't want to think how much worse the chanting would be if I'd taken Princess Arielle's place instead.

The fae might have thrown rotten fruit at me. Or stones.

What was the king thinking by excluding a princess? Of course, no one is attacking Lady Pepper for being chosen ahead of Princess Mora. They're attacking *me*. Amberle Kindra. The girl no one has heard of.

As we approach the front steps of the palace, I see the underwater and summer fae contestants waiting on the steps, including Princess Mora. My stomach lurches at seeing her and Arielle. Mora is trying not to look victorious hearing her name chanted through the crowd, but I can see it pleases her that the people are voicing their opinion. It's clear that they want Princess Mora to have a chance to become their queen.

I can't even look at Arielle. I'm afraid of what I'll see. Was she happy or angry when she heard my name called? I don't dare look to find out, but it's Princess Mora's eyes I should have avoided because she throws daggers with her gaze.

I didn't know Mora well when I left the palace, besides her being a lovesick youngling—she is much younger than myself, Prince Rion, and Princess Arielle—but I can see how much she hopes this incident will change the king's mind. As we walk past the summer contestants, her expression is triumphant and faux pitying.

She grabs my arm before I walk through the doors. I have to resist the urge to snap it from her shoulder.

"Enjoy this while it lasts," Mora hisses, her nails biting into my skin. "When the king hears about this, he'll reverse the mistake he's made. He'll put me in my rightful place and send you back to yours."

I jerk my arm from her grip. Her nails rake across my flesh, leaving angry red marks. "If you enjoy having your head attached to your neck, I'd think twice before pointing out the high king made a mistake."

The exchange is so brief, I doubt any of the others noticed, but I feel the hardened gaze of Princess Mora and the masked one of Arielle next to her as we continue into the palace. I offer a wane smile to my former friend, almost hoping she might be on my side in this even after all these years, but I can't read the expression she returns.

With the vitriol of the kingdom aimed at me, I don't know that I'll last a day. And I fear the fury of a disappointed high king. And he's my strongest ally. My insides churn.

I should have disappeared to the far side of Faerie the second the king left Rosewind. I should have gone to Sandtide in Autumn, or even Stardale, where I'd blend in better with my fellow star fae. I should have disappeared into the human realm.

I should have gone anywhere but here.

The king dangled my father as bait, but I don't see how I can possibly do what he's asked. Especially with so many of the contestants suspicious of me! The winter princess already knows I'm star fae and suspects a conspiracy, Princess Mora is angry about not being chosen, and Princess Arielle acts as if we're strangers. I think she's unhappy that my name was drawn too. Beyond three powerful royals, with all of Faerie watching my every move, my task is impossible.

"Isn't this amazing?" Didi whispers as we walk into the grand entrance of the Isi Aura palace. She sidles up and slips her hand through my arm that still burns from Princess Mora's claws and cranes her head up. "I knew the palace was opulent, but I never imagined it was this magnificent. I thought the spring fae were the master architects, but the things summer fae can do with light? It's breathtaking."

She's not wrong, I begrudgingly admit to myself. While it was spring fae who constructed the walls and floors, the ethereal light created by the summer magic creates an ambiance that feels as if we've entered the mansion of a sun god. Golds and whites and a glow that banishes even the darkest shadows bleed from the very walls.

But the sight of it has the opposite effect on me.

A deep familiarity plows into me with such force it steals my breath and pricks my eyes. Memories of my happy childhood, of growing up here, and fond thoughts of my father all twist up with renewed grief. My chest tightens and my breathing quickens.

I shouldn't have come.

I glance at the windows and doors, forming exit strategies in my head. Maybe it's not too late. Maybe I can still disappear.

Three sharp staccato claps capture our attention.

"Ladies!" Gnacia Evernet stands on the grand staircase just ahead. The golden crest on her lapel seems to shine. "Good, I see the summer and underwater contestants have joined us."

My stomach hops up into my throat, and I turn to see Arielle standing several paces behind me. Her attention is riveted on Gnacia, and she keeps the Underwater Court contestants between us. I can't help but feel a pinprick of hurt at the effort she's putting in to keep her distance.

At least I don't see Mora anywhere.

"Most of you have traveled for many days, so you will be shown to your rooms where you can clean up and rest. A light luncheon will be delivered to you shortly." She turns and gestures that we follow her up the staircase.

I side-step slowly, heading for a window. I'm not staying.

"When will we see the prince?" Princess Shay asks, flicking a strand of curly hair behind her and pressing her full lips together. I note her lips are a darker shade of green than the rest of her, and although I haven't met many winter fae, I had assumed the color was more common in spring and summer fae.

I pause as Gnacia turns with a practiced smile and clasps her hands in front of her. She looks controlled, but by the shuffling of her hooves on the steps, I see her impatience and the way she carefully chooses her words.

"At breakfast. Tomorrow," she says.

I press my lips together to push back a smile. Gnacia Evernett is the complete opposite of Conall Erlar, the slow-moving, always bored-looking elf who last held the faun's position as the king's assistant. I was already thieving in Rosewind when I heard the word that Conall met the wrong end of a troll's spiked cudgel. I didn't realize how fond I was of the old elf, but after learning of his death, it was the first time I cried since my father was taken.

But even though Conall seemed to have a laissez-faire attitude toward his position, I'd seen how out of sorts he could become when something disrupted the management of the courts. I can only imagine how much this Tourney has disrupted Gnacia's schedules. Conall would have hated it.

"The king has announced the breakfast event so all of Faerie can make themselves available to watch the momentous first meeting with each one of you," Gnacia continues, smoothing her already smooth navy skirt. "Tonight, you have the option of dining in your rooms, or together in the small dining hall."

Her eyes flit to me, and I freeze as some sort of knowing or realization lights her eyes. She doesn't look away for several moments. Does she suspect I'm ready to run? Or is she signaling that she's keeping a special eye on me?

I can't escape. Not yet.

With a snap of her fingers, four servants I didn't notice standing near the wall fly to her side.

She directs three of the servants to escort the underwater, winter and autumn contestants. Her eyes only briefly leave me to ensure her orders are being obeyed.

But I don't dare move because she looks back at me before saying, "Ysnet, you will take the spring ladies, and I will escort summer."

I nearly follow Didi with the others from spring when my new friend releases my arm and gives me a small smile. I remain still as the rest of the contestants climb the stairs until Lady Pepper, Princess Arielle, and I are left alone with the king's secretary.

Then, with only a pointed glance at me, Gnacia spins on her hoof and walks up the stairs.

"The princess is accustomed to the ever-present possibility of being watched. The only place you can be assured to have a small amount of privacy is within the walls of your own room," Gnacia explains when we've arrived at the landing of the fifth floor.

If I were staying, I might feel a slight relief, knowing that I could be myself when I was alone in my room. But I'm not staying.

"But that rule could change," she adds.

Lady Pepper glances at Arielle, but the princess doesn't seem alarmed.

We walk in silence with only the sounds of clacking shoes and hooves, and the swishing of our skirts. Gnacia points out Lady Pepper's and Princess Arielle's rooms after mentioning that each court has their own wing on this floor and the one below. Spring, Autumn and the Underwater Courts are below us, and Winter is housed at the opposite end of this level.

My room is at the end of the wing on the other side of Arielle's suite and next to a large floor-to-ceiling window. Without even looking, I know it looks toward the Sigmus River. The slow-moving river is the only thing standing between the Isi Aura Palace and the Infernus Forest.

When I glimpse the view, I press a hand against my chest as more memories surface with a jolt. I feel the shape of the key beneath my dress, which is enough to distract my thoughts and help me forget about my past and the forest, and I think of Clay instead.

The distraction works. After I escape, I'll search for my friend and see if he's up to traveling far away and working with me again.

I avert my eyes away from the window and direct my focus into my room. Twisting the knob, I push the door inward. Immediately, I scan the room: three windows on the far wall facing East and an arched doorway that likely leads into a washroom with one or two more windows inside.

I make a plan. Flying from the window is probably best. I'll just close myself in the washroom and—

"Leaving so soon?"

I whip around. Gnacia follows me inside and closes the door behind her.

"I know why you're here," she says when I don't speak.

A stone sinks in my gut.

"I know why the king wanted you as one of the chosen— well... not an official chosen, of course." She gestures with one finger in the air.

Gnacia orbits me as she walks further into the room. She briefly glances at our surroundings, at the extravagance of the guest suite assigned to me. A nobody.

"The king has been very generous with you."

I resist the urge to scoff. *Taking my father is generous? Using him as bait to get me to do an impossible task is generous?*

"He could have taken you the day he took your father, but you were innocent in your father's crimes."

"What were his crimes?" I blurt. "My father was a loyal servant of the king for centuries. We left on good terms and then suddenly one day he was taken without explanation."

Gnacia's smile is cruel. "Your father knows what his crimes are, but all will be forgiven if you do exactly as the king has asked."

Exactly as the king has asked.

I want to flee. I should flee. But, more than the difficulty of running or hiding from the king, my duty to my father roots me in place. I touch my promise mark, remembering how it burned like a fire having it needled into my skin. I can't leave. My fear will not stop me from holding fast to courage. Not until I find a way to free him. The accusations of a crime are ridiculous. My father could have done the smallest thing to upset someone in the court, or even nothing at all, and the king was within his rights to throw him into prison. The compassionless royal court sickens me.

"Need I remind you that your appearance in Herdan, and

being present for the choosing, was your formal acceptance and agreement to the high king's terms?" Gnacia continues.

With horror, I realize I've unknowingly entered a bargain. A fae bargain. How could I have been so foolish? I know better! My father's freedom on the line or not, breaking a bargain could be catastrophic.

If I don't fulfill what the king wants, exactly what the king wants, my punishment could range from being an indentured slave, to exile in the human realm. But more likely, breaking a king's bargain could mean... a slow and painful death.

Eleven

How did I miss it? How did I not realize my agreement was a binding bargain?

Being almost caught lifting those beads, being ambushed by the high king in my hideout, and then unknowingly entering a bargain with that same king, I can't help but wonder if something else is happening. Have I been enchanted or cursed with something that is making me careless?

"But what he wants is impossible," I say to Gnacia Evernet, and even I hear the defeat in my tone. "How can I possibly find out if the other contestants are conspiring or if they're truly here for the prince if we're always being watched?"

"You're smart. I've heard stories about the antics you played as a youngling here at the palace, and the rumors of the expertise of the Silver Shadow are famous in all of Faerie. Some think the Silver Shadow must be an otherworldly being." The faun's eyes widen in mock awe. "But some of us know the truth."

"The truth?"

"Yes. That the legend is merely a very talented halfling."

I bite down on my tongue, hard.

"And they will not always watch you," Gnacia continues, walking toward the windows and peering out briefly before turning back to me. "There will be plenty of moments when the winter magic is absent."

"How will I know when it's absent?"

"I trust you'll figure it out." When she turns, she winks. "But pay attention and take advantage of those times to learn all you can from the others."

How? I want to ask, but grit my teeth instead. "The winter princess is already suspicious," I say, folding my arms. "And she knows I'm star fae. She thinks there is a conspiracy since I took the place of Princess Mora."

The king's assistant lifts a brown eyebrow. "It is not difficult for the pure to sniff out a halfling," she says. "I assure you; the rest of the contestants also know you're a star fae. Besides, they chose Lady Pepper over the princess, not you."

"That's not what the rest of Faerie thinks," I say, and realize if the king chose Lady Pepper over a Summer princess, she must be a serious contender. Another one to watch and pay attention to.

"It does not matter what the rest of Faerie thinks."

"It does," I mumble. "They don't want me here." It could become dangerous, but I don't dare mention that. I can't let her see my fear.

Gnacia walks toward me, her hooves clacking against the smooth tile of my room. "Then make them love you," she says. "While the magic will not always work, much of the time it will. So you must be believable. Make them at least like you enough that you can stay until your task is complete."

"And Rion? What does he think?" I don't worry about using his shortened name. The faun said she heard about my antics as a youngling, so she must know my connection to the prince.

"Prince Orion doesn't know. And it will stay that way."

"He doesn't know? Then why does he think the king called my name?" I throw my hands in the air and walk backward. "It's been a long time since I was here, but I doubt he's forgotten me completely. We never got along."

"He has been told you're here because of your father."

I stop walking. The half-truth is not enough to tempt the prince to keep me around. "I don't think you understand... Prince Rion *hates* me. What's stopping him from sending me away the second he sees me? How can I do what the king asks if he doesn't know why I'm here?"

"He won't send you away. You are guaranteed to stay through the first round."

"How can you be so sure?"

"Because the prince will be flexible and will defer to his advisors' suggestions. Besides, I saw the prince's reaction when you were named. He was merely stunned, not angry that you are one of the chosen from Summer."

Merely stunned. My wings twitch. I want to scoff at her careful framing of the situation. The situation being me.

So I'm guaranteed for the first round. But that might not be enough. It feels like I'll only be set up to fail. "There's a lot of contest after the first round. How do I make sure I'm here until I've completed my task?"

Until I've freed my father.

"There is no guarantee. After the first elimination you are on your own, but if you win over Faerie and be amiable enough that the prince isn't in a hurry to send you away, your chances of staying could increase."

Fantastic, just fantastic. Make a kingdom who thinks of me as a disgusting half-fae love me. And convince the prince not to despise me too. I don't know which task will be tougher. Staying long enough to succeed might be impossible.

Gnacia is mistaken. She must believe Rion is actually open to listening and trusting his advisers, but they'll have to have a very convincing argument because I clearly remember the prince hating me. The wicked smile he would flash after besting me at a game. The way he tugged at tiny strands of my hair and blamed it on invisible pixies. His unruly hair framed his intense glare and hardened mouth watching me from a window when my father and I left for good. He was glad to see me go.

But... she says it's been guaranteed that I won't go home immediately. At least I have a little bit of time.

When Gnacia leaves and I'm finally alone, I take in the elaborate room and laugh out loud at the absurdity of my situation. They gave me this room of luxury, for my use, all to keep up a farce. To keep up a lie. I'm not here to become a princess or a future queen. I was given this bedroom to be a spy.

This room isn't the grandest thing I've seen in my life; I grew up in the palace, after all. But I've had nothing so grand set aside just for me.

Obviously, it's a giant step up from the lifestyle I've gotten used to—lumpy beds, cracked washbasins, and forgotten rooms full of cobwebs. But it's also more than I had when I lived here in Isi Aura.

Our family quarters at the palace were nice. They were clean and private. I had my own bed, and we had a private washroom. There was even a small chest where we kept personal items, like the few toys the queen gave me when she remembered I existed.

It's no wonder that the huge bed with a rich blue velvet covering seems more like a dream than anything real. A pearl-colored vanity decorated with gold leaf swirling patterns sits opposite the bed with a mirror as tall as I am. I imagine the contestants will spend many hours sitting in front of identical vanities as the servants ready them for majestic balls and revels and outings with the prince. Every stroke of a brush, every curl of hair, every jewelry piece picked with the hope it'll make Rion fall in love with them. Maybe the girls will confide in their servants about their growing feelings for the prince while they sit on their cushioned seats and express how desperately they want him to choose them.

A sitting area is arranged near the window with two plush chairs covered with fabric that coordinates with the bed cover. I walk through the archway on the right and am pleased to see a washroom with a deep copper tub as its centerpiece. I hope to enjoy a hot bath at least once before I'm sent away.

A light knock on my door brings a simple luncheon of chamois cheese, various fruits, and fluffy white bread. I sit in one of the chairs near the window and enjoy my meal while contemplating Gnacia Evernet's words.

She said I'm smart and should be able to gather information while keeping the truth of my presence a secret from the others. But my experience tells me my chances are slim, and I'm not entirely confident that she or the king worry about what will happen to me if I fail. Not only will I lose my father forever, but thanks to the winter magic, everyone will know my face. I imagine the king will spin the story and make me the villain, denying that he had any part in it. Maybe he'll even find me guilty for the very thing he demanded I unveil—that I'm a contestant here only to earn a crown and plan an assassination.

But I'm committed to my father. And even if I wasn't, I am bound by a bargain.

I'm trapped, but hopefully my imprisonment in this luxurious gilded cage will be temporary. As long as I do as I've agreed, there's still a tiny chance I can free myself and my father. I must try.

Gnacia advised me to make everyone like me enough to stay. Faerie, Rion, and most importantly, the other contestants, since it's their secrets I must unveil. Then I can pass those secrets along to the king and earn mine and my father's freedom.

Easy.

I stare blankly out the window, my mind spinning with ideas to garner the trust of the other girls. The clouds passing are a cottony white blur and what feels like only minutes are actually hours, because when I hear another rap at my door, the clouds have flattened into long fingers and the sky is stained with orange and purple.

"Will you be joining the other girls in the dining hall?" Gnacia asks, after letting herself in. "Or should I ask the servants to bring your evening meal here?"

I think about my options. If I go to the dining hall, I have to act the part immediately. I would be wise to get started on gathering information, but I'm not ready. I need a decent strategy. A plan.

"Please have my meal brought here," I say. I'm not hungry anyway, I tell myself. The simple luncheon was enough to get me through until morning, at least. My body isn't accustomed to regular meals.

Gnacia nods once, then excuses herself.

My eyes trail back to the window where a raven has perched outside on the window ledge. Its silky black coat shines with the setting sun and I wonder absently if it's a shape-shifting morrigu —an autumn fae—or if it's just the common bird.

"If you're here to spy on the high king, you've come to the wrong window," I say to the bird.

Before I can wonder if the raven can hear me through the pane of glass, it turns its head, looks at me with a beady eye, then lets out a loud *kraw*! but only steps to make itself more comfortable on its perch.

"I promise, I'm not interesting!" I call, leaning forward in my chair and cupping my hands around my mouth. "The real action is in the small dining hall where a bunch of females are likely tearing each other's eyes out because they all want the same thing."

The raven doesn't even turn this time and ignores me instead.

"Just a bird," I mutter under my breath, and slump back into the chair. But then something twists my insides. "Or a lousy spy."

What am I doing? I realize I'm giving the bird advice I should be acting on myself. I don't need a full plan. An evening of observation will help me form one, anyway. I should observe the tearing out of the eyes and keep notes about the contestants... while making sure my eyes remain in their sockets.

If I want to free my father, I must take action.

Twelve

There are protocols about wearing certain clothing to a formal meal. Meaning, the dress I bought in Herdan, then subsequently wore throughout the journey from Spring Court to Summer, is not appropriate attire. It's exquisite enough, but it needs a good cleaning.

But I'm out of time.

Instead, I merely run my fingers through my silver tresses before marching out the door.

"Oh!" says a servant I nearly bowl over, carrying a dinner tray. "I've come with your evening meal."

"I'm dining with the other ladies in the dining hall tonight," I say apologetically. "I had a change of heart."

Her cheeks flush. "Th-The others have already gathered." She fumbles with her tray. "W-Would you like me to show you the way?"

I have to bite my tongue from telling her I know the way—I could find my way in my sleep—but the fewer people who know my history, the better. "Yes."

She shifts the tray to her other hand, holding it upright with a bent elbow and gestures wordlessly that I follow.

It's strange being back in these familiar hallways. My habit of moving like a ghost wars with my memories of running carefree through the castle. And strangely, the instinct to walk tall is winning. Perhaps because I lived here before I was forced to live in the shadows. Before the need to be invisible was necessary for my survival. I lived here before I became a thief. Well, besides the occasional sneaking of pastries.

The rugs lining the hallway are the same deep blue with golden swirls and the Summer Court crest in the center.

As I follow the fae down the staircase, I can't help but smile as I notice one of the gilded mirrors lining the wall still has a chip in it. It's a wonder no one has noticed and had it repaired. I had taken one of Rion's toy soldiers without asking and was sliding it down the railing when he caught me. Although I had slid the toy at least a half dozen times without incident, he wanted to try, and one miscalculated twist of his wrist sent it careening down in a destructive path. It hit the mirror with enough force it fell from the wall. Luckily, I was quick and flew down to slow its fall enough that the mirror didn't shatter. But the mirror was still heavy, and I was small, so it struck a stair and chipped the corner.

Rion helped me hang it back up on the wall and promised to take care of any fallback. I figured he'd admitted to the accident because I was never punished. I also assumed it would be fixed immediately.

But the chip is still there. As I stare at it more, I notice a shimmer of light surrounding the chip and realize it has a small amount of glamour around it. No one would notice the damage unless they knew it was there or specifically looked for it.

And I realize: Rion told no one!

Did he place the glamour to hide it? Prince Rion is a summer fae, and I'd expect by now his magic would be stronger, but the magic looks like a light glamour even I could manage. Maybe he placed it when we were younglings and forgot about it. Maybe that's why he never enhanced the magic when he grew older and his magic became stronger.

"I-Is everything alright?" the maid asks, pulling me from my thoughts and I notice she's struggling to balance the tray.

"Yes, I was just admiring the palace," I say, waving a hand into the air after briefly pointing at the mirror as I slowly descend to meet her.

"The Isi Aura palace is admirable," she says, but her expression shifts into one of horror as the tray teeters and tips backward.

I fly down to right it mid-fall, but I'm too late and only manage to catch a sloshing bowl of hot soup before the remaining contents of the tray spill. But the servant's reflexes are quick and she conjures a thick vine from the floor that quickly twirls around itself, creating a bowl-shaped, small tree to catch the remaining food before it can soil the pristine rug below it.

I've always liked the spring fae. It's the reason I spend so much time living in Rosewind.

"That was impressive," I say, gesturing at the vine that slowly sprouts tiny flower buds and leaves as the spilled food settles. We both breathe heavily, but she seems much calmer and more tranquil than she was when she first brought the tray to my room.

"You're different from the others."

"Different? How?" My wings flutter in unease.

She points at the bowl still cupped in my hands. "The others would not have tried to help."

"Well, it seems you didn't need my help."

"You didn't know," she says, then fidgets and shuffles her feet from side to side. "D-Do you think you can find your way from here? I should get this tree removed."

"Of course. But what will you do?" I point at the foliage that is very out of place, with its earthy brown and green against the gold and white and blue of the staircase landing.

She smiles at her little tree. "A-An autumn fae who works with the water horses owes me a favor. I'll ask him to decay it before anyone sees it."

Again, I'm impressed. "You'd better go find him, then."

She curtsies and scurries away without another word, and I

can't help but smile after her. I should've asked her name, but she reminds me of Clay and seems like the type who would be good to have on my side. An ally.

I could use an ally.

As I make my way to the dining hall, contemplating how to get the spring servant assigned to me as a maid during the Tourney, I become distracted by the different tapestries and paintings on the walls. Some I remember, some look newer. I don't have a specific memory tied to each one, but I linger as the familiar smells and textures and light ignite happy memories.

New portraits of the royal family hang farther down the hall. It will only take a moment to inspect them. I pass right by the dining hall, closing in on the largest painting.

The portrait of the high king looks just as he does in person, from his flowing summer-blonde hair to his smooth and pointed elfin chin and ears. The queen, Siora, a summer fae beauty with white-blonde locks and pale pink skin, wears a crown of blood-red roses that matches her lips.

And finally...

A familiar, sly smile paired with walnut-colored hair and golden cat-eyes stare back at me. He's a very close likeness of the stranger I kept running into, dressed in elegance, and encased in the large portrait.

My throat tightens and my vision blurs as I think of a thousand reasons why the young fae I once knew could not possibly be the stranger I recently met. The fae who helped me escape my would-be captors could not be the prince because Rion would revel in my capture. The fae who wished me luck at The Choosing could not be Rion because he would sabotage me. He would reveal me as a thief and ruin everything.

"Have you lost your way?" a guard asks. I can't tear my eyes away from the portrait to address him. "If you were headed to the small dining room, you've just passed it."

I clear my throat. "Could you tell me who is in this portrait?"

"That's the prince," he says. I hear the smile in his voice.

"Prince Orion Illuminae. As a contestant in the Consort Tourney, it's curious you didn't recognize him."

I press my hand to my churning stomach. "We have not yet met the prince," I say, turning to him and managing a pseudo-embarrassed smile. "I suppose I didn't recognize him from the images I remember seeing of him as a youngling."

"Yes, well, he's grown up now."

"Excuse me." I abruptly leave, walking as if I'm heading back to the dining room. Once the guard turns the corner, I sprint past it, blindly climbing stairs without thinking about where I'm going.

How could I be so stupid? How did I not see it? How did I not recognize him?

Angry tears burn my eyes, which only make me even more frustrated and upset that my human nature has suddenly trumped my more controlled fae one. My forearm collides with a banister as I turn and stumble down a hall.

I knew his eyes seemed familiar! But the last time I saw those eyes, they were attached to a cruel smile, gangly limbs, and greasy hair. He always had an air of arrogance about him. That memory of the toy soldier and the mirror was a rare one. He usually enjoyed tormenting me.

But I saw none of that arrogance or that cruelty when he saved me in Rosewind, helping me escape capture for stealing, or when I saw him in Herdan and he wished me luck in being chosen for the Tourney. It was as if he was a different person.

Did he know he was talking to me the entire time? The instant he realized I didn't recognize him, did he take advantage and turn it into one of his games? One of his cruel glamours?

'My father's in town on business.' he'd said. Of course. It all clicks. The day he was in Rosewind was the day his father, the king, appeared in my bedroom—*business in town.*

And then in Herdan when I saw him before The Choosing— The Choosing his father personally announced from the Spring Court capital—*business in town.*

I thought it would be hard to pretend to like the prince I used to loathe—who I still loathe. But now, after he'd toyed with me already? Some fae are always cruel, never leaving behind their childish ways. And I'd fallen for the tricks of the one person I was supposed to manipulate.

My plan was failing before it even began.

But I have too much at stake to give up. I must regroup and strategize. My heart pounds. My stomach twists. The other contestants can't see me. Not like this.

I stumble through the hallways and my feet take over as my head and emotions reel out of control. Soon I recognize the path my feet are taking me. Back home. Back in the direction my feet traveled thousands of times toward my old quarters. My old home. The place I was most happy. But when I see the edge of the door, I quickly realize my mistake in not heading back to my room immediately.

Because leaning against the wall near my old doorway, tousled walnut-colored hair and golden cat-slit eyes, in his full princely attire, is Rion.

Thirteen

"Why?" The word flies from my mouth and I feel the familiar burning in my cheeks, accompanied by emotions I haven't felt in decades.

Unease. Self-consciousness. Discomfiture. Awkwardness. Embarrassment.

Pull yourself together, Amberle.

Memories flood my head in succession, and I'm forced to close my eyes because I can't even look at the prince standing right in front of me. My childhood horror when I realized he'd turned my hair into seaweed. The time he trapped me on the palace roof for three days, until it forced me to use my not-quite-developed wings to fly down. The day he shouted at me after I called him out for being a spoiled prince in front of Princess Arielle and Princess Mora.

You can't speak to me like that, Amberle! I'm the prince! he'd said.

His tantrum afterward only proved my point.

I knew seeing him would bring up a lot of buried emotions, but with all the tormenting and teasing in the past, when we were younglings, I expected I could see past it and do what I came here to do.

I've matured, and I assumed he had too.

But if he's up to his same tricks of making me feel foolish and lowly and unimportant, I don't know how I can possibly pretend to like him, let alone stay to do the king's bidding.

Yes, you can, I tell myself. *Amberle, you can. You're not the same girl you were back then.*

I can do this. I take a deep breath.

"Why didn't you tell me who you were?" I ask, controlling my anger without dampening it.

Rion's eyebrows furrow and he steps toward me. "I could ask you the same question, *Amberle.*"

"I didn't recognize you, *Rion,*" I say, holding my ground and leaning on his name the way he leaned on mine.

"Yes, well, we could have resolved that little miscommunication if you'd just told me your name in Rosewind."

"Ha!" I don't try to hide my incredulous look. "I was running away from pursuers!" The *S* comes out with a hiss. "I had just stolen from a noble autumn elf. I wasn't about to introduce myself."

"Neither was I!" he shouts. "When I traveled to Rosewind, it was to have a moment of anonymity. Since I had no other duties to attend to while traveling with my father, I glamoured myself enough to not be recognized."

"Well, your glamour wasn't very good," I mutter, folding my arms. "You don't look much different now. Well, besides your clothing." I wave a hand at his royal attire.

"It worked, didn't it?" he scoffs. "You said you didn't recognize me!"

I shrug, but drop my arms.

"What are you even doing here?" the prince asks, resting against the wall and oozing with disapproval.

"I told you in Herdan. I received an invitation from the king. Then he called my name, and here I am."

His cat-eyes narrow and his arms cross. "Just like that?"

My stomach clenches.

"Just like that," he repeats, frowning, "you decided you wanted a shot at winning the Consort Tourney?" His eyes narrow in disbelief.

My pulse quickens.

"Just like that, you wanted a chance to become a queen of Faerie?" He pushes away from the wall, taking a step toward me and drops his arms. "You wanted a chance to become my *mate*?" He seems to spit out the hard *T* as if he's trying to expel the distaste from his mouth. The word echoes through the hallway.

My throat tightens, but before I panic, I think about what the dark elf, Ralvano, taught me. We worked one job together long before I met Clay, but we kept in touch for a few years. Rav taught me some vital lessons, such as improvisation and controlling emotions—the best skills in a sticky situation.

Lean into what he knows. Rav's words fill my head. *Why he thinks you're here.*

"I agreed because it's what my father would want," I say, then walk toward the door to my former home. I assume Rion doesn't know my father has been in a dungeon for more than half a century as Gnacia said they told the prince I'm here because of my father. As I reach out to touch the smooth wood of the door, I run my fingers over the grain that runs from side to side instead of up and down. The unique direction of the wood grain has always reminded me of an embrace.

My hand jerks back from the door as an overwhelming and suffocating feeling of belonging and home and the family I lost overcomes me.

"You and your father left in the middle of the night." The prince's voice is so quiet, I barely hear it. "And you never even tried to contact me. All those years you could have come back, and you never did, so why now?"

Because I didn't want to land myself in a cell next to my father. But it's more than that. There was nothing here I wanted to come back to. I don't answer Rion's question because that would require me to spill more than I'm willing. Like the real reason I'm here.

So I turn it back on him, quickly picking out a truth that would reveal the least. "I was a youngling. My choices were not completely my own. Besides, we're both grown now, and it seems like we've both changed. Why did you help me in Rosewind? You're the crown prince and you helped a thief escape capture. You didn't turn me in, and you didn't demand that I return what I had stolen."

"That's a complicated question." His mouth twitches, and he glances at the floor before securing his expression back to his former stoic one. "But you reminded me of a silver-haired, winged star fae I used to know."

"You don't mean me?"

"Well, I didn't see your wings when we first met. They were concealed. But you still looked familiar." He shrugs. "You looked a little like Amberle Kindra. Perhaps I wondered what had happened to you."

I stop myself before rolling my eyes. A prince could have approached me far easier than the other way around. But of course, he couldn't be bothered to look for the star fae he never cared about.

"Wings might be uncommon on a star fae, but silver hair isn't," I say. "But what about Herdan? You saw my wings in Herdan before the choosing. Did you know it was me, then?"

"I was distracted in Herdan. I was about to hear the name of my future wife and mate, read by my father in front of all of Faerie." His glare shifts to one of my wings. Without permission, it flutters, feeling watched. His shoulders tense at the sight, but he continues. "And when I finally saw your wings, I wasn't convinced who you were because you didn't have that when you left either." He touches the right side of his eye, gesturing at my promise mark. "An enhancement tattoo?"

I bite down hard on my tongue at the insult. "I wouldn't

stoop so low, even if the spelled ink actually worked. I'm not ashamed of my weaker magic, Prince Orion."

Rion presses his lips together tightly.

Careful. I remind myself. I can't anger or irritate him so much that he sends me home before the Tourney has even begun.

"Everyone assumed you would watch from Isi Aura," I say, forcing a softer voice as I pivot the conversation and gesture at the walls. "From here."

"I didn't want to be observed," he says. "I didn't need anyone analyzing my reactions to each of the chosen—especially Princess Arielle—so I traveled to the Spring Court capital to watch from the crowd."

My eyes narrow. His mention of the princess is the sort of information I should pay attention to. Especially his current feelings toward her. "What do you mean, especially Princess Arielle? Did you know she would be one of the chosen?"

His nostrils flare, and he pauses. I think he's about to end the conversation when he finally speaks, his voice low and crackling like badly conjured summer magic. "Yes, and I believe the entire realm expects I'll choose Arielle in the end. But I don't believe any of the chosen were random."

At that, he lifts his eyes to mine with such intensity that I feel he might bore holes right through me. I'm forced to look away because he's too close to the truth. But he can't know what I know. Gnacia said he was in the dark as far as my true reasons for being a part of the Tourney, and I can't let the king's secret slip.

"I think most of the girls assume you'll choose Arielle in the end." I gently prod for more information.

His mood shifts, and the tension turns thick. "They have painted her as the favorite for over a century."

"Is she?" If she is Rion's choice, I'll merely need to focus on one contestant.

His expression is stony. "Perhaps you should ask her yourself. You were friends... or at least you were before you left."

Is that venom I hear in his tone?

"Well, she didn't look thrilled to see me," I mutter under my breath.

"What was that?"

"She hasn't said two words to me since I arrived," I confide, hoping it'll build goodwill, although I'm boiling with frustration. "She acted like she didn't even know me."

"Can you blame her? You left! And without so much as a goodbye."

"I..." I start, but the words choke. Princess Arielle was mad that I left? Is Rion upset because I hurt a friend we both cared about?

"I never meant to hurt Arielle. And if she's your choice, she will be a lovely queen." And I'll have to rekindle our friendship if I want to spy on her. Even though she's lived in the king's castle walls, he'll expect me to look under every pebble of her life. And I will.

"Shouldn't you be recommending yourself?" He smirks, but I know he's calculating behind his cat-eyes. "Not one of the other contestants?"

I can't help the scoff that flies out.

"What? You don't think you're an option?"

But don't make him like you too much, because you won't be the one he chooses. Yeah, I don't need the memory of the king's words to remind me.

"I'm a star fae, My Prince." I let the words sink in. Even if I were honestly selected and Rion and I could actually tolerate each other, I'd be the least likely candidate to win.

"Right." Rion's smirk wipes away and is replaced with a frown. "Clearly you're not here for me. Perhaps you enjoy the life of a thief." He walks a few steps down the hallway. "I suppose you're here for a hot bath and palace meals. A vacation."

There's the charming prince I remember.

He turns to look at me. "Unless you truly do thieve for pleasure? In that case, should I ensure the crown jewels and everything of value is not within reach of your grubby hands?"

By his tone, he's clearly meaning it as a joke, but there's something in his voice. A pain I can't figure out. "I have no need for the crown jewels."

"We aren't supposed to meet officially until tomorrow. Can you get back without being caught?" His words are clipped. But before I can respond, the corner of Rion's mouth twitches upward. "My mistake," he says, with a shallow bow. "Of course you can."

Then he marches away without looking back.

I don't make it to dinner.

Fourteen

Despite the exhaustion from traveling and the comfortable bed, I toss and turn until the first rays of dawn fill my room around the cracks of the curtains with muted light. It takes considerable time for the embers of my frustration and anger at Rion to extinguish after our run-in last night.

Still, I've lived with one eye open long enough that even when blissful sleep finally pulls me under, the sharp knocking at my bedroom door isn't what jolts me awake. Gnacia's hooves in the hallway are enough.

"Come in," I grumble behind closed lids.

The door swings open, and her footsteps clack toward the windows and three consecutive swishing sounds are accompanied by blinding yellow light invading the room.

"In the tub," Gnacia orders. "Now."

I pry my eyes open and fling off the bedcover.

"Wash and dress, then meet in the dining room for breakfast. Quickly."

"Why the rush?" I ask but feel a flash of panic, remembering that Prince Rion will be at breakfast, too. If he hasn't already decided to send me home, this morning he and I will have to put on a performance of meeting for the first time while Faerie watches.

"The other contestants are nearly ready. Hurry."

"I thought we were being assigned lady's maids," I say, not even trying to hide my annoyance as I walk toward the washroom. Not that I need or want help bathing, but if I've woken late, it's because I've had no one to wake me.

"Yes. But yours refused to come." Her tone is very matter-of-fact.

"What?"

The faun sighs with irritation—directed at the absent maid, I assume—and moves toward the wardrobe. "Apparently, some think that you are not fit to be a part of the Tourney and would rather face the wrath of their kin by abandoning their duties. And I assure you, she will scoop *cabyll ushtey* excrement for the next century, at least, if I have any say." She opens the wooden doors wide and rifles through it. "A new maid will be assigned to you shortly."

My shoulders sag. Part of me would prefer to scoop water horse droppings along with the soon-to-be demoted maid rather than deal with Rion. "We are meeting the prince for the first time today."

"We both know it won't be the first time you've met the prince," she says, flipping toward me with a deep blue dress clutched tightly in her hands. My stomach drops.

Does she refer to my history with the prince? Or does she know about last night?

"Your reason for being here is not to attract Prince Orion," she says, tossing the gown onto the unmade bed.

"Yes. I'm aware, but those watching might notice my lack of fancy hair arrangement and glowing, powdered cheeks." My tone is mocking, but... why am I concerned in the first place? Why do I care?

"There will be no hair arranging or powder today," Gnacia says. Her voice is calm. "Your tub is filled. Clean yourself, then put on this dress and tie up your hair. Then meet downstairs. I assume you know the way?"

It's an insult, since she knows I grew up in the palace, but I won't let her see my re-ignited frustration toward her shared Isi Aura snobbery with a certain royal. "I know the way."

"Good," she says, then leaves.

I do as she says. My bath water is near frigid, and although I didn't hear it, it must have been filled hours ago—perhaps with underwater magic. But it feels good to scrub my hair and skin with the lemongrass-smelling soaps. The cool water and the fragrance help wake up my last bits of grogginess and I quickly dry, then pull the dress over my head.

The dress is simple, with a round neckline, a skirt that ends just above my ankles, and a sash around the middle. Normally, I'd be grateful for the simplicity of it. It's not confining, and I'd even consider such a garment to do a job back in Rosewind with Clay, but I can't help but feel as if I'm being consciously singled out from the others. A simple look for a simple star fae.

My appearance is not what I imagined I'd be wearing the first time I saw the prince.

Get over it. Clay's words fill my head as my eyes trail over to the key discarded on the table near the window. I can't help but smile. If Clay were here and saw the way I'm bemoaning, as he would put it, over how difficult my lot is, he'd suggest something absurd, like letting him meet the prince. *I'd do a better job,* he'd say.

And he'd probably be right, if he could somehow glamour himself to look like me.

But he's not here.

I put the key back around my neck and march out of the room. As I make my way downstairs, bracing myself for political vying and insults in small chat, I run my fingers through my damp tresses then pull them up to tie with a ribbon. When I enter the dining room, the broad smiles that greet me send me back to my previous dour mood—despite my imaginary pep talks. Everyone is putting on their best faces and sitting tall in their chairs as they compete for the prince's attention with the batting of their eyelashes and sparkling teeth.

Bile crawls up my throat until I realize... the prince isn't in the room. What in Vejo's name is going on?

A booming voice says, "And finally, the mysterious summer fae has deigned to join us!"

My head snaps to the charismatic, cerulean-colored elf with hair the color of midnight and lips the shade of sunshine standing on the dais. He flashes his pearl-white teeth at me before speaking to the air next to him.

"Amberle Kindra!"

Applause erupts and I'm left dumbfounded and silent as all the girls in the room are suddenly cheering my arrival.

Well, that's new, I muse. I'm not sure how to react, so I mirror the other contestants and flash the best smile I can manage—the easiest fae lie.

"Now that everyone has gathered, we will allow the contestants to eat a quaint summer court breakfast. Be sure to watch my announcement of their first trial!" The elf executes a graceful bow at the air. "And I have a hint: Prince Orion is at the center of it!"

Several girls gasp while others let out loud exclamations. I watch the theatrical elf as I try to ascertain what is happening. But when the elf's posture and smile drops, I understand. It's the winter magic. I've stumbled into a broadcast across the realm. That's why they cheered my arrival. That's who the smiles were for. Those watching are the ones I need to convince to give me a chance. Internally, I groan. Showing up late was not the best way to endear myself.

With the eyes of the entire realm no longer watching, the girls' warm, welcoming looks disappear, leaving a chill in its wake.

A brief terror floods through me as I realize the winter magic might've been watching last night in the hallway. That everyone might have seen the argument between Rion and me and learned we already know each other. They would have seen our mutual loathing and have already joined Rion in their opinion of me.

But the king didn't send me to be eaten by a *biloko*. My fear wanes. Slightly.

I turn to figure out which of the round tables to sit at and catch Princess Arielle's eye. Her wings briefly flutter and her eyes flit away as she turns to speak with Lady Pepper. I feel a brief twinge in my gut, but pretend I'm not bothered.

"Amberle!" Didi calls from the far end of the room. "Over here!"

The tightness in my belly releases. At least I have one friend in the Tourney. Although, it shouldn't matter. I'm here to do a job. Not make friends or compete for the crown.

Still, I slide in next to the red-haired spring fae, reminding myself that she is a wealth of information and will help me achieve what I came here to do.

Just as I sit down, I nod at Raine and Clove—the other two spring contestants—who also sit at the table.

"Who is the elf?" I ask, gesturing at the energetic fae who now sits with one leg crossed over the other in a tall chair across the room. He holds a mirror in one hand as a small trouping faerie stands on the armrest—on her tiptoes—to powder his face.

"Nieven Morphyra," Didi says. I know the name but allow Didi to continue. "He's one of the king's entertainers. They said he'll be hosting a variety of events, give Faerie a summary of what happens each week, and he will interview the contestants when only five remain."

"Interviewing fifteen was too many?" I joke.

Didi shrugs. "I wonder if it's more than just talking. He implied the realm will get to see more into the lives and personalities of the remaining five."

My stomach plummets, and I twist my mouth to the side to hide my reaction. I can't afford for anyone, let alone some loud-mouthed, gossip monger, Nieven Morphyra, to be digging around my past. The king can't be expecting me to try and make it to the final five. Can he?

"What do you think the first trial is?" Didi asks.

A towering grundel places a stone plate in front of me with disinterest. It's piled with nuts and berries and a piece of flatbread I recognize from the human realm but can't remember the name of.

Tearing a piece of the bread, I chew it slowly and shake my head. "I have no guesses. I thought we were just meeting the prince today, not beginning trials."

"Well, whatever it is, I wish they'd allowed us to wear something better than this drab dress." Didi plucks at the dark green fabric of her dress that is the exact cut as mine even to the sash around the middle.

I look around the room and see that all the girls wear the same dress, just in different hues. It puts me at ease. At least now I know I'm being treated the same.

"What's the point of the trials?" Clove asks across from me as she moves her fork around her food. "If Prince Orion is trying to decide who should be a future queen, shouldn't he be spending time with us? Courting us?"

Didi looks at me. "She has a point."

It isn't my job to question the specifics of the Tourney, just to play along with it, but her question is valid. Shouldn't the prince be spending time with the contestants?

"The Tourney isn't only for the prince to find a mate," Princess Shay says, leaning from her chair behind Clove at the table next to ours to interrupt the conversation. A shiver runs down my spine, and I know the sudden chill in the air is more than just her winter magic. "It's also to see which girl can handle being a princess first, and eventually a queen." Princess Shay's dark eyes look pointedly at Clove, when she reminds her—and everyone around—that the girl the prince chooses won't be a queen right away and should remember that.

"You're already a princess," Frost says, also butting into the conversation. She sits next to the winter royal and speaks with an airy, fawning tone.

Princess Shay smiles widely at her and sits taller. "I am."

"Which means, she thinks she'll have an advantage," Didi mutters to me.

"Maybe she does," I say.

Didi turns back to her food.

"There's nothing fair about it," I say. "But I don't think they intended it to be."

"Then why include the rest of us? Why invite those of us who aren't royal?" she asks. "Why not just have a Tourney with the princesses if that's what they want?"

"Because that wouldn't be as entertaining?" I say, but smile because it might be entertaining to watch if they threw Princess Mora into the mix. Even if it was just the three princesses. Princess Shay would eat Mora, pan flute and all.

"Or because you're wrong," Raine speaks up. She turns to see if the winter princess heard, but Shay is absorbed in the compliments Frost showers on her about being the 'perfect choice' for the prince.

"Maybe they don't want a princess," Raine continues. Pleased with herself, Raine stabs a piece of melon with her fork and pops it into her mouth. After she swallows, she says, "Maybe they invited them to appease the other royals even though they're not actually a choice."

I glance first at Princess Shay, who revels in the admiration Frost still pours over her, then across the room at the summer princess, Arielle, and our eyes lock. I see a ghost of a smile flit across my former friend's features, and she tosses her long blonde hair over one shoulder before turning back to Lady Pepper.

When she engages back in quiet conversation with the other summer contestant, Rion's words last night, about Arielle missing me, fill my thoughts. I realize that I've missed her, too.

"That sounds like wishful thinking," Didi argues, pulling me back to their predictions.

"Then why do you think we were invited?" Raine asks, lifting a cherry-blossom pink eyebrow that is a shade darker than her hair. "Why were *you* invited?"

The flatbread in my stomach turns to icky mush. Raine's question is directed at Didi, but she could easily flip and ask me the same thing.

Didi shifts in her seat and tosses her head to swing her single braid behind her. "Because my parents are ambassadors to the king."

Raine narrows her eyes with a knowing smile that causes Didi to squirm, but she keeps her head high and seems to shoot back a dare with her own glower. The only people in the room who are aware of the tension are the three of us. Didi, Raine and myself. The rest of the room continues to chatter and the dull tapping of the woodware against stone plates fills in the space between.

Didi eventually wins the silent battle because Raine jabs her fork into another melon. But then she says, "Didi Beechriver, right?"

"Yes," she says.

Raine swallows. "I know the name. You're star fae."

I keep my face neutral despite the rush of shock and panic that courses through me. But it doesn't matter because Raine snaps her head at me.

"Don't worry," she says. "Your wings have fooled no one. You're star fae too, Amberle Kindra. Everyone knows you're the only two halflings here. And that neither of you have a chance."

Fifteen

"File out of the dining hall and make your way to the lavender fields," Nieven Morphyra announces.

Raine is the first out of her seat.

"You're star fae?" Didi asks me after she and Clove leave us.

"I am." I stand, and Didi does too.

The idea of the lavender fields simultaneously fills me with pleasure and dread. I loved the fields as a youngling and often lost myself in them. I was small enough that the plants towered over my head so I could walk a few steps into the field and be surrounded by green and purple and the soothing, calming scent. I would lose sight of everything around me, including Isi Aura and the palace.

They won't tower over me now, and my memories of them will surely be tainted by whatever our trial is.

"I don't think I've ever met a star fae with wings," Didi says, a half-pace behind me.

"They are uncommon." My stomach clenches.

"Is one of your parents full fae?" she asks. "Are you the offspring of a full fae and a human? Or are both star fae? Both of mine are star fae."

Her questions seem innocent but put me on edge. Maybe it's

the nervousness in her tone. Maybe it's the jabbering. I don't know why, but my instincts are on high alert. I've made so many careless mistakes lately, it's about time. I was beginning to wonder if I'd lost my touch. I just didn't think they'd go on high alert around the red-haired, seemingly harmless spring fae. Maybe it's because I don't enjoy talking about my family or my past.

Maybe it's because I didn't know she was a star fae too.

"My father is star fae," I say.

"What about your mother?"

What about my mother? My father spoke little about my mother. I have little memory of her. Whenever I tried to bring her up, to ask if she had been killed or if she just left us, my father never gave me an answer. He avoided the topic. I rarely pressed him because to me, he was enough. But one time he hinted that my mother's parents didn't approve of their relationship.

"I don't know much about my mother."

"I hate that they can sniff us out a mile away, but it's harder for us to recognize our own," Didi comments. Her voice is low. Almost dejected at the revelation.

I'm grateful for the subject change away from my parentage, but it has always bothered me too, even if there's nothing I can do about it. I can't strengthen my magic to hide that I'm star fae, or hope my uncommon wings are enough to disguise it.

"But I'm glad I'm not the only one," she adds, finally walking next to me.

"Me too."

We walk through the palace and outside in silence, but as we near the lavender fields, my breath catches.

"Whoa," Didi says, voicing my awe.

The plants are massive.

Lavender towers at unnatural heights, bees disappearing inside the magically enlarged blossoms. The perfume heavily permeates the air, making the hair on my arms raise in warning. We both gawk—as do the other contestants—at the solid wall of the flowering plant. It's so densely packed together it would be near impossible to walk into the field without a blade. Not like I used to.

"How many spring fae do you think it took to grow that?" I ask.

She mumbles something unintelligible, then whistles low.

Nieven Morphyra stands at the base of the wall, bathed in the shadow of it, with his sunshine smile secured in place.

I force a smile, too. Faerie must be watching with winter magic again.

Nieven holds both arms up as we near him. "Welcome ladies!"

The quiet chatter around us dies.

"This is a labyrinth," he says, gesturing at the lavender with grandeur. A part of the wall decays. The flowers shrivel and curl on themselves until it collapses and finally disintegrates to ash, revealing a pathway that quickly splits into three more paths. "This maze was designed specifically for the first trial, which is simple: Prince Orion Illuminae, our very own crown prince and the fae you've long waited to meet, hides somewhere inside the labyrinth." He draws out his words for dramatic effect.

It works because *eeks* and *oohs* erupt around me.

"The first fae to find him will not only be the first one to meet and make an impression on our prince, but that lucky fae will also get additional time with him later, after he meets each of you."

Didi squeals next to me and grabs my hand. I smile and squeeze her fingers.

"Use your wits and your smarts to find the prince." Nieven's smile widens, and he raises both hands high in the air. "And... go!"

He drops his hands, and the contestants rush toward the entrance.

Tierney and Juniper, both autumn, take to the sky. Lady Pepper flies up on their heels. Aqualis, who doesn't have wings, shoves her fellow Underwater Court peer, River, to the ground and rushes inside just ahead of Clove and Raine. Although Princess Arielle has wings, she doesn't fly up and jogs inside with Princess Shay just behind her.

"That doesn't seem fair," Didi says, pointing up at the two autumn fae and Lady Pepper, who fly up high. She still has my hand and pulls me forward.

I don't want to be the first one to find Rion, but after Raine's derogatory comments about Didi and I being star fae, the vindictive part of me wants Didi to have a fair shot at winning this first contest. Besides, since they chose her for this Tourney, the king must not be so prejudiced against my kind as I thought. So the king is unlikely to be angry if I help her.

"I'll fly up, then come down and tell you where he is."

She releases my hand and I flair out my iridescent wings, flexing them. Then, pushing them downward with one powerful motion, I lift into the air, rising above the lavender wall. The wind from my wings rushes through the flowers, kicking up pollen and filling my nose with the calming scent as I gain altitude.

I expect to see pathways and dead ends and some sign of where the prince hides in the center, but as I fly upward, I see no pathways. Instead, a solid wall or roof of lavender flowers covers everything. Most of the labyrinth must be made of tunnels.

The other flying fae have already abandoned their first strategy and are no longer in sight, but I want a sense of the size of the maze and travel south, toward the Sigmus River, toward the Infernus Forest, and see that the field is twice the size as it was when I was a child. It covers dozens of acres. It's massive.

Flying back toward the entrance where I've left Didi, I silently congratulate whichever fae had the idea of concealing the correct pathways from the air to even out the chances for winged and non-winged fae. But when I descend, Didi is gone. She's likely already rushing down pathways to find her way toward the prince, hoping to get to him first. I don't blame her. The rest of the fae are gone, too.

Rushing into the maze, I take the left path when I come to the fork and jog down the long stretch that quickly becomes covered by a roof of flowers and leaves. I slow my steps as my eyes adjust and the sunlight is mostly blocked, so I'm moving through a haze of deep violet and green.

There are no other options of pathways to go down, which feels too easy. As I reach the back wall and turn right—my only option—the pathway stretches out again. It looks like it turns right again, but as I approach it, it appears to be a dead end.

But it isn't. On the right-hand side of the wall, I see a narrow pathway that leads to a hidden path on the other side.

Turning sideways and flattening my wings against my back, I squeeze through until it opens. The pathway continues forward, but this time, I see more options of directions to choose farther ahead. I'm about to take the first left I come to, but then I hear a loud sneeze to my right, and I stop. Because I recognize the sneeze.

Fae don't get sick. At least not often. With our part-human heritage, in the rare case when a star fae falls ill, it's nothing like a human illness. And it's even more rare for the full fae to fall ill. Which is why I always thought it was funny when Prince Rion would sneeze. The scent of my childhood surrounds me in one of my favorite sanctuaries—the lavender fields—causing my memory to prick that Rion always sneezed around the flowers. His nose hated them. It was one reason I loved losing myself in them, because I knew he couldn't follow me without making himself miserable.

I don't know why lavender causes the prince to sneeze, but I've found him.

He is on the other side of the wall. I don't know the exact path to get to him, but I know where he is. And I find myself in a dilemma because I don't want to find him first. I don't want to be last, but until this moment I doubted the former would be the issue because navigating labyrinths isn't my forte. None of my thieving jobs required me to work through a maze to get to the item they hired me to take. I know how to pay attention to minor details, but Rion sneezing is an obvious, blaring clue, and now I've accidentally found him first.

Well, *almost* found him. Instead of turning left, I continue straight until the path turns right and I can see that it immediately turns right again to where I imagine Rion stands, waiting for the first fae.

So, I have a choice. Do I walk around the corner and be the first to meet him? Or pretend like I didn't hear him or know where he is and turn back? I also have to remember that Faerie might be watching.

I take a breath and keep walking forward, pretending to look more curious than fretful. But, to the right, there's another wall that quickly turns left.

And no Rion.

Maybe this isn't as easy as I'd feared. Still, I'm getting close. When I follow it around, I glimpse another of the girls rushing forward and disappearing around the corner. I follow her, but I thought she turned right and although I keep walking, there is no opening to the right. Just dense lavender.

Where did she go?

I keep walking until I reach a dead end and finally see another narrow opening to the other side. Like before, I shimmy my way through it and find myself in a small L-shaped area, and the narrow entrance behind me rustles. I flip back to look and see that the narrow opening is quickly closing on itself.

Is it closing on its own? Is there a spring fae close by?

Whatever is happening, I must continue moving forward because I can't go back. When I follow the *L*, I stop... because Clove Farabella, the sweet girl from the Spring Court, stands directly in front of me.

Did she close off the path?

"What are you doing?" I ask when she grins wide, showing her sharp teeth.

"Nieven Morphyra never said we couldn't use our magic to find the prince," she says. "Or to stop others from finding him first."

Lifting one hand, thick lavender closes the path between us, trapping me with no exit.

Sixteen

Clove flashes a wicked smile before the lavender stalks are braided too closely together to see through. But I can hear her laughing and singing a familiar tune about weakling star fae. It's a song I haven't heard since I was a youngling, but her singing fades to silence, and I'm left alone.

I stare at nothing. Lavender surrounds me, but my vision blurs as the reality of my situation settles in. And I feel foolish. Again.

For the love of the djinn... what is wrong with me?

But with the question, a thought drops into my mind like summer fire cutting through winter's ice: What if this isn't completely my fault?

I've depended on my own survival, for sniffing out threats for seventy years. I've never made so many mistakes in such a short timeframe. And as much as I'd like to blame the prince or his father, my trouble started before I ran into Rion at the market, before I received the invitation from the king. I might have escaped Nightfall's cottage with the deeds that night on my last job with Clay—that feels so long ago—but I was nearly discovered.

I'd brushed it off, but looking back, I see a pattern. It's so obvious now. How I was nearly caught lifting a simple bracelet. How I didn't realize the king and his retinue were in my apartment. And now this. Something else is at work.

But what is it?

Nothing makes sense. Am I under an unlucky charm? An enchantment? A spell? A poison?

I touch the key around my neck. The one Clay gave me that opens the trunk in Nightfall's cottage. It reminds me of Clay and our time together, but it's also a reminder of that night. How close I was to being discovered by the fae with the flicking lion's tail and permanent frown. But also, how Clay created the distraction that helped me get away. Just thinking about that night makes me smile.

Is it all connected? Is it all some long, complicated trap that will eventually lead to a dungeon cell? And if so, why? I've done nothing horrible enough to warrant this much planning and scheming. I'm just a thief. For better or worse, I'm not important enough to target.

I must consider that someone might have cursed me by mistake—collateral damage in a scheme gone wrong. Did I inadvertently trigger a spell or some other nuisance? If so, the timing couldn't be worse.

But purposeful or not, it's subtle, but damaging enough that my keen observation skills and instincts are severely weakened.

I doubt it's the king. If he wants me in jail next to my father, he could snap his fingers and it would be done. Even now, in the middle of the Consort Tourney, if King Estelar wanted me out of the castle, a simple smear on my behavior would bring the kingdom to his side without question.

No, I'm here for the king, working for the king, which makes my predicament extremely dangerous. If the fae responsible is merely attempting to thwart my chances with the prince, they might inadvertently find out too much as my carelessness continues.

Prince Rion needs to cut me as soon as possible while I still keep my promise to the king. But I must get out of this L-shaped, dark violet trap made of lavender.

It's ironic that my childhood sanctuary—the lavender fields—has become a prison. And especially because the seemingly innocent Clove trapped me. The girl who is only here because her sister fancied another and rejected her invitation. Not that any fae could be described as innocent, but the fact it was Clove was unexpected.

Walking around the small space, I search for another narrow opening, but find none. Clove's magic is just as strong as the spring magic that created this labyrinth. The plants she's grown are indistinguishable from the walls that were already there.

Still, I try to push through her new wall, attempting to press myself through it the way I did as a youngling. But the plants are too tightly pressed together.

What if I can't get out and I'm forgotten in here? What if I'm the last one to find Rion? I don't want to be the first, but what will the king say if I come in last? He warned me that I must convince the prince and Faerie that I'm here for the same reasons as all the other contestants.

What sort of thief and spy am I if a spring fae can so easily trap me?

And what's worse is that it's possible that I'm being watched right now. I imagine fae are booing at my projected image.

Jumping upward, I fly to the roof, trying to find an opening. I use my hands to feel for any loose or weak stalks. Overhead is dotted with pinpricks of light, but the shafts are so deep and narrow, I can't even reach one finger through.

But it's difficult to keep myself hovering just below the roof as I dig my fingers into the tightly woven flowers. My wings quickly tire from the rapid beating to keep me in the air, especially at the awkward angle of lying on my back, while my fingertips become raw from the effort. It's all I can do to slow my descent to the ground enough that I don't snap one of my limbs or tear a wing.

My wings lie limply at my sides as I gulp in panting breaths and wring sore hands. I wish I possessed a blade. I wish my summer magic was strong enough to ignite even a small spark to burn down the entire maze. But weapons and tools weren't offered, and my star fae magic is too weak.

Then suddenly, as if conjured directly from my thoughts, a spark lights in front of me at the base of the lavender wall and ignites a fire.

I jerk back, tripping over my wings. My right wing folds awkwardly underneath me, pinching it with the force of my weight. A sharp stabbing pain radiates in all directions along my wing and down my back. I bite my tongue until I taste blood and tears prick my eyes.

My throat burns as thick, perfume-heavy smoke fills my cage. The fire has grown into hungry flames that lick up the stalks of the lavender. It's hard to breathe and makes me cough. But I don't panic because it's clear that the fire is controlled.

Eventually, it carves out the perfect door-shaped hole that extinguishes as quickly as it started. As the smoke clears and clean air rushes through my lungs, my hacking stops, and my body settles. I blink away burning tears until I see the summer fae standing in the doorway. The one who started—and ended—the fire.

A tall lithe form with long, golden hair and wings the color of a sunset, wearing a deep blue dress the same shade as mine, is none other than the girl who was my friend... once upon a time. Princess Arielle.

With no one else around to talk to and nothing else to focus our attention on to act as if the other doesn't exist, the summer princess and I stare at each other for several breathless moments.

When she finally looks away, her eyebrows pinch together. "It's you. How did you get in here?"

"Clove trapped me." My voice grinds and cracks.

"Clove?"

"Yes, she's a spring fae."

Arielle nods and walks further into my temporary prison,

touching the wall with perfectly manicured fingers. "Why did you come?"

"I received an invitation, and King Estelar called my name," I say. "Why did you?"

"You know what I mean."

"So do you."

Arielle watches me with an openness on her face, but doesn't divulge anything and neither do I. The tension mounts as the silence grows, while neither of us break it. Finally, her face turns to flippant indifference, and she says, "Well, this is clearly a dead end."

Then she turns on her heel and walks away.

Seventeen

I'm freed from my temporary prison, but after my run in with Princess Arielle, I pause before walking out the charred door. I'm an expert thief and an expert spy, but this job differs vastly from any I've done before.

This one is personal.

I don't hesitate long, and fold my wings tightly against myself, wincing as my right wing aches with the motion.

The path winds back and forth with several short switchbacks heading in the general direction I think the prince is in—I have no idea which way Arielle went—but I'm glad there are no split paths because I'm so distracted in thought and would have difficulty keeping track.

I knew agreeing to come would mean seeing Princess Arielle, and of course, Prince Rion, but I didn't expect that seeing both would churn up so many emotions. I didn't expect that I'd suddenly feel as if my life of nearly a century had never happened. That the Silver Shadow never existed. I didn't expect that all I'd be left with was a chasm of missing. Missing the life I once had filled with fae and home and carefree joy.

But those years did happen. I've lived a life as a thief for too many decades. I've learned to live in shadow and not get too close to anyone. I've learned not to care about connections or friends. I've learned to be alone.

Except Clay. But he was a rare exception in my solitary life.

As I round the corner, I glimpse dark hair and immediately jerk back.

I've found him. The prince.

My heart pounds and I feel a rush of energy that courses through my limbs until I'm hyper-aware. I look behind me and take a few steps in the opposite direction to see if any of the other girls are on my tail. But I see no one. I'm alone.

Taking several deep breaths to calm my racing heart, I step silently toward the prince. At least it's one thing I'm still good at. I assume none of the other contestants have found him yet because I don't hear chattering or girlish giddiness, but I peek around the corner, anyway.

He leans against the lavender wall, one ankle crossed over the other, examining his fingernails with obvious boredom. I was correct. He is alone.

Turning back to remain concealed, I press my side into the lavender wall on the other side of Rion and strategize.

Nieven Morphyra said the first girl who gets to Rion will get to spend extra time with him after he's met all the contestants. That time could be beneficial to me because I could find out the prince's initial impressions of each fae and narrow down which ones I need to pay close attention to.

Being the first to meet him could speed up my task and get my father freed and both of us out of Isi Aura and far, far away from the reach of the king the quickest.

On the other hand, being the first to meet him could paint a target on my back. It would put me in the limelight, and other girls are certain to feel envious of the extra time I would get. Some could become jealous and dig into who I am. Into my past, my life. Others, like Clove, might directly attack me. The subtle might even plot to sabotage me. That's all I need... Especially because I suspect someone, or something already is.

The extra time also might be broadcast for the entire realm to watch, meaning it might not be as informative as I'd like because I would have to play the part of adoring contestant instead of interrogator.

So, I decide to stay hidden and let someone else be first.

If I'm ever asked why I hesitated by those who are surely watching, I'll just have to be vague with my answer. Hint that I was nervous, or that I wanted to give Didi a chance to be first—which is the truth.

I brush specks of dirt from my dress, attempting to smooth the invisible wrinkles. Compliments to the seamstress who magick'ed this material because it's in excellent condition even after my losing battle with the lavender.

I casually stretch out my wings, pretending to preen, but really checking my right one to ensure I can still fly. I might have to leap up and press myself against the roof if any of the girls use this path on their way to the prince.

But the rustling of dried plants decaying over themselves—the way they opened the labyrinth when we first arrived—captures my attention. It's coming from around the corner, near Rion.

By the stench of decay, I know it's one of the autumn fae.

"Ooh!" a surprised voice says. "I've found you!"

I inch to peek around the corner and see the button-nosed girl with orange hair piled high on her head. I recognize her as one of the fae who flew up at the beginning of the labyrinth.

"It seems you are the first," Rion says. His tone is formal and cheery, but I hear the edge of irritation and boredom in his tone. It grates my nerves and reminds me of an attitude I well remember. He doesn't sound happy that she is the first. "What is your name?"

"Juniper!" she squeals. She doesn't know him well enough to have heard the slight in his tone, which is fortunate for her. "Juniper Faeven! From the Autumn Court!"

"Congratulations, Juniper."

"That means I get extra time with you, right?"

"Yes. That is the prize for being the first." Rion's tone only increases in annoyance. "Why don't you tell me about yourself while we wait for the others?"

I roll my eyes at him. I feel bad for her.

"Yes! Well, as you might know by my name, I'm the eldest daughter of Lord Faeven of Sandtide and I'm just so thrilled to be a part of this Tourney!" Juniper speaks faster with each word. I struggle to keep up. "I know you keep cabyll ushteys, so you should know that I have captured a cait sith I keep as a pet. And I love—"

"Aww. Juni, you beat me!" another contestant interrupts in a mock-whine.

"And you are..." Rion prompts.

"Tierney Doyra, of Autumn."

The other autumn fae who flew off at the beginning.

"Nice to meet you, Tierney." Rion sounds a touch more interested to talk with Tierney, but perhaps only because she stopped Juniper's rambling.

For several minutes the two of the autumn fae—who are clearly friends—bowl over each other to tell Prince Rion about themselves and how wonderful they are and which qualities each of them thinks would be best as the high queen of Faerie and to be the prince's mate. I can't see his face, but Rion might as well be asleep for as many words that escape him.

I might have stifled a laugh at his obvious disinterest, but both girls are earnestly trying to earn his approval. Sure, they're both a little ridiculous and spoiled—but my anger flares. It doesn't seem like Rion is taking this Tourney seriously. He isn't giving either girl a fair chance, and he's just met them.

I should round the corner and reveal myself now that Juniper has already won the labyrinth task, but my blood heats the more I listen. Just in case I'm being watched, I shake out my hands, hoping it comes across as nerves and not anger. Once I'm near the prince, the entire kingdom will be watching. I'll be a performer on a stage.

I must gain control of my emotions before I act the part of doting contestant, eager to make a memorable first impression. I pace to act the part and bite my bottom lip as if pushing back nervousness while continuing to eavesdrop. I'm listening for information about my mission, even though nothing I hear sounds remotely important. At least not until he shows the least bit of interest in either of the autumn fae.

Juniper must have carved quite the path with her decaying magic through the labyrinth because soon I hear the raspy voice of one of the underwater fae, followed by three more contestants including a voice I recognize, laced with sharp teeth named Clove, who all arrive from the same direction. It makes me wonder why Juniper didn't find him sooner, if she just cheated by decaying walls instead of winding through them.

It's funny that I'm the only one who has found the actual path. But, star fae like Didi and I don't have strong enough magic to use to our advantage in a task like this maze. Didi might have what one would call a green thumb in the human realm, but her spring magic is nothing like her full fae relatives. And although I'm adept at glamour by manipulating my light magic, I struggle to create even the smallest of sparks, let alone a blaze large enough to burn living flowers.

I don't muse about it long though, because soon I feel an icy wave wash over me. I don't have time to leap up before the dark curls of Princess Shay round the corner and I'm greeted with her chilly smile.

"Don't tell me you've won," she says.

"I haven't," I say, and can't help but glance in the direction of the chittering of fae around the wall.

The Winter Princess mock-pouts with a pitying look. "What, did he send you away? Are you not allowed to play with the nobles and royals?"

"It's not..." I ground my teeth, but then shake my head. It's not worth arguing about. "I was giving the others a chance with him before I introduced myself."

Princess Shay folds her arms. "Well, isn't that arrogance at its finest? Did you think the others would not have a chance the moment Prince Orion laid eyes on you?"

My mouth trips over the words, but I quickly regain my composure and turn the question back on her. "Why, is that one of your worries? Shall I give you three quarters of an hour before I reveal myself? Give you a chance to woo him before he—as you said—lays his eyes on me?"

She glowers at me, then walks closer. The temperature drops with each step and I have to resist the urge to rub my hands along the goosebumps that raise along my arms.

"Let us walk around the corner to meet him... together," she says as her cheeks flush, making her green skin more yellow. She directs a fierce challenge from her dark eyes that seem to bore holes right through me.

But I keep my head held high and flutter out my wings, keeping my face neutral and ignoring the pain in my right one when I repeat, "Together."

One corner of her mouth lifts into a smile and the two of us walk side-by-side around the lavender wall until we come face-to-face with the contestants who are already congregated... and Rion.

"My prince!" Princess Shay croons. "It has been so long since we've seen one another!"

"Princess Shay." Rion nods slightly at her and I see the glimpse of a smile.

I hear exclamations from the other girls at the sudden revelation that the winter court princess and our high crown prince know each other. I didn't know they were acquainted, but it's easy to imagine. Royalty are often thrown together when summits are called, or treaties are formed. And when there is no fighting or wars between them, month-long revels for the solstices and equinoxes give royalty reason for celebration.

But my cheeks heat when cat-slit eyes slide to me and I remember the part I must play.

"I'm Amberle Kindra," I say. "I'm a summer fae."

"Ah yes, it was good of my father to include some star fae in the competition." He grins widely at his audience, prompting their reaction.

He's immediately rewarded with both fawning over his goodness and quiet snickering and gossip at my expense.

I ignore them and Rion steps closer to me.

"Tell me, is there something specific you are looking forward to during your stay at the palace?" he asks. "Any specific type of food?"

My face burns at his rude assumption that I'm only here for the food and comforts of the palace.

Two can play at this game.

"Absolutely!" I say with mock-cheer that I hope only he catches. "I've been longing to have a piece of dragon fruit pie."

It's subtle, but I'm rewarded with an eye twitch at the mention of his mother's—the queen's—favorite dessert.

"Then I'll inform the kitchen to make you some during your stay." He emphasizes the phrase. Another jab implying I won't be here long. Well, the joke is on him since I don't actually want to be here. The sooner I leave, the better.

But when he winks at me, I want to punch his face.

Eighteen

I don't know how long it takes Didi or Princess Arielle or any of the remaining contestants to find Rion, because I take advantage of the commotion to slip away. I'm sure no one notices my absence because they're all tripping over each other to recommend themselves as the girl the prince should fall in love with.

It's ridiculous.

I hate how long I take to find my way out of the labyrinth. If Clove hadn't closed off the way I'd come, it might have been easier, but I reach too many frustrating dead ends and turn in too many circles before I finally break free of the maze.

As soon as I breathe the fresh air that is no longer heavy with lavender perfume, I waste no time and take to the sky. My right wing still hurts from tripping over it, so it's a pathetic limping flight, but the Isi Aura palace isn't far, and I soon land on the balcony to the third floor, right next to the servant's stairwell.

I remember where Gorwin Erlar's office was when I lived in the palace, and I hope it's now Gnacia's. I also hope she's here instead of back at the maze.

The servant's floor is open, and the salt of the sea burns my eyes and chases me through the corridors. Gorwin's office is the largest. It's tucked in the back of a hallway since the king's secretary requires privacy for their work.

Instinctually, I turn my head in the opposite direction when I pass by my father's former office. I can't bear to see it empty of his things—his worn coat hanging next to his herbs and his spices stacked neatly in jars alongside his pile of books—or full of someone else's. I also hold my breath, fearing what it will do to me if it smells familiar... or not familiar.

But I don't hesitate when I reach the large wooden door that I hope is Gnacia's and rap with forced determination.

When Gnacia answers, I push through her and into the room without greeting and gesture that she shut the door. She quickly masks over her momentary shock and offense at my rude intrusion with the stoic expression I know.

"Why aren't you at the labyrinth with the others?" Gnacia asks, then picks an invisible stray hair from the side of her face and tucks it back in place. I note that her office is less cluttered than it was when it belonged to Gorwin, but I recognize the large cherry wood desk that serves as its centerpiece piled neatly with lists and notes—likely cleaning tasks for the maids and menus for the kitchen.

"I didn't think I would be missed."

"You are a contestant in the Consort Tourney, Amberle," she says with an exasperated tone, as if speaking with an unruly youngling, then lifts a missive from her desk and opens it to read. "With Faerie watching, someone might notice your absence."

"My bargain was to be a spy for the king," I say. "What better time to slip away to give a report than when the prince and other contestants are engaged with one another?"

She drops the letter back on the desk and looks at me with a stern expression and crossed arms. "Alright then, what is your report?"

"Clove Farabella trapped me in the labyrinth. She's clever and will do anything to win."

"An ambitious fae," Gnacia muses. "Did she say anything

about harming the prince? Anything that is a threat to the royal family or the crown?"

I stand straighter, wincing as the movement smarts my wing. "No."

"There is nothing wrong with wanting to win."

"Yes, but I think she is someone to watch closely."

Gnacia's hooves clack on the floor as she moves toward me. "Then watch her."

I want to say more, I want to complain that I cannot last until the second elimination, let alone the first. I've only had two inter-actions with the prince, and both left me wanting to blacken his eye.

"Is there something else?" Gnacia asks as she moves behind the desk to sit, then picks up a stack of papers and flips through them. "You were supposed to remain at the labyrinth until all contestants found the prince."

I shake my head, no.

She flicks her wrist, dismissing me. "Then scurry back before anyone notices you're missing."

"I'll head back."

"And remember, Prince Orion intends to have formal intro-ductions with each of you immediately following the end of the trial. Don't disappear again."

"Formal introductions?"

"Yes. A sit-down with each one of you for all of Faerie to watch."

"When were they planning to inform us?"

She looks back up at me. Pleased at my obvious unease at the news. "After all the fae find the prince. In the labyrinth."

I nod and swallow over the newly formed lump in my throat.

Gnacia's eyes crease with amusement, but I see a bitter chill behind her eyes. "Flit there quickly, little bird, or your game will be over before it's begun."

Nineteen

We're herded like erluitle goats to the picturesque balcony in the Isi Aura Palace. The one that overlooks Aura Pond and the sparkling Northern Sea in the distance behind it. The sun sits low in the west, splattering the sky with wispy pink and coral siren colored clouds and casting shadows all around.

Thick, granite columns carved into the images of past summer kings—most of which were also high kings of Faerie—hold up the balcony above it and surround us on all sides. I lean against one of them with folded arms, resting on my left shoulder and trying not to look too irritated at the spectacle in front of me.

Prince Rion and Juniper Faeven sit on a pale blue loveseat with their backs to the view. Juniper was the winner of the first trial, and therefore was granted the first official introduction with the prince. The rest of the contestants stand in a huddled group a stone's throw away from me, waiting for their turn.

I should join them, but I just don't share their same enthusiasm.

The winter magic watches the couple, and I imagine all of Faerie is in enraptured attention and bated breath as the prince has his first official conversation with each fae. One of whom will become his queen consort and mate.

We're all distanced enough that we cannot hear the conversation, but the group is silent. Perhaps each hope to hear a single word here or there, as if it will tell them whether the prince is falling in love with the orange-haired autumn fae, or if they still have a chance.

The conversation is brief. Rion lifts a hand, gesturing to Juniper that their talk is over and that the next girl—Tierney Doryra—should join him. She saunters to him with her head held high and her delicate painted lady butterfly wings fluttering behind her.

We are being introduced to the prince in the same order we found him in the labyrinth, so there are a few girls ahead of me. But first or last, I expect my conversation with him will be the shortest. If coercion of the prince wasn't in the plan to keep me through the first elimination, I imagine I would be the first to go. I wonder how they plan to convince him, or what tactics they'll use if he insists he can't stand me, let alone consider me for his future mate. The thought makes me smile because I don't like him either. At least we can be miserable about it together.

"Where did you disappear to after you found Prince Orion?" Didi whispers, siding up next to me. "You found him before I did."

I grin when she hooks her arm through mine, hoping my smile hides the guilt. "I didn't think the prince would care that I'd left—"

"C'mon. I want to show you something." I don't think she was truly curious to hear the answer to my question because she interrupts and pulls me away from the group.

"Where—"

Didi cuts me off, when she shoves me into a small side room that's more of a large broom closet. But before I can ask her what she wants to show me, I see it. A group of maids along with

Raine, Cerule from Autumn, and two underwater fae huddle around a small plate-sized disk. A miniature projection of the scene in the other room sits on top of it.

"It's against the rules to watch," I say as the tiny version of Tierney stands to let the next girl 'meet' the prince.

"Since when are you, of all fae, a stickler for the rules?" she asks, nudging me.

My head jerks to her. Does she suspect who I am? After my heated negotiation with Gnacia, I'm on edge about my identity being exposed.

Didi eyes me with amusement. "The human side of you is strong, I see."

"It wasn't a complaint, just an observation," I say, then walk toward the projection enraptured with the scene unfolding because... Clove is next and a fury that I fear might result in me punching her right in the mouth the next time I come face-to-face with her is near overpowering. It hurts my injured wing as it radiates through my limbs. I'll have to find a healer.

Clove's sharp teeth don't look as menacing when she smiles. Or maybe it's because I'm staring down at a tiny version of her that makes her look more innocent, though I doubt she's fooling anyone. Pretend friendliness is one of the fae's greatest, but most predictable, deceptions.

Prince Rion stands as she approaches.

"If you remember from the labyrinth, I'm Clove Farabella. From the Spring Court," she says with mock meekness.

"Yes. It's nice to know you, Clove," the prince says. "Please, sit."

She obeys and sits next to him on the loveseat.

"Tell me about yourself." Rion's tone doesn't sound quite as bored as it did in the labyrinth, but he's not entirely genuine either. I wonder how much say he had in this Tourney, or if it's truly a political ploy invented by this father like Clay suggested.

And if so, I wonder the reason.

"My elder sister is practicing her art," Clove drones. "She's much improved, but still does not compare to my skill. I must show you some of my best pieces."

"You should have them sent to Isi Aura," the prince says, but I can't tell if he's truly interested, or appeasing Clove and the audience.

She continues talking about her family and their status in the Spring Court, then clumsily segues into mentioning how everyone in Spring agrees that spring and summer fae—meaning Clove and the prince—are a perfect match because of light and all things good... or some nonsense.

I peer into the other room to see if her comment perturbs any autumn or winter fae. It's not the first-time spring and summer fae have decided they were the superior races. But the growth and the light would eventually deplete Faerie's resources if they were not kept in check by the autumn fae's ability to decay and winter's control of darkness and shadows. Without that balance, the growth of spring would eventually suffocate and crush everything.

But I suspect they didn't hear because none of them react.

It's funny that the Underwater Court was never dragged into such arguments, but it isn't surprising that Clove would pull out every argument she could. She's holding nothing back. She wants to win.

I've heard enough and stop listening, but note Rion talks with Clove longer than he did the first two girls.

I approach a maid watching the scene and ask, "Is Kali Island-wort still a healer at the palace?"

She nods. It lifts my mood.

"Where might I find her?" I ask, fearing that Kali has risen so far in the ranks that she'll be unreachable for a Consort Tourney contestant like me.

Kali's quarters have not moved, which surprises me, but it's comforting at the same time. I signal to Didi that I'm leaving. It's nearly my turn and I want to prepare mentally, but my ears prick when I hear my name on Clove Farabella's lips.

I turn back toward the projection.

"What do you mean, trapped her?" Rion asks. His tone shifts. It's subtle, but enough for me to notice.

"I told you I was clever," she says, leaning toward him and placing a hand on his arm. "I lured her into an area, then closed it off with more lavender walls. Let me show you the location. My magic is as grand as the architects you employed to erect the maze. The added wall is indistinguishable from the rest."

He discretely brushes her hand from his arm as she gloats, but Clove doesn't seem to notice because she's so pleased with herself.

"I trapped her like an unwitting human stumbling into a faerie ring." Clove laughs. "I'm astonished she escaped and didn't need to be rescued since, you know, she's star fae and can't spark anything to save her life. Without her flimsy wings, she could easily pass as a human without glamour."

My fingernails dig into my palms, and I grind my teeth, irritated that all of Faerie now thinks I'm a perrifool. I keep my eyes firmly on the projection even as several sets of eyes—including Didi's—flit to watch my reaction.

It's all I can do to keep my expression neutral.

"She must be clever, too, if she managed it." Rion's tone is flat with a hint of thinly buried rage.

"That was a compliment to you," Didi whispers, leaning into me.

"That's the human side of you talking," I snap. "The prince is likely looking for someone who is clever and ruthless." It is an applauded trait of the fae.

"Perhaps?" Didi smiles. She's unperturbed by my flash of anger. "But Prince Orion is the one who mentioned your skills."

I don't have an answer for that and focus back on the scene in front of me.

"Thank you, Clove," the tiny projected version of Rion says, forcing cheer into his voice. "I think it's time that I meet the next fae."

"I hope we will have many more talks?" Clove asks, leaning closer. Even as a small image, it's clear that she bites her lower lip. Her attempt at seduction is vomit inducing.

Rion's smile is forced. I wonder if he feels the same. "We shall see. Now, if you will please allow the next lady to step forward."

"Of course." Clove curtsies and practically skips away.

Twenty

It's my turn.

Princess Shay and I met Rion together in the maze, but since she spoke to him first, her interview was ahead of mine.

I hope the audience doesn't see my stiff posture and forced smile as I walk toward Prince Rion. It's my turn to meet him in front of all of Faerie. I doubt the winter magic watched us last night in the hallway, but there's a good chance they broadcasted most of the trial in the labyrinth. Still, I don't know if they could hear all our conversations as each of us found him.

But this moment is being scrutinized by the entire realm.

Which means, whatever the prince says, no matter how cruel or mocking, I'm not allowed to claw his eyes out.

My heart clings to my ribcage as my fear spikes. I must put on a performance, but I don't know how Rion will act. Will he give away that we know each other? It might not paint a target on my back the way Princess Shay might have when she alluded to their history together, but I'm the daughter of a former servant and not a Winter Court princess. Still, it would pique interest. On the other hand, the prince might pretend he doesn't know a lowly daughter of a servant at all.

I prefer the latter.

Whatever happens, however he acts, I must ensure that he tolerates me enough to keep me, and I also must win Faerie's affection.

Whether or not anyone likes it—me included—I'm staying at least a little while.

I imagine the small projection in the other room where the maids and other contestants watch isn't the only crowded room with females analyzing the conversations. I wouldn't be surprised if high stake bets are being placed on this very day throughout Faerie. Especially on the isle of Erato. The fae on Erato are known for their gambling and other sordid activities.

We could not change or clean-up for our tête-à-tête's, so the stretchy fabric of my dress clings to my back between my wings and under my arms from the exertions of the maze. And although my hair is up, I must fluff out the loose strands around my face to prevent them from sticking to my forehead and temples.

The prince stands when I walk toward him. His golden cat-eyes watch me with an intensity that doesn't match the easy smile playing on his lips.

"Amberle Kindra," the prince says. "Please, sit."

The blood drains from my face. Clove and the others had to re-introduce themselves, but he used my name. The one small action told all of Faerie that he remembered it.

"Thank you, Prince Orion." I'd rather play this off like we don't know each other. Hopefully calling him by his formal name will be hint enough.

"It seems the other contestants view you as a threat."

It's all I can do to keep my wings still and my smile secured. What is he doing? I fight the intense urge to fly away. I thought we were making faux introductions and discussing safe topics like how much I wish to become his princess and which colors I'd choose for the queen's rooms once I hypothetically win.

Leaning toward him, I grit my teeth to keep my smile and ask quietly, "I thought this was the part where we are supposed to get to know each other better?"

He lifts his hand, pretending to clear his throat as he whispers, "You and I both know there's no need for that." Then he backs away and says louder, "Tell me how you escaped Clove's little trap in the maze? I'm sure everyone wants to hear it." The prince glances at his audience—at the air next to us—and flashes a smile before turning back to me. "I know I do."

I resist the urge to narrow my eyes and say something cruel because Clove wasn't the first fae to trap me. Once, when I was much younger and much more naïve, Rion lured me into a hollowed-out tree in the human realm. He told me a fantastical story about how humans obtained their sweets from hollowed-out logs and that this one had not been emptied yet. After I crawled inside, looking for treats, the young prince rolled a large boulder in front of the opening, trapping me.

"It's a good thing I'm not claustrophobic. I'll say that much," I force a laugh, hoping Rion will get the hint and change the subject.

He catches my meaning but doesn't seem ruffled by it.

"Don't be modest," Rion flashes another grin at the audience. "Indulge us."

I'm not keen on bringing up the fact that my star fae magic really couldn't help me escape Clove's trap, but it seems he has trapped me again.

Fine. If this is the game he wants to play, I'll play along. And hopefully I'll bring at least the summer fae around to tolerate me.

I sit taller. "Princess Arielle rescued me."

"Arielle?" His voice pitches in shock. His eyes flit to the crowd of girls at the end of the room. Arielle is among them.

"Yes," I say, following his gaze. "She burned a doorway for me. She didn't know someone trapped me, but it was kind of her, all the same."

I spot her across the room, but don't know if the warm smile is real or imagined.

"It was kind of her." Rion turns back to me, staring for several seconds as if he's at a loss for words.

Could he have feelings for the summer princess? Is that the cause for his reaction?

I force myself not to look at her again and lower my head demurely. If she's his choice, I need Faerie and Prince Orion to know I'm a supportive citizen. I won't win this Tourney, but I can't lose, either.

"I believe I can speak for everyone when I say that most of Faerie thought you and the princess would make a magnanimous match. Many fae believe you two were intended for each other." Glancing at the invisible audience next to us, I offer a shy smile. "Of course, I'm happy to be here as a contestant in the Tourney." I turn back to him. "But I wish you happiness with whomever you choose."

Something flashes in Rion's eyes and I feel a brief burst of heat ignited by his summer magic. It's subtle enough that I doubt anyone else notices—unless they know him as well as I do—but his expression smooths just as quickly and he quips, "I think you misunderstood my confusion at Arielle's help. I think I assumed a capable fae like you would have the smarts and skills to escape on your own."

Don't you dare tell the entire realm about my profession. I fight down the spike of panic coursing through my veins.

"That assumption implies you know me and my skills," I warn through gritted teeth.

He flashes another smile at the audience, making my stomach flip before turning back to me with eyebrows raised in fake innocence. "Well, I have to admit, I learned a bit about each of the fae before you came, and I know you were raised by your father, but the rest of Faerie don't know about your upbringing. Why don't you tell us about him? Tell us about your life as a youngling?"

Rion wants to expose me right now! He wants me to unveil too much. He's clearly angry, but this is cold, even for the most depraved fae. Once the prince forces me to reveal that my father has been in prison for seven decades, I'll quickly have the attention of all of Faerie. And not the good kind.

"I love my father," I say, balling my hands into fists at my sides. "He is a simple man, with a generous heart, and I am here because of him."

"Then I suppose he might be upset if I sent you home tonight?"

He's angrier than I thought. My anger turns to horror as I realize his mention of it suggested he is seriously considering it. What would the king do if the prince is hellbent on tossing me out? "Do you plan to send me home tonight?"

The crown prince shrugs and glances at his audience, then leans toward me, resting his elbows on his knees. "No one is safe tonight."

I imagine it could get messy if the prince makes rash decisions that his father must remedy later. I swallow over the hard lump in my throat, attempting to push away the sudden flash of panic. Gnacia won't be thrilled, but I don't want to imagine the type of platter the king will demand my head served on.

Fix this. I can practically hear the king's voice in my head.

I swallow the rising bile. "I'd like to stay."

He watches me for several breathless moments. The prince still leans on his knees, and I realize our faces are a mere handbreadth apart. "You're here because of your father?"

"Yes, I said that, but—"

"He wants you to marry me? The prince?"

Fix. This. The king's imagined voice sings.

The king knows I cannot lie. I might be star fae; part human with all its weaknesses and mortality, but even with that, I was not born with the ability to lie. Despite Didi's teasing about my humanness, the fae in me is too strong to allow it. And Rion knows it.

"My father wants me to be happy," I say, touching the promise mark near my eye. "And being a part of the Consort

Tourney is an enormous step toward making us both happy." *Interpret that, Prince Orion Illuminae.*

The prince sits back again as one surprised eyebrow lifts. He also dons a careful smile, but I can't tell if it's genuine or forced. His expression smooths before he says, "I look forward to talking more, Amberle, but I have one more question."

I nod and sit straighter with my chin lifted. He can't see the relief at hearing his words that he intends to keep me at least a little while longer. Whatever he asks next, it seems I am safe from elimination tonight.

"What is one thing, one attribute or talent the high queen must have?"

"Humility." It flies out and I can't help but wonder if it isn't the blasted curse that triggered it. He was looking for answers such as cunning or beauty or diplomacy.

Prince Rion's eyebrows pinch together. "I'm not familiar with the word."

"It's a human word," I explain, grasping at how to salvage this very vulnerable position I've put myself in. "I don't expect many full fae are familiar with it, but I learned it from my star fae—my half-human—father." I don't add that it's an attribute I can safely assume most of the fae do not wish to possess.

"Well then, educate us." He leans back on the couch and waves a dramatic hand that settles on the backrest behind me.

I'm suddenly very aware of the closeness of his fingers to my wings and try to ignore the electricity that crackles along the length of them.

"Humility is letting go of pride. It's realizing that sometimes we make mistakes and we're sorry for them. Like hurting a friend without realizing it, then attempting to make amends." I glance at Princess Arielle across the room. I don't think she can hear what I'm saying, but by her expression—one of softness and hopefully forgiveness—I hope she can.

It might not pay the debt I owe her for saving me in the maze, but it's a start.

I expect Rion to quip at the audience about how foreign and undesirable the concept is to him, but he doesn't, and I feel his eyes on me. When I meet his gaze, I see his lips pursed in careful consideration.

"Is there anything else you want to know about me?" I ask, wishing it was acceptable to excuse myself without his blessing.

"No. That is entirely enough for now."

Twenty-One

I don't stay to watch the rest of the interviews. Instead, I wind through the corridors of the Isi Aura palace down to the lower levels. The servant's levels.

The sconces are still ornate and lovely, made of the same intricately sculpted white marble as the rest of the palace, but they're placed farther apart. Now that the sun has set, the light they provide is scarce, but warm. For ten steps at a time, I'm left in shadow until I reach the next umbrella of light, but I know my way.

This was once my playground.

As an esteemed member of the court staff, my family quarters were on a higher level in the palace, but most of the servants reside and work down here. My shoulders relax as scents of rosemary and citrus laundry soap waft through the halls.

My feet easily find their way to the worn door I'm looking for, but I don't knock right away. Instead, I run my fingertips over the charred mark in the wood frame.

It's still here. Just like the chip in the mirror upstairs, it's more evidence of my life here.

The burn mark resulted from my first—and last—attempt at using my summer magic. It escaped my weak control and sent a massive spark careening down the hallway. I'm sure I imagined it much larger than it actually was, but I feared catching the entire palace on fire, so I never practiced again.

Knocking quietly, I'm greeted by the tall, slender, black-eyed elf. I don't shove myself in the way I did with Gnacia Evernett, but hold bated breath, waiting for her reaction.

She brushes her sleek, emerald-colored hair behind one shoulder and sighs.

I exhale and can't help the smile that forms.

"Come in," she says, stepping aside to allow me to enter.

I resist skipping inside and acting as if no time has passed since I left; I take my cues from her.

"You know they have healers for the Tourney Contestants, Amberle." Bitterness laces her tone.

"How did you know I wanted a healer?" My voice softens. "Maybe I just missed you, Kali."

Kali's eye twitches. I wonder if I imagined it. But she invites me into the healer's room. It hasn't changed. A small apothecary cabinet with drawers is labeled in neat handwriting, a long table covered in herbs and spices, and two infirmary beds. The full fae rarely get sick and injuries are uncommon, so the beds aren't used often.

The elven healer pats the closest raised bed, gesturing that I sit. Just like she's done thousands of times in the past whenever I hurt myself doing something foolish. "I saw you favoring your right wing during the interview. Hop up. I'll take a look."

I'm torn between the comfort of being in one of my favorite places as a youngling and hating the awkwardness between us. Perhaps Rion was right when he said Princess Arielle felt hurt when I didn't return. Perhaps others felt the same.

Doing as she says, I move to the bed. My wings instinctively flutter to assist. A shock of pain accosts my right wing, and a hiss escapes my lips.

Cool hands gingerly grip the edges of my wing, extending it fully. "Did you fly after you injured it?"

"Yes," I say, lowering my head. "Ow!" I jerk back when she pinches the top.

"You've strained a tendon," Kali says, gently pressing the sore part again.

I wince. "Can you fix it?"

She rounds the table to face me. "I can speed up the healing, but you shouldn't fly for at least a week."

"A week?" I groan.

"Or I could leave it as is..." Her eyebrows narrow into a look I remember a bit too well.

"No, no. A week is fine," I say. "I'm sure flying won't be part of the trials."

Kali walks behind me again and I hear the familiar spark of her summer healing magic before she places hot hands on the point of my injury. It's near burning, but not unpleasant. The warmth stirs memories, and I regret not sending any messages to Kali. Perhaps I should've done things differently.

"I really have missed you." My voice comes out in a whisper.

"You've had seventy years to come see me, but you waited until the king summoned you."

I didn't think I was missed. When my father and I fled in the dead of night, I didn't know why we had to leave. I ached to return to my former home. But after they took my father, I wanted nothing to do with the palace or the royal family, and I assumed everyone felt the same way about me.

I clear my throat, blaming my emotion on the combination of pain and memories. "I didn't think I'd be welcome."

Another long pause fills the room. When Kali finally speaks, her tone is different. For the first time since I walked through her door, she sounds hesitant. Vulnerable. "I must admit, Amberle, it shocked me to hear your name called as one of the Tourney Contestants. And I wasn't the only one. What compelled you to come?"

Her question is layered, but I don't know what's hidden beneath the actual words.

"The king," I say. I don't dare get into the rest of it. But her comment makes me curious. "Who else was shocked? Was anyone... angry?"

"Angry? No! Hearing your name gave many of us... hope."

Kali's words send a jolt through me more than her magic ever could. If she wasn't using a concentrated dose of light magic that can irreparably damage as easily as it can heal, I might whip around in shock. Because no full fae with their wits about them wants a lowly half-human daughter of an imprisoned servant to win the crown.

If that's what they hope, they'll be sorely disappointed when I'm not chosen.

The heat subsides, and Kali steps back. "You know the routine."

I stretch my wing. It feels better already.

"Amberle?" she prods.

I twist on the bed to face her. "Yes, yes. Plenty of sunshine and elderberry wine."

"The kitchen keeps elderberry stocked. I'll have some sent to your room."

"There's no need for that. I can get it myself."

"I'll have some sent," she insists, leaning forward and placing both hands on my shoulders. "Contestants of the Tourney shouldn't be fetching things for themselves."

"But—"

"If you won't act the part, then you definitely won't win." She clasps her hands. "Don't give anyone a reason to eliminate you."

"I'm afraid I can't exactly help that." I shrug, wondering at her genuine tone. Not that it matters.

I hop down from the table.

"Then change your stars!" she snaps. "Believe in yourself! You won't win if you tell yourself you won't."

I tilt my head to the side. I want to remind her just how much I loathe Prince Rion, but her passion confounds me. "Why do you care so much?"

Kali steps to the door and peers out briefly before shutting it again and facing me. Then she speaks in low tones my half-human ears strain to hear, "Many of us believe the crown prince can make an excellent high king to the full fae and the star fae."

"What do you mean Prince Orion... can?" I understand her caution. She's criticizing King Estelar's rule without using the actual words. She's merely hinting the current high king is a bad king. It's treason. And it could get her killed if the wrong fae overhear.

It could get us both killed.

But I was never one who couldn't take a risk. "You believe he will be different than his father?"

"I believe he is still malleable. With the right mate at his side," she thrums nervous fingers across her lower lip before practically mouthing the rest of her words, "he could be an advocate and a just king for both species."

"And you think I'm the right mate because I'm star fae? We hate each other!" I shake my head and raise one eyebrow dismissively. "And what happens if he's with the... as you say, wrong mate? What happens then?"

"Then he'll be just like his father. But worse."

"I disagree. Prince Rion will never be like his father." I might dislike the prince, but I'd never put him in the same category as the king.

Kali frowns and her shoulders sag like she carries the whole of the world on her shoulders alone. "I've seen too much, Amberle. You've been gone, but I've been here—a witness to things I can't unsee."

"Is that why you were never raised to a higher level of healer?" I ask, almost dreading her answer. If Gnacia Evernett went from not employed by the crown to the king's secretary since I've been gone, why hasn't Kali risen in the ranks? Why hasn't she been promoted? What had she seen? A secret worth locking away in the lower corridors? "You're the best in the entire palace. Why aren't you the High King's personal healer? Or at the very least, the royal family?"

"I am happy to heal the servants."

"But..."

"The royals don't need healing services often." She walks to the door, ready to dismiss me.

I don't move. "Kali? Why haven't you been elevated?"

She sighs. "Because of Barrow and Flint."

"Your sons? Why? Have they done something?"

"Yes." She sighs. "They exist." Her forced smile is pained and paired with welling tears. "Star fae do not recognize other star fae, so you probably never knew, but Barrow and Flint's father was a human."

"They stunted your status because of who you chose to love?"

"Yes."

"You think if a star fae sits next to the crown, the kingdom will be forced to treat all fae equally. I don't know if that's true, but that's why you want me to win."

Kali walks toward me and places her hands on my shoulders again. "No, I want you to win because you're you."

"But how can you know who I am?" I ask, blinking rapidly to banish my own brewing tears. "I've been gone for nearly a century."

"I know you never changed in here." She points at my chest. At my heart. "And I remember how you were with the prince. He was always better with you around. He was kinder. He tried harder to be good."

I lift one eyebrow. Kali is wistful for innocent days of yesteryear. But she looks back through rose-colored glass. Those days never existed. Not the way she remembers.

Not wanting to rob her dreams, I simply joke. "Are we talking about the same prince?"

Her smile falters.

"I told you," I quickly add in a light tone, not wanting her to get her hopes up. "I don't think he cares for me." At all.

"You're here, aren't you?"

"Yes, but—"

"Please, Amberle."

I bite my tongue before confessing that I have the same dislike for Rion that he has for me, and there's no way I'm winning this Tourney. Even if the king wasn't pulling the strings. But... Kali reinforces an earlier, fleeting thought I'd brushed off: I can make sure Rion picks a fae who will make him better.

"I'll do my best not to be eliminated by something... foolish," I say.

Kali's shoulders relax before she straightens and heads for the door. "We shouldn't speak of this again."

I slink off the bed, assuming this is her way of telling me not to return. "Of course. I understand."

"Come visit any time, though." She smiles with gratitude. "If there's anything I can help you with, please let me know."

I nod, my mood brightening. Kali doesn't hate me. Perhaps I can fix things with Princess Arielle, too. I nearly walk out the door, but something comes to mind. "Actually, would you know how to get a curse removed?"

"What's the nature of the curse?"

"I'm not exactly sure," I say and think about all my recent mistakes. "Poor decisions? Maybe? And weakened reflexes. Oh, and loose lips?"

Kali scratches her chin in thought. "It sounds complicated. And old."

"Old?"

"Yes, what you describe sounds powerful and subtle. Something a sly fae would curse another with so the victim would think the mistakes were their own. I'm impressed you noticed. The curse is on you, isn't it?"

I nod, but don't mention that I noticed because of my line of work. The average fae might not notice, but mistakes in my line of work can mean the difference between getting paid and being sent to a cell.

"I suggest you look in the library for answers. Alexander still runs it, and he was always fond of you. But you might want to bring a peace offering for staying away for so long. He still loves rainbow tarts."

"I appreciate the tip."

"But I should warn you, subtle curses have always been a favorite for summer royalty."

"Do you mean..." I step closer to whisper. "Do you think the king... or someone close to him?"

"I can't say for sure, but be careful."

Twenty-Two

"Amberle Kindra," Alexander says when I present him with the rainbow tart I procured from the kitchen. He's blocking the entrance to the library with arms crossed and horns turned downward in disapproval.

The tart is arranged prettily on a plate with a dollop of cream on the side. It's a risky move, offering him something that makes any fae inebriated, but Alexander was always more agreeable when he was drunk on cream.

He eyes the plate with skepticism, but his expression thaws. Especially when he licks his lips.

"This is for you," I say, raising the plate higher. "I remember how much you liked these."

He eyes the plate again, keeping his arms folded. Alexander turns up his nose. "So, you're trying to win back my favor?"

I lower the plate. "If you don't want it, I'll eat it myself."

Alexander snatches the plate from me and I hold back the smile that threatens to emerge.

"What do you want?" he asks, scooping a finger through the cream and sticking it into his mouth. "You never came here just to bring me treats."

"You're right," I say. "I came here for something."

He eyes me.

"It's better than asking for something with nothing to offer!"

Alexander sighs, then moves to the side, allowing me entrance into the grand library. Windows line one wall from floor to ceiling, looking eastward toward The Sea of Neptulus. From here, the beaches can be seen. At the right time of day there are groups of fae on the sand, hosting revels and bonfires, or louche rituals and pranks pulled on the poor humans they trick into following them through a portal.

I know this because I used to sneak out and spy on them, not because I did the tricking.

The other three walls are covered in floor to ceiling bookshelves lined with books and scrolls from around Faerie and even some of the other realms. And in the center is a massive tree. Fifty fae could circle the base with their arms outreached and only be able to touch fingertip to fingertip. Shelves are carved into the bark from the ground up to hold even more books. The tree climbs far above the ceiling, where it disappears above it with more books and scrolls shelved on the next level.

I don't know of a single fae—star fae or full—who knows all that is contained in the Isi Aura Library. Not even Alexander himself, and he's curated it for nearly a millennium.

"Is there something I can help you find?"

I'm not sure how much to tell Alexander. Kali mentioned that royal summer fae tend to favor subtle curses. So while Alexander might know who cursed me since this is the library for the royal summer fae, it's unclear if his loyalties would be to me... or them. He might tip them off that I've been snooping and researching.

But... I doubt I can find what I'm looking for on my own.

I'm left with little choice. "Could you point me toward books about old curses?"

"Old curses?" he asks around a mouthful of tart and cream. "Is there one in particular you want to know about?"

"The subtle kind? The kind a fae may not realize right away that they've been cursed?"

Alexander grips his pointed black chin and wags his eyebrows at me. "Trying to get a leg up in the competition, are we?"

I smile. It would certainly help me in this competition if this curse was removed. "Something like that."

Luckily, Alexander doesn't ask more questions and leads me to the tree. I think the cream is doing its work because he doesn't seem concerned when he says, "If you can't find what you're looking for here—" He gestures to a section of the tree by drawing a large circle in the air with his hand. "It might be further up—" He points, indicating the floor above us. "In the north section of the tree. The lift will take you up there."

"Thank you, Alexander," I say. "I think I can manage from here."

He lifts his plate with a grin, then leaves me to enjoy his treat. I don't expect to speak with him again today since he'll likely fall into a drunken slumber as soon as he consumes the rest of the cream.

It will give me plenty of time to research.

An hour later, I've found an alcove and have dozens of books piled around me. Most are useless and contain the ramblings of bored and eccentric fae with only the occasional mention of curses, but I've found three written by humans which are promising.

Most curses I know of rely on some potion or hex bag containing fingers or toes or claws of various creatures; then it's ingested or placed near the target of the curse. Old curses are in a class of their own. The more I read, the more I realize that the older the curse, the less straightforward:

When the moon is high and the sea is low.

Or, *as the bulbegger climbs or when the pixie falls.*

And, *when you can see your image in the green of his eyes.*

None of it makes any sense, and my vision blurs.

A shadow falls over my page, but then quickly retreats.

I look up to see Princess Arielle standing above me. "Is this where you've been hiding? You slipped out before the interviews were over."

"Yes. I missed yours," I say. "I hope it went well." I close the book in my lap and rest both hands on it, covering the title.

She smiles. "Mine was dull. We couldn't act as if we didn't know one another the way you and the prince managed. So we just talked about the past."

"I'm sure it wasn't dull," I assure her. "I imagine the entire realm held their breath as you two reminisced. You must know you are the favorite to win."

"Not for everyone," Arielle says softly.

I don't know what she means, and I don't dare ask, but to dispel any oncoming awkwardness between us before it even begins, I say, "It was good of you to help me in the labyrinth trial, although I imagine you didn't free me on purpose."

Arielle looks at me until I meet her eyes. When I do, the warmth and friendship I see behind them is intense. "I didn't know someone was trapped, that is true, but I was happy to help. If I had known you were on the other side of that wall, I wouldn't have changed my actions."

I stare at the ground, feeling uneasy at the sudden bubble of emotion filling my core. I feel her goodness. A goodness that is so unnatural to the majority of the fae, I wonder if she isn't part human.

After my conversation with Kali, I realize Arielle is—and always has been—the perfect fae for Rion. I think she could be a just queen for the full fae and star fae alike and she could help the prince become a good king. My task here might be easier than I thought if I can just focus on her. Still, it makes me wonder why King Estelar went to the trouble of the Tourney if Arielle was always the best choice. Unless he doesn't want the two of them together.

It's definitely worth digging into.

"What are you looking for?" she asks, gesturing at the sea of books around me.

"An old curse." The words fall out and I imagine it's exactly *the curse* at work.

Arielle is royal summer fae, but it's too late to take my words back now.

"A subtle one," I add.

"And for what reason? Do you intend to cheat to win the Tourney?"

"No." I look at her and can't help the way my expression falls.

"Oh! Someone put a curse on you?"

I look back at the books. For being away so long, she still knows me well.

"What's the curse? When did it happen?" she asks, as she folds her legs underneath her and joins me to sit on the ground.

I scan the library before I look back at her.

"If we both search, I'm sure we can figure out what happened quickly and get it removed." Arielle scoops up a book next to her and flips through it. When I remain silent, she pauses. "Unless you don't want my help?" She closes the book slowly and places it back on the floor.

"No, I just—I... why do you want to help me?"

"I uh... I just thought that we were once friends and maybe we could..." There is a sincerity in her voice and a kindness in her eyes. She might be a summer princess, but she's not like the others. She rubs her hands along her skirts as if expelling invisible dirt, then rises to her feet.

I grab her hand, stopping her. "We were friends, Princess."

She settles again, and I draw my hand back.

"It's just been a long time, and I've lived a life of distrust in the shadows for decades." I force myself to look her in the eyes and sigh.

"Well, if you'd rather do this alone..."

Between the curse and Gnacia's demands, my chances of freeing my father are slim. With help, my chances could improve immensely. If I must trust someone—by choice or not—my best bet is Princess Arielle.

"No. I mean, I'd like for us to be friends again."

She smiles. "Me too."

If nothing else, I can keep her close and find out for sure if she is the perfect match for Rion, but since I've known her since we were younglings, I think I already know the answer.

"I really wish I could have seen your interview," I say. "I'm sure it wasn't as dull as you fear."

Arielle waves a hand. "It's of little importance."

"Because you already have a strong connection with him."

"No, because..." She clears her throat and picks up the book again. "So, what is this curse?"

"But Arielle, you do have a strong connection with Rion." I pause. "Unless... did something happen?"

"No."

"Then what is it?"

She lifts her eyes to me and I can see that she doesn't want to discuss her and the prince. "Your curse? Can you tell me about it?"

Pushing harder won't make Arielle talk, so I stop and answer her question instead. "I'm making mistakes. Saying things I didn't mean to say. I almost—well, I'll just say that it has interfered with my... profession."

"Wait. It didn't start after you came to Isi Aura?"

"No."

"So it wasn't put on you by one of the other contestants?"

"If it was, it was before I even received my invitation. Most of the contestants didn't know who I was before the king called my name." I look away. "And those who do know me didn't know where I was."

The summer princess stares at the pile of books and asks softly, "Where were you?"

"When I received my invitation?" I ask, grateful she hasn't asked what my 'profession' was. "In Rosewind."

"Spring Court." She nods, pleased by my answer. "There were many nights I imagined you freezing in the depths of Winter. I'm glad to know you were someplace moderately warm." After a pause, she says, "I don't want to win."

My head snaps to her and my eyes widen. "You... you what? You don't want to win... the Consort Tourney?"

"Look, I've known Prince Orion my entire life." She smiles, but it's a sad smile and she won't meet my eyes. "You know that. We've both known the prince since we were young."

"Well, you have. I missed out on nearly a century."

She looks at me through lowered eyebrows. "You understand what I mean."

"I do."

The princess sits straighter and lifts her chin when she says, "Orion is a romantic. I am a romantic. But we don't love each other. At least not that way."

"He's like a brother?" I guess. A very annoying, demanding, entitled brother who broods and chastises.

"Yes. And I think if we were ever to become more than that, it would have already happened."

"So, what will you do?" I ask.

"I don't know."

"Does Rion know?"

"That I don't love him? Yes, he knows. But he doesn't know that I'm considering leaving the competition."

"Wait. You're leaving?"

"There's no point in staying, Amberle. Orion and I would have a comfortable life together, but not a happy one."

"When will you go?"

She shrugs. "Likely soon. Especially now that I've told you."

I don't know what to say. I can see that she's decided, and there's no convincing her to reconsider.

"Think of it this way. If I was the favorite, now I'll be out of the way for everyone to see the prince's true options." She reaches out to place a hand on mine. "And although I never saw the two of you together until the Tourney, I think you're the best one."

"I don't— "

"Your curse." Her face alights. "It sounds a lot like a mixture of the Hex of Mania and the Clumsy Vex."

My mouth slams closed, and I realize that with Arielle, Rion's hurtful words were honest and actually helpful. Princess Arielle was my friend. She's still my friend. I must give him credit for helping me mend our friendship.

"Unfortunately, it doesn't narrow down the perpetrator, as both are well known to the summer fae," she continues.

"But if I was in the Spring Court..."

"Fae travel between courts. Both are easy to place on a fae since they only require the victim to touch the object with the curses."

"How do I remove it?" I'm feeling a stroke of luck knowing that my friend has knowledge that could have taken me months or years to figure out on my own. Especially since she suspects I have not one, but two curses affecting me.

"Well... that's the tricky part. You have to find the object first."

Twenty-Three

The stars shine against the dark new moon outside the window of my quarters as I sit in the stiff, royal-worthy seat and force sips of elderberry wine from my glass. I feel its healing effects in my injured wing—which is worth the bitter aftertaste I've always hated—but it also rejuvenates my bleary eyes and blooming irritation after reading for so many hours about old curses.

Fiery anger radiates through my limbs. I shove away the books at my feet, unable to even glance at the offending pile of even more books scattered all over my bed covers.

The books have been no help.

I've learned nothing. My brief conversation with Princess Arielle told me more than the hours and hours of pouring over tomes and scrolls. I was glad for her company, but I couldn't let her ruin her entire evening in study, so I excused myself and spent more hours in the solitude of my room with the handful of promising volumes I borrowed from a very drunk librarian. It was a waste of my time.

At least Arielle and I are friends again, but I wonder if she'll stay in the palace or leave it once she bows out of the competition. Now that she's told me her plan, she warned it would be soon, but maybe I can convince her to stay long enough to help me get the curses lifted.

As I gaze at the stars, I think about Clay. I wonder how he's fared since I left. Has he taken on any jobs? Has he been successful? I have little doubt he's just fine on his own—he will be a better thief than I am someday.

I take another sip of the elderberry, then hold the key still slung around my neck that Clay gave to me before we parted. Wearing it grounds me and helps me remember my former life. I wonder if he will be open to teaming up again when I get back.

If I get back.

Although returning to the Spring Court to find my former partner might not be the wisest decision. Even if I pull this off and free my father, it might be better to disappear for a while. Maybe we should leave Faerie altogether and spend some time in the human realm once this is over. Get as far away from the royals as we can.

Even so, I cannot allow myself to become too soft while being pampered in luxury as I pose as a possible future queen. Because I won't be the next future queen. I will always and forever be a thief.

Ursa Major shines brightly tonight. Although I prefer to call the constellation Fisher, as my father always did. Fisher was the fox-like creature who tore a hole in the sky with his friends to bring summer to the earth, which was formerly plunged in never-ending winter.

It was one of my father's favorite stories to tell. It was a human story he learned from his mother, who spent years in the human world with her human father.

I want to learn more human stories someday. They often teach humility and goodness and sacrifice. Three things the fae horribly lack. Fisher sacrificed his life so humans could have summer. I've always admired him for that.

Knock. Knock. Knock.

My thoughts are interrupted by the quiet rapping at my door.

I set my glass on the table and rise to answer it. It's late, which means Gnacia has probably come to scold me about something. Although I hope it's Arielle. Perhaps she remembered something else about the Hex of Mania or the Clumsy Vex and has come to tell me how I can be rid of them.

But when I swing the door inward, it's neither female. Instead, golden cat-eyes stare down at me with a guarded expression beneath tousled dark hair.

"It's late, Rion," I say.

"I'm aware," he says with exasperation. "Can I come in?"

I smirk and hitch one hand on my hip, but step aside and gesture that he's welcome. "Is that allowed?"

"I'm the prince, Amberle," he says, walking past me and into my room as I shut the door. "I'm allowing it."

"All I have to offer you is elderberry wine," I say, remembering my dusty manners as I follow him into my sitting area. "But I'm sure you could call for something at this late hour since you're the prince." I poke.

"I won't be staying long," he says, but makes himself comfortable in one of the plush chairs.

I sit across from him.

"Where do you keep disappearing to?" he asks.

"What do you mean?"

"I mean at the labyrinth, and then during the interviews. You didn't stay like the others."

After the interview. I don't want to tell him I needed space after the interview. Not after he nearly exposed my profession and the location of my father to all of Faerie. Not to mention that little conversation about humility.

"I didn't know I was supposed to stay." I lift my shoulders, then reach forward to take my glass from the table and drink from it. My cheeks pucker from the bitterness.

He watches me with careful consideration, then gazes out the window at the clear night sky.

"The stars are bright tonight," he muses.

"Yes, I was just admiring them."

"What's that one called?" he asks, pointing at the sky. "The one that looks like a soup ladle?"

"Ursa Major?"

"Yes, but you always called it something else." He looks at me. "Fox, or Fish?"

"Fisher?" Funny. I was just thinking about that story.

Rion snaps his fingers, then looks back out the window. "I always loved the story you used to tell me about Fisher."

"I told you the story?"

The prince smiles and looks at me with a shrug. "Well, you were telling it to some younglings once, and I overheard."

"Ah, you were eavesdropping," I accuse, folding my arms and leaning further back in my chair. "You know what they say about eavesdroppers?"

He rolls his eyes. "How did it go? The story? All I remember is that it was something about the sky people?"

"Something like that."

"Tell me again, Amberle. I need a distraction." Rion leans back in the chair and closes his eyes.

Is this what it means to be in the Tourney? Distracting the prince?

If it will keep him from sending me home...

"Well, Fisher and his friends wanted to bring summer to the earth, but the Skyland people kept it all to themselves," I begin. "So they took turns trying to break a hole in the sky. When Wolverine succeeded, the friends all scampered around Skyland, enjoying the warmth of summer."

"Ah, yes, summer. That's why I always loved that story," Rion says, keeping his eyes closed. "Continue."

"Fisher wanted to make the hole bigger so that the warmth and growth and abundance of summer could pour down on the earth for the humans to enjoy. He became so busy with his task, he didn't see the arrow notched and aimed at him.

"When the shaft shot through him and he fell to the earth, the hole in the sky was only big enough to allow summer on the earth for half the year. But the gods honored his sacrifice by hanging him among the stars as the constellation."

Rion doesn't respond and I wonder if he's fallen half-asleep. I lift my glass from the table and take another sip.

"I thought you hated elderberry," Rion says, peeking at me through his nearly closed eyelids.

"Well, I don't love it, but..." I drink more before replacing it on the table.

The prince lifts an eyebrow. Waiting for me to finish the thought.

"But... when Kali tells me to drink it, I obey."

"Kali? The servant healer?" Rion sits up. "Have you fallen ill? Are you injured?" His eyebrows pinch together.

"My wing," I say, lifting my injured wing slightly and trying to dismiss the way my insides twist. The movement doesn't hurt as badly; Kali's healing and the elderberry must be working. "I tripped over it in the labyrinth. Kali says I've injured a tendon."

"Is that why you kept disappearing?" he asks.

"I didn't think I would be missed."

The prince laughs once, then leans forward, resting his elbows on his knees. "You're a contestant in the Consort Tourney, Amberle. Weren't you told that you would always be watched? Of course you were missed."

I fold my arms. "Are we being watched right now?"

"No," Rion says, then does something I don't expect. He lifts my glass from the table and drinks some of my wine.

"I thought you hated elderberry."

The prince lifts one corner of his lips into a half-smile and wags his eyebrows. "Maybe I need healing, too."

Before I can ask more, Rion stands. I do too, thinking he's about to leave, but instead he walks toward the bed and lifts a book. "What is this you're studying? Curses?" He lowers the book and looks at me. "Why?"

"I don't want to say." I stand and take the book from his

hand, then move in front of him to gather up the rest and shove the stack in the bottom of the wardrobe. Out of sight.

"You don't want to say? Are you planning to place a curse on someone?" His eyes harden, but the smile doesn't leave his lips. He's amused. "Do you plan to hex your competition? I must say, I'm impressed, but it's not the way to win."

Why does everyone come to that conclusion first? I wonder. *That I want to cheat in the competition?*

"That's what Arielle thought, too." It just comes out. The symptom of the blasted Hex of Mania!

"Arielle?" The smile wipes from his face.

He looks panicked, and I wonder if Arielle was wrong about his feelings for her. She suggested there was nothing romantic between them, only a brother-sister bond, but the mention of the summer princess always triggers a reaction from the crown prince.

I should dig more. I need to find out his feelings for her. If she exits the competition and he cancels the entire thing because of a broken heart, the king will have my head.

"Yes. Arielle found me in the library. We've mended our friendship."

That brings back his smile. "I'm glad to hear."

"Are you?" I ask. "Can I ask why you're glad to hear it?" *Because you love her and you don't want to see her hurt?* I bite my tongue.

"Because you were friends as younglings. Because she missed you."

"And you don't want to see her hurt?"

"Of course not, and more than that—"

"Because you love her?" I press my lips tightly together. I hadn't meant to spout it out. I tried to hold it back, but well... curses.

Rion steps toward me. "Because if you could mend your friendship with Arielle... perhaps you could also mend your friendship with me."

What? We were never friends. There is nothing to be mended.

"Why?" I close my eyes and cover my mouth with my hand as my stomach does a flip. I meant to say nothing. I meant to let him think what he wanted.

His smile is pained, and he looks at the floor.

"I-I mean… I just didn't expect…" I stammer.

The prince lifts a hand, silencing me. Which is probably for the best before I say something else really foolish. This damned curse is going to get me sent home! Especially with so many slip-ups in one small conversation with the prince.

Rion turns and walks toward the window, looking out into the night. "Why do I want to be your friend?" he asks the stars. "Because if you become my queen at the end of this, I want us to like each other. I want us to enjoy each other's company."

I bite the inside of my cheek and swallow over the hard lump that has formed in my throat and pray I can keep my thoughts to myself. Blurting that I'll never become his queen will ruin everything.

He turns back. Perhaps to watch my reaction. Luckily, no other sentences escape without permission.

"I don't know how to tell you this…" he continues, a smile tugging on the edge of his lips. "Because it's probably cheating… But well, as I said before, I'm the prince and I say it's allowed."

"If it's cheating, then maybe you shouldn't," I blurt.

He watches me for several painfully long moments. I want to crawl into a hole or hide in the wardrobe with the books on curses. I want to disappear.

"If that's what you wish," he says, then lifts my glass of elderberry wine and finishes it in one swallow. "I said I wouldn't stay long. I'll leave you now."

I nod once. I've hurt him, I can see that. But I don't know how to fix it. Especially because I fear opening my mouth will do more harm.

And so I say nothing as the crown prince walks out my door.

Twenty-Four

At breakfast the next morning, they arranged the dining hall with three tables covered in sky blue linens and fragrant floral arrangements. My preference would have been to stay in my room and have my meal brought to me, especially since I'm used to a tiny breakfast, but after the prince scolded me about my disappearances, I should begin doing what is expected of me.

And what is expected of me is to join the other contestants for breakfast.

It also means I should probably stop sending the servants away when they come to help me dress.

I feel like I managed well enough on my own this morning. My dress is proper and my hair—although not intricately plaited or arranged—is clean and neat in my natural soft waves that hang over my shoulder like a silver scarf. But as I scan the room to find Didi, I notice the others wear back-laced dresses and fancy hairstyles. No one else sent their servants away like I did, but at least I'm here.

"She exists!" Didi teases, leaning over to nudge me with her elbow as I sit next to her. Raine sits across from Didi, but I'm glad Clove is at another table, sitting with my fellow summers. Next to

Clove, Princess Arielle is feigning a smile as she listens to her babble—probably bragging about trapping me in the labyrinth. Arielle catches my eye and flashes a look of annoyance. I stifle a laugh. The princess was always better than I was at pretending she liked a fae when she didn't.

"Tierney." Didi waves at the autumn fae as she arrives and gestures to an empty seat at our rounded table. It's sweet how Didi tries to make friends across courts. Naive, but sweet. Tierney sits, her back ramrod straight, as Didi turns back to me.

"I was beginning to think you were a figment of my imagination or some type of rare light-wisp that shies away from crowds," Didi teases, hooking a loose lock of red hair behind her ear.

"Yes, I realize I haven't been as present as I should," I say, recalling her earlier chiding. "But in my defense, I injured my wing and went to have it attended to by a healer."

"I hope your wing is better. But that couldn't have—"

Didi is cut off first by a collective yammering of excitement, then a hush that falls over the room. She, and everyone else, straightens in their chairs. I do the same.

I expect to see Prince Rion walk in the door, or maybe the king or even Queen Siora, but when I turn to look, it's none of them.

"Juniper!" Tierney calls to her friend, then gestures that she join us at our table.

The entire room has grown quiet... for Juniper. The orange-haired fae who first found Rion in the labyrinth stands in the doorway, her mouth in an 'o' before she smiles at Tierney and walks toward our table.

While Juniper stops to chat with another table of fae, I lean closer to Didi and whisper, "Are we still applauding her for winning the maze task? Or have I missed something? Has Juniper already won the crown?"

"None of those," Didi says, muttering from the side of her mouth. "But she is the first fae to be courted by the prince."

"Courted?" Something about that word irritates me. "What do you mean, courted?"

"She and the prince ate their evening meal together after the interviews last night. She's the first to have any amount of private time with him."

"Well, private, while being watched by all of Faerie," Raine says, inserting herself.

"If you had stayed through the interviews, Amberle, you would have known." Didi winks as Juniper sits next to Tierney.

With all the contestants now present, they serve our breakfast. Plates of fruit and meats and pastries are set in the center of the tables for us to help ourselves. I reach for a peach and nearly bite into it when I notice Raine cutting her fruit into dainty wedges. I do the same. Manners.

"Well?" Didi asks Juniper, leaning across the table to whisper at her. "How was your date with the prince?"

"Yes, Juniper, you must tell us!" Raine says, leaning forward. "What was he like?"

"Are you already in love?" Didi asks, her hands clutched together tightly on her lap.

I look at Didi. I'm as curious as the rest—in fact, I've become hyper-aware as I need to pass on to Gnacia this intel about Juniper for the crown to assess her qualifications for becoming the next high queen. But Didi is leaning forward, and I can't help but wonder if Didi is already falling for the prince even though she's only spent a few moments with him.

"Now that's not fair," Princess Shay says, as she hovers over me. She's brought her plate and sets it next to mine, then snaps her fingers, ordering a servant to bring her chair. "We all want to hear about Juniper's outing."

Princess Shay squeezes in between Didi and me as more of the contestants also bring their plates to crowd around our small table.

"Yes, we want to hear it too," Clove says, elbowing in to sit on Juniper's other side.

"Well, then make room for everyone," Juniper says, gesturing to the three Underwater Court fae huddling awkwardly on the outskirts of the table. With a few groans and several nasty looks, the chairs are adjusted again.

The fifteen of us are soon all arms and wings and plates overlapping each other. Pretending I'm completely comfortable, which is ridiculous, I casually stretch my right wing behind me so it doesn't get accidentally bumped. I'm tempted to move to one of the now empty tables, but I need the information, too.

"Oh, I just love that coral bracelet," Juniper gushes over the nearest underwater fae. "I mapped the west coast of The Sea of Neptulus in cartography as a youngling. And I believe that deep shade is found in—"

"Juniper!" Clove snaps. "The date. Tell us about the date."

Juniper blinks, seemingly half-surprised to see fourteen fae staring at her. "Well, as you all know, I was the first to be interviewed so that I had time to bathe and dress. My gown was exquisite—"

"Yes, we all saw it," Princess Shay says, flicking a piece of her dark curly hair behind her shoulder. "We want to hear about Prince Orion."

Several heads bob and there's collective muttering of agreement around the table.

"Oh." Juniper nods, but doesn't seem convinced that we don't want the details of her dress. She gazes over our head and smiles.

I realize this conversation is exactly the type of thing the court would show. Is Faerie watching? I sit up straighter. I wonder if there's a way to replay the magic at a later date. If the autumn fae who earned the first outing with the prince becomes the queen, will this moment be played and replayed for future generations to watch as some of the first moments of their romance and eventual union?

"First, we took our evening meal on the upper balcony overlooking the Northern Sea," Juniper says airily, yet with no hesitation and no qualms about discussing her private moments with the prince. "He asked about my life as a youngling and inquired after my father's..."

I stop listening as her soft voice babbles about her family's ties to the Autumn Court royalty. I can't help it. My wing aches from holding it up behind me during her never-ending tale. So, I take a pastry and more fruit for my plate, then stand and step into the background, picking at my food as I listen to the dull details. They ate pheasant in a cranberry sauce with the best mulberry wine ever. The sunset was vermilion and phlox. What color was phlox, anyway? And the prince looked at her like she was the prettiest thing he'd ever seen. Obviously, it's her interpretation of his expression since none of us were there to see it ourselves.

Tierney nods in agreement. "Yes, he seemed to admire you."

"Wait, how do you know, Tierney?" Clove snaps. "Were you there?"

"Or did you watch?" Princess Shay adds.

"N-no, it's not allowed for us to watch," Tierney says. "I-It's just that Juniper came to my room right after and told me everything."

Just as I thought... Interpretation.

It looks like Princess Shay is about to complain about the unfairness of it, but she looks at her fellow winter contestant, Luna, and the two of them share a glance. Perhaps it's an unspoken agreement that they'll tell each other about their moments with the prince immediately afterward, too.

"Then, after dinner, we took a stroll through the gardens," Juniper continues with a sigh. "It was dark by then, and the stars shone like a million pixies."

"Pixies don't glow," Clove mutters under her breath.

Fae cannot lie, but there's no way to know if Rion is falling in love with her based on Juniper's opinions of the truth. It's also impossible to know her intentions or potential plots of murder after they wed. However, I might be able to watch for telltale signs that a fae isn't truly in the competition for the prince if I can observe these moments. Then, I could possibly determine his feelings for each contestant, too. I think I know him well enough. It's against the rules to watch, but Didi and I broke that rule during the interviews.

"It was a beautiful night," Juniper continues dreamily. "I held on tightly to his arm and he leaned close to me…"

My stomach twists.

"But then we were interrupted by some radicals," Juniper says.

My ears perk. Radicals?

Princess Arielle finally speaks. "Did you fear for your life?"

"It was just one, actually," Juniper says. "He spouted something about a secret the king was hiding from Faerie for decades and that Faerie deserves to know it."

"What secret?" Didi blurts.

Juniper shrugs. "Prince Orion didn't say. And the fae was quickly dragged away."

Clap. Clap. Clap.

Our heads all snap with the staccato claps to see Gnacia at the head of the room.

"Ladies, if you could please spread out, Nieven Morphyra has an announcement to make," the faun says.

Everyone returns to their former seats, and I move to sit next to Didi again, who still peppers Juniper with questions in a hushed tone.

"The prince didn't say, but do you have an idea what the secret is?" Didi asks, leaning forward.

Juniper glances at Tierney and bites her lip before turning back to my friend. "It's always carefully concealed, but while I was with the prince, I noticed—"

"Tourney Contestants! All of Faerie!" Nieven Morphyra, the king's entertainer, interrupts.

"You noticed what?" Didi hisses.

"As you all watched last evening," Nieven continues, obviously speaking to those watching around Faerie. "One of the fae has already begun her journey with the prince to determine if they are a good match and if she can be the next high queen consort. Juniper Faeven, will you please join me up here?"

Juniper cocks her head, as if seeing Didi for the first time, then whispers, "I think I know what the secret is."

Then she stands to join the elf.

"Tell us Juniper," Nieven says. "What are your thoughts about our prince?"

"Well, he's very attractive and agreeable," Juniper says.

Nieven winks at the air—at the winter magic. "Yes, but tell us something we don't know."

The other contestants let out humoring laughs.

Juniper looks at her feet briefly with her hands clasped in front of her before looking up again, and we all see that her cheeks are flushed. "Well, I think I could easily love the prince."

"And do you think he could love you?"

"I hope so."

"You took an evening stroll in the gardens after your evening meal," Nieven continues. "Now, you don't know this, but the winter magic vanished before Faerie could see how your night ended. Indulge us. Tell us how you parted."

Juniper opens her mouth to speak, but Nieven interrupts.

"There's no need to tell any secrets that should not be shared with the realm, but tell us something Faerie will surely regret they missed afterward. Did the prince share his feelings with you? Was there a kiss?"

Nieven is warning her. He wants her to gush about her romance with the prince and leave out the portion she told the rest of us about the radical and the secret the king has apparently kept from us.

"No kiss." Juniper's blush deepens. "Not yet, anyway. The prince was proper and respectful, exactly as I'd imagined. He escorted me back to my quarters, wishing me happy dreams, then headed back to his quarters."

"Well, that is a disappointment," Nieven says.

I bit the inside of my cheek, keeping the truth to myself—the prince didn't retire after he left Juniper. He came to my room.

Juniper takes her seat again, and Nieven looks around the room with a dramatic pause. Then he announces, "The first elimination ceremony will be this evening. Ready yourselves, ladies, because some of you might be going home tonight."

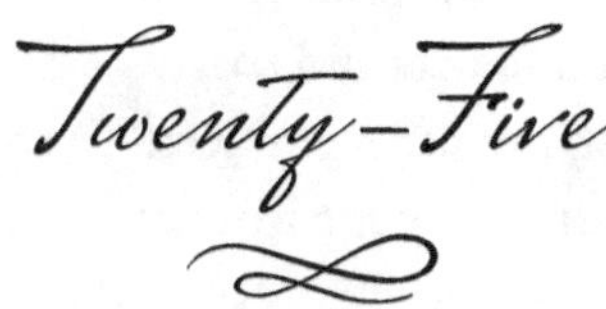

Twenty-Five

The other contestants squeal and rush about in a blur of fluttering wings, horns, and swishing chiffon as they all scramble over themselves to get out of the room after Nieven Morphyra's announcement.

Elimination. Tonight.

I know I'm staying tonight, but my heart pounds as if I might not.

Gnacia waits for me in the corridor with arms folded and one eyebrow lifted. I know what she's about to say before she says it. She wants me to quit sending ladies' maids away.

"Can I request which servants attend to me?" I ask.

A triumphant smile tugs at the edge of Gnacia's mouth before she hides her amusement away. "That depends on who you request."

"The spring fae who brought my dinner the first night. I want her." The way she skillfully conjured a tree when she spilled the dinner tray impressed me.

Gnacia scoffs. "If she brought your meal, she is not a ladies' maid—"

"I want her."

Gnacia walks toward me, her hooves clacking on the tiled

floor. With the other contestants gone, her prim facade drops. She lowers her voice when she says, "Need I remind you that you are not in a position to make demands? You are not a royal."

I don't flinch away from her stare. "Yes, but you and I both need me to succeed in my task. In the brief conversation I had with her, she felt like a fae I could trust."

"You don't trust my advice? Need I remind you, I strongly suggested you not turn up your nose at a ladies' maid. Then you saw the wisdom in my advice. Now I'm suggesting you have someone experienced to help you."

"Then someone who won't have loyalties to another contestant or fae. What about Kali Islandwort? The healer?"

"She is not a ladies' maid, either. And the king would never agree—" The faun pauses as if something has occurred to her, then sighs. "There's a human girl who attended a noble lady in the human realm. She's recently come to Faerie and so has no loyalties or strong ties. If you agree to allow her to assist you, I'll ask the kitchens to send this spring fae, too."

I bite the inside of my cheek to stop myself from grinning like a maniacal cait sith.

"Yes, that sounds acceptable," I say, then nod and turn to walk back to my room.

Half an hour later, I'm seated at my vanity. A new ivory dress is slung over my bed while the human girl, Kenna, is fumbling around with my hair. Kenna is a dull girl with brown hair tucked underneath a gray cap and rounded ears. Her eyes are a bit too close together, but her looks aren't ogrish like some humans. The spring fae, Posey, hovers next to her, watching her work.

I try hard not to think about the situation I'm in. I remember watching servants fawn about the queen's hair when I was young. I don't remember why I was in the queen's chambers watching her servants attend to her, but I remember feeling glad that I would never be subjected to it.

And yet here I am. An imposter. In the mirror, I barely recognize myself. I shift in my seat, uncomfortable with my farce. I grip the arms of my chair, reminding myself it won't last long. A means to an end.

"This is called a chignon," Kenna says to Posey as she wraps my silver hair around itself and into a low knot.

"I-It seems simple," Posey says. "Perhaps too simple?"

"It's elegant," the human argues.

"Simple doesn't turn heads or win crowns," says the spring fae. I sense a shift in her. An assertiveness I've never seen. "Do you know any other arrangements? We want Amberle to shine among the other contestants. We want Prince Orion to keep her past this elimination."

The human girl glances at Posey in the mirror, her hands frozen.

"Or else you and I will be out of a job," Posey adds.

Kenna drops my hair, allowing it to bounce against my back. "What do you mean?"

"I'll go back to the kitchens, and you'll go back to... wherever you were before they sent you here."

Kenna's eyes widen.

I swivel around to look at them full on, instead of through the vanity mirror. "I assure you both, I won't be going home tonight."

Even if I wasn't sure, I doubt my staying or going would have anything to do with how fancy my hair is.

"What if Kenna shows you the simple chignon tonight," I suggest. "Then we can practice the more difficult hairstyles later?" I smile at them both.

Posey nods, then gestures that the human continue. She steps forward and lifts my hair again, twisting it the way she did before, then secures it with pins in silence as Posey watches.

"How did you end up in Faerie, Kenna?" I ask, remembering the panic I saw in her eyes when Posey reminded her of the possible consequences if they sent me home. I wonder if she would go back to the human world or be sent to serve another fae. "I'm told you worked for a noble lady in the human realm?"

"Yes," Kenna says, glancing at me briefly in the mirror before turning back to her work on my hair. "But then when the famine came, it threatened even the noble families with starvation..." she pauses, then sighs. "They sold me to a leprechaun for a bag of flour."

"Famine? I didn't know," I admit. "How long has it been going on?"

"Two years. I think?" Kenna says. "I know time in Faerie is different. Perhaps the famine is over now. It could well be the fifteenth century for all I know. The year was thirteen hundred and sixteen when I left."

"It's funny the way humans mark time," Posey comments.

"The fae are immortal," I point out. "Time is an affordable luxury, so we view it differently."

"Yes, but even the star fae who aren't immortal don't obsess so much over time the way humans do."

"Perhaps because we live longer than a human."

"What's star fae?" Kenna asks.

"Part-fae," I say. "It's what I am."

"What is the other part?"

"Human," Posey says.

Kenna's thin eyebrows furrow. "You're part... human?" she asks me. "Was one of your parents human?"

"No. But that is true for some."

Kenna finishes my hair, so I stand for her and Posey to help me into the ivory dress. It has a criss-cross pattern of thin, interlacing ribbons that go from my throat and down through the bodice to my waist. The back hovers low, allowing my wings to be completely free. The skirts reach the floor in a flowy silk that has the appearance of spilling milk.

Posey turns me to look at her and she looks at me with intense concentration, gripping her chin with one hand. After a moment, her eyes widen with a thought and she gestures that I sit at the vanity again, this time facing her.

"If you worked in a noble lady's house, how do you not know

more hairstyles, Kenna?" Posey asks as she waves her hands around. I feel the spring magic tug and pull at the hair near my crown, though not enough to hurt.

"It is improper for ladies to show their hair in public," Kenna says. "A chignon or a bun is sufficient to then be covered with a bonnet or hat to hide it."

"Well, that is not how it is in Faerie," Posey says.

Kenna's cheeks flush. "Yes, it has been an eye-opening experience coming here."

"You are scandalized by the fae?" I ask.

"I was at first," Kenna admits. "But I have grown accustomed to your... ways."

I glance at Posey who hides a partial smile.

Kenna straightens in my peripheral. "I realize your customs are not the same as mine and I am not the one to judge."

Posey finishes, then smiles and twists her finger in the air, gesturing that I turn and look in the mirror. I do and my breath catches. I lift my hands up to my hair, but don't touch it because the diadem she's created with an intricately woven golden vine and five golden daylily blossoms make me look like... well, a princess.

I turn and stand, reaching forward to grip Posey's hands. "It's perfect."

Kenna sighs, and I turn to her.

"You're beautiful," she says, then lifts both hands briefly. "All the fae are beautiful. I don't see why any of the fae—even a part fae like you—would seek a human to... have a child with. Not when you're all so healthy and lovely." Her cheeks color again. "And why aren't there more of you? If you are immortal—" She points at Posey. "And your kind lives to be... how old?" she asks me.

"Our life expectancy is around one thousand years," I say.

"Yes, then why aren't there more of you?"

"The fae cannot produce offspring as easily as humans," I say, eyeing Posey. I wonder if I should tell so many of the secrets of the fae, but strangely, in this situation, I hold a higher rank than the spring kitchen servant. "So some fae go to the humans in order to have younglings."

"Yes, it was a miracle our queen had a child at all," Posey says, and my head snaps to her.

"A miracle?" Kenna asks.

"It is a miracle for any fae to have a child," I add.

"Yes, but the king and queen tried for a child for well over a thousand years before the king brought a human physician to examine the queen," Posey continues.

"Surely you heard wrong, Posey," I say.

"No. I lived it. I remember the centuries of worry that King Estelar would never have an heir. Then I remember when word spread throughout all of Faerie that the physician declared Queen Siora barren."

"Then he was wrong," Kenna says.

"Yes, of course, because it was less than a year later that Prince Orion was born."

"Then it was the will of God," Kenna says.

"I believe this is why the king is taking such pains with this Consort Tourney," Posey says. "He is always celebrating his son."

A chime rings through the corridor outside, alerting us that it's almost time for the elimination ceremony.

My stomach twists in knots as Posey touches my cheeks with a bit of rouge and paints my lips with crimson.

"There. You're lovely, Amberle," Posey says, turning me toward Kenna for her approval.

"Beautiful, my lady," she says and curtsies.

I glance in the mirror once more, noting the way the crown on my head shines in the sconce's light and the brightness of my blue eyes—the right one highlighted by my swirling black promise mark next to it. Even my blue iridescent wings seem to glow, though they weren't touched by my ladies' maids.

I keep my back straight and my head high as I walk through the corridors. When I reach the hallway for the throne room—

where the ceremony will happen—several of the other fae are waiting outside among the busts and statues of past kings and queens and heroes that stand as forever-frozen reminders of the past. Every Tourney contestant is dressed in fine gowns of different shades from blue to ruby to plum to bronze and every color in between. Mine is the only white gown, but none of the dresses are alike.

I find Princess Arielle who wears a gown the color of sunshine and stand next to her, using the excuse in my head that I should stick with the summer fae for such formal ceremonies.

"We are being announced one at a time," she says.

"In what order?" I ask, so I can prepare myself.

"I don't know."

But Arielle is called first. She offers me a nervous smile before walking into the throne room where a roaring applause can be heard.

The cacophony amps up my heart rate. How many fae are in the audience?

Princess Shay is next, followed by Aqualis, one of the Underwater Court contestants. Then Lady Pepper. I can't see a logical order and assume it's random until Clove says,

"We're being called in order of importance."

"What do you mean?" Raine asks.

"Ranking. First the princesses. Then the nobility. Then those with positions in the court and so on."

"Aqualis's cousin is the queen of the Underwater Court," Lily, another underwater fae, says.

"Yes. Then, Lady Pepper, who also has royal blood." Clove's eyes snap to me and look between me and Didi, who has moved to stand next to me. Her hair is down now, in soft red waves. "Which means you two will be last," she sneers at us.

"Why will we be last?" Didi asks. "My mother and father are ambassadors to the king."

"It doesn't matter what your parents do," Clove says. "Halfling automatically puts you at the bottom."

I reach out for Didi's hand and squeeze it in a silent *don't let her goad you,* gesture. I think she gets my meaning because she says nothing.

Clove is right because soon Didi and I are the only ones left in the hallway. They call her next because the ambassador to the king is surely higher in the ranks than a thief and I am left alone with the stone kings.

But finally it's my turn, and I hear Nieven Morphyra's voice ring out with my name.

The double doors open wide, as they have for the other contestants. I straighten my shoulders, fluttering out my wings. My injured wing still smarts, but I march through the doors with my chin high.

I don't expect the applause to be as grand as it was for the other contestants. Especially the favorite, Princess Arielle, but I completely miss the volume and excitement and the energy of the room because as soon as my eyes find Prince Rion's and I see the look on his face, seeing me, everything else fades away.

Twenty-Six

It's for the viewers, I tell myself. I'm sure Rion looked at every contestant that way when she was announced and walked into the throne room. He wants all of Faerie to think that he could fall in love with any of us.

Well... any of *them*.

But the king's words echo in my head: *Don't make him like you too much, because you won't be the one he chooses.*

I shake off the shiver that skitters down my spine as I walk toward the two rows of contestants—seven in the front, eight in the back—all facing the prince. I take my place next to Didi in the back, and although I look forward, I can't bring myself to look at his face again.

"Now that the contestants are all gathered," Nieven Morphyra says, turning toward us and gesturing with his arms. He wears a suit of ebony to match his hair, which also nicely contrasts against his cerulean skin. "Which, by the way, you all look lovely, ladies." He keeps his eyes on us for a moment, smiling with his yellow lips and watching the reaction to his words. He's rewarded with curtsies and blushes and hands touching faces. It's absurd, but fae pride their beauty, even though all have it. Nieven claps his hands. "It's time for the Invitational!"

"Invitational?" I whisper to Didi.

"The prince thought *elimination* was too harsh a word," she explains, ducking her head as she speaks quietly. She wears a dress of deep blue. "So he's calling it an *Invitational* because he's *inviting* those who he wishes to stay and continue on in the journey with him."

I nod and straighten.

A servant hands Nieven Morphyra a small box of white wood, engraved with gold leaf swirls and adorned with precious jewels. I can't help but notice it's small enough to easily take and conceal. Stealing such an item would mean an easy pay day if a client ever requested it.

Now is not the time for such thoughts, but I cannot push away that part of me. I'll be going back to that life after this is done.

With a flourish, Nieven opens the box to reveal small shining droplets against jade-colored silk.

Several of the contestants' gasp. Including myself.

"The prince will call you by name and he will present a crystalized sunbeam to you," the elf says, flashing a debonair smile as if it's nothing. As if one could pluck a crystalized sunbeam out of the sky with the same ease one might pluck a flower from a garden.

Didi gasps. "I thought they were a myth."

"Then," Nieven continues. "It is your choice whether to accept Prince Orion's gift and remain in the competition, or rather, the journey to his heart." The king's entertainer pauses and looks at the rows of us. "Or refuse the sunbeam and leave the Consort Tourney."

Another servant carries out a pedestal for Nieven to place the box on. He gestures at the prince.

"Now I leave it to you, my prince," he says, then bows to Prince Orion and walks from the room.

Rion waits until the announcer leaves before clapping his

hands in front of him. He clasps his fingers together then smiles at us.

I wonder if anyone else can hear the pounding of my heart that rushes through my ears, or if they notice the quivering of my wings, even though I desperately try to keep them still. Or if they're all too anxious for their own sakes. I was so certain of Gnacia's promises that I'll stay through this elimination—or *Invitational*—while Kenna and Posey fussed over my appearance. But now that I'm here, standing in front of the prince who holds all the power of who is staying and who is going, I can't help but feel the metaphorical sharp point of a blade pressed against my throat.

If I've angered Rion enough, or if there is too much past between us that he cannot see any sort of future for us, he could cut me from the Tourney right now. This very night, as a defiance to his father. I try to replay our last conversation when he came to my room, but everything comes up blank. I can't even remember if he looked at me in a certain way or if I angered him.

"River Lyn," the prince says.

River. Underwater Court.

I force myself to focus and observe.

"At least he's not going in order of *importance*," Didi says.

I don't know River well, just that she's a selkie with ties to a group of selkies who live in the human realm. The underwater fae have kept to themselves so far.

She walks to stand in front of Rion, who then lifts a sunbeam from the box. "Will you accept this gift and remain in the competition to see if we might make an agreeable match?"

"I will," River says.

The sunbeam is attached to some sort of cord—it looks invisible from where I stand—which he puts over the selkie's head to hang like a necklace.

He calls Lady Pepper next, followed by Raine and then Princess Shay. Each is presented with a sunbeam, and each accepts, then returns to their spot among the group. Soon, half the contestants wear the glowing drops around their necks, filling the room with warm, bright light.

"Didi Beechriver," Rion says.

My friend lets out a little squeal next to me, then reaches out to squeeze my hand before cutting through Cerule and Luna in front of us.

"Didi, will you accept this gift and remain in the competition to see if we might make an agreeable match?" The prince repeats the phrase. He's recited the same phrase to each one of them.

"I will!" Didi says, and I can see the excitement bubbling as her shoulders tighten before Rion loops the sunbeam around her neck.

She walks back to stand next to me and I stare at the crystalized drop of sun, noting that it's held by a thin strand of silver. The glow highlights the ends of her red hair that hangs over her shoulders, igniting it with an orangish hue.

"Princess Arielle Lieawarin," the prince says.

Since Arielle entered the throne room first, and I last, she's in the front row on the other end. The opposite position and the furthest contestant from me. But even from my vantage point, I can see the heavy weight pushing her down as she walks toward the prince. Something is wrong. Something—

No.

"Princess Arielle," Rion says. His words are becoming dull and repetitive. He would snap to attention if he saw what I see in her.

Not now, Arielle! I want to shout at her.

"Will you—"

"I can't," the princess interrupts. I can barely hear her, but I'm probably the only one who knew this might happen.

"What did she say?" Didi asks and I hold a hand up to my lips, silencing her and gesturing that we both listen.

The easy smile Rion had planted on his face falls. He dips his head lower, bringing his face closer to hers and forcing their eyes to meet.

Arielle says something so low, I can't make out her words, but her wings flutter briefly behind her. Rion then glances up at the group of us and gently grips her elbows before saying, "If you'll excuse us, Princess Arielle wishes to speak to me privately."

He guides her to the other side of the room where they can't be overheard, but I note a shimmering magic zips over to them, following them. It must be the winter magic. He'll get a moment alone with Arielle apart from the other contestants, but Faerie still watches.

"Excuse me," I hear Princess Shay mutter to the fae near her before she walks the other direction, out the door and into the corridor.

"Where's she going?" Didi asks.

"I don't know, but I'll find out," I say, lifting my skirts and following the winter princess. Being royalty makes her a favorite to win. Especially if Arielle is using this moment to bow out of the competition. Whatever she's running off to do while the prince is occupied is worth investigating.

I slip out into the hallway quietly. If the princess merely stepped out for air, it might be suspicious that I followed her. But I don't immediately see her, so I stand in the center of the hallway amid the marble statues and lift both wings higher to better amplify the sound toward my ears.

"I can't do this, Orion." It's Arielle's voice, coming from my right, but it's small and tinny.

I lower my wings and hide behind the hulking form of Queen Tatiana, wearing long, flowing stone robes.

"I cannot stay in this competition," Arielle says. "It would be a farce. A lie."

Slowly, I peer around the statue and see the dark curly locks of the winter princess. Luckily, her back is toward me, but I see she holds a miniature projection in her hand atop a small stone disc of Prince Orion and Princess Arielle. Their *private* conversation.

"This is exactly what I have feared," tiny-Rion laments. I can't tell if the shimmer I see in his eyes is a trick of the light or if the winter magic has captured the glisten of gathered tears.

Small-Arielle reaches forward to take the prince's hand in hers. "But we don't love each other." She ducks her head. "At least not like that. If you and I were ever to fall in love, it would have happened already."

The prince watches her as she speaks, but lowers his head again. "We have known one another since we were younglings."

"Yes, we have had near a century together, but can you tell me if there was ever a time when you thought about me that way? Like you wished for us to be mates, to marry?" she asks. "Has there ever been a time when you wished for that? Have you ever even wished to kiss me?" The last part is so quiet, I wonder if the prince even heard her.

Rion doesn't speak.

"Before your father announced the Tourney," she continues, "everyone assumed we'd end up together since we are both Summer Court royalty and our fathers were friends, but now that you have these fourteen other fae to choose from, do you really see yourself ending up with me?"

Don't do it, Rion. Don't let her go, I think selfishly. Not because I think they should end up together despite not loving each other, but because I can't bear to see her leave. Not yet. We've just become friends again and I fear she'll leave Isi Aura. At least until the Consort Tourney has ended. If not longer.

"My father will be furious if you are the first eliminated."

"High King Estelar could have forced us to marry, Orion. Instead, he wanted you to choose your bride through this Tourney." It's just like Arielle to speak this way. The king is surely watching, and she has earned more of his esteem by praising his choices. "There are plenty of other eligible fae still here. Fae who are ready to fall in love with you, and I'm sure you could love."

"I admit, you are right," he says. "You and I would not have ended up together."

"Which is why I'm pulling out now, so you can focus on the others."

"I appreciate your friendship, Princess."

"And I appreciate yours," she says.

"Please take your place in the line again while I get through the rest. When I'm finished, you may say your goodbyes."

She nods, then they both walk away. Back toward the awaiting group.

I rush back to the throne room door to enter back in before I'm missed, but when I pull on the door handle, it's stuck. It won't open. When the cold marble bites into my hand, I realize the door is *frozen.*

It won't budge. I can't get back inside.

"Oh, it's just you," Princess Shay says.

I whip around to face her. "You've locked us out!"

"Yes, well, I already have *my* sunbeam, don't I?" she says, fingering the glowing droplet around her neck.

"You'll still be missed, even if you're just trying to sabotage me," I say to the winter princess, keeping my voice even as my heart pounds.

First Clove and now Princess Shay? What have I done to capture enough notice that they feel the need to thwart my efforts? Is there something they see and I can't? Or is it just my star-fae heritage that draws their ire?

Princess Arielle just asked to leave. What if Prince Rion thinks I've left too? What if he assumes I wished to pull out of the Tourney, but I couldn't say it to his face?

His expression when he left my room last night burns in my memory. Somehow, I hurt him by stopping whatever it was he wanted to tell me. I have an inkling I knew what he was about to admit, but it terrified me to hear it.

I still feel regret for treating him with sharpness.

Strange, I never thought I'd regret that.

But it might not matter anymore. It might be too late.

Twenty-Seven

Princess Shay walks up to me with a hard gaze in her dark eyes as she looks me up and down like she's stepped into the excrement of a bullgegger goblin. A sneer arches her lip.

What can I possibly say to convince her to unfreeze the door? Any bargain I make would be disastrous.

But she flicks her wrist and rolls her eyes, then emits an icy ripple-like-wave outward. "You're not worth sabotaging," Princess Shay says. "Clove was a fool."

Without another word, she pulls open the now unfrozen door and waltzes back inside. I'm shocked, but quickly follow her in case she changes her mind about keeping me locked out, but she doesn't even glance back.

"Forgive me, your highness," Princess Shay says as she saunters back to her spot on the front row. "I had to step out for a moment." She fans herself. "This room is slightly warm for my winter blood and I needed some air while you were occupied with the summer princess."

The prince nods at her, seemingly distracted and unperturbed by her absence.

I make no apology and simply scurry back to my place next to

Didi, hoping the winter princess's excuses divided his attention long enough to allow me to slip back into place unnoticed.

The prince brings his attention to the group again and takes a breath.

"Princess Arielle and I have decided not to continue this path together, but there are no hard feelings between us and I wish her happiness."

Another prince might have subtly cut down Arielle for walking away from the Tourney, but Rion made it sound like they'd decided together, and he reinforced their friendship. His careful language might curtail the most salacious gossip, but I wonder if every contestant will suffer hurtful conjecture when their turn in the tournament ends.

I know I will.

"Let us continue." The prince pauses briefly before saying, "Juniper Faeven."

From where I stand, I can see a visible difference in the prince's demeanor. Where he looked almost bored before as he called the names of the contestants, now—after Princess Arielle's request to leave—his question seems almost... panicked.

"Juniper, will you accept this gift and remain in the competition to see if we might make an agreeable match?" he asks, then his face pinches into a subtle wince.

"I will!" Juniper clearly doesn't notice the change. She doesn't see that he fears more will ask to leave the competition.

This Tourney means more to him than I assumed.

But he doesn't love Arielle! He agreed with her when she gave her reasons for leaving. So why does he look so terrified now?

The question grates me. For as long as I've known the crown prince of Faerie, he's become a mystery to me.

Prince Rion drapes a crystalized sunbeam over the autumn fae's neck, then calls the next. His tone and attitude are the same for each following. The hesitant question, the almost imperceptible wince, but always followed by an enthusiastic, *I will!*

The more names he calls, the more agitated I become. *He's*

worried Juniper will leave? And Luna? And now one of the Under-water Court? I don't have time to wonder if he will eliminate anyone when I realize he has offered fourteen crystalized sunbeams, including the one Arielle rejected, and there is one left.

"Amberle Kindra."

I walk toward the prince, keeping my posture straight and my wings still. My frustration vanishes, replaced with a knot in my gut.

"Amberle," he says, lifting a sundrop from the box. Beads of sweat gather at the edge of his hairline. It's something I couldn't see from my place among the group and even though I noticed the change in him and the obvious fear of more wishing to leave, it astounds me. "Will you accept this gift and remain in the competition to see if we might make an agreeable match?"

Don't worry. I'm not leaving yet. I lift my gaze to meet his. Funny, only moments ago, I thought he would defy his father to send me away. Now I see that he feared I wouldn't accept his proposal to stay. His pupils dilate, and I have an urge to grab his hand and assure him. Calm him. But I simply say, "I will."

He lifts the necklace over my head in careful concentration. His fingertips graze my neck, and I wonder if it's his magic making my skin spark at his touch. One corner of his mouth lifts, but only briefly, before it falls again. I wonder if he did that with all the fae and I missed it? Or was the almost-smile just for me?

I dip in a small curtsy before turning to return to my place, but he grips my hand before I can walk away. My eyes are captured by the molten gold of his.

"And I would like us to be friends, Amberle." His voice is so quiet, I doubt the others can hear.

"I would like that too," I say without thinking. It surprises me that the honest words tumbled so easily. I'm unable to lie, but I didn't even need to think of a clever way to word my agreement.

After everything I've witnessed in these few moments, I can see the prince wants a friend. He *needs* a friend.

I walk back to my spot. My hand tingles and my ears buzz

from my interaction with Rion. I can't name the feeling, as hard as I try.

"What did he say to you?" Didi asks.

"He wants us to be friends," I say.

Didi's face pinches into confusion, but she nods and I'm left back to my thoughts.

Nieven Morphyra re-enters the room, then greets us and the invisible audience with open arms. When he drops his arms, he smirks, then winks at the prince. "That was quite the ceremony, Prince Orion."

Rion nods, but doesn't speak.

"I don't know about those of you watching, but I did not expect the summer princess would leave tonight." Nieven turns to Arielle and bows. "We will miss you, Your Highness, but we wish you the best."

The princess nods her head in response.

"In just a moment, the prince and the other ladies will have a moment to say goodbye to Princess Arielle," the announcer continues, but I stop listening.

My eyes are on Rion. I can't help but be impressed that he tried to include everyone, not wanting any fae to feel rejected at the first ceremony. He didn't have to be so generous. Still, there was a cost. The tight shoulders and the anxious posture relax and are replaced by what I now recognize in myself. *Relief.*

He's glad no one else asked to leave.

Just like I'd worried I'd be one of the first eliminated.

I'm glad I'm still here. Perhaps Rion is, too.

When I'm back in the solitude of my room, I stand in front of the vanity mirror, mesmerized by the way the light from the crystalized sunbeam seems to pulse. It creates dancing shadows across my face that almost look like they're controlled by winter magic.

Or being pushed away by light use. Summer magic.

I rarely pull on or arrange light the way full summer fae do and even other star fae with summer blood. They create glamours to make themselves look more benevolent or more beautiful. I find both ridiculous and vain since a fae could never pretend to be virtuous, and our beauty—a summer fae's beauty—is so commonplace.

The only time I have used it was the rare occasion I wished to disguise my appearance. If I remain in Faerie after the Tourney, I imagine I'll have to become an expert if I wish to remain a thief.

I use the light from the sunbeam now, twisting it and highlighting different parts of my face. I make my nose appear bigger, then smaller. My eyes shift in color, then my eyebrows disappear. I mess around with the light until my eyes look large and wide and my nose has nearly disappeared. Until I look like some hideous gryla.

I remember Princess Arielle doing something similar when we were younglings. She used her more powerful glamour to disguise herself once as a ghoul to scare off some visiting dignitary younglings who wouldn't stop pestering me, and sometimes her and Rion and Princess Mora. Afterward, the younglings kept to their rooms for the rest of their stay, and we were free of their taunting.

Why did I not recognize Arielle's friendship so long ago? I ponder. Back then, I assumed she did it only for the royals, but now I realize her primary concern was for me.

Thankfully, when Princess Arielle said her goodbyes to the group tonight, she whispered she wasn't going immediately, and we could have a private goodbye later.

Smiling to myself, I remove the key over my head—the key from Clay—and set it on the vanity, then finger the sunbeam still around my neck and release the light from my grip. It springs back to its original radiant glow and the appearance of my face returns to its natural state.

My thoughts turn to Rion and all the events of tonight. I had assumed Rion was merely taking part in this Tourney at his father's insistence. But the thinly veiled emotion I saw just underneath the surface showed me that his heart is fully invested in this competition. Much more than I assumed. This is more than just a game for him. It's his life. His future.

I keep the necklace on as I climb into bed and think about the best way to make this Tourney a success for the prince. For my *friend*. The king asked me to ensure he picks the right fae, while keeping in mind that the prince is a romantic. King Estelar has his son's best interests at heart, but I imagine if the *right fae* and the *fae he loves* aren't the same, he'll be forced to choose the former. But maybe I can make sure they're the same. Somehow.

I don't land on an answer before I fall asleep, but I continue to think about it when I wake up the next morning. I change my dress and comb through my hair before heading down to breakfast with the sunbeam pinched between my fingers.

When I enter the breakfast room, I wish I had done more than change my dress, because Nieven Moyrpha is standing at the head of the room.

I walk over to Didi, who eyes my necklace.

"I should have put mine back on," she says, frowning.

I look around to see more eyes looking at my sunbeam with regret in their eyes. Only two others, besides myself, wear theirs.

"Especially since the prince will be here soon," Didi adds.

"Now? Why is he coming?" I ask. I don't tell her I never took my sunbeam off because I'm too focused on the thrumming of my heart.

She doesn't answer because the crown prince walks in. My eyes follow him as he walks to the head of the room, standing next to the announcer. The prince's expression is guarded.

Nieven flashes a smile around the room, then lifts both hands and says, "I have some announcements this morning, then I'll leave you to your meal." His hands lower as he continues, "First, starting today, the prince will have several more one-on-one outings with some of you before the next Invitational. He wishes to get to know those of you here to win his heart, and he can only do that by spending time with you."

Didi grips my upper arm and lets out a quiet squeal. "I hope I'm one of them!"

I turn to her and smile in a way that suggests I wish the same thing.

"But before I announce the first lady chosen," Nieven says. "I must tell you the second part. The *twist.*"

Nieven Morphyra has everyone's attention, and he knows it. He takes advantage with his long pause before saying, "Because of the unconventional way Princess Arielle Lieawarin has chosen to leave, it has been decided that another summer princess should be given the chance to win the prince's heart."

No.

The girls exchange mixed looks, from surprise to confusion to worry to fury. All in attendance know which name the announcer is about to say.

"Princess Mora Rolen will join as a Consort Tourney Contestant immediately."

The princess waltzes through the doors before Nieven even finishes saying her name.

Mora. The love-sick youngling I knew before I left the palace. The princess everyone thought would be the last summer called for the Tourney, instead of me. The princess whose name they chanted as we walked through Isi Aura into the palace. The princess who raked her nails across my arm and hissed that she would find her way into the Tourney. And she did.

I groan, remembering her other promise: to get me booted out.

Mora's white-blonde hair hangs in waves around her head held high in triumph. She acts as if she's already won.

"Since the summer princess has not spent time with the prince," Nieven continues. "Princess Mora will have the privilege of the first outing with him. Beginning now."

Maybe she has already won.

Twenty-Eight

There are looks of shock and bewilderment at Nieven's announcement of Princess Mora's entrance into the Consort Tourney. And the news that she'll immediately receive alone-time with the prince spurs several exasperated sighs and frowns. But as soon as the announcer and the pair leave the room, the complaining turns verbal.

She just got here!

It's not fair!

Why is Mora special? It's not like we've had loads of time with the prince.

It's because she's a summer princess.

Do you think the Tourney is rigged?

Will this happen every time someone leaves?

Mora lives in the Summer Palace! She already knows the prince!

Why are you complaining, Juniper? You already had a one-on-one outing with him!

Once Juniper pipes in, the rest stop complaining about Mora and go after her. I can't help but shudder at the way they so easily turn on each other. Like rival divs—with their dripping fangs and hypnotic stares—after the same prey. They've suddenly forgotten about the princess and the unfairness. I grab a pastry and an orange, then slip out before anyone decides to turn on me next.

My injured wing feels stiff this morning, and I have spent no time in the sun to help its healing process, like Kali suggested. So, with the prince occupied, I intend to sit on the southern balcony for the bulk of the day.

"Amberle." Gnacia's hooves clack behind me.

Her voice has begun to grate on me, but I can't protest because she's my best ally in helping me rescue my father. As long as our goals align, she'll help me. I stop and touch the promise mark next to my eye, then inhale through my nose to steel myself before I turn to greet the faun.

"He has some questions."

He. The king. And I assume *he* has sent her to ask them.

I present the best fake-smile I can muster. "Yes? What questions?"

"In private. Follow me to my office."

I keep my smile from falling. "Of course. Lead the way."

I eat my pastry as we walk through the hallways. Despite the sweetness of my breakfast, it tastes bitter on my tongue. Between the viciousness of the other contestants and Princess Mora's blind obsession with the prince, my stomach twists.

Why was *Mora added to the competition?* The Tourney is obviously manipulated in some ways, otherwise I wouldn't be here. But Mora's entrance is unexpected. Suspicious. What message is the king sending by inviting her at this late hour? Is he set on a summer fae winning? Or is he weak, cowed by the voice of his subjects? Or worse, by Mora's family? No, the king hasn't shown signs of weakness. Still, inviting Mora feels like rules don't matter. So, why bother with this ridiculous Tourney at all?

I finish my pastry by the time we arrive at Gnacia's office, but my stomach churns and I can't even look at the fruit in my hand, let alone eat it. I plan to set it on Gnacia's desk once we enter—a snack for the faun later.

But when we enter, my hand clenches around the orange.

King Estelar himself sits on the other side of Gnacia's desk. His magnificent summer-blonde wavy hair beneath a crystal crown reminds me of his son's locks—the waves, not the color—and it proves his heritage and his position better than the crown does. That, and his pointed elven ears and chin. Guards stand in the corners near the door, but I note there's only two this time.

"Sit," the king says, gesturing at the seat across from him.

I turn back to Gnacia. "I thought—"

"I said that *he* had some questions," she whispers as she yanks the squashed fruit from my hand. Then she nods at the king and backs out of the room and shuts the door.

Slowly, I walk toward the chair and sit on the edge of the seat.

"What's the matter, Amberle? I don't recall you ever quaking in my presence before?" The king is amused, but his goad snaps me back to myself.

"I didn't expect you, is all," I say, lifting an eyebrow and relaxing my posture a bit. "You have a throne room and a private office. You shouldn't have to lower yourself to using your assistant's workspace."

King Estelar smiles, then leans forward, steepling his hands together on the desk. "Yes, but then it would make this meeting official and would raise questions."

"Alright then, as this is unofficial, may I speak freely? I have a grievance."

He chuckles silently and leans back, interlocking his fingers over his middle. "By all means."

"If you plan to bring in new contestants whenever something doesn't go the way you want, why don't you just tell Prince Orion who he's allowed to pick?" I ask. "Or... if you have a particular winner in mind, why not just force him to marry whichever fae you've already chosen?"

"There's the Amberle Kindra I remember." The king leans forward again, then stands and clasps his arms behind his back. "But I don't have to explain my motives to you, *halfling*. You will do as you're asked and not ask questions. *I* will ask the questions."

"Fine, but you've asked me to spy on the other girls," I say, trying to forget the way he said *halfling*, like it's an expletive. "They're in a tizzy about Princess Mora. But when they stop and think it through, they'll become suspicious of this event, which could create unintended problems."

"Are *you* in a tizzy about it?" He stops and looks at me with a frown. "Need I remind you that you are *not* an option to win?"

I want to assure him I don't *want* to win and almost expect it to fly out of my mouth because of the hex, but I'm able to control my lips and my words just fine. "I know. But, I *am* annoyed. It's hard to do my job with twists like this. I should have been informed."

"What are these *unintended problems* you speak of?"

"Others might ask to leave like Princess Arielle did if they feel the Tourney is a farce." I stand to face him, gesturing with my hands.

The guards step forward, but King Estelar holds up a hand and shakes his head, telling them I'm not a threat. They settle back in their corners.

"None of these contestants want to look foolish. Not to mention their families who will be angry if their daughters are hung to dry on a public stage due to ever-shifting rules that *you* control."

The king's brow furrows. I'm sure my questions are an annoyance, but I fear he has underestimated the contestants' fervor. And if his miscalculation could cost my father his freedom, I must be bold.

"What if all the *acceptable* fae decide to leave?" I continue. "You may not want me asking questions, but they are." I point at the closed door as if all thirteen of the original girls stand on the other side, demanding answers. "At least to each other." I drop my hand. "They're irritated. There's nothing keeping the ones with the best intentions here if they don't think it's worth it to stay."

"You do not tell your king how to run the Consort Tourney." His rumbling voice causes the ground to tremble. Or maybe it's just my nerves. "Sit down, *halfling*. I have questions. I hope you have suitable answers." He gestures across the desk again, ordering me to sit, and sinks back in Gnacia's chair.

I obey.

"What do you know about Juniper Faeven?" He asks when I've settled.

"Juniper? The autumn fae?"

"Yes."

I pinch my eyebrows together as my eyes drop and unfocus. It wasn't a question I expected. Why does he want to know about Juniper? I form my answer carefully. "She was the first to find the prince in the labyrinth. And because she was first, she had the first interview and the first outing with him." I pause. "But I gather you know that?"

"I do."

I rack my thoughts for anything out of the norm about Juniper. Anything or any reason why the king would be interested in her.

"I think her peculiar personality causes others to underestimate her." I lift my gaze back to him. "Is she already winning the feelings of the prince? Do I need to focus on her because she might be his first choice?"

I don't like the way my chest tightens at the thought. But it seems quick. Rion has only had one so-called *date* with Juniper.

"Has Juniper said anything about her private time with the prince?"

My eyes narrow. It wasn't an answer to my question, and immediately brings up the memory when the other contestants were clamoring to hear the details.

"It was a dinner, if I recall correctly," I say.

The king's nostrils flare, but he smiles. "Yes. That is something else I *already know*." His frustration is showing, which piques my curiosity. "Did she merely talk about the food? Or was there any discussion about their conversation?"

"You want to know about their conversation?"

King Estelar leans forward with fire in his eyes. "Do not play the fool with me, Amberle. You know what is at stake. You know what will happen if you do not do exactly as you're asked."

"My father, yes," I say, but lean forward too, daring to call his bluff, "but you need me too. What will you do without a spy on the inside?"

"Don't flatter yourself. You're not the only one."

Not the only... My heart speeds and my palms become clammy. I wipe my hands alongside my dress so he doesn't see. "Another spy? Who is it? Is it Clove? Princess Shay? No, a princess wouldn't have reason to spy." I'm mostly talking to myself now, but when he doesn't answer, I keep going, "When did you plan to tell me about this? Does *she* know about me? Are there more than one? Are *any* of the Consort Tourney contestants *actual* contestants?"

"No more questions!" The king pounds both fists on the desk. "I will do the asking and *you* will answer. If you cannot do as you're asked, I promise you will not be missed."

How can I possibly do what the king wants if there are so many variables? Secret variables.

"I promise I will be more effective if I have all the information," I say through gritted teeth.

"Then perhaps the Silver Shadow is not as skilled as I was led to believe."

That stings. "F-fine. Yes. She went on about the f-food," I stammer. "And the way the prince looked at her, she thinks he's falling in love with her—"

"Is he falling in love with her?"

"I don't know—" His daggered stare stops me and I amend. "No. I know the prince enough to know he wouldn't fall in love so quickly." Especially since she seems so flighty and distracted. Like her thoughts live high up among the stars.

"Are you certain?"

"Yes."

King Estelar's eyes narrow. "Did she say anything about her walk with the prince? In the garden?"

Yes. She spoke of the radical who interrupted their stroll. About the *secret* he claimed to know about something the king was hiding from Faerie. But how do I bring it up without losing my head in the process?

"Be careful with your words, Amberle Kindra," he warns, "or else it won't just be your father's life on the line."

I have no choice but the truth. I'm meant to be a spy for the king. Anything else renders me useless to him. And to my father.

"She said a radical interrupted them."

The way his mouth twitches, I know he knows about it. Of course, he knows. Juniper said the lone interloper was dragged away by the guards who undoubtedly reported the incident to the king.

"Did she tell you what this criminal said?"

I inhale and hope King Estelar doesn't have a fondness for decapitating messengers. "He said you were keeping a secret from Faerie. He said Faerie deserves to know the secret, but Juniper said guards intercepted him before he could tell her more."

For once in my life, I'm grateful I can't lie, but I still hold my breath as I wait for his response.

He seems satisfied and rises, gesturing that I may leave.

"You will tell me at once if Juniper *remembers* anything else?" he says as I stand.

"I will." I exhale, but only a little. He thinks I'm holding back. "I'm sure she was mostly focused on the prince and her relationship with him."

"You may go."

I want to sprint to the door, but my damned curiosity prompts me to turn back again. "Can I ask why Juniper is in the Tourney? For spying purposes. She doesn't seem particularly special or highborn."

"Her family has powerful magic," he says, surprising me with his sudden candor. "The labyrinth trial was child's play for one as strong as the Faevens."

I nod and turn, remembering how easily Juniper decayed the

maze to get to the prince. But then something else dawns on me and I face my sovereign once more.

"Actually, I remembered something else," I say. "After Juniper told us about the radical, she said she noticed something about Rion—about the prince."

The king shows interest and ignores my informal use of the crown prince's name. "What did she notice?"

"She never said. The announcer interrupted her, but she implied it had something to do with the..." *Downplay it. Pretend you don't believe the king is hiding anything.* "Something to do with the *so-called secret.*"

"My assumptions about the Silver Shadow were correct after all," the king says. "You may go."

I should feel pleased. I should have hope that the king found something I said helpful. But as the guards slam the door behind me, I can't help but think I've somehow missed something. I need to find out what Juniper knows. About the secret. It could make all the difference in my father's freedom. Or condemnation.

<h1 style="text-align:center">Twenty-Nine</h1>

The healing effects of the sun soaking into my wing as I lean against the rail of the southern balcony of the Summer Palace lifts my mood. But only slightly.

After my *unofficial* meeting with the king, I searched for Juniper. I didn't know what I planned to say to her or how I'd get her to open up about the secret she knows or what she suspected about Rion, but when I learned that she and several other winged-fae took a picnic up to the highest tower, I knew I couldn't follow.

First, because the tower doesn't have stairs. And second, because flying now would set my healing back. Kali said I shouldn't fly for a week.

It's not like they invited me, anyway.

Still, I am glad to have some solitude. Outside. Away from the stuffy extravagance of the palace. Hearing the trilling of birds and the sweet fragrance of plumerias feels almost like a typical afternoon *before* the Tourney. Standing in the open air feels... like home.

"Here you are."

I turn at Princess Arielle's voice and greet her with a smile.

"I've looked everywhere for you." She walks forward and

193

stands next to me at the rail. Her tone is lifting, but her expression —with pinched eyebrows and creases lining her mouth—tells me everything.

"You're leaving."

"I am."

"Where will you go?" I ask, turning to look out toward the Sigmus River and the Infernus Forest behind it. "You've lived here all your life."

"I'll go to my family's estate on Clio Island." She grips the railing. Her voice is regal, but there's a tightness to it. "It's nice there. I'd like to see my brother and his mate. They have a youngling I've never met."

"I'm happy for you," I say, twisting my mouth.

"I cannot stay, Amberle." She drops her hand from the railing and faces me. "Not now. Not until after the Tourney has ended. I should have refused my invitation, but I thought Prince Orion would want a friendly face around, a friend."

I could beg her to stay, but a supportive friend wouldn't do that, so I hold my tongue.

"But he doesn't need me for that because he has you."

I want to blurt out that the prince and I are not friends, but that's not entirely true anymore. At the Invitational, he said he wished for us to be friends. Perhaps I can be a friendly face around —whilst spying on the others, of course. I look out at the river again.

"Have you learned anything else about the curses?" Arielle asks after several silent moments.

I shake my head no and keep my eye on the horizon.

"Any idea what object could have been hexed?"

"No. I wish you were staying longer to help me figure it out."

Arielle blows a puff of air from her lips. "I'll keep researching. It will give me something to focus on since I'll be out of the public eye for a time."

"I appreciate your willingness to help."

"I wish I could do more." Another pause. "Why aren't you up

with Juniper and Tierney and the others? It seems they've started a wings-only group." Her half-smile is amused. "They invited me to come, but I declined since I'm leaving tonight."

"My wing," I say, lifting my right one in a shrug. I have kept my injury to myself, not wanting anyone—especially Clove—to know I was injured. Still, Arielle is my friend, and she might have advice for me. "I injured it during the maze trial, and I'm not supposed to fly for a few days. That's also why I'm out here." She doesn't need to know that I wasn't actually invited to the winged-fae's little picnic.

The princess nods and flutters her own red-orange wings. "Sunlight healing."

"Yes." As much as I like Arielle, it bothers me a little that she was invited, and I wasn't. But I'm not surprised. "It's too bad I couldn't go because I wanted to talk to Juniper about something."

"Why?"

Princess Arielle might be out of the competition, but I doubt King Estelar wants me to reveal my true reason for being here. It was foolish of me to mention Juniper. But I blame it on the curse.

"I wanted to hear more about her time with the prince," I say. "She didn't get the opportunity to tell us the rest."

The princess stares at me for several seconds as her eyebrow slowly lifts and her mouth makes a mischievous shape.

"Come with me." She reaches for my hand and drags me into the palace.

"Where are we going?"

"*Shhh.*" She stops and presses a finger against her lips with her free hand. "I want to show you something, but you definitely *don't* want the others to know about it."

I nod and allow her to drag me through winding hallways and past open balconies until we're in the east wing. She releases my hand, and we walk down a flight of stairs. I have an inkling where she's taking me, but I'm uncertain until she stops halfway down and gently pushes aside the dark portrait of nereids and a raging storm on the wall to reveal a well-concealed door.

My half-smile gives me away.

"You know about this?" she asks, then shakes her head as she smiles. "I only found it a decade ago!"

I lift my good wing. "Yes, but you're a princess. They always expected you to be places and attend things. As the daughter of a servant, I always had more free time. And I could move about, essentially invisible." I frown. "But I don't know what's in the library that I wouldn't want the others to see."

She doesn't answer my question and walks through the secret door that leads into the upper level of the library. I follow her through. This floor of the library is empty of fae, but I can hear muffled voices below. Princess Arielle hugs the wall of books opposite the balcony that looks down to the lower floor. She doesn't want to be seen by whoever is below. I wonder what she would have done or said if a fae was on the upper level and witnessed our entrance.

Halfway down the wall, between the bookshelves, she leads me into a private room. One with a large table and cart for books. A thin layer of dust covers everything. Except a familiar disc resting on the table.

"The ease we have in watching the events of the Tourney lends me to think the king doesn't mind if the contestants watch each other with the prince," Princess Arielle says.

I nod and smile, hiding the way my chest tightens as I realize we are about to watch Rion and Princess Mora.

"Typically, we would need a winter fae to make the magic work," Arielle explains. "But since the king wishes for all of Faerie to watch the Tourney, and winter fae are scarce in four of the courts, winter magic discs—like this—have been injected with their own magic and placed all over the realm."

Without another word, a miniature version of the prince and princess appear. They're riding inside a carriage. Sitting side by side with Mora's arm looped through Rion's, her mess of blonde curls lay on his shoulder and a contented smile rests on her face.

But I can't read his.

"But that's not what I brought you here to see," Princess Arielle says, stepping forward and turning to me. She pauses. Studying me. Then turns back to the scene. "He doesn't care for her. Not like that. See how she's draping herself over him, but he is trying to find a reason for her to lift her head and scoot away?"

I look at his face again. His expression is guarded. Unreadable.

"How can you tell?" I ask, but wave a hand. *It doesn't matter to me. It* shouldn't *matter to me,* I tell myself. This only concerns me if Princess Mora is the one he chooses. Then I must learn if she deserves him.

"Just trust me," Arielle says. "This disc is special because while it shows what the king wants the fae to watch, it can also show us what *we* want to watch."

"What do you mean?"

The princess doesn't answer and merely turns back to the disc and says, "Show me Juniper Faeven."

In an instant, Rion and Mora dissolve into the image of the autumn fae and her winged friends. I gasp. Amazed at this happy little spying tool. The winged fae sit shoulder to shoulder at the edge of the tower with their legs dangling over the side. Tierney sits at Juniper's left with her delicate butterfly wings stretched out behind her. Lady Pepper is on her right and the winter fae, Frost, is on the other side of Lady Pepper.

I turn to Arielle with wide eyes. "We can see *anyone* with this magic?"

"Anyone who is being watched by the winter magic."

Twisting my body around, I scan the small study room. "Is there a way to know when we are being watched? Might someone be watching us now?"

"Princess Shay put a block on this room. The winter magic cannot watch us in here. It's subtle in order that those controlling the magic for the Tourney don't notice it, but this is a place you can come to for privacy." She grins. "You can also watch the others in here. Or the prince."

"Why would she do this for me?"

Arielle's eyebrows lift in apology. "She did it for me. And I imagine she'll use it herself, so be careful and perhaps learn her whereabouts before coming. She doesn't know I planned to show you."

"So she could walk in at any moment?"

"She could, but Shay was invited to tea with the queen. I assure you she is otherwise engaged and won't bother us."

Tea with the queen. I file that away for later. If Princess Shay has gained the notice of the queen, she is already in a place of importance. The queen is a private fae who defers most important meetings and tasks to the king. I wonder what spurred her to invite the winter princess to tea. I turn back to the projection on the table.

"And she won't suspect anyone else using this room since only she and I knew about it," Arielle adds. "But be careful."

"I will," I say. As the Silver Shadow, moving about unseen is one of my strengths. And the last time I encountered Princess Shay, she looked at me as if I was nothing more than a nuisance. I'm nothing to her. As long as I'm careful, she won't suspect me.

From the projection, Juniper says Mora's name, and my attention jumps back to the winged fae.

"She has lived in Isi Aura since she was a youngling," Lady Pepper says.

"But do you think she has an advantage?" Tierney asks. "Since she already knows him?"

"It is the same as with Princess Arielle," Juniper says. "If she was going to form a romantic connection with the prince, she would have by now."

I look at Arielle.

"My conversation with the prince was not a secret," she confirms, the skin around her eyes tightening.

"Perhaps he always saw her as a youngling though, and now she could be an option for him," Lady Pepper says.

Even in the small projection, I notice Juniper shift at the summer fae's comment.

Her friend, Tierney, notices and pats her knee with a hand. "But that doesn't mean they will have a connection. Not like you do with the prince."

Juniper's shoulders drop. "I know. It's just that after my time with him... the way we were together, it feels like he's already mine." She looks around at her small group with a sad look. "You have not experienced it, so you don't understand, but it feels as though my mate has gone off with another." Her voice is airy, and she talks like she's speaking to herself, but I feel deep sympathy for her that is mirrored on all the faces of the fae she sits with. "And I know we are all a part of this Consort Tourney and he's not officially mine yet. But it's still hard. That's why I couldn't watch him and Princess Mora."

"Let us speak of something else then," Tierney says. "Take your mind off it. That's why you wished to have this picnic, wasn't it?"

Juniper nods and smiles at her friend.

I wish I was there to continue the questions. If I were there, I'd encourage Juniper to talk about her time with the prince, then lead the conversation to the question of what she noticed about him, or what she knows of the king's secret. But I'm not there and the fae don't know I'm listening.

But this gift Arielle has given me, an additional ability to spy, could prove very useful.

"I appreciate you showing this to me," I tell her as we leave the room the way we'd come.

"I was glad to help," she says. "And I'm sorry to go, but I promise I will contact you if I learn anything about the curses."

Arielle takes my hands and gives them a squeeze. "What Juniper said was just her perception."

"What do you mean?"

"I doubt he feels for her as much as she thinks he does."

My eyebrows pinch in confusion, but she doesn't say anything else and releases my hands. As she walks away, I can't help but think that my trip here might be worth it, just to mend a friendship I didn't know was ever mourned. If I'd had an inkling that Arielle even cared, I would have attempted to send her messages occasionally. Share funny stories with her. As a child, I didn't know Arielle could miss me with all the trappings of court and adoring fae surrounding her. Hopefully, when this is over, I'll have gained back my father and a friend.

Determined to heal my wing as quickly as possible, I spend the rest of the day in the sunshine. The tightness in my back loosens and my wing stops aching. My stomach growls and I finally flex my wings. No pain. I could cry with joy, but instead I stride to dinner.

At our evening meal, I note Juniper's smile. She's scrubbed away the sorrow she showed on the roof. And there's no sign of triumph on Princess Shay after getting face-time with the queen. I wrinkle my napkin in my lap, clutching it into my tight fist as I realize my tremendous disadvantage without the disc. The king should've offered me one.

Princess Mora hasn't returned, so there is no need to clamor for a spot at the same table to hear about her time with Prince Rion. They're probably still together. The idea makes my stomach roil, and the food I just ate threatens to make me ill.

I'm on my feet in a flash, ready to retire for the night. When I turn the last corner to my room, my feet turn to lead and my jaw drops. Rion is standing outside my door, waiting for me.

"Do you plan to make this a habit?" I ask the prince, folding my arms and checking my peripheral for signs of winter magic. Signs we're being watched. "Coming to my room after your dates?" One eyebrow and one corner of my mouth lifts. Though I don't know what I'm looking for, the temperature hasn't dropped.

"There's no winter magic here," Rion assures me, gesturing at the hall.

"How can you tell?" I ask, impressed but also wary that he read my worry so easily. "Gnacia promised privacy in our rooms, but not forever."

"I know because I demanded privacy after I parted from Mora. I might only get an hour, but…" he pauses and winks. "But that is only if the winter magic can find me."

"So you're here to hide?" I smirk. It's unexpected how pleased I am to see him. A big part of me *hopes* he will make it a habit.

It will be the best way to learn firsthand about who he is most interested in, I tell myself. *It will take the guessing out and depending on the hearsay of the others. It will save me time so I can focus only on the ones he might choose.*

I'm rewarded with a half-smile that matches mine, and a shrug.

When I catch the mischievous glint in his golden eyes, I roll my eyes as if I'm annoyed. But when I enter my room, I leave the door open for him.

He accepts the unspoken invitation and walks in, then closes it gently behind him.

"I came to see if your offer of elderberry wine was still good," Rion says as we walk to my sitting area.

"It's gone. We could call for some?"

"Do you need more?" Lines crease his forehead as he glances over my shoulder at my wing.

I lift it steadily. "My wing is much better," I say. "Since I wasn't invited to spend time with you, I spent the day in the sunlight. It feels nearly healed now."

"That explains the glow of your necklace." He points.

I look down and see the brilliant radiance of the crystalized sunbeam. I've become so accustomed to it in such a short time, I hadn't noticed how bright it has become after a day soaking in more sunlight. I meet his eyes, lifting the sunbeam and rolling it between my fingers.

The prince sits in one of the blue plush chairs and leans back with both arms on the armrests, but his expression of worry doesn't wane.

I let the sunbeam rest below my throat again and sit across from him.

"What's weighing on you, Rion?"

"I assure you, it wasn't my idea to spend time with Mora right when she entered the Tourney." Rion glances out the window and rubs a finger along his temple.

"While you were on your date, I was able to say goodbye to Arielle," I say, as if his comment was an apology for not choosing me. Which it wasn't. "But Mora's entrance made quite the stir."

He looks at me with dark eyes, but I can't read his expression. In one motion, he stands and walks toward the door.

My heart feels heavy. *What did I say wrong? How can I persuade him to stay a little longer?*

"I'm calling for some refreshment," he says, then pokes his head out the door and speaks in hushed tones with a servant in the hallway before rejoining me.

I ignore the lightness in my chest that follows.

But he doesn't sit. Instead, he walks to the vanity and touches the cord attached to the key. The unusual pendant used to hang around my neck—where his gifted sunbeam now hangs.

"What does it open?" he asks, lifting the cord to hold it up.

I stand and walk toward him. "It's just something from my former life. A gift."

"From a lover?"

Heat rushes into my cheeks. "No, no! Nothing like that. This was from a... job I did with my partner, Clay. He's like a younger brother to me."

"Clay? You haven't mentioned him before." Rion smiles. "I didn't think thieves had partners."

I bite down hard on the inside of my cheek until I taste blood. I shouldn't have said his name! Even if I implicitly trust the crown prince, Clay's identity is his to share, not mine.

He sets the key down, then bridges the gap between us and places both hands on my shoulders. My thoughts scatter. The heat from his palms permeates through my layers of fabric. "Don't fret. I won't reveal what you've said."

I exhale, wondering when Rion became so thoughtful. Wondering why I want to melt into his touch. I brace myself to look up and feign indifference, like his nearness means nothing. I intend to look him straight in the eye, but my attention snags on his lips. His mouth opens as if he's about to say something else. Air escapes my lungs and I lift my chin. But his lips snap shut and his attention jerks back to the key on my vanity. His hands drop like I'm made of molten iron.

Rion steps back, and I flush at my childish reaction. I lift my hand to my forehead, wondering if the curse could be blamed for my flustering.

The prince moves and points at the key. "You treasure this. Even though he is—as you say—like a younger brother, you wore this key every day until…"

"Until you gave me this." I hate how tight my voice is. I try to play it off by fiddling with the necklace at my throat. "Something as rare and precious as a crystalized sunbeam should either be locked away in a well guarded vault, or worn for all to see."

He studies me, as if waiting for me to finish my unsaid thoughts. What he doesn't know is I'm on the verge of blurting out a demand for him to leave so I don't accidentally say something I regret. But that would be rude and I don't want to implode our tenuous friendship.

Because we are *friends.*

He frowns with his eyebrows. "Yes, I suppose you're right. Both are reason enough, no matter how the sunbeam was acquired. I wonder…"

"You wonder what?"

The prince shakes his head and lowers it. "Forget I said anything."

He needs a friend. With Arielle gone, I should be that for him. I *can* be that for him. *Right?*

I step forward and reach out to touch his hand, but refrain. "Rion?" His eyes lift to mine, and I'm close enough to swim in the browns and greens within the gold of his eyes. I force myself to speak. "What's wrong?"

He studies me for several breathless moments, and I can smell the musk of cut grass and fresh rain rolling off him. The smell of summer.

"I think my father is manipulating the Tourney," he says.

Oh no. What does he know? What does he suspect? Iron-like dread fills my veins.

A quiet knock at my door saves me from responding. I hope I'm discreet enough in wiping my suddenly clammy hands on my dress as I walk to answer the door that he doesn't notice. I admit a dark-haired brownie servant inside, a tray of fruit, cheese, tea, and a slice of pie balanced in his hand.

The brownie waits for the prince's nod of approval, which seems to take ages, all the while wondering if Rion suspects the king placed spies in the tourney. That *I'm* a spy. Is he here to confront me?

Finally, the prince dismisses the brownie, who sets the tray on the table, bows low and excuses himself.

I wipe my hands again, wondering if I'm leaving a streak of sweat.

Rion sits again and eats a piece of cheese, then pours a cup of tea and looks at me, silently asking if I want a cup, too.

I nod, hoping he doesn't notice my tight smile, and sit.

"What makes you think the king is manipulating the Tourney?" I ask when he hands me a steaming cup. The bitterness of the herbs burns my nose as I take a sip.

The prince drinks, too.

"You said Mora's entrance made a stir?"

I relax a little. It's a simple question. "Yes. The others were upset."

"It wasn't my idea to bring Mora in. I was just as blindsided as the rest of you."

"It was the king's idea?"

"Yes."

"Why do you think your father did it?" I ask, relieved that his suspicions have nothing to do with the king's meddling by putting me in the competition as a spy.

The prince sighs, then sets his cup on the table as if suddenly not interested in it. "Because I don't think I actually have a choice in who I end up with."

He's not completely wrong. I know that. The king wants his son to end up with *the right choice.* I carefully mask my face, hoping he doesn't see the truth in my expression as I deliberately select my words. "But... the Invitational? Wasn't that all your choice?"

"I thought it was." Rion looks out the window. The sun is setting, and its orange and reddish colors highlight the edges of his brown hair. The waning sunlight frames his face in an ethereal glow. "But Arielle leaving wasn't my choice."

I frown. "No. But it was hers." When he doesn't answer and keeps his gaze on the horizon, I continue. "You see her leaving as the king manipulating the Tourney?" I don't have to work hard to inject questioning into my tone. "Arielle left of her own accord. I spoke with her and her decision had nothing to do with your father."

"She said she didn't love me and wanted to withdraw."

"Then why do you think the king is meddling?" I ask. "We were told by Nieven that it was our choice whether to accept your gifts and stay or refuse and leave."

"I know."

"Then why is there a problem if one of them asks to leave?" *Them.* I shouldn't have said *them,* I should have said *us* since in his eyes I'm a part of this too. "Won't it help you narrow down your options if some contestants walk away?"

"I suppose, but what if more want to leave?" He shifts his attention to the floor. "What if I grow feelings for—" His words cut off when his cat-slit eyes rise again, and the intensity pierces me. "What if I fall in love with one of the fae? Then they ask to leave?"

He doesn't mean you, Amberle. Every fae feels special when Rion spends time with him. Juniper swore he was falling for her. It's his fae allure, and I refuse to fall blindly for the illusion of attraction.

We are friends. Friends. Just friends.

I shove my treacherous thoughts away and dig deeper. This is my chance to win back my father and help Rion along the way.

"Do you love Arielle?" I ask. "Are you heartbroken that she left?"

"No."

"Then you are being a perrifool."

Rion's eyes snap to mine at the insult.

"When did you turn into this sniveling, whimpering princeling?" It's harsh, but friends don't sugarcoat. I can't let myself be caught up in shallow attraction—or whatever has been happening between us. I must help him find a match so I can get this agonizing Tourney behind me.

His eyes narrow. My words have smarted, but at least I have his attention.

"What happened to the prince I knew? The one with a backbone who didn't wallow and feel sorry for himself?" I bridge the small gap between us and jab my finger into his sternum. "You are the *crown prince*, Rion. Those ladies are already falling for you, I assure you. They thought that with Arielle leaving, they had a better chance. But then Mora showed up and got all your attention. *They* should be upset. Not you."

"How do you know they're falling for *me*? Maybe they're all just falling in love with the crown."

"Perrifool. Again." I sigh and grip my forehead with one hand. "Look, you've known Arielle your entire life. You were practically raised as siblings. It's easy to see why you both have trouble feeling anything romantic toward one another when you knew each other as younglings."

"You and I knew one another as younglings," the prince points out.

I wave a hand, dismissing it. But the mention strikes a chord and I realize how dangerous my situation could become if the others find out. "Yes, and I fear what will happen when they learn of our history, so perhaps you shouldn't pull any more of these shenanigans. Showing up in my room after your dates? Spending time with me, even while the winter magic isn't watching? Someone is bound to find out."

Not to mention that I am bound to say or do something I shouldn't.

"I don't care what the others know."

"Well I do!" I shout. "I'm already a target for Clove. Princess Shay doesn't seem threatened, not yet. But you and I both know the servants will gossip. If any of them are loyal to other contestants, they'll know about this secret meeting before the moon rises."

His expression tells me he didn't even consider what the others thought.

"Don't show me favoritism, Rion. You're only doing me a disservice."

"Favoritism? Coming to speak to you as an old friend is *favoritism?*" His voice rises, and I can't help but focus on 'old friend.' Of course, how could anyone deign to think of me as an actual option to win? "I'm just trying to navigate this the best I can," he laments.

"Surely you have advisors—"

"Who tell me what to do, but cannot give me any actual advice!"

I try not to flinch at his shout. "You want my advice? Why?"

"Because you're the only one I trust." He sounds weary.

A churning, uncomfortable sensation begins behind my ribs and drops into my gut.

"I told you, I need a friend in this."

"You and I were never friends, Rion," I say and immediately clamp a hand over my mouth. *Rotting curses.*

"Then what are you doing here? Why did you agree to enter the Tourney?"

"I told you. My father." I wish the curse would swallow me up rather than make me into a perrifool.

"No other reason?"

"I-I don't want to answer that."

The prince storms to the door. "Fine, then. We are not friends." He grips the handle but doesn't leave. Instead, he straightens his spine and lifts his chin. "You will stop with the casual use of my name. I am Prince Orion Illuminae to my subjects, and you are one of them."

An invisible knife twists into my heart. "Yes, Your Highness."

"Enjoy your dragon fruit pie. You did say you longed to have some of my mother's favorite dessert before you left."

My eyes drop to the forgotten tray with a single piece of pie as something inside me fissures.

Thirty-One

I messed up.

The prince came to *my* chambers to have a conversation with *me* because he was looking for a friend. He was looking to decompress after his date. And why wouldn't he? Princess Mora is a vapid, energy sucking vampire.

He let down his guard. Sat right in my chair, comfortably pouring tea. He let down his guard, and I let him down.

Foolish, Amberle.

I pace my room. It's late, but sleep has fled as I consider my options.

Foolish. Foolish, Amberle.

I catch a glimpse of my reflection while passing the vanity mirror and I pause, touching my promise mark and loathing myself. My face crunches as a sharp regret pierces my chest. I came here for the opportunity to free my father and I let my pride get in the way.

How could I be so obtuse? So inept?

When the prince showed up at my door, I should have taken the opportunity to draw him closer—imbue enough warmth that he might feel comfortable confiding in me. It would have been easy. He was already in my chambers!

But I pushed him away. Maybe too far. He's definitely sending me packing at the next Invitational, if not sooner. The dragon fruit pie was a nice gesture, but maybe it was part one of an upcoming goodbye.

I don't need the fire of the king's voice in my head to demand I fix this. Now.

I must find Rion.

Fleeing my room, I rush down the corridor in the direction I think the prince might have gone. I see no signs of him, but I know the palace better than any of the other contestants—probably even better than Princess Mora. And I know all the best hiding spots.

Daring to test my wings, I fly up the stairs to the upper levels and keep my footsteps light on the tiled hallway so I don't alert anyone of my movement. I hope Rion hasn't retired to his quarters—the one place I might have difficulty sneaking into. My thoughts whir as I search other locations.

He's not on the balcony I spent the afternoon on.

He's not in the library.

He's no—

I shove myself behind a wooden bust of a dead king in a hallway full of floor to ceiling windows when the heavy footsteps of a group of guards come my way. Pressing myself tightly behind it, I take shallow breaths. The roar of blood thumps a rhythm in my ears as I strain to make out their footsteps. They're drawing closer.

I fist my hands, chastising myself; I'm not a prisoner. It's not forbidden to wander the hallways at night, but my instincts are too ingrained. I curse myself. I've made too many mistakes tonight. Now that I've rushed into the shadows, it would only make me look guilty of *something* if I popped out of my hiding spot now. Or if the guards see me.

I lean into my instincts and skill to remain hidden. Tucking the sunbeam beneath the collar of my dress to hide the glow, I regret not grabbing my dark cloak. I'd bolted so quickly, the idea didn't even cross my mind, but I wish I had a way to hide the bright silver of my hair from the moonlight that pours in through the tall windows. As the group passes, one could spot me from their periphery.

Tucking my hair behind my ears, then twisting the bulk of it and shoving it down the back of my dress, I do the only thing I can think of to stay hidden and slowly rise up the wall and onto the ceiling where I cling to a hanging chandelier.

The fixture cannot hold all my weight, so my wings strain to keep me hovering and silent. Sweat beads along my brow and I mentally will the guards to march faster. My back aches, but I can't afford to drop. Every moment stretches as the guards conduct their patrol. But they don't look up. I exhale in relief when they pass and are out of sight.

As I slowly descend, something outside the window catches my eye. I turn and see the prince walking into the summer garden. My pulse quickens at my stroke of luck. I know the exact back corridors and stairwells to reach him in minutes. And there's a balcony that will get me to him even sooner.

But what do I say to him?

I didn't mean what I said, won't come out right because it's not the truth. *I do want to be friends* is also a lie, except for the purpose of freeing my father.

What *truth* can I possibly say that will fix things?

I come up with nothing as I make my way to the balcony and leap over it to glide down to the entrance of the summer garden.

The sweet scent of gardenia, hyacinth, and of course, plumeria fills my nose as the evening breeze lifts tendrils of my hair, tickling my cheeks. Glowing vibrance of *will-o'-the-wisps* weave among purple rosebushes and blue nightshade, giving the garden an eerie, yet celestial ambiance. It might have been romantic if I wasn't in a panic to convince my childhood nemesis not to hate me.

I spot him sitting on a stone bench, but he rises the instant he sees me with angry eyebrows, and with the obvious intent to cast me from his presence. I can practically see the shimmer of ire radiating from him.

"Ri—" I choke on his name, remembering too late his scolding. "Prince Orion Illuminae," I amend slowly with a stiff curtsy. "Allow me to speak?"

"We have nothing to say," he says, lifting a hand of dismissal. "You made it very clear that you wish to have nothing to do with me. We are not friends, remember?"

"That's not what I meant. I didn't mean to say what I said." I close my eyes briefly, trying to catch my breath.

He steps toward me. "There are other girls who wish to be here for *me.* They came to Isi Aura because they want to see if they can form a connection and become my mate and my queen."

"Surely you aren't that naive?" I clamp a hand over my mouth and shake my head slowly, but I see the way he flinches and his expression hardens. This curse is going to be the end of me.

"Did you follow me to throw insults?"

"No, I—" *Do something!* My pulse increases and my eyes burn. I've made such a horrible mess of everything, and I don't know how to fix it. I don't know what to do.

Fiery summer heat radiates from him. "Amberle Kindra, I hereby—"

"Rion no! Please no!" I whimper and throw myself at him, gripping the fabric of his shirt as tears stream down my face.

I think I've confounded him because he doesn't finish his sentence and his summer magic wanes.

"I've been cursed!" The words fly out. "There's a damned curse on me that's making me say things I don't mean to say."

His eyes narrow, but I see the hue of the gold brightens slightly. Melting slightly. Softening slightly.

I foolishly keep going. "I don't know who put it on me or even how to get it removed, but it's the truth. Princess Arielle was helping me try to rid myself of it before she left, but I promise you I want to be here! I promise! Please don't send me away!"

"Star fae cannot lie," he says coolly. "Even a curse cannot make a star fae lie."

"But I didn't lie." I loosen my grip on his shirt and take half a step back, dropping my gaze. "We weren't friends." My voice is a ragged whisper.

His hands fist at his sides as his entire body turns rigid.

I keep my chin lowered as I dare to look up at him.

When his eyes flit downward toward my lips, mine trail to his, too. But when I feel heat prickle up and down my spine, I snap my eyes back to his.

What was that?

But the prince's expression hardens again.

"I think the interpretation of our memories as younglings doesn't match up," I say, then bite my tongue at the wince on his face.

Fix. This.

I *must* salvage things, but I can't trust that my words won't make matters worse and convince Rion to cut me from the competition anyway. So I do the one thing that words can't mess up. With a flick of my wings, I rise on the tips of my toes and grip the fabric of his shirt tighter.

His eyes widen.

Mine slowly trail down to his mouth, then back up again. My heart rate speeds like dragonfly wings against my ribcage.

The moonlight highlights the flush that spreads up the prince's neck.

Heat rushes to my cheeks.

His eyes lower.

Mine do, too.

He bridges the gap, but stops less than a wing's thickness away.

"Kisses can be lies," he whispers.

The pounding of my heart threatens to break through my chest.

"Then lie to me," I manage through hitching breaths.

He pulls back. His eyes have grown dark as the moon passes behind the clouds.

I try to ignore the surprising, but heavy devastation that has burrowed through my center at his rejection.

"Tell me why you're here." Rion's voice is a low growl. His cat-like pupils have grown in size. He looks almost predatory.

I know what he wants to hear. That I'm here for him. That I *want* him. But I can't because it isn't the truth. Silent tears stream down my face. Tears that can do nothing to get my father out of his cell. But I am here to help him. At the behest of the king, but it is true that I'm here for him. To help him choose a mate.

My tone is direct when I say, "I'm here for you."

His eyes narrow. "You said you're here for your father."

"Yes, that's also true."

The prince breaks from my grip. My words weren't enough to convince him.

"I want to stay!" I reach for him again, but he dodges my grasp. "Just because I came here for my father doesn't mean I don't want to be here!"

He stares at me for several more agonizing moments before he lowers his head and turns to walk away. "Don't follow me."

"Prince—" I start, but the jerk of his raised hand silences me.

Rion turns slightly to look at me, but doesn't come closer. "You are not the only one in the competition, Amberle, so stop pretending that you are. I have fourteen others to focus on, so you will excuse me if I don't speak to you for a time."

I nod and watch him walk out of the garden before staggering toward the stone bench, reaching it just in time to collapse onto it. I feel pitiful as more tears burn my eyes and a heavy weight crushes my heart.

He nearly sent me home and was mere syllables away from casting me out. I press a hand to my aching chest. But he didn't send me home. I'm still here. So why does it hurt so much?

Thirty-Two

After I drag myself to my room, I fall into a fitful sleep. I'm startled awake the next morning by a sharp rapping at the door, and my head pounds with every knock.

"Come in," I call to Gnacia.

I lift my heavy head from the pillow as the door opens, and sit as Gnacia clip-clops through the door. When the king walks in behind her, I'm quick to my feet.

"Wh-what is happening?" I ask.

Did the prince complain? Am I being thrown out after all?

Gnacia shoots a sidelong glance at the king as if asking permission to speak. When he nods, she turns back toward me.

"Your conversation in the garden with the prince last night was broadcast."

My stomach lurches, and I wrap my arms around my middle. I confessed the curse to the prince in the garden. I hadn't planned to. It just came out. But *it came out.*

"H-how much of it was shown?"

The king's eyes narrow as he studies me for several moments. It tells me he didn't see everything, but he wonders what he missed. "Enough that those watching are demanding to know the history between you and Prince Orion." His sigh is heavy. "They want to see more of the two of you."

"Why?"

"Because suddenly you're the talk of Faerie."

I let King Estelar's words sink in. Rion told me the winter magic wasn't watching when he came to my room last night. He said—

My thoughts tumble from their perch.

The prince said the magic wasn't watching when he came to my room, but he said nothing about the magic—whether it was present or not—when I sought him out. I *need* to figure out how to detect the winter magic and how to skirt it. Soon. I've been so focused on my curse, it hasn't been a priority. But it should be.

So Faerie didn't hear Rion's suspicions about his father manipulating the Tourney. We only discussed that in my room. They also didn't see my insults after he lamented whether any of the fae were there to win his heart or only the crown. Or my cold insistence that he and I were never friends.

My chest tightens. But the discomfort quickly turns to a cringe of horror because Faerie must know about the curse.

"What happens now?" I ask, swallowing over a hard lump in my throat and focusing on the king's previous words. About the fact that Faerie is demanding to see more of Rion and me together. "Am I to spend more time with the prince in the... public eye?" And how am I expected to act?

Gnacia looks at the king standing near my door, then back at me. "Not immediately. There are some things that need to be put in place, but yes, you will have some time with him that will be watched by the masses."

"We cannot let Faerie think the competition is being directed by anyone other than Prince Orion," the king adds, his voice a low rumble. King Estelar prides himself on control, so the thinly veiled fury behind his eyes frightens me even more than the day he showed up in my apartment above the bakery. "Gnacia will give you instructions, but I wanted to come personally."

I nod, but my knees turn to jelly. The king's presence alone tells me what an epic mistake I've made.

He steps toward me with his elven chin pointed directly at me. "The magic followed the prince out of the garden, so Faerie did not see your pitiful display of human emotion after he left, but I warn you that any attachment to my son on your part will not end happily."

"It's not—" I choke. I want to tell him what he saw had nothing to do with my feelings for the prince, that it was my devastation for failing my father, but I can't form the words. The heavy intimidation pulsing in waves from the high king has cut off my voice. My knees threaten to collapse.

"Do you understand?"

"Yes."

The high king leaves, and I lean onto the vanity table, discreetly gripping the edge.

I feel Gnacia's eyes on me, and I turn to her. "I don't—"

She lifts a hand and shakes her head. "That's not what I'm here to discuss."

Unsteady, I forget propriety and sit on the edge of the bed.

"An outing with you and the prince would have happened eventually for the purposes of showing equality in the competition, as King Estelar pointed out." Gnacia is all business. "But the plan was for a forgettable outing. What happened last night complicates things; no matter how unforgettable the circumstance, Faerie is now paying attention. So, first you will be invited to a group activity with the prince and several of the contestants."

Group activity. Sounds manageable.

"Shortly after, there will be a one-on-one where you are to talk about your past together naturally for the audience to hear. You must appease their curiosity and make it sound as unromantic as possible."

I make an educated guess. "And I am to show Faerie that we aren't a suitable match."

"You are correct." She pauses. "Now about this *curse* you've mentioned. What do you know about it? Who else have you told?"

I study her. Watching for any sign that she had something to do with it, but then dismiss it because it was placed on me long before I met the king's secretary.

"It seems all of Faerie knows now, so does it matter who else I've told?"

"Faerie does not know. That part was... *eliminated,*" she says. "Another benefit of having winter fae around with powerful shadow magic. What are the symptoms of this curse? How does it affect you?"

Despite my relief, my eyes narrow and I fold my arms, but there's no point keeping it a secret from Gnacia any longer. "I say things I don't mean. I've... made mistakes."

"This curse could be detrimental to all of us. We must find out what or who caused it and have it removed."

I hold back the smile that threatens to build. She knows my curse could be dangerous for her, too. Maybe I should have told her about it sooner.

"I'll see what I can find out and divert questions about it to other things. You may need to play up your relationship with Prince Orion in the meantime in order to do that."

I nod. Play up the relationship while also making us look like we're not a suitable match? Sure. Sounds easy.

She walks toward the door but stops with her hand on the handle and turns back to me. "Pretend as if we didn't talk when you arrive at breakfast. If you were an actual contestant, you wouldn't know they watched you." Gnacia closes the door quietly behind her.

Great. That means I can't hide out in my room all day.

I dread the inevitable scrutiny I'm about to endure, but being the last one will add more pressure and more eyes on me, so I quickly dress. As I make my way to breakfast, I distract myself by revising my plan.

Rion and Faerie might think I'm an utter love-sick fool, so

how can I use that to my advantage? Play the simpering half-fae who just isn't good enough for the prince? The idea of turning myself into a silly, nonsensical ball of fluff makes me nauseous, but I basically already did that. And it might be the best way to stay in the competition, but get everyone's attention off me.

Surely, I can think of something better.

More than half of the fae are already seated, but I still feel every eye in the room as I make my way to sit next to Didi. I don't return any of their glances, fearing what I'll see.

I have no appetite but reach for a pear and nibble at it, keeping my focus on something other than the thick, judgmental atmosphere.

"Why did you never tell me you and the prince knew each other as younglings?" Didi whispers.

I straighten, pretending I don't know what she means. "Did he tell you that?"

"Amberle, we all saw your conversation with him in the garden last night. They broadcast it everywhere."

I don't have to force shock into my expression, and I feel my face pale when I turn to my friend. Her red hair is a tumble of curls cascading down her back with parts of it held up with pins.

"What did you mean when you told him your memories differed from his?" she adds. I hate the pitying look on her face.

"How much did you see?" I ask. "*What* did you see?"

Didi keeps her eyes on the room, but only directs her voice at me. "Well, he looked angry. Like he wasn't happy you went looking for him." She lowers her tone more. "A lot of the fae aren't happy you sought him out like that. Unofficially."

"What do you mean? *Unofficially?*"

"You bent the unspoken rules. Getting time you weren't granted."

I venture a glance around the room and catch a piercing glare from Clove, which isn't surprising, but every fae has the same expression with varying degrees of severity. I jerk my attention back to Didi.

"But if they assume as you did—that he was angry because I went looking for him—why do they care if I broke the rules?"

"Because most of them were smart enough to see that Prince Orion was furious about more than that. What happened? Why was he so angry?"

"I was foolish," I say, rolling my eyes and trying to diminish the seriousness. "I said something I didn't mean to say. And it came out all wrong."

Didi looks skeptical. "C'mon. You're telling me you didn't mean to say…" She pauses long enough to plant her elbow to the table to conceal her words with her palm when she says, "*Lie to me.*"

My hand flies to my mouth and flaming heat rises in my cheeks.

Didi laughs at my reaction, and I whip my attention back to her. "Wait. It doesn't bother you that I was trying to kiss him?" I ask. "We are both in this Tourney."

She shrugs. "It's part of the process. But I'm also cheering on a fellow star fae." Her expression has fallen serious. "I think a lot of things could change for the better if he ends up choosing you."

Thirty-Three

Something in my chest twinges at Didi's words.

Partly because I know I'm not long for the competition to make her statement even a remotely fleeting idea, but partly because Kali had said something similar after she healed my wing. I dismiss the feeling as flattering appreciation or acceptance, both of which I'd had little of in the last decades.

"Or if he chooses you," I deflect, reaching for my glass and taking a sip of pineberry juice. "You're star fae, too."

"Yes, of course. But I can care about your relationship with the prince and separate it from my own feelings about him."

I study her face as I spot Nieven Morphyra entering the room in my periphery.

"Your human side is showing," I tease, but I'm grateful our breakfast is about to be interrupted and no one has accosted me.

Didi smiles, but it doesn't reach her eyes. She looks down and runs her finger along the linen tablecloth. "What did you mean when you said you came here for your father?"

"Ladies! May I have your attention?" Nieven wears a suit of powdered blue that sparkles as if it's been encrusted with diamonds.

I lean toward her and whisper while keeping my eyes on the

announcer. "Didn't you ever wonder how a nobody like me was in the competition? There aren't any other true commoners. My father used to work for the king. So yes, I entered the Tourney for my father." *Literally, to ransom him back.* "I hope to honor him."

While my last sentence is true, it's not the reason I entered.

"Not because you're hoping to end up with the prince?" my friend asks.

Careful, Amberle.

When I turn toward her, she's scrutinizing me. "I initially came for my father, but I want to stay."

My words seem to satisfy her because she smiles again and turns her attention toward Nieven.

"In this envelope, I have the name of the lady who will have the privilege of spending the entire day with the prince," he says, holding up a cream envelope with a golden seal.

With a flourish, Nieven makes exaggerated movements as he breaks the seal and unfolds the note.

With a smile, he says, "Didi Beechriver! The prince invites you to spend the day with him!"

My friend gasps and clutches a hand to her chest.

"Do you accept his invitation?"

Didi looks at me with a gaping mouth before turning to Nieven. "Yes!" She stands. "Of-of course, I-I'd love to!"

She's in such shock she doesn't glance back at me as she walks to take the announcer's outstretched hand as he leads her from the room.

For a moment, I'm panicked that I'm about to be swarmed by the other girls with accusations and questions about what they saw last night, but everyone remains in their seats, ignoring me. Perhaps they're taking notes from Princess Shay. Not wanting to tempt chance, I sneak out. I have no appetite, anyway. Now that I've been *officially* told of my humiliation—the more I think about my conversation with Rion in the garden, the more I cringe —I'll find somewhere to hide out for the day.

But I'm not out of the room for three paces before someone

follows me. I slow my steps to allow them to catch up. I want to get this over with.

"It's not fair what you did, you know." It's Princess Mora. She brushes past me like it's the only thing she plans to say, but then pivots and folds her arms. Her lower lip juts out. "I was supposed to be the one he's known for decades. I'm supposed to be the one with a *history* with him."

"I don't understand. I can't just *erase* my past with Rion."

"*Ugh!*" she growls. "That's not what I mean. That was *my* angle! I was supposed to be the fae he's known most of his life, but now he sees with new eyes."

"No one informed me the role was taken," I say, trying hard not to smile at the princess's tantrum. "Tell me, what was my role supposed to be?"

"The token common fae, of course." She throws her dark hair over her shoulder. "Or the token star fae, but the spring red-head fills that spot just fine."

Part of me flares at the slight—especially for Didi's sake—but it's Mora, so the feeling of offense easily extinguishes.

"It's not worth getting worked up, Mora," Princess Shay says, entering the hallway. An icy wave washes over me, but I can't tell if it's coming from the winter princess, or if it's my feeling toward her. "That display in the garden was pathetic. Everyone thinks so." Her eyes rove over me from head to toe with a look like she's discovered a rotting bulbeggar corpse. "The way she threw herself all over *our* prince. Really, she should spare herself more embarrassment and leave the competition."

"Or maybe you want me to leave the competition so that you'll have a better chance with him," I say between clenched teeth.

Princess Shay smiles, then steps closer to me. "I'm just trying to help you. You don't belong in the court, let alone with a prince."

"Why? Because I'm star fae?" My chest feels tight and my jaw aches.

"You're low born." Her insult is a frigid slap, so unfeeling it's as if she's been too insulated in her lofty tower to realize that common fae bleed.

"Why don't you let the prince decide who he belongs with?" I want to spin and leave, but don't want to look like a coward.

Princess Shay watches me for several long moments before gesturing to Princess Mora that they should go back to their breakfast.

They think they've won, I think as I walk toward my room where I intend to spend the day. But after Gnacia and the king's visit this morning, I can't wallow and feel sorry for my mistakes. If I'm ever going to be released from this nightmare of a job, I must find out the information the king wants. And I need to find it soon.

Since I actually want Didi to win, her being chosen for the date with the prince today is perfect, and I intend to find every reason I can to make the king see her as a worthy contender. So I pivot and head for the upper level of the library instead.

With Princess Shay still at breakfast, I have a moment to spy within the room Princess Arielle showed me without interruption. After last night, I welcome the thought of being somewhere the magic can't watch me, while taking notes on Didi's date.

I shut myself in the study room and ask the disc to show me the two.

"Where are you taking me?" Didi asks the prince as she clutches his arm.

Physical contact. It's a good sign.

Her hair was down in curls when I last saw her, but now it's piled high on her head. And she wears trousers.

"You'll see." Rion smiles down at her.

He's pleased and relaxed around her. Also a good sign.

They're walking on sand, so I assume they've traveled to the shoreline and are headed down the beach to the water's edge. "I've heard this is more exhilarating for star fae."

I frown as an uncomfortable feeling churns in my gut.

Didi spots them as soon as they appear in the magic, but my assumptions were ahead of both. Two horses, one the color of Oris Lake at midnight and the other a sea-foam green, stand at the edge of the water nibbling on seaweed.

Cabyll-ushteys.

"A-Are we going to ride them?" Didi's voice is barely a squeak.

"Yes."

Red-hot jealousy fills my veins. It's a good thing I'm alone. I've always wanted to ride a cabyll-ushtey across the sea. The water horses are carnivorous and can make a meal out of a fae as easily as carry them to the far islands at the edge of the Sea of Neptulus. I've always wanted to have the thrill of riding one. If I met my end while galloping over white-capped waves, it would be an acceptable way to die.

The two mount the horses, Rion on the dark blue and Didi on the green, and they trot out into the surf.

I move closer to the projection to watch as the snouts of the water horses elongate into hooks, their teeth turn to sharp points and their manes lengthen and the textures shift to look like sea grass.

Didi's eyes are wide, but the prince is ecstatic.

Rion kicks his heels into the sides of the horse and takes off. Didi follows without prompting close behind.

But the magic doesn't follow. It stays on the edge of the water, watching the two disappear into the horizon with longing. The magic cannot follow over water? Interesting.

I watch for several moments but realize it could be a while before they're back where the winter magic can see them again. So instead, I ask the disc to show me someone else.

"Show me Juniper."

The Sea of Neptulus evaporates and is replaced by... nothing. Did the magic stop working? I hope not. It's not like I can go looking for a winter fae to fix it for me.

"Show me Princess Shay," I say and the space above the disc

reveals the winter princess sitting in the dining hall, eating a leisurely breakfast with some of the other contestants.

I breathe a sigh of relief.

Just to double check, I say, "Show me Princess Mora."

The magic doesn't dissolve, but merely moves around the table until Mora is in full view, eating a pastry.

Not broken.

But I'm not interested in watching royalty eat breakfast, so I try again. "Show me Juniper."

The dining room disappears, and the space above the disc is empty of projections.

Juniper must be somewhere the magic isn't watching.

It's just as well, since breakfast won't take all day and Princess Shay might come here to spy on others. She doesn't know that I use the space and I wish to keep it that way.

I leave the study room with no plan or destination except that I want to find Juniper. Maybe I can convince her to tell me more about the secret she suspects about the prince. I need good information to bring to the king.

The most logical place Juniper might be is in her rooms. Gnacia said it was the most likely place to have privacy, so I head toward the floor where the autumn contestants live. I don't know which room is Juniper's, but I lean into the comfort of my skills and look for clues.

Halfway down the hall, I hear muffled voices. It doesn't sound like they're behind a door, but just around a corner. *Even better.* Now I don't even have to make small talk. I can just eavesdrop.

Pressing myself against the wall, I slink toward the voices and push as much of the light away from me that my minimal magic can handle. It's not the best form of concealment, but it also won't draw attention.

"I asked her if the king knows, since it's a big secret to keep, but she didn't know for sure." I recognize Tierney, Juniper's friend, and my ears perk with attention. "Still, it seems like something he would have to know. Don't you think?"

"Unless the queen kept it hidden," another girl says. I don't recognize her voice, but it isn't Juniper.

What are they talking about? It smells of secrets. The dangerous kind. I move closer.

"True... but don't you think someone would have told him by now?" Tierney asks. I glimpse her painted lady butterfly wing as it flutters into view, and I stop. I'm close enough to hear them clearly.

"Are you thinking that someone should tell him?" the other girl asks.

"I wasn't, but you're right. Someone should tell him."

"The king deserves to know. I wonder... do you think one might gain favor with the king if they told him?"

"That could be very dangerous, Cerule."

Ah, Cerule Rostina. The third autumn fae. I should have guessed.

"Then why does your face tell me you're thinking about doing it yourself?" Cerule asks.

This information could be huge. I lift my hand to my mouth and bite down on my nails. *Or it could be horrible.*

"Because I want to figure another way to gain favor with the king other than having to throw myself at the shallow prince!"

"Tierney!" Cerule snaps, but she lowers her volume. "What you speak could be considered treason!"

"We're in the private halls," Tierney says flippantly. "The winter magic can't watch us here. Look, I know Juni is head over heels for Prince Orion, but I just don't see what she likes so much about him. I'm only here because it might win me a crown. But... if I can gain influence and status another way..."

Keep talking, Tierney. I smile. *This is exactly the sort of thing the king wants to know.* Tierney is definitely not here for the right reasons.

"How can you say that? Don't you like him even a little?"

"Look, he should have to win us over, too. It shouldn't just be us trying to impress him, and I have to say that so far I'm not impressed."

The feeling is unexpected, but I want to wring her throat. But I keep my feet firmly planted where I stand.

"Well Juniper is." Cerule's voice is tight. "Do you think the prince is really falling in love with her?"

"I don't know, but staying close to her is good for me, too."

Oh Juniper. I think about the button-nosed girl who always seems in a daze and is so naive and vapid. Faerie is unforgiving to fae like her. I'm surprised she wasn't stomped out of the competition long before she was in it.

"How did Juniper figure out... you know?" Cerule asks. "Did he tell her?"

"No. She noticed it. She said if you look hard enough, you can see it. But the Faeven's magic is so much greater than ours, so I don't know if you or I could see it as easily." At least I hear pride in Tierney's voice as she talks about Juniper's powerful magic. "She said if you look past the glamour, you can see it."

Cerule mutters something I can't hear.

"C'mon, Juniper is taking forever. Let's go watch the halfling on her outing with the prince," Tierney says. "It probably won't be half as entertaining as watching Amberle sniveling in the garden, but let's watch anyway."

It's hard not to react and stomp over to confront them, but I resist and rush back the way I came. I slip through a hidden door that leads to a servant stairwell the autumn fae aren't familiar with.

Forcing myself to let go of the slight, my thoughts chew over something else Tierney said, *if you look past the glamour, you can see it—*

But I clamp a hand over my mouth to stifle the scream. I've nearly tripped over the lifeless body of the button-nosed fae the two autumn fae were just gossiping about and waiting for.

Her wings are torn and crushed, and her burnt-orange hair is spread in a fiery mess around her head on the smooth, stone floor. But by the way her mouth hangs agape, and the way her eyes are wide and unseeing... it's clear that she isn't merely injured or unconscious.

Juniper Faeven is dead.

Thirty-Four

Acrid bile rises in my throat and I stumble backward into the wall, mashing my just-healed wing against the cold stone. But the fresh wave of pain barely registers as I continue to stare at the lifeless body that was once Juniper Faeven.

Death in Faerie is not a common event—full fae are immortal unless hewn down by blade or poison. Even star fae can live a millennia, so death in Faerie is rare.

Until this moment, I had only seen a dead fae once. Ever. I was a youngling. It was over a century and a half ago, and it was my mother.

It was my mother.

I thought I had no memory of her. But I do. The images, as vague as they are, roil through me. Bending forward, I clutch my stomach as the memory surfaces.

I barely reached my mother's waist, but I remember the dark sackcloth she wore to cover her hair and face in those last days and weeks. Father said she had been poisoned, but I couldn't believe she would die. Fae did not die. But perhaps that is only in my memory of her. And perhaps it is flawed since I've blocked it.

Until now. Staring at Juniper only brings about another

memory of that time since it was here, in the Isi Aura palace, where my mother drew her last breath.

Rion was in the memory.

"Your mother has died," Rion said, bumping into me outside the dining room. His tone was flippant. Dismissing.

"She hasn't. She merely sleeps," I argued.

"No. My father confirmed it. She has died. And whatever the king says is the truth." Rion's chin jutted upward and his commanding stance with folded arms only caused the blood in my veins to boil. Why did he always have to pester me?

"Just because your father can't lie doesn't mean he knows all truth. He's mistaken." I believed my words but couldn't understand why frustrated tears burned my eyes. "I just saw her. She is resting. Tomorrow she will wake and we will travel to Melpomene Island where I will ride cabyll ushteys every day and never have to think of you again."

Rion frowned and his eyebrows turned angry. "No. You're wrong, Amberle. Your mother is no longer alive. Your mother is dead, and you will have to live here forever."

I remember shoving past him, hating the way he could hurt me with his words and the upturn of his lips. I rushed to my family's guest quarters—that would soon become our permanent ones— just so I could prove the cruel prince wrong. My mother wasn't dead! She was recovering! And the next day my father and mother and I would leave.

I remember the soul-racking sobs coming down the hallway as I neared the room, and when I pushed through the door and into my parents' bedchamber, I saw my mother. Ashen and limp, her lips had turned a dark gray. Her hair was the same colorless silver as mine, but now the ends were black as night. The tips of her fingers were also black.

I would have continued to convince myself that she only slept despite her stillness, but seeing my father lay prostrate across her body and learning that he was the source of the weeping was proof enough.

My mother was dead. Death was real. *Fae can die.*

Though my mind still didn't believe it, my sobs soon harmonized with his.

It was the worst day of my life, and along with the sight of Juniper's broken body, the memory of it crashes over me like an unforgiving wave on the Sea of Neptulus. I flee back the way I'd come, back through the concealed door, and collide right into Tierney and Cerule. The two fae I was trying to hide from.

Their surprise and angry exclamations, *whatwereyouwhyareyou,* are quickly cut off by what I assume is the reaction to my expression.

Tierney opens her mouth to speak again, but she's immediately silenced before she can even form a word by Cerule's scream.

The world spins and I'm pinned under someone. It's Tierney, and she's shouting at me, but I can't make out the words. My wing is pinched, and a shooting pain radiates along my back.

All I can think about is getting away. Making the pain stop. Run and hide from my memories. Desperate, I flick my wrist and create a spark. Tierney screams as I singe her arm, but jerks off me and I roll onto my stomach.

Without a plan, I push to my feet and bolt down the corridor and straight into the guards who have run toward the commotion.

My words are jumbled, but the guard grips my shoulders, steadying me. I'm not sure which guard holds me, but my vision tilts and I'm unceremoniously dragged off to my room.

Thirty-Five

My insides are still in a tangle as I report to the throne room. The king has summoned anyone with information about Juniper's death and since I was the one who found her, I'm not exempt from questioning.

I try to ignore the venomous stares of accusation from the autumn fae, Tierney and Cerule, as they huddle together in front of the closed door.

"We know you were jealous of Juni's connection with the prince, but you didn't have to kill her!" Tierney accuses. Her tone high-pitched.

I don't respond, and thankfully I'm ushered into the room before she or Cerule can say more. I can't blame them for hating me. My assumptions would be the same if the situation were reversed.

My heels clack against the smooth stone beneath my feet as I walk the long trek to the king seated on his crystal throne. Someone once told me the throne was made of crystalized sunbeams, but I can't remember if I actually heard that or if I dreamed it, so I don't know if it's true.

The tall, curved windows behind King Estelar blind me with summer light, casting him in shadow, and I cannot see his face.

But the domed skylight in the center of the room gives enough light that it highlights the crown on his head and his summer-blonde hair.

I expect to see the entire privy council flanking him, but besides the king, only Gnacia is present. She stands on his right with hands tightly clasped in front of her.

I want to speak, but this could be much worse if I lose my composure.

"What were you doing in the servant's corridor?" King Estelar asks. It's to the point, but it angers me.

"My job," I say, trying to keep the snark out of my tone. It's not hard since my shock and grief have made my voice shaky. "I was listening to a conversation between two fae and needed a quick getaway. I remembered the hidden door that leads to the servant's stairwell." Why else would I use the lesser-known passageways?

"Faerie will want to know why you were there," Gnacia says.

"You plan to make it public?" I ask. "If I explain what I was doing in the servant's hall, everyone will know the real reason I'm in the Tourney. Why do they need to know?"

"Because the other autumn girls know about the fae's death," the king says, "we cannot hide her murder. And since she comes from the Faeven family, they will demand a tribunal."

"Her name was Juniper, and I didn't kill her," I say. I cannot call her the *deceased girl* or the *dead fae.* "I'm not a killer."

"We know," Gnacia says.

"What would you have me say?" I ask. "I'm sure you don't want me telling them I'm a spy for the king."

"Gnacia, handle this," King Estelar gestures to his assistant with exasperation and pinches the bridge of his nose. "I need to speak with more of the fae."

The faun ushers me out through a side door as the main one is opened again.

"Where is she taking her?" I hear Cerule say, but we're soon separated by a door in a small sitting room. Still, I hear Tierney's reply, "Hopefully she's banished from the Tourney."

My eyes burn as I turn toward Gnacia. "The king expects me to get out of this, but how can I without revealing the truth?"

"Let's worry about that when it comes. For now, say nothing. We will contact the Faeven family today. The high king does not expect the autumn king to get involved, but it's a possibility. It is likely that a representative of the Faeven family *and* King Carpus will want to speak with you, but we will deal with that if it comes to it."

A sharp twisting sensation buries itself between my ribs and forces the air from my lungs.

"But for now, the attention on the unfortunate event will wrap up quickly," she continues, "and the focus can return to the prince and his journey to find a mate. Now, prepare yourself, because tomorrow will be the group outing we spoke of previously. It will be just what we need to pull the attention back on the Consort Tourney."

I pace my rooms as the stars come out, waiting for Rion to show up at my door. He said he did not wish to speak to me for a time, but once he learns about Juniper, he'll surely come. He has to. I've been forbidden to talk about Juniper's death with the other contestants, but they did not forbid me from talking about it with Rion. They'll tell him that I found her and he'll come.

But the garden conversation last night assaults me as I wait.

I told you; I need a friend in this.

You and I were never friends, Rion.

Squeezing my eyes tightly, I hold my breath and clench my teeth, trying to rid my mind of the memory and the way my chest compresses as if trapped in a vice.

He'll come.

There are other girls who wish to be here for me. They came to

Isi Aura because they want to see if they can form a connection and become my mate and my queen.

Surely you aren't that naive?

He has to come.

I don't know what I'll say to him or how I'll even face him after seeing one of his potential mates... dead. But I'm confident he'll come and somehow things will be right again.

Last night was merely a fight. He'll come.

Time passes and my pacing slows. And slows. To a stop. I curl up on a plush blue chair near the window and wait. More time passes and when there is finally a knock at my door, my eyes flutter open, then squeeze shut again against the dawn.

I fell asleep. He didn't come.

Another soft knock beckons, and I drag myself to the door. It's not the prince. It's Didi.

"You missed breakfast."

I don't respond and stiffly walk back to my seat.

"I would berate you for not asking about my date with Prince Orion, but I heard about Juniper," she says, sitting across from me. "They told me you found her body."

Was I the only one sworn to secrecy?

"How was your outing with the prince?" I don't want to talk about Juniper.

A conflicted grin splits her lips. "It was amazing. *He* is amazing." She ducks her head as a blush colors her cheeks. "But you know that."

My head snaps to her, but I stop myself, close my eyes, and nod. "The garden. When I..."

"Well, yes, that and the fact that you knew him when you were younglings."

My eyes open, and I look at her with my mouth twisted. I know it's common knowledge—mine and Rion's shared past— but having so many fae know so much about me feels intrusive. I feel as if I'm standing on a stage, naked, for all of Faerie to see.

Some full fae wouldn't bat an eye at the thought of being

undressed in front of a crowd, but the human side of me finds the idea humiliating.

"But I'm not here to talk about you and the prince." Didi pauses. Studying me. "Nieven announced a group activity with Prince Orion and several of the contestants."

"Who was invited?" I ask, knowing my name will be among them.

"One from each court. Princess Shay from Winter, Raine from Spring, Lily from the Underwater Court, Tierney from Autumn."

I turn my head to look out the window at the mention of Tierney. I'm not sure I'm ready to face her. Or anyone.

"And from Summer?" I ask, although I know the answer.

"You."

"When is this *activity?*"

"Today. Now, actually. You're planning a revel for tonight."

I snap back to her and let out an incredulous laugh. "A *revel?* Tonight?"

"Do you think they will bring in someone else from Autumn, since the way Juniper left was..."

I rub a hand along my forehead, but she doesn't see the gesture since she has already risen and is moving toward the door. How can anyone celebrate tonight?

"You know, since Arielle left unconventionally, and she was replaced by Princess—" She turns and stops talking. "Aren't you coming?"

"Didi, a fae... *died!*"

"You're right. It might offend the Faevens if Juniper's spot is filled again. But that means less competition for us."

I cover my face with both hands and groan.

"Amberle?"

In one motion, I drop my hands and stand. "Is this how everyone is acting? That we should indulge ourselves in drinking and dancing at a revel as if losing one of us is just part of the process? That we should move on as if nothing happened?"

"I uh—"

"Tell them I'm not coming." I lift a hand. "Or don't. I really don't care, but I cannot plan a *revel* and act as if I didn't trip over Juniper Faeven's body only yesterday." Or the fact that Rion never came last night.

Didi takes a cautious step toward me. "Were you and Juniper close? Were you friends?"

No, but it causes memories of my mother I didn't know I had to resurface. *Your mother has died.*

"No. But she was one of us." *Well, one of* them. *And they think I'm one of them.*

Didi leaves without another word. I expect the wrath of the king, or of Gnacia, to command that I attend the group activity, but the only thing that interrupts my self-inflicted solitude is a note on a parchment paper slipped underneath my door.

I stare at it, but don't move to fetch it. I'm not in the mood to be chided by Gnacia for refusing to attend the group date.

But she wouldn't send a note. She'd march in here and scold me herself.

Is it from Kali? Is she asking about my wing? Perhaps it's a discrete invitation to visit the healer. I should visit my friend.

Or maybe it's from Princess Arielle with information about my curse. Although now that I think about it, I haven't had much trouble with the curse lately. Or at least it's ebbed. *Strange.*

I walk toward the note, but before I even pick it up, I see the familiar golden seal. I don't need to see the intricate details of a raven wearing a crown to know it's the prince's seal.

I should have guessed, but I didn't think Rion would send a note. Has he heard that I refused to meet him? Is this his goodbye note? My stomach clenches. When we were young, the prince was quick to be cruel if his feelings were hurt. Maybe he is asking me to pack my things and leave immediately.

I inhale... then crack the gold wax and unfold the missive.

· · ·

The group date has been postponed until tomorrow so we can grieve today.
—Rion.

I exhale.

Then climb into bed. I pull the covers over my head, cocooning myself in protective darkness. I can't be bothered with questions about my curse or visiting old friends. Tears well and I'm not sure if I'm crying about my father or Juniper. Or my fight with Rion. Probably all three. And I don't know how I'll pull myself together before tomorrow. But right now, I don't care. Today I'll let myself mourn, and tomorrow I'll fight again.

Thirty-Six

As I walk to the grand ballroom, I brace myself for what's coming. I'm grateful Rion pushed the group date back one day, but I don't feel much better. Even though sleeping and crying for an entire day is a luxury I've never had, I'm still haunted by Juniper's death.

As a thief, I usually worked at night when the world was quiet and dark. When clients were scarce, I spent daylight hours picking pockets. Sometimes I had to do both to survive.

The option of lying around without pain gnawing at my stomach and bare cupboards mocking me is oddly discomforting. So I can't help but feel a little ashamed. I am on a job. I'm here to spy and gain information which can't be done while hiding under soft bed covers.

My simple, but elegant dress for the date is deep blue, embroidered with silver vines and flowers at the bodice and the hem near my ankles. Kenna plaited my hair down the middle and it trails down my back.

I straighten my spine while keeping my re-injured wing absolutely still as I walk down the hallways and adjust my mindset. Four other contestants will be in attendance on this outing, and it will be the perfect opportunity to learn more about each of them.

Didi said they invited one fae from each court. I don't know much about the underwater fae, Lily, but I've had interactions with the other three. So far, I don't like what I've seen. Beyond my frustration with Rion, I wouldn't wish any of them to become my future queen.

When I overheard the conversation between Tierney and Cerule before finding Juniper's body, it was clear that Tierney is here for selfish reasons. She isn't attracted to the prince and only wants to gain power by winning the crown or gaining the loyalty of the fae who does. While I don't think Tierney would hurt the prince, it's enough evidence to bring to Gnacia and the king, but I should learn more. Still, if the king really wants Prince Rion to end up with someone who truly cares for his son, the advisers will be alerted, and they'll push for the prince to send her home.

Most of my interactions with Raine have been uneventful or negative. But the more I've gotten to know her, the very idea of spending the day with her makes me want to gag. She's an entirely new level of snobbery. Her vitriolic tone when she spoke the words *star fae* while discussing mine and Didi's heritage is enough to make me want to lock her in a closet for the duration of the date. But I'd have to lock away everyone else too because, even if the others aren't saying how much they hate star fae, I know they're thinking it. Her opinion of the half-fae is a common sentiment.

I miss Princess Arielle. She was truly a rare rose among thorns.

Princess Shay might be the most dangerous one of all. While she's ignored me because she believes I'm not worthy of her notice —to the extent that her almost-sabotage during the invitational was abandoned when she realized she was trying to thwart me—if I cross her, her payback could be a thousand times more painful than Clove's schemes. However, I may not like her, but that doesn't mean she's not the right fae for the prince. She is a royal in her own right, so she might be here for more than just power. She has history with the prince, after all.

I shudder, then steel myself before walking into the grand ballroom.

I'm the last contestant to arrive, and I note that all wear finer gowns than mine. All are floor length with delicate lace, satin ribbons, or intricate beading. It's not uncommon for a spring fae to wear live flowers, but the orchids that swirl around Raine's jade-green skirts are breathtaking, even drawing a nearby white butterfly. How are they not wilting? If I were a flower, I'd wither instantly, being so close to her.

Tierney's cherry red dress has a plunging neckline and a slit to her knee.

Lily's scaled dress is fitted through the bodice and hips, then flares into lovely swirling material that almost looks like waves as she moves.

Princess Shay's fragile and sharp white gown almost looks like the sleeves are made of lace, but upon closer inspection, I notice it's actually millions of snowflakes. Of all the dresses, the winter princess's nearly steals my breath away.

But none of the dresses look like appropriate clothing to be planning a revel.

Only Lily even glances at me when I walk in, but her eyes are so large and open that she seems to look at everything at once. Tierney leans toward Princess Shay and whispers in her ear. The winter princess doesn't respond, but Raine grins and moves closer, her back to me as she speaks to them both.

I stand awkwardly and pretend to study a piece of art on the wall until the prince walks into the room and all conversations stop. Every set of shoulders straightens, and I notice the slit on Tierney's dress slowly splits further up her thigh as she decays the fabric. I wonder if the slit and plunging neckline were there to begin with, or if both are evidence of Tierney's autumn decay magic at work.

But I don't dwell on it and watch for Rion's reaction when he sees me.

Prince Rion's eyes briefly flit to each of us without changing the expression on his face, then he glances behind him where Nieven Morphyra walks into the room with arms upheld in a dramatic gesture.

Feeling a subtle rush of something—*magic, maybe?*—the air seems to crackle and sparkle. It also feels familiar and without realizing it, I've come to associate the feeling with the announcer. Wait! It must be the magic that allows Faerie to watch. I can sense it!

"Ladies!" Nieven smiles brightly at us. "Prince Orion." He turns to the prince with the same wide smile. "And all of Faerie," he addresses the air. Though I felt the magic enter the room with Nieven, I didn't know exactly where it was until he looked at it. Perhaps I could learn to track it like he did. "Today, the prince and these five contestants will prepare an exclusive revel that will commence this evening. Why are they planning a revel, might you ask, when a revel has no need of planning but merely enjoying?" Nieven turns to the prince with dark eyebrows raised before turning back to the *audience*. He pauses for only a moment before allowing his face to drop the jubilant mask. A somber one replaces it. The announcer looks pointedly at the air in front of him and continues. "Rumors and gossip spread like summer fire through our realm, but if you're living under a rock—I'm looking at you, the underjordiskes and the trows—you may not have heard that one of the contestants was recently found dead."

I press my lips tightly together at the mention and close my eyes when I hear the collected gasps coming from Raine and Tierney and Princess Shay beside me. They act as if they were unaware of Juniper's demise until this moment.

"That's right. Juniper Faeven from the Autumn Court... has died."

Tierney lets out a choked sob. Raine reaches a comforting arm around her. Both actions are unexpected because full fae rarely show their emotions. Especially because although they have them, emotions are typically dormant or well-controlled in the fae.

"And so these ladies will plan a revel that will also serve as a wake for the fallen fae. We hope that their interactions with each other and our prince will distract all of us. The queen recently attended an event in the human realm, a sort of carnival with festivities that are not unlike a revel, but she said it had a certain intangible *substance* about it that she wanted re-created here." The announcer pauses. "And so they will attempt to create what the queen loved for us to enjoy."

Nieven excuses himself and we are left to stare at each other. None of us is certain what to do.

"Is the queen coming to give us direction?" Princess Shay asks the prince.

"I believe she plans to see our progress, but wants to see what we come up with first," he says.

"Well, that's ridiculous." The winter princess moves toward the door. The thousands of connected snowflakes at her skirts click against each other and sound like tiny wind chimes.

"Where are you going, Shay?" the prince snaps.

She turns around slowly, then walks back to him with hooded eyes and a half-smile. The light from the tall windows reflects off her dress and sends rainbows skittering across the hardwood maple floor. "To find your mother," she says, drawing a pointed finger up the length of his chest. "If we are to satisfy her with this event, we should know what it is she wants."

My veins burn. I've never seen her speak to him that way until now. But Rion seems unfazed by the gesture. He merely nods and Princess Shay leaves.

Is it a common way they interact with one another? I swallow the bile that rises.

"Well, I've traveled to the human realm many times, and I think I know exactly what the queen wants," Raine says.

"And what is that?" Tierney asks brightly.

"Grand decorations, lots of food and light. And entertainment." She winks at the prince, who offers a half-smile and folds his arms.

"It seems like you have a clear plan, Raine," the prince says. "Why don't you instruct us on what to do?"

"Yes. Well, I think it's obvious that a spring fae should oversee the decorations," Raine says, pointing to herself and offering a self-satisfied smile before tucking a lock of her pink, cherry blossom hair behind an ear. "But I'd love your help with the lighting, Prince Orion." Raine lowers her chin and doesn't take her eyes off the prince when she instructs with a flippant hand, "Tierney, Lily, and Amberle can take care of the food and entertainment."

Rion glances at me, but not long enough for me to communicate anything with him—not even a *thank you* for postponing this date, or *how are you doing after Juniper's death,* or *are you still angry at me*—before he turns back to Raine who is gripping his arm and talking excitedly about something. Despite Raine's instructions, Tierney follows her and the prince to the other side of the ballroom, leaving just Lily and me.

"I didn't know humans had revels," Lily says. "Isn't that the reason we bring them to Faerie? So they can experience it themselves?"

"I've never been to the human realm, so I don't know," I admit.

"But now the queen wants to create a revel like one in the human realm?" Lily mostly mutters to herself as she also wanders out of the ballroom.

"Where are you going?"

"I'll head to the kitchens and plan the food," she says without glancing back.

I'm glad for the sudden solitude but wonder what I could possibly plan for 'entertainment' on my own since Tierney clearly doesn't intend to help. I've spent so much time hidden in the shadows and avoiding any sort of spotlight—

"Amberle!" Rion calls. His arm is raised, and his smile is warm. It ignites a rising lightness inside me. *Perhaps he's no longer angry with me.* "Come help us decorate. We can all plan the entertainment afterward."

By the sudden stiffness of Raine's shoulders and the frown on Tierney's face, I can see he didn't ask their opinion before beckoning me over. I don't know if my smile is in response to the prince's grin or to the two fae's irritation. But I can't care too much about either. This is my opportunity to learn some things.

Thirty-Seven

Suffering through an afternoon spent with Raine and Tierney to decorate for a revel pays off. Raine's skill at growing flowers is something I've never seen. Most spring fae can grow flowers, of course, but her creations are especially unique. I'm no expert, but they look like mixes of different breeds. It's curious.

And she's excellent at barking orders ... I mean, 'delegating.' She chirps for hours at both Tierney and me to deliver her creations at various spots in the ballroom to spill over tables and hang over doorways.

I learn that despite Tierney's insistence that she has no feelings for the prince, she would fool even me as she endlessly fawns over him—finding any reason to touch, or link arms, or flutter her lashes. She's as talented an actress as she is with her carefully controlled power of decay. And the slit in her dress edges higher with every passing hour while her neckline plunges lower. Too much further and she will cut the dress in half.

But nothing is too scandalous for the fae.

My wing begins to ache as I haul an armful of fuchsia roses, orange lilies, and Viking pompons to the long mahogany buffet table at the far end of the room. It's the third arrangement I've

"

transported while *thinks-she's-already-Queen*-Raine has remained in one spot.

"I thought your wing had healed." Rion's voice comes from behind me.

"It did," I say. I'm glad for the interruption from my thoughts and observations. "But when I found Juniper I—" My words choke off unexpectedly. I twist my mouth and blink a few times.

He touches my shoulder, the tenderness grounding me.

"Did you see who... " he trails off and swallows hard. "Were you attacked?"

"No. It's not that." I shake my head, quickly reassuring him. I lift a hand, causing him to drop his from my arm. "Just seeing her... startled me and I fell backward into the wall."

He nods slowly. A rose thorn presses against my arm, and I move to put the flower centerpiece on the table.

"I won't make you talk about it," he says as I place the flowers. "But I wondered, how are you faring? I know Tierney is sad about her friend, but the others seem to have moved on."

Slowly, I turn to face him. My throat tightens and my eyes burn as I see a glisten in his. He's concerned. It's endearing and something I never expected. I'm confused. Prince Rion is full fae. How could he possibly understand the tormented feelings swirling within me? A lock of his dark hair falls over his forehead and I itch to move it away, but keep my hands tightly fisted at my sides.

The prince looks over his shoulder at the girls at the other end of the ballroom, then back at me with downturned eyebrows. "I can see you struggle. Allow me to ease your burden."

Tears well. I wipe my eyes and step back, dazed. I haven't forgotten the words we exchanged that night. I haven't forgotten how close he was to banishing me from his presence. Throwing me out. I can't even fathom what that would have done to me. And my chances of seeing my father again, of course. "And how would you—the crown prince—do that?"

"Talk to me, Amberle," he whispers.

A shiver raises the hairs at the back of my neck and I frown at the way my heart does a little flip.

"Amberle?"

The second mention of my name wraps around me like a caress, and when he reaches out to take my hand, my words tumble out, "I'm half-human and am unfortunately subject to human emotions and feelings." A tear escapes. Then another. But I smile through it. "I wasn't close to Juniper, but she did not deserve what happened to her."

I close my eyes against the image of her crushed and broken body as more tears spill from beneath my lids. But that's not the only reason for the tears.

Suddenly I'm pulled into an embrace that causes the air to fly from my lungs, but I lean closer to him, loving the summer warmth radiating from him.

But it doesn't last forever, and soon some urgent message pulls the prince away and out of the ballroom. Without him, I'm unshielded from the new, icy glares from across the room.

With the prince gone, Raine marches toward me and pushes another flower arrangement into my arms. "Put that up there," she says, pointing at the ceiling. "Drape it around the chandelier."

My wing twitches and sends a piercing ache radiating down my back. I know my face is streaked with tears, just as clearly as I know that Raine cares more about a single orchid on her dress than she does about me.

"I can't," I say, pushing it back into her arms. "Ask Tierney to fly it up there."

Raine's mouth hangs open, but I can't bring myself to care as I excuse myself and walk out.

I'm not even two steps out of the ballroom before running into the prince. I hadn't intended to follow him, only to get away from everyone and find a moment of peace.

"I was not away long, Amberle," he says. "What did I miss?"

"I uh... " I pause and shake my head with closed eyes. "I had to get away from *them.*" Hooking a thumb over my shoulder, I look at him again. I realize that I can't make a habit of running away when I'm irritated by the others, but it was more than Raine's orders that sent me from the room.

An amused smile lifts the other side of his mouth, and he crosses his arms. "I've heard that females can become like vicious *cait sith's* when in competition for a male."

Don't flatter yourself, I want to say, but bite the inside of my cheek instead.

Rion steps toward me. "Speaking of... did a *cait sith* steal your tongue? Where's your quip about my arrogance?" His smile widens. "I recall the last time we were alone you weren't afraid to call me a *sniveling, whimpering princeling.* Putting me in my place is not a weakness of yours. It never has been."

"Yes, but in that same conversation, you reminded me that I'm not the only fae in this competition." My smile is feeble. This is not the prince I remember. "And you said you didn't want to speak to me." Why the sudden change?

He winces.

"Those were your words."

"I know."

"I guess I was merely trying to navigate how I should talk to you, Prince Orion Illuminae." When I bow and speak his name, I make sure my tone is reverent, not mocking.

Rion's jaw tightens, and I brace myself for his regal stone façade to appear, but it doesn't. "I regret the words I said that night."

Regret? I didn't know the word was in his vocabulary. If Didi had used the word *regret,* I would have teased that her human side was showing. It's not a word often used by the fae.

"After what happened to Juniper... and the fact you were the one who found her..." He takes a breath. "Everything sour between us has been forgiven."

That quickly? I wonder, but I won't question it. The tremendous weight I didn't realize had been laying on my shoulders since that night lifts in an instant. Emotion threatens to bubble up again, but I shove it down.

"I also realized that the way I remember things from our past might be... different from the way you remember them."

I consider his words. There's a fiercely genuine intent behind them that jumbles my thoughts and twists my gut.

"I didn't realize you hated living here, but it would explain why you never returned," he continues, and I can't help but notice the hint of hurt in his tone.

"I-I didn't hate it here," I say. It was my home. I loved living in the palace. "But we saw things through different lenses." We might have lived under the same roof, but the life of a commoner and a royal might as well be worlds apart.

The prince's shoulders lift. "I hope that someday you'll tell me what it was like for you."

Sucking in a shallow breath and tearing down a few walls, I say, "Perhaps we can have that conversation soon."

"Good."

When Rion lightly grips my elbow and I find my arm suddenly draped through his, it feels like a natural, yet foreign reaction to his touch. But I feel a rush of heat flood my body from the crown of my head to the skin of my toes. Trying to sound natural, I ask, "What pulled you away?"

He doesn't respond right away and leads me back to the ballroom, acting as if we've walked like this—arm in arm—a thousand times.

The prince frowns as if he can't share what urgent message tore him from the group date, but I can see the war behind his eyes. He *wants* to tell me.

Getting over my self-consciousness, I push myself closer to him and whisper, "Was it about Juniper?"

He nods. "It terrifies me to think it could happen again. The moment I heard about Juniper, I sent for Wyn."

My heart lightens. I always had a fondness for Wyn Firetail. Although he spent little time with us when we were younglings, since his father often dragged him all over Faerie—being one of King Estelar's most trusted ambassadors—I considered him a friend too. And one who was vastly less cruel than the prince.

We also had a commonality the prince couldn't share. Neither of us were royal and were merely the children of important fae who worked for the king.

"Will his father accompany him?" I ask.

Rion shakes his head. "He spends all his days gambling on div fights on Erato Island."

"Oh." I don't hide my shock or astonishment well.

The prince laughs, then nudges me with his elbow. "Funny thing to do after working for the king for so many centuries, huh?"

"It is," I agree.

"Your Highness? Might I have a word?" Raine interrupts in a high, lilting tone. She smiles sweetly up at the prince while fluttering her eyelashes. When he reluctantly agrees and releases my arm and allows her to take my place, she flashes a glare at me.

"She's complaining about you," Tierney sings, coming up from behind me.

I turn and don't have to inspect her dress too closely to notice the plunging neckline has neared her navel. I try to hide the sigh in my voice when I say, "Why? Because I wouldn't fly her flower arrangement to the ceiling?"

Tierney's butterfly wings twitch—in what I assume is frustration for me guessing correctly—but she keeps the emotion off her face with a triumphant look.

I ignore it and glance around the room. "I think we have *plenty* of fauna, Tierney. Any more and we might as well move the revel out to the garden."

"Commoners cannot comprehend the importance of this event, let alone *star fae*." She lifts her chin, genuinely seeming to believe my brains are inferior. "Let me explain in a way you can understand. *We* must impress the high queen. The atmosphere sets the tone for the entire revel." She pauses and a few tears escape, cutting a path of destruction down her smooth skin as if acid eats at it. She turns slightly, and I suspect she senses the magic as I do, watching us. The tears mean nothing, though—a trick of the autumn fae to make themselves look pitiful and fierce at the same time. "Besides, we're doing it for Juniper too."

"Of course," I say, lowering my head in a respectful bow. For a moment I feel remorse for not throwing my full energy into the décor, but quickly catch myself, recognizing Tierney's manipulation. She's using Juniper's name to justify being tricked into being Raine's servant for hours on end. She's trying to save face.

The lamenting huff Raine lets out across the room is so loud that both Tierney and I turn and watch her march out of the ballroom. I press my lips together to stop myself from smiling. Whatever she said to the prince didn't go quite as she'd hoped.

The prince seems unfazed as he walks back toward us. "This group date has not gone as I intended," he says. "I didn't expect so many of you to excuse yourselves. Come, let's see what is keeping Lily in the kitchens. Perhaps when we return, Raine and Princess Shay will have decided to rejoin us."

The two never did rejoin the planning, but both were in attendance—wearing even finer gowns—when the revel begins.

It's clear that the time and effort Princess Shay has put into her relationship with Queen Siora has paid off because from the moment the queen enters the revel and her eyes alight with wonder and joy at the flower arrangements accented with Prince Rion's light magic, and the entertainment of summer fire jugglers, and the magnificent gold and burgundy carousel erected by the most skilled spring architects right in the center of the ballroom, she calls the winter princess to her side and the two are quickly inseparable. As they move around the ballroom, with arms linked, they talk in confidence with each other. Their smiles are frequent, and their laughs add a layer of harmony to the lutes playing and the guests chattering and the pipes of the carousel.

I can't help but feel frustrated that Princess Shay is receiving equal credit when she never lifted a finger or even offered a suggestion to make the revel a success. But it seems she knows how to play the game better than the rest of us.

If the game is to win over the current high queen, of course.

The rest of the contestants are also in attendance, so the prince's attention is pulled to and fro. Lady Pepper steals him for a waltz. Then one of the underwater fae, Aqualis, has his ear for at least half an hour at the refreshment table. Clove glowers at each fae who spends time with him until she snatches the prince for a ride on the carousel. Her on a golden unicorn while he rides a burgundy dragon.

I weave through the party, pretending to be lost in thought, but simultaneously observing the contestants while I practice feeling for the buzz of winter magic. I'm sure it must be present and watching. The magic seemed so obviously *there* when Nieven announced to Faerie about the group date this morning, but with the music and the noise and the other fae around, with the low hum of their own buzzing magic, I can't pinpoint the location of it.

Could it be everywhere now? Can Faerie watch all of us?

"No, I didn't kill her. That would be premature."

My pulse flutters against my ribcage as my ears prick at the female voice behind me. No other fae are near enough to hear, and the voice is coming from one of Raine's flower arrangements pouring out of a large vase.

"There are still too many contestants to know which ones might be in the way," she continues.

I slow my steps to a stop as naturally as possible, keeping my back to her, and pray my eavesdropping isn't obvious.

"But I can't talk right now," the same voice says, then pauses.

"No. I've blocked it temporarily, but the *other* magic will be able to listen soon." Another pause. "Yes, yes. Contact me tonight."

An icy chill runs down my neck when I note it sounded like a one-sided-conversation. I know there is only one type of fae who can project images and sound, and therefore only one type of fae who—by projecting their voice to another—could have a full conversation at a long distance.

My mind reels at the new information as my thoughts whir around what I've just overheard.

Killing her would be premature?

Killing who? Killing Juniper?

It's hard to know which contestants might be in the way?

In the way of what? The Prince? The Crown?

The other magic might be listening?

And the mention of *other magic* confirms exactly the type of fae I overheard.

She—whoever *she* is—and whoever *she* was talking to... are winter fae.

Thirty-Eight

It's not surprising that a winter fae is involved in something sinister. General peace doesn't last long, especially with the Winter Court. It seems they're always up to something. Creating chaos, causing havoc, trying to steal crowns and thrones. Conspiring to murder in order to get what they want. Typical.

During the conversation I overheard, *she* said she didn't kill Juniper, but she's waiting for *something*. Likely for the competition in the Tourney to narrow down. And she was very clear that killing those who stand in the way is a possibility to ensure they meet their goal.

Meaning... there is more than one dangerous fae in our midst. The one—or group—who killed Juniper, and the Winter Court group with a future, murderous plan.

Someone walks toward me from the other direction. I hope they'll pass by while I learn the identity of the conspiring winter fae. Making no sudden movements, I shift slightly, straining to spot a face, or even a swish of fabric or a glint of jewels.

"I hate seeing him with her," Didi says, stopping right next to me. Of all the creatures to approach me right now, it had to be my one friend. At least I heard her coming. It's an obstacle of being an undercover spy that I could get interrupted right when I learn something interesting.

I internally curse, but miraculously keep my face neutral as Didi gestures with her chin toward the carousel where Clove and the prince still ride their magical mounts.

"I think we all do," I say, carefully hiding the irritation from my tone.

It works because she laughs, then sighs.

"What is it?" I ask while discreetly looking over my shoulder. Seeing no one, I clench my teeth and my fists. The fae I overheard has mingled back into the party.

"I know I sound just like her," Didi says. "But after my time with him last night, it feels like he's... well... *mine.* And now it feels like you're all trying to steal him away." Her voice is dreamy and wistful and sad.

With the fae gone, I roll my shoulders, then focus my attention on my friend. "You sound like *her*? Her... meaning Juniper?"

Didi nods, causing the red ringlets around her face to bounce as she touches the crystalized sunbeam at her throat. Since the morning after the first Invitational when I wore mine, I have noticed more of the contestants wear theirs regularly. But not tonight. The others seem to prefer their fancier jewels for this revel, so only Didi and I wear ours now.

I resist the urge to touch mine, too.

"Do you think he really had a strong connection with her?" She pauses, then lowers her voice to a whisper and drops her hand. "Juniper, I mean?"

Whether Rion cared for Juniper shouldn't matter. What were a fae's feelings compared to Juniper's life? This stupid competition robbed a creature of her future. Her family had lost a beloved member.

"We could ask him," I say, "but it doesn't matter anymore."

"I suppose not. This competition isn't going as I'd expected. I feel..."

"Everything," I answer for her. "The full fae are buffered from emotion. We are different, but that's not a bad thing." I attempt to console myself as much as Didi because I feel like my emotions could sink me.

"The carousel has stopped," Didi says, stepping away from me. "I want to snatch Orion away before anyone else does."

"Go get him." I smile.

The spring fae seems honestly confounded at her growing feelings for Prince Rion. But what else did she expect to come out of this experience? The prince is here to find a mate and a queen to rule by his side. He wants someone who cares for him. He wants to fall in love. That is the purpose of this Consort Tourney. To find his future consort queen. Did the number of contestants squash her expectations of getting quality time with him? Or did she expect him to be less attractive? Did she expect he wouldn't be the type of fae she could care for?

Aside from my thoughts and feelings that Princess Arielle would be the best match for the prince, Didi is the fae I have been rooting for from the beginning. I've been so focused on other things that I haven't spent time increasing the chances for the pair. I thought I may have to nudge them into each other's arms, but it seems they've already done it on their own. It's the best-case scenario, isn't it?

Back to work.

I must figure out which of the winter fae I overheard. Fortunately, I can easily narrow down the list because only three winter fae are at the revel. The three Tourney Contestants. Princess Shay, Frost Neige, and Luna Diables. I know Princess Shay's voice well enough to know it wasn't hers, but that doesn't mean she isn't involved. I must do more digging.

I weave through the crowd, looking for the dark elf or the winter dryad. If I hear the other contestants' voices, I'll know which was the one I heard.

Luck seems to be on my side, because I spot the white hair of Frost standing near the lute players watching as they—

"Amberle?" Rion's hand grips my arm gently and turns me toward him.

But I thought Didi—

I tilt my head and point in the direction I thought Didi ran off when she went looking for the prince.

"Are you looking for someone?" he asks with a grin.

"I uh—" I stop my words, then shake my head. Perhaps Didi's feet turned cold before she could speak with him. Perhaps she stepped out? "No, I'm not."

The prince holds out a hand. "Would you like to dance?"

My mouth opens to protest and insist that he dance with someone else. Someone with potential to be his companion. Someone other than me. But he believes I am here for him, so I nod and take his hand and allow him to lead me to the center of the floor.

Another obstacle of the job. Frost will have to wait.

He places a hand at my back and I rest my arm on his shoulder, then I take his other outstretched hand. Rion turns to the lute players and nods once, prompting the waltz to begin.

"My mother said it takes humans lots of practice to get the steps right," he says, leading the dance.

"Then I hope my fae side prevails now," I say. "Has she witnessed humans dance this way?"

"She has. She says that despite the clumsiness and rigidness we often associate with the humans, with enough practice, they can move nearly as gracefully as the fae."

"That is very kind of your mother to say." I can't imagine the king would have such favorable words about humans, but don't bring it up.

We fall silent and move around the ballroom. It's been many decades since I've been to a revel or even danced, and this one is especially unique with its human influence the queen has requested. And I find myself entering a dream-like state. My eyes trail to the flower arrangements around the room, and, erasing their association with Raine, I can see their unique beauty. Each is highlighted with tiny lights that attract several *will-o'-the-wisps*. I barely hear the music, although with Rion's guidance, we move absolutely in sync with the melody.

For a breath, I forget I dislike my dancing partner and the pomp of the creatures surrounding me. I let go of my life as a spy, a deceiver, and a thief. In this moment, I'm not swallowed by chaotic emotions. I'm swimming in the beauty around me. For the first time in days, calm assurance envelopes me, and a spark of joy flits in my chest.

Maybe the obstacles of this job aren't so bad.

The prince's arm shifts, and I snap back to reality. My senses become hyper-aware. Rion's firm arm radiates heat through his shirt where my arm rests on his. His hand is hot, near-scorching, at my back. It might feel as if it was burning if I were anything other than a summer fae myself.

When my face lifts upward to his, he's watching me with molten-gold eyes—his earlier grin has vanished, replaced by an intense, alluring expression—I feel as if his gaze could ignite my entire being in an instant.

My heart speeds. My task forgotten.

My breath escapes and I see the fae I met, what feels like so long ago, when I was escaping from capture after stealing the bracelet off that haughty elf. The strong, capable *mysterious* fae, who was so adept and skilled at helping an *expert thief*. I have not been drawn to anyone in a long time, but I can admit now that *he'd* interested me. What if this Tourney had never started? What if I never left the Spring Court, and this fae had still entered my life when he did? And *stayed* in it. I would have wanted to learn more about him. I might have liked more of what I saw.

I could have easily fallen in love with that stranger who rescued me in Rosewind.

Thirty-Nine

"What is on your mind?" Prince Rion asks as he whirls me around the ballroom.

My face heats in realization; I've been thinking about the way I feel in his arms. How it feels to have his hand at my back. The way his golden eyes look at me as we dance.

I've been thinking that under different circumstances—like if I was with the intriguing stranger in Rosewind who helped me escape capture—I could see myself falling... well, I don't know that I would've let myself fall in love, but he would've at least been a delightful distraction.

But I can't tell him any of that!

Rosewind, Amberle. You were thinking about Rosewind!

"I was just thinking about... the past," I say, hating how breathless my voice sounds, but grateful I can answer with something less revealing.

Rion stiffens, then forces a smile. "*Ah* yes. We did say that we'd talk about our past. I had hoped we could have the conversation later, but we could discuss it now."

A tingling sensation wraps around my core, then up and around my shoulders, feeling like a small whirlwind that will rise and lift my hair, but it never does. I send a questioning glance up at him. *What is going on?* I want to ask. *What was that feeling?*

He winks and gestures with his eyes looking up briefly, then mouths, *"It's watching."*

My pulse quickens. *The magic. Right.* The physical sensation is new, but I try to ignore it. I should have guessed that any mention of our past would bring it into hyper-focus. Does all of Faerie have a close-up of every pore on my face and the pent-up tension in my wings?

"Remember when we were younglings, you told me that humans gathered sweets from hollowed-out-logs?" he muses. At least the prince doesn't notice my nerves at the watching magic.

"Wait. No, *you* told me that—"

In one sweeping motion, he stops our dancing and leans his face very close to mine. Our noses nearly touch. Our breaths mingle together in the shared air between us. I fear he's about to kiss me when he whispers, "Tell me... when was the last time you had *cryspes?*"

My mouth waters, and I can't help the way my eyes glaze over at the mention of the sugar-coated funnel cakes.

Rion laughs and backs away to lead me in the waltz again.

"Not since the Summer Solstice celebration before my father and I left. I haven't had *cryspes* in decades!" I lick my lips; grateful he didn't misunderstand my idiotic reaction to the mention of the treats as my desire to kiss him. "Why? Do you have some here?"

The prince frowns. "No. But I wish I did."

"They're my favorite."

"I remember," he whispers.

"So, why did you bring it up?" I scowl.

"You mentioned the past. It came to mind." He pauses, then cocks his head to the side. "What part of our past were you thinking about?"

"I never said I was thinking about *our* past." But my cheeks burn, betraying the fact that I was very much thinking about *us.*

"Amberle?" he prods when I don't immediately answer.

"I-I was thinking about the day," I stammer. "In Rosewind."

"Oh?" He grins, signaling he's eager to play this secret game. "What made you think about that day?"

The flush deepens and trails up my neck, so I turn my head away, pretending that something has caught my attention across the room. I wonder if the magic can see it. But when I catch the furious stare of Princess Mora, I look away again and back up at the prince.

"You were different," I say. "I mean, I didn't recognize you..." I drop my head and trail off while biting the inside of my cheek. Hard. What am I trying to say? What am I confessing? *But I kind of thought that if you stayed in my life, I might fall for you?*

Prince Rion tilts his head down, forcing my eyes to look at him. "I was glamoured."

"Yes, but even if you weren't magick'ed," I say, remembering his terrible glamour; he looked exactly the same as he does right now, "I wouldn't have recognized you. You were..."

So different? Mature? Dangerously alluring? I scramble to change the subject.

"If I remember right, *you* were the one who told me about sweets in logs," I say. "I climbed into one because you said it contained cryspes and you trapped me inside!"

"I had a good reason." He smirks.

"Which was..."

"I don't want to say."

He captures my eyes, his flitting back and forth between mine.

"What's on *your* mind?" I ask.

"I'm thinking about cryspes," he jests, but pulls me close and whispers in my ear. "And about what you were about to say before you changed the subject."

Part of me melts and the other part wants to bolt from the room. I don't know what's come over me, but my skin is buzzing. Thankfully, Rion recognizes my alarm, and the tension on my back slackens as he changes the subject.

"Thinking back on the day we met in Rosewind," he muses,

mostly to himself, "you didn't look much different than you do now. And you look so obviously like *Amberle* now. I don't know why I didn't recognize you then." The prince's face has taken on a sort of dazed look.

"Then why didn't you recognize me?"

He presses his lips together tightly, staring at me with an intensity that steals my breath, but I can't look away. We're being *watched*. Possibly by all of Faerie. Probably by the king. Definitely by Gnacia.

"My memory was flawed. I remembered your beauty, but it wasn't accurate."

My beauty? What?

I hadn't realized that we'd stopped dancing again. Rion drops the hand that held mine and lifts it to cup the side of my face. His fingers send sparks along my skin and it's all I can do to remain still. "I always thought you were beautiful, but my memory didn't do it justice—"

"Prince Orion?" a familiar voice interrupts.

It's *the* voice.

It's the winter fae I overheard earlier. The one with a sinister plan.

I close my eyes and drop my head, grateful for the interruption, annoyed by the interruption, but most of all... thrilled that *she* interrupted so I can identify her.

"I wondered if I could have some time with you, too?" Her voice is sweet, but I don't dare look at her yet. I don't trust my expression. "You've been dancing with Amberle a long time..."

"Of course," the prince says, his tone and volume back to his princely, proper self. He releases me from his arms, but keeps my hand clutched in his and lowers his head. "I trapped you in that log because I thought it was the best way to keep you."

My eyes fly to his, and I'm suddenly terrified for him. He's about to take this fae into his arms.

"It was a pleasure dancing with you, Amberle."

Forty

My mouth is full of spider webs, so all I can do is nod as the prince lowers his lips to brush the back of my hand. The heat of his mouth sends a jolt that ignites my skin, then trails up my arm before skittering down my neck and spine. I force my body to remain still, hoping the shiver doesn't show.

I glimpse snow-white hair, then shift to see the profile of Frost Neige, the winter dryad, as the prince waltzes with her.

Frost? Internally, I scold myself. *Frost is a conspirator?*

When I learned the prince liked wings, I determined to get close to Frost, thinking she'd be a serious contender. But I didn't. When I realized befriending a winter fae would be beneficial to getting around the watching magic, I also thought of Frost. But I never put the time in to form a relationship with her. Instead, I've been so focused on other things, she's slipped through my notice. If I'd just gone with my initial instincts to get close to her, I might've uncovered her nefarious plot sooner. Maybe I'd have more information about it. Maybe I'd already be gone from this Tourney, with my father freed.

She admitted she didn't kill Juniper, but what if she's

connected to her death? What if I could have prevented her murder?

But I cannot change the past, only move forward. I pivot and try to act casual as I search for Gnacia.

The faun is nowhere in the ballroom, although I assume she's watching the revel from *somewhere*. I wish I could just whisper to the winter magic that she should find me, but at least a few curious fae could still be watching me.

So I make another plan and find Tierney instead. With the right choice of words, I can convince the autumn fae to find Gnacia for me. It's easy to spot the orange-and-black colors of her painted lady butterfly wings, so I hurry through the other contestants and the fire-breathing entertainers to the small group she's huddled with.

I see that she's opted for a different decaying strategy than she did while we decorated. Instead of a plunging neckline and slit up her thigh, the midnight blue fabric that covers from her throat to her ankles has varying sizes of tears in strategic places that show nothing and everything at once.

It's not unexpected to see her with her closest friend Cerule, but I quickly realize that she's chatting with my fan club: Princesses Mora and Shay, Clove, and Raine. But I don't let it dissuade me from enacting my plan.

"Tierney, do you know if anyone had planned to say a few words about Juniper at this revel? It is supposed to double as a wake in remembrance of her."

Tierney's eyes narrow, and Cerule leans closer too.

"What do you care?" Cerule interjects.

I lean closer to both of them and look Cerule in the eye when I say, "I assure you, I had *nothing* to do with her death. I liked Juniper. I would never harm her."

"She's right," Tierney says. "C'mon Cerule, let's find that king's assistant. Someone should say a few words."

Within minutes, the music has stopped, the fire entertainment has paused, and everyone gathers around a makeshift platform erected by Raine and Clove themselves, two spring fae who wanted to show off their building skills.

On the platform stands Nieven Morphyra with Tierney and Cerule. They're suddenly distraught about their lost friend again with dramatic open wounds where they allowed their tears to mar their faces.

Gnacia stands on the other side of the room, but the plan worked. Tierney fetched her, and she summoned Nieven. Now I must wait for an opportune moment to speak with her.

"The purpose of this revel was to allow Prince Orion time with his potential future mates, the contestants of the Consort Tourney, but it is also in remembrance of the autumn fae who lost her life in these very walls." Nieven holds his head high, but his tone is somber, and his movements are graceful and respectful. "And so first, we will have a moment of silence to remember the fallen. And then, if anyone would like to speak a few words about Juniper, we invite them to stand on the platform to share them."

Nieven bows his head, which prompts the entire audience to do the same.

"I would like to say some words," King Estelar interrupts the silence, standing in the doorway. The audience parts and bows lower as he makes his way to the platform. Tierney and Cerule step down, followed by Nieven, as our sovereign stands before us.

"What happened to the Faeven girl was tragic," he says. "And I want to send my deepest condolences to the Faeven family—"

I stop listening and slowly make my way to Gnacia. But she spots my movement and shakes her head slightly before looking back at the king, but holds one finger out at her side.

Not yet.

The king's speech is excruciatingly long and is full of pomp and placating of the autumn fae who might put blame of Juniper's death on the king for not protecting her. He somehow points out that all of Faerie should be even more grateful that the Summer Court is the current High Court and while the faces of the contestants show they believe every word, I know only Lady Pepper and Princess Mora truly do.

When he finally finishes and leaves the room, I look back at Gnacia. I raise my eyebrows and hope she understands my signal that I want to talk. She lowers her head briefly, then gestures with her horn that we step outside the ballroom.

She leaves as Tierney steps up to talk about Juniper. Her words are equally nauseating as the king's, and after a few sentences, I follow Gnacia.

I smile with my teeth when I ask, "Are we being watched out here?"

Gnacia grips my arm and pulls me further down the hallway and into a small sitting room. She shuts the door behind us. "The magic is focused on the events in the ballroom. You may talk freely here. I assume you have some useful information?"

No longer do I feel the crackle of the magic, so I nod. "I overheard a conversation between two winter fae. I think they were using the projection magic to talk to one another."

"Did they know you were listening?"

"I don't think so. They were behind one of the large flower arrangements and that area of the ballroom was vacant of anyone else before I happened by. No, I believe they were certain they were alone."

"Good. Did you identify who?"

I take a breath. "I identified one fae by her voice: Frost Neige."

Gnacia's lips tighten.

"I don't know who she was talking to, but it sounded like they will kill any fae who impedes their plans."

"And what are their plans?"

"I don't know, but there was something in her tone. A sinister edge, even for a winter fae."

Gnacia steps closer to me, places both hands on my shoulders, and wills me to look into her eyes. It's the first time I've noticed their exact shade of deep violet. Different from a faun's typical dark brown. "Amberle, this is important. What exactly did you hear?"

"She said she didn't kill Juniper..." I speak slowly, repeating the exact words.

Gnacia drops her hands and folds her arms.

"She said it was premature and..." I close my eyes briefly as I recall the rest. "And that there are still too many contestants to know which might be in the way."

"Go back to the revel, Amberle. We will take it from here."

I nod, then slip back into the revel before Tierney has even left the platform.

Forty-One

RION

My eyes can't help but fall on Amberle when she re-enters the ballroom. Her presence draws me in like a moth to a flame. No, the feeling is even more deadly. I'm reeled in like a trow's fiddle.

She still favors her injured wing. It hangs a hair lower than the other. But it's not her wing that causes my chest to tighten and my jaw to clench. There's something about her expression. Something has happened between when we danced and now.

Did our dance affect her? Did she leave because she was upset another stole me away?

My heart flutters against my ribcage, filled with a levity that is forbidden with her. But it's a levity I haven't felt in decades, not since I was a youngling.

No assumptions, Rion, I remind myself.

I cannot assume anything. Amberle has kept her distance and her heart locked away in a gilded cage despite her outward show of wearing my gift: the crystalized sunbeam.

I hate that it gives me hope.

And I hate that I must remind myself of her words to squash that hope.

But I didn't lie. We weren't friends.

I suppress my curiosity and turn back to the speaker, Tierney. This moment is for Juniper Faeven. Not Amberle.

Tierney's words about her friend have been as heartfelt as a full fae can make them. Though fae abhor the wailing emotion of humans, fae are immortal and death is rare, so they still feel sadness. They still mourn.

As I listen to Tierney's memories of Juniper as a youngling playmate back in the Autumn Court, I get a better picture of who Juniper was. Her magic was powerful, her family was influential and wealthy. However, it almost seems as if Tierney is faulting her friend for not being *cruel* enough.

Being too *kind* is a failing, but I can't help but feel even more respect for Juniper Faeven because of that specific trait.

I glance back at Amberle. I don't know if I'm trying to decipher her thoughts or her reactions as a half-human, but my eyes are drawn to her wing again. She was injured when she found Juniper. It was minor compared to poor Juniper. However, Amberle's accident was indirectly inflicted by whoever murdered the autumn fae. Amberle was still hurt, and I can't help but feel responsible for it. Amberle is fortunate. She's still breathing, but Juniper isn't.

My gaze returns to the dais.

These fae women are here to become my potential bride. Only one will take that role, but broken hearts and injured pride are a real and expected possibility. Still, I wanted none of them to receive bodily harm.

Juniper's senseless death was a tragedy. I hope Wyn arrives soon and can investigate what happened. I dread that he'll discover it's related to the Tourney, but I need to know. None of the fae's lives are worth my hand in marriage.

Although I fear my father will feel differently.

Tierney drones on. Her words soon veer into a speech that sounds more about her than about her friend. I can't listen to it anymore, so I make my way to the dais.

Tierney's eyes flit to me, but I keep moving forward through the parting crowd.

"She would have made a wonderful queen. I think Juniper could have been very happy with Prince Orion," Tierney says as she turns to me as I step up onto the platform. Her misty eyes turn predatory for an instant.

"Prince Orion," she says, "would you like to say something about Juniper?"

"I would," I say and take her place.

She curtsies but doesn't step off the platform. Instead, she stands just behind me, acting as if this dais is hers. Or that the place next to me is *hers*. I see what's she's trying to do, and I could send her away, but I won't take away from this moment any more than she already has by humiliating her.

Instead, I ignore her presence and address the audience.

My memories of Juniper are limited, but I share the story of our date at the beginning of the Tourney and my regret that she and I were robbed of any future conversations. I wish I could say more, but anything else would sound shallow. Juniper deserved genuine honesty.

"If anyone else would like to say something about Juniper Faeven, we would like to hear them," I say.

Nieven Morphyra claps me on the back and takes over. "What an honor for us to hear from the prince himself." His flattering tone is just a bit too honey-sweet, but I ignore it. "It shows the graciousness of our future king, and how beloved the Faeven family is to find friends in the Summer Court."

I hide my grimace as I continue down the steps and Nieven speaks again, "Cerule Rostina, would you like to speak?"

I feel the eyes of nearly every fae in the room, watching me as I pass Cerule on her way to the platform. My feet take me toward the exit. Toward where Amberle stands. I tell myself it's because it's away from the attention of the crowd, but that would only be a half-truth.

Amberle's blue eyes flit to me as I near her, but quickly look away when I slow and stand beside her.

My heart twists when I think of her cutting words again—that she never considered me a friend. Even the thought burns like iron. I pushed my own feelings away to comfort her earlier, but it's not sustainable. I can't keep her here for long. I can't bear it.

Especially not after the way I allowed myself to forget about her earlier look of loathing and lost myself when we danced. I shouldn't dwell on the idea that she might have become lost in it, too.

Some eyes turn back to Cerule, but not most. As much as I wish to hear from the others, I feel like a distraction. I should step out, but the only way to leave without a half dozen ladies following is if I take one of them with me.

I look at Amberle again. She isn't my first choice, not with my maelstrom of emotions, and I'm in no mood to be wooing anyone else right now. Still, I'm curious why Amberle left earlier and came back clearly unsettled.

I'm fooling myself if I think it was jealousy.

"Walk with me?" I ask, keeping my face forward. I feel her eyes on me, so I turn to her and continue, "I fear my presence is taking the attention away from Juniper's memorial."

She nods once, then takes my offered elbow. The touch sends a spark that jolts through my veins. By the twitch of her good wing, I think Amberle feels it too, but she doesn't comment, and we walk out of the ballroom.

"Your speech was lovely," she says when we're a few steps down the corridor.

"I don't want to talk about my speech."

She stiffens. "What do you want to talk about?" she asks, then blurts, "Or do you not want to talk at all? I can be silent. I can—"

"Is everything alright?" I interrupt.

"Whatever do you mean?" She attempts flippancy, but her voice is tight.

I hazard a glance at her, but her expression is unreadable. "Where did you go... *before?*"

She turns toward me, her bluebell-colored eyes watching me and shining in the light of the sconces. There's an openness in them and a pinch between her eyebrows. It's different from the shocked and flushed look that came while we were dancing, and I asked her about funnel cakes.

I hate that *that* expression is etched in my memory. But this one... it changes my earlier curiosity into sincere concern. *What happened?*

"What is it?" I whisper.

"Prince Orion." A breathless servant rushes to us, balancing a wooden tray holding a single crystal glass filled with some type of berry wine. I wonder if it's elderberry for Amberle's wing. "Frost Niege sent this for you." The servant lifts the tray and bows. "She wanted to tell you that your speech 'spoke to her very soul' and she would like another audience with you."

I take the glass, but feel Amberle's arm tighten on mine. "Send her my gratitude," I tell the servant. "And that I'll return shortly."

"Yes, your highness." He bows again, then turns and walks away.

When the servant has disappeared back into the ballroom, I lift the glass to my lips, but Amberle's free hand knocks it from my grip, spilling its contents and shattering on the floor.

"Amberle, what is going on?"

"I shouldn't have left a mess for the servants," she says with remorse, but I can see she doesn't regret knocking it from my hand. It was intentional.

"What's wrong?" I ask, but I don't wait for her answer and release her arm to take her hand instead. "Come. I need to talk to you."

Forty-Two

We step outside, rounding the palace on the northern side, and walk through the tall grass toward the sea. No one followed us, but I feel the buzzing presence of the watching winter magic. I can't say a word until I find a way to evade the invisible eyes and ears of Faerie.

"We're away from the ballroom now," Rion says. "Can you tell me what is going on?"

My heart jolts as I consider how to answer his question and when I duck my head, I realize we're still holding hands. I pull away and fold my arms, then look up at him.

"The magic is always nearby, of course," he says.

My good wing lifts and tenses. He knows what I want to say is dangerous. If I told him what I've learned and the wrong fae overhear...

No, I can't think of it.

Rion steps forward and grips my elbows, then whispers, "What is it?"

My eyes fall to the sand, and I chew on my lip as I dig my toe in the sand. How do I warn him? What could I possibly say to tell him what I need to say without the entire realm listening? Or... understanding.

We are supposed to talk about our past. It gives me an idea.

"Do you remember the games we used to play on that beach?" I ask, glancing at the darkened sea before looking back at him. I hope he'll catch on to what I'm about to hint at.

Rion's eyebrows pinch.

"Remember the one where we'd switch places, acting as if you and Princess Arielle were court servants and Wyn and I were royals?"

The prince still looks confused, and my hope falls down a rung. This might not work. "We only played it once. Remember? Wyn had come back from an excursion with his father to the human world where he learned about something called *pretending*. He said it was something human children enjoyed."

"Yes, he said humans even had troupes of actors pretending as if they were anything and everything but their true selves," he says. "But I remember the game didn't work in our favor."

"Because you couldn't even pretend to be a commoner!" I say and can't help the smile that erupts as I poke him in the ribs. He remembers.

"We're fae, Amberle!" he says and laughs. "None of us can truly lie, not like the humans. And if I recall, none of us were practiced in the fae art of carefully constructing our words for the illusion, so the game failed."

"Those are just excuses, Ri—Prince Orion." I catch myself, remembering that we're being watched. "You didn't even try! Wyn became frustrated, and we never played it again."

"I remember," he says.

Now I laugh. I keep the levity bubbling, but this is the part I want him to pay attention to, so I grab his hand and gently pull him to continue walking down the beach. "Remember that Wyn wanted the scenario to be a... an assassination attempt on the prince—him being the prince and you being the guard who was supposed to protect him?"

"I remember. Arielle was the supposed assassin, but Arielle

wouldn't hurt a pixie!" Rion looks away as if he doesn't want me to see the expression on his face.

I watch him with curiosity, willing him to look back at me, hoping that he will catch onto my hints that I'm trying to warn him of someone and that he—and some of the other contestants—could potentially be in danger.

He feels my eyes and leans closer. "See? We were friends."

It catches me by surprise and as a thrill rushes down my spine, sending a tingle all the way to my toes, I'm suddenly captured into the depths of his gaze.

"I regret ever saying we weren't," I whisper as my heart beats against my chest.

His eyes fall to my lips.

Forty-Three

RION

I yearn to do the one thing I've wanted to do since the instant I found out exactly who she was, standing on that platform in Herdan and accepting the invitation to be in the Consort Tourney. That the reason for my attraction to her while in Rosewind was because I already knew her. I already cared for her. I already wanted her.

I always have.

Amberle's acceptance to that invitation has given me hope because she willingly entered this Tourney for me, even though I sense the wall she's put up around herself.

I pull away, scattering the magic between us. I want to imagine I see disappointment in her eyes, but my memory has made her into someone she's not. She's a blind spot I must recognize. I can't fawn over a childhood crush when my heart's desire is to find a partner who reciprocates my feelings. I must let her go soon. Perhaps at the next Invitational.

We continue walking.

When we reach the edge of the sea, Amberle gazes into the dark waves for several moments. The breeze lifts the white-blonde locks around her face, and her lashes slowly flutter as she ponders on the horizon.

Glutton. I tear my gaze away from Amberle and toward the sea.

"Remember how the game didn't work?" Amberle asks the waves. Her voice is light and airy.

"Our sad attempt to pretend to be something we weren't?" We're still talking about this?

She smiles while slowly turning her head toward me, but I keep my focus on the waves. She heaves a heavy sigh, then brushes a piece of my hair away from my face. I hold my breath as she strokes a finger across my cheek. I close my eyes when the sparking touch sends a shiver that skitters across my brow and down my jaw, spreading like summer fire across my skin and down my neck.

She's acting. That's what her story is about. She's just acting.

"I pray to Vejo that there's never an actual assassination attempt on your life," she whispers into the small space between us.

Wait. This... talk of childhood memories has a hidden purpose. She's trying to tell me something else.

I think back on the memory. On the words she's used.

Pretending.

Assassination.

Is someone threatening to assassinate me? A thrill of fear pulses through my veins. I feel like Amberle wishes to tell me more but is holding back. But why—

The magic.

Thinking quickly, I take her hand and flash one of my disarming, innocent smiles at the magic. "Remember the sandbar that stretches out so far, it feels as if you could walk the entire length of the Sea of Neptulus without sinking?"

"I remember—"

"Come. At this time of night, if we can go out far enough, we might glimpse wild cabyll ushteys as they come up to feed!"

"Doesn't that mean they might come up to feed on us?" Amberle lets out a breathless, nervous laugh, but doesn't resist.

Soon, we're splashing through the water, the bottoms of my

fine trousers soaking in the surf. We slow when Amberle's gown becomes weighty with the water and her steps grow heavy, but we keep moving until we're a fair distance from the beach.

When the magic fades, I say, "We don't have much time. The magic can't follow water into the deep, but it can hover over the sandbar. We have maybe a minute before it navigates to us."

She glances behind us.

I pull her hand close and whisper, "Quickly."

Her eyes snap to mine.

"Is someone plotting to assassinate me?" I ask. "Is that what you've been trying to tell me?"

"I don't know what they're planning," Amberle blurts. "All I know is that it isn't good, and Frost is involved."

I clench my teeth and nod. That's why she knocked the drink from my hand. "Is it connected with Juniper's death? Did Frost have anything to do with her murder?"

"I don't know, Rion. I just couldn't bear it if something happened to you. I had to tell you."

My chest tightens. She couldn't bear it if something happens to me? My hope threatens to blossom and is in real danger of blooming out of control.

The buzzing of the magic zips toward us, creating its own wake through the waves. I turn away from it and wrap an arm around Amberle's back to resume our act of watching for the water horses, but she hisses, and I jerk away.

My hope wanes.

"It's just sore," she whispers, leaning into me with closed eyes and lifting her limping wing.

Of course. I touched her injured wing. I hurt her.

"You should see a healer. Soon."

"Yes, before the others use the weakness against me," she mutters under her breath.

I pull back.

Amberle looks up. "One of them trapped me in that labyrinth, Rion. You know some contestants will do anything to get ahead. I bet Raine already complained to you about how I refused to fly up to hang one of her stupid nine hundred flower arrangements for the revel."

I remember Raine's lengthy monologue on the subject. "She said I should send you home."

Amberle scoffs and rolls her eyes. "I'm not surprised."

Perhaps sending Amberle home would be the wise course of action. But I'm torn. I'm not ready to lose her again. Besides, I need to better understand our shared history or my questions will haunt me forever.

Either way, I'll confer with Gnacia to make a change. I will move the next Invitational up to tomorrow night because it's time to send some fae home.

"Prince. Orion. Illuminae," his tone is mocking, but he's the only one in the entire realm who can get away with it. "Your Highness..." He bows so low, his dark hair tied at his neck flips forward.

"How did you get in here?" I ask, turning from my starry view on my private balcony. I greet my friend, squaring my shoulders with all my crown prince pride and barely suppress a grin. "I should toss you into the stocks for breaking into my chambers!"

"You couldn't if you tried," he quips as a smile splits his face.

I laugh once and he takes large steps toward me, clasping my hand and pounding my back with his other.

"Thank you for coming, Wyn." Although I wish he hadn't disappeared to the Winter Court the moment the Tourney began.

He ducks his head in a bow and steps back to lean against the jamb of the open balcony doors with arms crossed. "I should have guessed that you wouldn't be able to handle fifteen fae women all on your own." He smirks. "You needed to bring in someone who could take a few of them off your hands, did you?"

Wyn doesn't know how close to the truth that is, but dealing with the women is my duty. And it's not why I sent for him.

My humor fades. "No, I hope you can investigate a fae's death. I contacted you the moment I learned of it."

Wyn's arms drop, and he straightens. "Death? There was a death?" He strains to swallow. "Who?"

"Juniper Faeven."

He blows out a breath, although his shoulders are still tight.

I tilt my head. "Haven't you been watching the Tourney? We had a memorial for her tonight."

Wyn grips his temples with one hand briefly before responding. Then looking everywhere but at me, he responds, "I haven't."

I study my friend for several seconds with narrowed eyes. There's something he's not saying. What is it? I think about all the reasons a fae wouldn't watch the Consort Tourney but come up blank.

"Let's go inside," I say. "I'll call for some honey wine."

I wait until Wyn drains one glass while draped over the chaise in my lounge before asking, "Is there an issue with the magic? Is that why you haven't been watching?"

The idea fills me with a thrill I didn't expect, but I already know it's the wrong assumption. I didn't realize how badly I wanted a little privacy.

Wyn sits up, then leans on his knees, cupping his glass with both hands when he says, "I'm sure the magic is fine. I just..." He chuckles low at the ground, then rises to refill his glass. "I just can't watch."

"Why?" I blurt, tossing my free hand, but still sloshing my half-empty glass in the other. "Of all people, I thought my closest friend could watch this very public display of me choosing my future. This is my life, Wyn! I'm not some imm—" But I stop myself. It's too dangerous to admit. Even if he knows the truth. I take a breath, then calm my voice and continue, "I called you because I need your help and I assumed you knew what has happened and what has transpired during this contest since my father insisted the entire realm watch. Now you're telling me you're useless? That your keen observation skills cannot be used because you were not observing?"

He fills his glass to the brim and sips it down before looking at me. "I guess I just don't see the purpose in this... Consort Tourney, Your Highness," he spits with bitterness, then grips a fistful of his hair. "Damn it! Just marry the girl!"

I blanch. I've never seen this sort of vitriol. What is causing it? What troubles him?

My thoughts immediately go to Amberle and last night.

Has Wyn learned how to lie since I've seen him? Has he been watching? Did he see me dance with Amberle? Did he see us slip out during the memorial?

Does he have feelings for her?

"It's not that easy, Wyn," I say with a sigh. Ignoring the brief, fleeting thought. First, there's the fact that I don't really know why Amberle is in the competition. Despite her regret about what happened in the garden, I'm still not sure of her feelings for me. And then there were all those decades she stayed away. But she's not the only star fae in the competition, and her father was once a beloved servant of the court.

But if Wyn has feelings for her... what could that mean when she sees him? Will she reciprocate his affection for her? He did say he was taken aback when he heard her name called. Has he stayed away because *she's* in the competition and he couldn't stand to watch?

"The Tourney... is a distraction, isn't it?" Wyn asks.

My eyes widen and I stare at him for several moments, feeling whiplash at the change in topic. Of course, there's no winter magic allowed in my apartments, which makes it easier to speak freely. But it is still a bold thing for my friend to ask. "You could lose your head if the wrong fae hear you say that."

"Then it's true?"

I scrutinize his expression, trying to discern if he knows the reason for the distraction. He could lose more than just his head for that knowledge. Friend or not.

It makes me wonder if anyone else suspects.

"If you cannot keep your thoughts to yourself, you might as well leave now," I say. "This is dangerous talk. Besides, it's not why I brought you here."

"Right. The Faeven girl." Wyn takes a sip of his honey wine, then settles. It seems he's dropped the topic for now. "What exactly happened to her? You said she was killed?"

I nod. "Behind a wall, in a secret corridor."

Wyn rubs his chin. "I'm sure the answer to my next question is moot, but were there any witnesses?"

"No witnesses, but Amberle found her."

His face lights, and he sits again. "I still find it strange that she is among your potentials. How is it having her back?"

"Actually, I'm glad you brought her up because I learned some information tonight from Amberle that might be important to your investigation," I say, shooting him a pointed look. "You know... the reason I asked you to come?"

"Right." He drains his glass, then sets it on a side table and stands with arms crossed. "What information did Amberle tell you?" Wyn cocks his head. "And how did she get it?"

"She's clever."

"Amberle has always been clever," he says with narrowed eyes. "And you're finally seeing it?" He shakes his head in disappointment, but shrugs it off. "I can't wait to see her. Do you have a date with another of your potential queens soon? Because I might steal our old friend away for an afternoon."

My blood heats. "Can we get back to the topic?"

Wyn stiffens.

"Of course, Your Highness," he says with a bow and without his former mockery.

Heaving a heavy sigh, I say, "I just..." I grit my teeth and close my eyes, collecting myself. "I just don't want to lose any more of them."

"Any more? Or a certain one?" My friend's tone is still sincere.

My eyes fly back open, but I don't comment. Instead, I tell him what Amberle told me tonight. "She thinks there is something sinister going on and it involves Frost Niege."

"Frost Niege? Is she certain?"

"Yes! We both agree that our old friend has always been clever. She knows how to see and hear without being seen or heard."

"How did you finally come to know this about her?"

My thoughts fly to the memory of Rosewind. But as close as we all were as younglings, I cannot tell Wyn her secret about being a thief. It's not my secret to tell.

"Never mind," he says in response to my hesitation. "Not important now. But Amberle mentioned Frost and not any of the other winter fae contestants?" He pauses and looks away. "Who are they?"

"Princess Shay and Luna Diables."

"Right. Not them?"

"No. Amberle didn't name either of them."

"Okay. Then it's hard to know if it's a Winter Court plot or something else."

I nod in agreement. "I plan to bump the next Invitational to tomorrow night. It's time to send some contestants home—"

"So you *are* having trouble with the ladies," he teases, trying to lighten the mood.

"You might have been right about fifteen being a lot to juggle," I confess. "But I plan for Frost to be one of the first."

"No. Don't send Frost home. Not yet."

"But she—"

"It might tip her off and anyone she's working with," he explains. "Better to keep her around until we know more."

"But she could be dangerous."

"True, but I'm here now," he says, but his arrogance is gone. His tone is very matter-of-fact. "Did Amberle say anything else?"

"Just that one of the spring fae, Raine, was giving her trouble."

Wyn waves a hand. "I bet it's nothing Amberle can't handle."

My mind is spinning, but I lean back. There was a crack in Amberle's armor tonight. A vulnerability, although I don't know exactly what it means. I want nothing more than to protect Amberle, but her intentions elude me and half the things she says cut me to the quick. And though I know Wyn is correct, I want nothing more than to get Frost far, far away from the palace.

No, I want her far from Amberle.

Forty-Four

My human attendant, Kenna, tugs and pulls at my hair while I sit motionless in front of the vanity. Although I face my reflection, my eyes are unfocused. I cannot pull my thoughts away from last night.

Tell me… when was the last time you had cryspes?

Rion's golden eyes made my stomach heat and my heart flip. I thought he might kiss me.

And I might have wante—

I suck in a breath and sit straighter. Tonight is the second Invitational. I need more time. I *thought* I'd have more time, but it seems that the prince insisted it happen sooner. I could be cut tonight.

So much for our one-on-one date to discuss our shared past. I should rejoice that I'm avoiding more opportunities to fail, but I don't feel as though I've succeeded, either.

"Did I hurt you?" Kenna's fingers freeze.

Posey steps forward. She's been watching the human with anxious scrutiny this entire time. I've tuned out most of their chatter, but Kenna has learned some elaborate hairstyles since the spring fae disapproved of the chignon at the last Invitational. Posey has asked a hundred questions and inserted her opinion dozens of times in her effort to ensure it looks just right. It warms my heart to hear she cares so much about my success in the Tourney.

As if success can be won with an intricate hair arrangement. I suppose it can't hurt, but I also fear Kenna won't have more opportunities to use her new skills after tonight. After tonight, they will be sent back to the places they don't want to go.

"I'm fine," I assure her. "It wasn't—" I lift a hand, dismissing it, then look at my hairdresser in the mirror. "You didn't hurt me."

Kenna's eyes flutter in relief, then she goes back to pulling and twisting.

At least Frost will leave tonight, and the threat I uncovered will be gone. Or at least the pawn in someone's deadly game. She might be a rook, or a knight, but she'll never be the queen.

The drink she sent to the prince last night may or may not have been poisoned, but I don't regret my actions. I still couldn't risk it. I couldn't stand there and watch him drink his death.

I couldn't bear—

A knock tears me from my thoughts and the three of us snap our heads to the door.

Posey looks at me briefly before moving to answer it.

When she cracks open the door, every earlier thought is gone —including the thoughts of my half-completed hair arrangement. The instant I see the familiar lightning green eyes and pitch-dark hair, I spring toward the door.

"Wyn!" I shout as I barrel into him, throwing my arms around his neck.

He catches me with a *humph*, surprised by my enthusiasm, but his arms quickly wrap around me, crushing me to him.

"Hello, Amberle," he mutters into my ear.

I didn't realize just how much I've missed my friend—the one friend I had no animosity or complicated feelings toward when my father and I left the palace all those years ago. I don't worry about the hurt I might have caused him because he was always leaving me. He often traveled with his father, and when he returned, he and I could always act as if we'd never been apart.

Wyn was my one and only star fae friend at the palace, and neither of us were royalty. We always connected on levels Princess Arielle and Prince Rion could never understand.

"When did you get here?" I ask when we untangle from one another.

I toss a glance over my shoulder at my two attendants. Kenna's expression waffles from confusion to devastation, while Posey's borders on fury while keeping her demure servant attitude intact.

"My hair," I say, lifting a hand to it. "Have I ruined it?"

"Of course not!" Kenna lies.

Posey's expression smooths. "It can be fixed," she says, straightening, then gently guides me back to my seat. "As long as you can control your passions, Amberle."

Passions? My face heats from embarrassment. "It's not—"

"I didn't mean to interrupt. I just wanted to see you," Wyn says, moving back toward the still open door.

"You don't have to go," I say. "Stay."

Wyn grins, then shuts the door behind him and walks toward the vanity.

Posey aims a finger at him, but is clearly flustered. I can see she wants to scold him but isn't sure if he ranks too far above her.

"As long as you can control your passions, I'll stay." Wyn winks at me, then drags a chair from my sitting area to sit closer.

Protesting his statement is pointless, so I ignore them. He always knew how to best me with words, anyway.

"When did you arrive?" I ask him when Kenna resumes her work on my hair.

"Late last night."

"And you waited until now to come see me?"

"It's not my fault you weren't at breakfast."

I fold my arms. I feared facing Rion after last night and

needed more time to gather my composure. Plus, I was anxious about seeing Frost.

"Prince Orion was the one who sent for me," Wyn explains. "I reported to him first."

Hearing that reminds me of the reason Rion sent for him. He said he contacted our friend the moment he learned of Juniper's death.

"Then you've heard?"

Wyn looks at my maids.

"They know about Juniper," I say.

He leans forward, resting his elbows on his knees with an unasked question in his eyes. "Do they know..."

I sense the words he doesn't speak. He's asking if they know I'm the one who found Juniper. I squeeze my eyes shut, but see her broken body on the back of my lids. My eyes fly open and I'm gripping the vanity, my knuckles white. I take a breath and shove my fists into my lap. I can't find my voice, but thankfully, Posey answers.

"We know she found the body," she says.

Wyn reads my discomfort and makes small talk with my maids while Kenna works on my hair.

"Could I have a few moments alone with Amberle before she's expected at the Invitational?" he asks when the human finishes.

Posey glances at me.

"Wyn and I are old friends," I assure her. "And you've already dressed me." I lift the silky violet skirts of my exquisite gown, making the hundreds of beads made of fine gems clink against each other in a pleasing, jingling sound. "All I need are my slippers, and I can manage those on my own."

"Of course," Posey says with a small curtsey, then takes Kenna by the elbow and the two of them walk out the door.

"You don't have much time, and I understand it might be difficult to relive the memory, Amberle, but can you remember anything that might help us catch the killer?" he asks. "Any clue? Anything?"

"Just that she'd clearly been attacked. Violently. But it couldn't have been Tierney or Cerule because they were in the main corridor when it happened. And they also likely didn't know about the hidden passageways."

"I'd like you to show me where you found her after this... ceremony tonight." He seems to chew on the word like it has a bitter taste to it.

After? My stomach twists, but I try to mask it. "What if the prince doesn't pick me and I'm sent back to my hole in the Spring Court?"

"Spring Court, huh? That's where you've been all this time? Is your father there too?"

I shake my head quickly. I've revealed too much. And I'll likely never go back to the Spring Court ever again.

"He's not." I quickly change the subject. "What are your thoughts on the other contestants? Have you discerned anything from the bits you've seen broadcasted?" I don't feel like I've gathered enough information to fully put my weight behind the best match for the prince. But I'm out of time to do it.

Wyn always had a good eye for details. I might be able to observe and move unseen, but I've never had Wyn's natural talent for extrapolating from the tiniest clues.

"Nothing useful. But now that I'm here, I'm hoping to have a better vantage point."

Now that he's here. Maybe he can take over and finish what I've failed.

"Did Rion tell you what I told him last night? About Frost?"

"He said you're as clumsy as ever and a poor goblet of wine was injured in the process."

I roll my eyes, but I'm glad Rion passed on my information.

"I should go," Wyn says, standing. He moves to leave but thinks better of it and walks closer to me with a smirk on his face.

"You know, at first I was surprised you were among the contestants."

Keeping my voice steady, I say, "Because I'm a commoner? A star fae?"

I don't think he knows the truth. Wyn doesn't exactly have the ear of the king. At least I don't think. I was also far from King Estelar's notice... until recently.

Wyn is a master at observation, though. At any time during the Tourney, he might have seen my façade slip. He might have deduced that I'm not exactly here for Rion. I might have to tell him myself before he figures it out on his own. If he hasn't already.

"I swear it was only a momentary thought," he says. "But anyone who knows the truth of the past knows that, of course, you'd have to be a part of it."

I'm not sure what he means, but I shrug and act like I do.

"It's good to see you again, Amberle," he says, his genuine tone filling me with an unexpected warmth that causes my chest to tighten.

"You, too."

Forty-Five

"What do you think the gift will be tonight?" Princess Mora asks Lady Pepper as we stand in our places, waiting for the Invitational to begin. "I didn't get a crystalized sunbeam, so it had better be special."

I tune out Mora's petty talk. It's too much. Especially while my throat is tight, and my muscles are wound.

"What makes you think you're receiving anything?" Princess Shay asks.

I nearly bark out a laugh. *Okay, maybe I do want to listen to this.*

"I told him I've always wanted an onyx pearl from the Underwater Court, you know, the kind that are dangerous for even mermaids to collect?" Mora's voice is light and airy, and on the verge of vomit-inducing.

Bold—requesting the rarest 'queen of the gemstones'.

"The kind they say is cursed?" Didi pipes in. "No, thank you."

My pulse quickens on the word *curse*. I resist the urge to press a palm against my chest to calm my racing heart. *No one here knows about my curse,* I remind myself. The king said that part of the projection was eliminated when I told the prince in the garden. Only Rion and the king and Gnacia know.

The summer princess whips on Didi with narrowed eyes, but a pleased smile. "So you'd *reject* the prince's gift? You'd go home if he gave you something you didn't want?"

"You'd like that, wouldn't you?" Didi snaps.

"Aren't you a cute little star fae!" Mora sings with thick superiority and bats her eyelashes. "The sooner you all go home, the sooner I get the prince to myself. Of course, I'd like that!"

I can't resist rolling my eyes.

The princess turns her attention to me. "Oh stop, Amberle. No one even knows why you're here. You're not royalty. You're not noble. You're just—"

"But everyone wants *you* here?" Princess Shay interrupts, stepping toward Mora.

Mora attempts to keep her confident air, but I see it crack, just a little. "You care about the halfling? Are you saying you're glad she's here?"

Princess Shay steps closer, and pulls shadows around herself, making her look more severe, more intimidating. Her smile is full of malice and distaste. Maybe I'm getting cut tonight, but I'm loving every second of this. "You're a spoiled little princess who thinks that because she replaced a beloved summer princess—"

"*I am* a summer princess."

Princess Shay bares her teeth, and Princess Mora flinches.

"Why do you think *you* are here, Mora?" Shay asks, injecting a sickly sweetness into her tone. "Because until Princess Arielle left, most of us believed this entire Tourney was a ploy to highlight the grand love story of the lovely Arielle and her Prince Orion." She looks around at the rest of us and is rewarded with a few head nods. "But when Arielle baffled us all and left the competition, the game changed. You are not a replacement for the *beloved princess*. You are *not* Arielle, so stop acting like you've already won. Personally, between the *halfling* and you, my coin is on the former."

Lady Pepper gasps, but everyone else seems delighted by Shay's cutting remarks. The double-insult doesn't get past me, of course, but I'm astonished that the winter princess dislikes someone more than me. And Shay *hates* me.

Nieven Moryphra walks in, but the two royals stare at each other for a few more seconds before directing their attention at him.

The prince walks in behind him with a tight smile and my pulse quickens. He looks different. Perhaps it's the way the light bounces off his walnut-hair, or the gleam of the gold in his eyes I can see even from here. Or maybe it's the way the embroidery of his dark blue, velvety jacket tied with a string at the side shines in the light of the sconces. Its deep v-neck shows off the flowy ivory shirt underneath.

I will him to look at me, but his eyes only briefly trail over all of us as something dark flutters in above his head. He glances up at it and watches as it perches on his shoulder. It's a raven with sleek, jet black wings.

Didi leans toward me and whispers, "Is that... Stjarna?"

Stjarna? "I uh..."

"You know, the prince's raven?" My friend cracks a smile. "I thought you had history with the prince? You don't know about his pet?"

"What is it? A *morrigu* or something?" I ask, eyeing the bird. Most morrigus, or raven shifters, are female and can change at will from a human form to a raven. I blink away the sudden spots that obscure my vision and ignore the hard pit in my stomach.

"No. It's just a common raven." Didi smiles and shakes her head, studying me. "You really don't know about him?"

Him. My vision clears and the feeling in my gut disappears. There was a raven outside my window once. I wonder...

"Stjarna has been Prince Orion's companion for near a decade," Princess Mora says, looking me up and down with distaste. "It's still shocking you didn't know. Have you been living in an underjordiskes mound all these years?" She hitches a hand on her hip and exaggerates her frown that stinks of contempt.

I don't answer her question and instead direct my attention back to the prince and his bird. Then mumble mostly to myself, "He hasn't mentioned him."

That part hurts a little.

"He's a beloved pet," Didi says without judgment in her tone. "But he's a lower creature, a wild bird, so he comes and goes."

My mind doesn't have time to question *why* Rion hasn't told me about him because behind him, several containers are wheeled into the room. They're of varying sizes and shapes and are made of different materials. Some are covered with cloth.

"I count six," River, one of the underwater fae, says.

"What's in them, do you think?" Lily asks.

"Whatever it is, it looks like six of us are staying and eight of you are going home," Mora declares, beaming at all of us.

The reality sets in. Vejo above, I'm going home tonight. A pit forms, and the acid in my stomach threatens to eat through my gut. My heart races, thumping a frantic rhythm, *it's too soon. Too soon.*

Why did the prince insist on pushing this Invitational to tonight?

It's too soon.

I informed Gnacia and Rion about Frost, but she must be working with someone else. She *has* to be working with someone else, but I'm out of time!

Maybe with Wyn here, they no longer see the need for me. Will he take over? Can I update him on what I've learned? He'll protect Rion's life. They're friends.

But that means... Will I get to see my father soon?

I try to picture my father's face, but is my recollection even accurate? How much has he changed in seventy years? I've changed from a youth to a woman in that time—he won't recognize me. I itch to see him, but I'm horrified that the king won't uphold his bargain. Will he find a loophole and not release him?

No. I've spied as he'd asked. I reported who didn't love the prince. I even discovered Frost's duplicity.

Maybe I'll see my father *tonight*. Maybe after tonight we'll both be free from the games of the court.

The king wanted me to reveal any fae who are not here for the prince. Not just threats to him. I'll share every drop of information. It will be enough.

I bite back the fear crawling up my throat and thundering in my ears ... *is it enough?*

I swallow and wipe my palms discreetly on my skirt, but they slide over the beads and cause a distracting jangling. Fortunately, no one seems to notice because Nieven lifts both hands and announces with a wide grin, "Ladies, it's time."

I sense the buzzing winter magic enter the room and feel the attention of it, like a bitter polar blizzard on my face.

All chatter among the contestants dies with the announcer's words.

"I think we all know just how close Prince Orion is with Stjarna."

Rion shares a look with the bird on his shoulder, then smiles at the floor. Stjarna lets out a clipped *kraa!* causing the ladies to let out nervous chuckles, but they share knowing looks.

But all I can do is stare. At all of them. At the contestants. At the crown prince. At his bird. I can't help but feel like an outsider watching the scene. I feel as if I've been asleep a hundred years, or actually living in an underjordiskes mound like Princess Mora suggested.

How did I not know? I've been completely blind to this pet— this fowl—that is clearly an important part of Rion's life.

"For tonight's invitational," the announcer continues. "The prince wants to give the fae he is inviting to stay a creature of their own." Nieven eyes the prince before turning back to us. "He wants the fae he chooses to have an animal companion. He has more than one reason for this decision, but the creature will be yours to keep if you choose, even after you leave the Consort

Tourney." Keeping up the dramatics, he drops his shoulders and his smile when he says, "But... Prince Orion won't gift a creature to all contestants. Some of you *will* leave tonight." He leans on the word, although we've all guessed it. The prince isn't keeping everyone this time.

The announcer steps back, then gestures with an outreached hand that the prince should take over.

"I am not well acquainted with all of you, but I have chosen creatures I feel fit you best." His smile is tight. He's nervous. "I hope you are pleased with what I have chosen for you."

Then he steps toward the containers and plucks the first one from the pile. It's medium-sized and dome-like and is covered with a silver cloth.

"Princess Shay Malov," the prince says.

The winter princess strides toward the prince with her head held high and a half smile on her lips.

With flair, Prince Orion lifts the cloth, revealing a snowy owl. Its head spins now that its view is no longer obscured by the cloth. Its dark eyes soak in the room until they finally land on the princess.

The owl tilts her head. Princess Shay does too, prompting the owl to *hoot* at her then flex her wings.

"Well, aren't you majestic?" the princess says.

Rion smiles. When Shay catches it, she straightens.

"Princess Shay, will you accept this gift and remain in the competition to see if we might make an agreeable match?"

"I will, Prince Orion." Princess Shay carefully takes the cage from Rion's fingers, then walks back to the group.

Tierney is next. She gets a chattering gray squirrel, followed by Luna, who is presented with a spider—unsurprising since the winter fae have an affinity for them. Frost's brows narrow; perhaps she suspects not all winter fae will be asked to stay. She's not wrong.

Didi's name is called next.

My friend practically skips to the prince, her excitement

evident in the tightness of her shoulders and the bobbing of her head.

The prince moves to lift a crate from the dwindling stack, then sets it on the ground between them. He snaps a finger, prompting a servant to rush forward with a tool to pry the lid from the box.

"Didi Beechriver," he says before the servant is finished. "Will you accept this gift and remain in the competition to see if we might make an agreeable match?"

Didi leans back with arms folded and says, "I'll stay, but I won't make any promises about accepting the creature until I see it."

Princess Mora chokes on the air, but I laugh out loud. The prince chuckles and gestures as the lid is lifted.

Didi squeals when her eyes land on the contents of the crate.

"Yes! Yes! Of *course*, I'll accept and stay and see if we might—" she cuts herself off when she leans down to scoop up the stripped gray feline with violet eyes. A cait sith.

She talks to it in a high-pitched voice as she walks back to the group, tuning everyone and everything else out. It's endearing and I can tell by the glimmer in the prince's eyes that he thinks so, too.

And just like that, there are only two containers left. My eyes drop to the ground, and I take a deep breath. I'll be a graceful loser. I dread the rejection—but remind myself it's just my pride. I'll recover.

The first container is another bird-like cage covered with a black cloth. It's about the same size as the one for Princess Shay's owl. And another crate at least twice the size of the cait sith crate.

Two left.

I look around at who hasn't yet received a creature. Besides myself, Lady Pepper and Princess Mora of the summer fae are empty-handed; plus all three underwater court contestants; Raine and Clove from Spring; Cerule of Autumn; and, of course, Frost from Winter.

I've done my duty—I'll see my father. I silently repeat the reason I've come to the palace over and over in my mind, preparing for the sting of rejection.

I'm leaving tonight.

I still care about Juniper. So, I will have to figure out a way to find Wyn before I go. I'll take him to the place of Juniper's death for his investigation. And though Rion does sometimes act like a spoiled child, he's not the same fae I remember. In fact, he might be one of the kinder fae I've had the displeasure of knowing. I don't want him to end up tied to a fae who doesn't see him for who he's become. The qualities I've come to admire in him are the very same that others will disdain. I don't want that for him.

I don't want a cruel queen ruling us *all*.

But I don't know who to recommend to the king. I thought I'd have more time. The king is exacting; he'll demand information on every single remaining fae in the competition.

And I don't have it.

My body trembles. Oh, Vejo, what if I don't have enough?

I've spied, but have I come up short? Not even the gatekeeper of the heavenly realm can intervene and help me dig up information after I've been eliminated from the Tourney.

After everyone has seen my face, how can I be a thief? I might have revealed my identity on the grand Faerie stage, only to fail to achieve the one thing I wanted: my father's freedom.

I fear how this will end. For all of us.

Forty-Six

Nieven Morphyra claps the prince on the back. "I think it's time we change things up before you gift these two creatures," he says, gesturing at the last two containers. He turns to us with a glimmer of knowing, and then winks. "Because not every creature Prince Orion wanted to gift would fit into a compact cage or crate."

The coil wrapped around my insides releases just a notch. There are more gifts? Several sighs of relief surround me, proving I heard Nieven correctly. But I don't have an assured spot yet.

The prince nods with a pleased smile right as a sylph floats into the room and heads in our direction. It's a rare one, iridescent and the color of a sunrise.

"Such as a wind spirit! A sylph!" the prince says as it flies over his head and aims for its intended. "I think she'll pick you before I can call your name, but Cerule Rostina, will you please step forward?"

Cerule's eyes widen and her cheeks flush with pleasure. She always seems to be in Tierney's shadow, but now all attention is on her. The autumn fae skips forward, then stands on the balls of her feet while she listens to the prince's words.

"Will you accept this sylph and remain in the competition to see if we might make an agreeable match?" he asks.

"I will," she says, but her eyes fixate on the air spirit. Cerule steps away, prompting her sylph to fly next to her, hovering at her side.

Next, a pale pink light wisp flutters in. It stops next to the prince with more patience than the sylph.

"Lady Pepper," he says.

Poised as always, Lady Pepper steps toward him and stands with fingers interlocked in front of her. She agrees to stay and moves back to her spot in the group, the wisp hovering just above her head. She beams up at her companion before facing forward again.

The prince has already chosen six to stay, and two creatures remain. I scrutinize the large crate and the outline of a cage and ponder who they're for. At least with so many fae leaving, there is a much smaller pool of fae to sift through and determine which might be the best mate for the prince. Prince Orion is unknowingly making this easier.

But is there any possibility that one of those creatures is for me?

I hate the fragile hope that threatens to shatter, then rob all the air from my lungs.

To distract myself, I clasp my hands behind my back to hide the slight tremor in them as I tick the remaining possibilities in my head. Readying for my recommendation to the king when this is all over.

Tierney cannot love the prince. I've heard her say so from her very lips. Rion wants romance, so it cannot be her. I have no qualms about Luna, but I know little about her. I won't have time to learn about her either.

The only fae I can truly endorse right now, right in this moment, is Didi or... Princess Shay.

Princess Shay might hate me, but she's royalty. She understands the ways of the court. And she seems open to a relationship with Rion. She's also clearly close with the queen. I don't oppose her.

But I must know who the last two will be.

It would be too deliciously perfect if Mora is sent home. Or Raine. Or Clove. All three getting sent away is more luck than I can hope for.

Lady Pepper has promise. I have nothing negative to say about any of the underwater fae, but the prince hasn't shown interest in any of them. None of them have pursued him, either, not like the other courts.

Didi must feel my trepidation because she adjusts her *cait sith* to hold it in one arm and reaches over to squeeze my fingers.

"He'll pick you," she assures me. "There's no way you're leaving."

"I hope so." My response is instinctual. The words astound me because I know she's wrong.

But I'm not ready to go.

I need more time to gather information, I tell myself. If I don't have the information the king asks for, he could keep my father imprisoned indefinitely. Or worse.

Rion's gaze skitters over each one of us. I think his eyes remain locked with mine a wisp's spark longer than the others, but I can't be sure and his focus skips back to the fae he intends.

"Princess Mora," he says.

Just like the youngling I remember, the summer princess lets out a little yelp, then hops in place before rushing forward to stand in front of him.

The prince lifts the covered cage, then in one fluid motion, removes the dark cloth and reveals a shiny, jet-black raven.

Princess Mora's hands drop to the side as her head snaps to the prince. I can't see her expression, but I can imagine the jaw drop.

A piercing sensation twists between my ribs.

Kraa! the bird cries when the summer princess ducks her head to peer into the cage.

"Princess Mora," says the prince.

He's gifted her a raven.

"Will you accept this gift..."

A <u>raven</u>.

"And remain in the competition..."

Just like his.

I stop listening. I've heard the words enough times already. And, knowing Mora, I know her response. But what does it mean that he gave Princess Mora the exact species that he cherishes and adores? Perhaps it's even *his* raven's mate?

My chest burns and I force myself to breathe again.

I haven't considered Mora, but she is worthy competition. She, too, knows how the courts work. She has lived in Isi Aura all her life. And Mora has a rapport with Rion. *Could* she mean more to him than I thought? *Might* Rion—*Prince* Orion—actually consider her?

The bird is removed from its cage, and it perches on a sconce directly behind Mora when she takes her place among the group again.

I'm torn between disbelief and revulsion, so caught up in possible meanings for the gift that the next name is already called before I can brace myself for the devastation that punches down my throat.

Because he doesn't say my name.

Surely, I misunderstand, because it can't be *her*. There's no way that *she* would be allowed to stay while I'm sent away.

But she marches forward, her white hair a blur, gripping her demure attitude with the folds of her dress and the upturn of her lips.

Prince Orion opens the crate, releasing a large cu sith that immediately rushes to her, rubbing his canine snout against her leg and wagging its thick tail high in the air until she crouches down and allows it to lick her face.

The prince laughs.

She laughs.

He asks the question.

She rises, pushing a loose lock of her bone-white hair from her pale face and lifts her chin when she answers, "I will."

Thick dread mixed with painful shards fills my gut. Frost Niege is staying.

And I'm being cast away.

Forty-Seven

My vision blurs and I feel sick. Quiet chattering erupts among the group as the rejected and the chosen alike discuss the prince's choices tonight.

Didi is saying something, denying that it's the end and exclaiming that the prince made a mistake in not choosing me, but I can't focus on her words. They're all tilted and sideways and falling like they're afflicted with autumn's wretched decay.

Nieven says something and the group silences, but the pressure surrounding my heart only increases, and I can only focus on the splintering and widening of the cracks that break it painfully apart.

"Yes," Rion says with a smile in his voice. I glance at him and he beams, striking another painful blow that shudders straight to the center of my bones. "There are *other* creatures I cannot bring inside." His smirk causes more than one lady to weaken at the knees and everyone not yet chosen to stand a little taller.

"Wait, what?" I ask no one.

The group shuffles out the door.

Didi grips my hand, pulling me along with her, and smiles. "He's not done gifting familiars. C'mon, we're going outside."

Snap out of it, Amberle! I scold myself. I must keep my head on until the very end, even though it feels like a death march as we walk through the corridors as a group. This is just delaying the inevitable because the prince doesn't intend on gifting a creature to everyone still remaining.

The sky is clear when we step outside, revealing the expanse of glittering stars and a pale moon that hangs over the sea.

Didi grips my arm with her free one—the one not cradling her cait sith. "He said we're going to the shore."

"For the underwater fae," I guess.

"Maybe?"

We reach the beach of the Sea of Neptulus and my thoughts immediately go back to last night when Rion and I came out here alone during the revel. My eyes trail to him and I can't help but wonder if he remembers it, too.

Of course, he remembers but it hardly matters anymore. He's already decided to keep Frost despite what I shared. I just hope keeping her doesn't turn out to be a deadly mistake.

My thoughts are interrupted by the splashing of a small, round creature that captures our attention, and we all turn to look at what it is.

"River Lyn?" the prince says, gesturing at the marine animal.

River steps forward, but then lets out a high-pitched squeal and rushes into the surf, not caring that she's soaking her skirts. When big, round black eyes and a spotted white pelt pushes to the surface, I see what River's creature is. It should have been obvious. As a selkie herself, it makes sense that the prince would gift River a harbor seal.

"Oh, she's adorable!" River squeals again and reaches down to stroke the head of her animal. It shivers and splashes in pleasure, leaving River drenched. But by her laughing, she obviously doesn't mind.

"River!" Rion shouts. He's laughing too. "Will you—"

"Yes, I will!" River says from the sea, lifting one hand without looking at the prince.

He laughs again, shaking his head and looking at the water,

then turns back toward us. "Do you see why we had to come out here?"

The prince is rewarded by joined laughter from those still dry on the shore. Some sound a little too forced. Especially the other two underwater fae. Perhaps the reserved water fae are more interested in him than I'd assumed.

"Well... should we head back?" Princess Mora asks, stroking the head of her raven perched on her arm. "I'm sure those you're kicking out would like to begin packing." Even in the dark, I can see the hard, satisfied look she throws at me. The words she said to me when I first entered the palace shout in my head.

"Enjoy this while it lasts," Mora hissed, her nails biting into my skin. "When the king hears about this, he'll reverse the mistake he's made. He'll put me in my rightful place and send you back to yours."

Forty-Eight

"Actually, there's one more," the prince says.

Lily and Aqualis, the other two underwater fae, stand straighter, but I've already accepted my fate. The last creature is surely a marine animal intended for one of them.

"Amberle Kindra?" Rion's voice is soft and warm. Hearing my name with that tone, with such... *affection?* No. It's not that. It *can't* be that. Gnacia said there was no guarantee that I'd stay. After everything that has happened, it would be best if Rion just sends me away. But it sends a heated spark up my spine.

Didi nudges me and whispers, "He said your name."

Realizing I've been frozen and unmoving for much too long, I stumble forward, taking his outreached hand. He didn't offer his hand to any of the others, so I feel a little strange, but once he has my fingers, he pulls me closer.

"I remember how fascinated you were with these when we were younglings," he whispers. "This isn't conventional and my father and Gnacia pushed against it because of the... danger. But I told them you could handle her. I *know* you can handle her."

I turn to look up at him and feel my very bones melt at the flash of *something* I see in his eyes.

My eyes widen. *No. It isn't... it can't be—*

A high-pitched *Reeeee!* sounds through the air, followed by a loud snort.

I turn to see her. Her hide is pale white in the moonlight with a long-braided mane to match. But it's her eyes that tell me what she is. Crimson red, gleaming like the deadly creature she is.

"It's a... it's a cabyll ushtey," I whisper.

In his excitement, Rion pulls me forward to greet her. She's in her land horse form so her nose is equine and not hooked and her teeth are flat, but I still feel the skipping of my heart, the adrenaline rushing to my limbs. My instincts scream a warning that this creature could kill me in an instant. Because she could.

"You can't see her as well in the dark," Rion says. He's very animated and using his free hand. "But she's a pale blue color and when she touches the seawater, her hide shifts darker to camouflage with the sea and to match—"

When his voice catches and he clears his throat and doesn't finish his thought, I turn to him with furrowed eyebrows. "To match what?"

"Your eyes." He turns away again and releases my hand.

I don't allow myself to think about that now. I'm too enamored with this creature, this water horse, this cabyll ushtey.

And she's mine.

Walking slowly, I keep my eyes locked with hers. When I get closer, she bows her head and when I reach out to feel the smooth skin between her eyes; she lets out a low, *huh-huh-huh,* of pleasure.

"She likes you," Rion whispers, his words buzzing my ears and his breath lifting the escaped wisps of hair from my neck. Before I can turn and comment, he straightens. "Amberle Kindra, will you accept this gift and remain in the competition to see if we might make an agreeable match?" His voice is low and rough.

I turn and lift my eyes to his. His gaze drops to my lips like they've done too many times lately.

He's asking me to stay.

I clear my throat and say, "I will."

His smile falls slightly. "Do you like her?"

My eyelashes flutter. "I love her."

"Good." His smile returns and he leans down one last time. His mouth is so close, I wouldn't have to move much to press my lips to his. "I hope we can ride together then. Soon."

Epilogue

RION

Saying goodbye to Lily and Aqualis—of the Underwater Court—is painless. Both are gracious and clearly look forward to going back to the comfort of their court. Neither bother returning to the palace to collect any mementos from the Tourney and merely bid River and a few of the other remaining contestants goodbye before quickly walking into the surf, and disappearing beneath the waves.

"You're making a mistake," Clove says when she approaches me. Raine sidles next to her with a matching look of fury.

A farewell to all the rejected is expected of me, but I didn't miss that several of the ladies still in the competition leave as soon as the ceremony is over. Including Amberle. It's not expected of them to stay, but I had wished at least she would linger.

Alas, she was one of the first. I can't even see the silver of her hair walking up the beach anymore.

"My father took you in when you wanted to hide in the Spring Court," Raine says, pulling my attention to her.

"If Prince Orion married every daughter of a noble who invited him into their house, the entire realm would be related to the high court," Wyn says, stepping next to me.

The spring fae glower at him. They're seething and I expect

they planned to attack my choices of keeping certain fae while they are being sent away—like Amberle—but lucky for me, Wyn's presence seems to curtail their plans.

Instead, Raine steps forward and eyes me. "Clove is right. You've made a mistake." She glances at Clove, then back at me. "Send for me when you've realized your foolishness and wish to remedy it."

She turns on her heel and walks across the sand in a huff.

Clove watches her go before turning back to me, flashing her pointed teeth. "Don't send for me."

She walks away too, and I feel my shoulders relax.

"I've changed my mind," Wyn says as we watch the fae retreat from the shore and back to the palace grounds. "I *don't* envy your position. You can have your, now ten, fae females to yourself and all the excitement that goes with it."

I sigh. "I imagine this part will only get harder."

"It will. The fae are not keen on rejection," he says. "I'm betting only two might have that... that *thing*, Amberle mentioned at your first 'meeting.' The human quality. What was it? *Humility?*"

"I thought you weren't watching the Tourney?"

"Alexander helped me to the tomes with the recorded events of the competition. I haven't watched every moment, but many of the important ones."

Important ones. *Like the ones involving Amberle?*

Every mention of her name, even in thought, sends pixies swarming in my gut.

"So you heard her say she was here for her father?" I ask.

"I did." Wyn speaks slowly. Deliberately. "I also heard her say she wants to be here." His tone in hopeful.

I turn to him. "Wanting to be here and wanting to be here for *me* are two entirely different things."

His face lights in understanding when he says, "and she has only said she wants to be here."

"Yes." My jaw tightens and I'm compelled to turn away in the direction of the dark sea and the crashing waves.

Wyn still stands opposite. His eyes on the lights of Isi Aura.

"I want to know why they left," I say.

"Who? Amberle and Ilthuryn Kindra?"

"Yes."

Amberle has been so adamant that she is here for her father, and yet, he was not with her when I stumbled upon her in the Spring Court. Nor did she mention him in connection to her life in Rosewind when I inquired about that key she always wore. At first, I thought it was a gift from him, not some thieving partner, named Clay. Does Ilthuryn Kindra know his daughter thieves to survive?

If so, where is he?

"And she won't tell you?" He looks at me.

I turn to him. "I don't think she knows the reason."

"Do you want me to find him and ask?"

"Yes. I find it curious that he hasn't reappeared. Especially with Amberle in the public eye."

"Consider it done."

Raine and Clove might be right about me being a fool and making a mistake in keeping Amberle. I should've cut her before my feelings grew deeper, but my damned hope refuses to let her go. She has secrets, she's holding something back and I cannot fully commit—to her or anyone else—until and unless those things are brought to light.

It seems that Ilthuryn Kindra is my best source in finding those answers.

"Start in the Spring Court," I say. "In Rosewind." Although I have a feeling he won't find her father there.

End of Book One

Get three FREE short stories when you join Joanna's email list at joannareeder.com

Thank you for reading!

Thank you for reading *Courting Fae Thieves and Crowns!*

If you enjoyed jumping into the land of Faerie and Amberle's world, please leave an honest review on **Amazon**, **Goodreads**, and/or **Bookbub**. Reviews are essential to indie authors like me!

Review on: Amazon
    Review on: Goodreads
    Review on: Bookbub

—Joanna

Acknowledgments

First of all, thank you for reading this book!

I also need to thank my Kindle Vella and Patreon readers who took a chance on this story in serial form so that it could shine when it was time to wrap it in novel form.

But it never would have come to fruition without the support of my family. From my sweet husband who may not understand my need to tell stories but supports me anyway, and my crazy kids who keep me on my toes, but also understand that mom needs to write.

Also my parents, siblings, and extended family who are <u>**always**</u> supporting me and encouraging me.

A huge thanks to my mastermind group (the Queens of the Quill), my cover designer, Angel Leya, my proofreaders Nicholas Reeder and Madeline Mortensen, and my amazing cheerleader PA, Gladys Atwell.

I also couldn't have done it without my dear editor and friend, Kristin J. Dawson, who made this story everything it could be!

About the Author

Joanna Reeder is a USA Today Bestselling author who takes her readers time traveling to the past and through the portals to Faerie (and ALWAYS have a dash of romance!).

She lives with her husband, three littles, a dog, and a cat. When she isn't writing or reading, Joanna enjoys bike rides with her family, vacationing at the beach, and cuddling on the couch with a good movie.

She's a believer in the paranormal (seriously, she has stories!) and her motto is, "A Dr. Pepper a day keeps insanity away!"

If you love time travel and fantasy, sign up for Joanna's weekly newsletter HERE.

You can also chat with her on Instagram @authorjoannareeder

Or on Facebook @joannareederauthor